THE

LIFE AND DEATH OF RICHARD

YEA-AND-NAY

12ᵗʰC.   .7.

THE LIFE AND DEATH

OF

RICHARD YEA-AND-NAY

BY

MAURICE HEWLETT

AUTHOR OF "THE FOREST LOVERS," "LITTLE NOVELS
OF ITALY," ETC.

Sì che a bene sperar mi era cagione
Di quella fera alla gaietta pelle.

Inf. i. 41.

New York
THE MACMILLAN COMPANY
LONDON: MACMILLAN & CO., Ltd.
1901

Norwood Press
J. S. Cushing & Co. — Berwick & Smith
Norwood Mass. U.S.A.

𝕿𝖔

HIS FRIEND

EDMUND GOSSE

(ALWAYS BENEVOLENT TO HIS INVENTION)

THIS CHRONICLE OF

ANJOU AND A NOBLE LADY

IS DEDICATED

BY

M. H.

CONTENTS

BOOK I — THE BOOK OF YEA

CHAPTER VI

CHAPTER VII

CHAPTER VIII

CHAPTER IX

CHAPTER X

CHAPTER XI

CHAPTER XII

CHAPTER XIII

CHAPTER XIV

CONTENTS ix

BOOK II—THE BOOK OF NAY

CHAPTER VI

CHAPTER VII

CHAPTER VIII

CHAPTER IX

CHAPTER X

CHAPTER XI

CHAPTER XII

CHAPTER XIII

CHAPTER XIV

CONTENTS

CHAPTER XV

BOOK I

THE BOOK OF YEA

EXORDIUM

THE ABBOT MILO *URBI ET ORBI*, CONCERNING THE
NATURE OF THE LEOPARD

I LIKE this good man's account of leopards, and
find it more pertinent to my matter than you
might think. Milo was a Carthusian monk, abbot
of the cloister of Saint Mary-of-the-Pine by
Poictiers; it was his distinction to be the life-
long friend of a man whose friendships were few:
certainly it may be said of him that he knew
as much of leopards as any one of his time
and nation, and that his knowledge was better
grounded.

'Your leopard,' he writes, 'is alleged in the
books to be offspring of the Lioness and the
Pard; and his name, if the Realists have any truth
on their side, establishes the fact. But I think he
should be called Leolupé, which is to say, got by
lion out of bitch-wolf, since two essences burn in
him as well as two sorts. This is the nature of
the leopard: it is a spotted beast, having two
souls, a bright soul and a dark soul. It is black
and golden, slim and strong, cat and dog. Hunger
drives a dog to hunt, so the leopard; passion the
cat, so the leopard. A cat is sufficient unto himself, and a leopard is so; but a dog hangs on a
man's nod, and a leopard can so be beguiled. A
leopard is sleek as a cat and pleased by stroking;

3

like a cat he will scratch his friend on occasion.
Yet again, he has a dog's intrepidity, knows no
fear, is single-purposed, not to be called off,
longanimous. But the cat in him makes him
wary, tempts him to treacherous dealing, keeps
him apart from counsels, advises him to keep his
own. So the leopard is a lonely beast.' This is
interesting, and may be true. But mark him as
he goes on.

'I knew the man, my dear master and a great
king, who brought the leopards into the shield of
England, more proper to do it than his father,
being more the thing he signified. Of him, therefore, torn by two natures, cast in two moulds,
sport of two fates; the hymned and reviled, the
loved and loathed, spendthrift and a miser, king
and a beggar, the bond and the free, god and
man; of King Richard Yea-and-Nay, so made, so
called, and by that unmade, I thus prepare my
account.'

So far the abbot with much learning and no
little verbosity casts his net. He has the weakness of his age, you observe, and must begin at
the beginning; but this is not our custom. Something of Time is behind us; we are conscious of
a world replete, and may assume that we have
digested part of it. Milo, indeed, like all candid
chroniclers, has his value. He is excellent upon
himself, a good relish with your meal. However,
as we are concerned with King Richard, you shall
dip into his bag for refreshment, but must leave
the victualling to me.

CHAPTER I

I CHOOSE to record how Richard Count of Poictou rode all through one smouldering night to see Jehane Saint-Pol a last time. It had so been named by the lady; but he rode in his hottest mood of Nay to that, yet careless of first or last so he could see her again. Nominally to remit his master's sins, though actually (as he thought) to pay for his own, the Abbot Milo bore him company, if company you can call it which left the good man, in pitchy dark, some hundred yards behind. The way, which was long, led over Saint Andrew's Plain, the bleakest stretch of the Norman march; the pace, being Richard's, was furious, a pounding gallop; the prize, Richard's again, showed fitfully and afar, a twinkling point of light. Count Richard knew it for Jehane's torch, and saw no other spark; but Milo, faintly curious on the lady's account, was more concerned with the throbbing glow which now and again shuddered in the northern sky. Nature had no lamps that night, and made no sign by cry of night-bird or rustle of scared beast: there was no wind, no rain, no dew; she offered nothing but heat, dark, and dense oppression. Topping the ridge of sand, where was the Fosse des Noyées, place of shameful death, the solitary torch showed a steady beam ; and there also, ahead, could be seen on the northern horizon that rim of throbbing light.

'God pity the poor !' said Count Richard, and scourged forward.

'God pity me !' said gasping Milo; 'I believe my stomach is in my head.' So at last they crossed the pebbly ford and found the pines, then cantered up the path of light which streamed from the Dark Tower. As core of this they saw the lady stand with a torch above her head; when they drew rein she did not move. Her face, moon-shaped, was as pale as a moon; her loose hair, catching light, framed it with gold. She was all white against the dark, seemed to loom in it taller than she was or could have been. She was Jehane Saint-Pol, Jehane 'of the Fair Girdle,' so called by her lovers and friends, to whom for a matter of two years this hot-coloured, tallest, and coldest of the Angevins had been light of the world.

The check upon their greeting was the most curious part of a curious business, that one should have travelled and the other watched so long, and neither urge the end of desire. The Count sat still upon his horse, so for duty's sake did the aching abbot; the girl stood still in the entry-way, holding up her dripping torch. Then, 'Child, child,' cried the Count, 'how is it with thee ?' His voice trembled, and so did he.

She looked at him, slow to answer, though the hand upon her bosom swayed up and down.

'Do you see the fires ?' she said. 'They have

been there six nights.' He was watching them
then through the pine-woods, how they shot into
the sky great ribbons of light, flickered, fainted
out, again glowed steadily as if gathering volume,
again leaped, again died, ebbing and flowing like
a tide of fire.

'The King will be at Louviers,' said Richard.
He gave a short laugh. 'Well, he shall light us
to bed. Heart of a man, I am sick of all this.
Let me in.'

She stood aside, and he rode boldly into the
tower, stooping as he passed her to touch her
cheek. She looked up quickly, then let in the
abbot, who, with much ceremony, came bowing,
his horse led by the bridle. She shut the door
behind them and drove home the great bolts.
Servants came tumbling out to take the horses
and do their duty; Count Eustace, a brother of
Jehane's, got up from the hearth, where he had
been asleep on a bearskin, rubbed his eyes, gulped
a yawn, knelt, and was kissed by Richard. Jehane
stood apart, mistress of herself as it seemed, but
conscious, perhaps, that she was being watched.
So she was. In the bustle of salutation the
Abbot Milo found eyes to see what manner of
sulky, beautiful girl this was.

He watched shrewdly, and has described her
for us with the meticulous particularity of his
time and temper. He runs over her parts like
a virtuoso. The iris of her eyes, for instance, was
wet grey, but ringed with black and shot with
yellow, giving so the effect of hot green; her
mouth was of an extraordinary dark red colour,
very firm in texture, close-grained, 'like the

darker sort of strawberries,' says he. The upper
lip had the sulky curve; she looked discontented,
and had reason to be, under such a scrutiny of
the microscope. Her hair was colour of raw silk,
eyebrows set rather high, face a thinnish oval,
complexion like a pink rose's, neck thinnish
again, feet, hands, long and nervous, 'good working members,' etc. etc. None of this helps very
much; too detailed. But he noticed how tall she
was and how slim, save for a very beautiful
bosom, too full for Dian's (he tells us), whom else
she resembled; how she was straight as a birch-
tree; how in walking it seemed as if her skirts
clung about her knees. There was an air of
mingled surprise and defiance about her; she
was a silent girl. ' Fronted like Juno,' he appears
to cry, ' shaped like Hebe, and like Demeter in
stature; sullen with most, but with one most
sweetly apt, she looked watchful but was really
timid, looked cold but was secretly afire. I knew
soon enough how her case stood, how hope and
doubt strove in her and choked her to silence. I
guessed how within those reticent members swift
love ran like wine; but because of this proud,
brave mask of hers I was slow to understand her
worth. God help me, I thought her a thing of
snow ! '

He records her dress at this time, remarkable
if becoming. It was all white, and cut wedge-
shaped in front, very deep; but an undervest of
crimson crossed the V in the midst and saved her
modesty, and his. Her hair, which was long, was
plaited in two plaits with seed-pearls, brought
round her neck like a scarf and the two ends

joined between her breasts, thus defining a great
beauty of hers and making a gold collar to her
gown. Round her smooth throat was a little
chain with a red jewel; on her head another
jewel (a carbuncle) set in a flower, with three
heron's plumes falling back from it. She had a
broad belt of gold and sapphire stones, and slippers of vair. 'Oh, a fine straight maid,' says
Milo in conclusion, 'golden and delicate, with
strangely shaded eyes. They knew her as Jehane
of the Fair Girdle.'

The brother, Count Eustace as they called him
(to distinguish him from an elder brother, Eudo
Count of Saint-Pol), was a blunt copy of his sister,
redder than she was, lighter in the hair, much
lighter in the eyes. He seemed an affectionate
youth, and clung to the great Count Richard like
ivy to a tree. Richard gave him the sort of
scornful affection one has for a little dog, between
patting and slapping; but clearly wanted to be rid
of him. No reference was made to the journey,
much was taken for granted; Eustace talked of
his hawks, Richard ate and drank, Jehane sat up
stiffly, looking into the fire; Milo watched her
between his mouthfuls. The moment supper was
done, up jumps Richard and claps hands on the
two shoulders of young Eustace. 'To bed, to bed,
my falconer! It grows late,' cries he. Eustace
pushed his chair back, rose, kissed the Count's
hand and his sister's forehead, saluted Milo, and
went out humming a tune. Milo withdrew, the
servants bowed themselves away. Richard stood
up, a loose-limbed young giant, and narrowed his
eyes.

'Nest thee, nest thee, my bird,' he said low; and Jehane's lips parted. Slowly she left her stool by the fire, but quickened as she went; and at last ran tumbling into his arms.

His right hand embraced her, his left at her chin held her face at discretion. Like a woman, she reproached him for what she dearly loved.

'Lord, lord, how shall I serve the cup and platter if you hold me so fast?'

'Thou art my cup, thou art my supper.'

'Thin fare, poor soul,' she said; but was glad of his foolishness.

Later, they sat by the hearth, Jehane on Richard's knee, but doubtfully his, being troubled by many things. He had no retrospects nor afterthoughts; he tried to coax her into pliancy. It was the fires in the north that distressed her. Richard made light of them.

'Dear,' he said, 'the King my father is come up with a host to drive the Count his son to bed. Now the Count his son is master of a good bed, to which he will presently go; but it is not the bed of the King his father. That, as you know, is of French make, neither good Norman, nor good Angevin, nor seethed in the English mists. By Saint Maclou and the astonishing works he did, I should be bad Norman, and worse Angevin, and less English than I am, if I loved the French.'

He tried to draw her in; but she, rather, strained away from him, elbowed her knee, and rested her chin upon her hand. She looked gravely down to the whitening logs, where the ashes were gaining on the red.

'My lord loves not the French,' she said, 'but
he loves honour. He is the King's son, loving
his father.'

'By my soul, I do not,' he assured her, with
perfect truth, then he caught her round the waist
and turned her bodily to face him. After he had
kissed her well he began to speak more seriously.

'Jehane,' he said, 'I have thought all this stifling
night upon the heath, Homing to her I am seeking my best. My best? You are all I have in
the world. If honour is in my hand, do I not
owe it to you? Or shall a man use women like
dogs, to play with them in idle moods, toss them
bones under the table, afterwards kick them out
of doors? Child, you know me better. What!'
he cried out, with his head very high, 'Shall a
man not choose his own wife?'

'No,' said Jehane, ready for him; 'no, Richard,
unless the people shall choose their own king.'

'God chooses the king,' says Richard, 'or so
we choose to believe.'

'Then God must appoint the wife,' Jehane said,
and tried to get free. But this could not be allowed, as she knew.

She was gentle with him, reasoning. 'The King
your father is an old man, Richard. Old men
love their way.'

'God knows, he is old, and passionate, and indifferent wicked,' said Richard, and kissed Jehane.
'Look, my girl, there were four of us: Henry,
and me, and Geoffrey, and John, whom he sought
to drive in team by a sop to-day and a stick to-
morrow. A good way, done by a judging hand.

What then? I will tell you how the team served
the teamster. Henry gave sop for sop, and it
was found well. Might he not give stick for
stick? He thought so: God rest him, he is dead
of that. There was much simplicity in Henry.
I got no sop at all. Why should I have stick
then? I saw no reason; but I took what came.
If I cried out, it is a more harmless vent than
many. Let me alone. Geoffrey, I think, was a
villain. God help him if He can: he is dead too.
He took sop and gave stick: ungentle in Geoffrey,
but he paid for it. He was a cross-bred dog with
much of the devil in him; he bit himself and died
barking. Last, there is John. I desire to speak
reasonably of John; but he is too snug, he gets
all sop. This is not fair. He should have some
stick, that we may judge what mettle he has.
There, my Jehane, you have the four of us, a fretful team; whereof one has rushed his hills and
broken his heart; and one, kicking his yoke-
fellows, squealing, playing the jade, has broken
his back; and one, poor Richard, does collar-
work and gets whip; and one, young Master
John, eases his neck and is cajoled with, " So
then, so then, boy!" Then comes pretty Jehane
to the ear of the collar-horse, whispering, " Good
Richard, get thee to stall, but not here. Stable
thee snug with the King of France his sister."
Hey!' laughed Richard, 'what a word for a
chosen bride!' He pinched her cheek and looked
gaily at her, triumphant in his own eloquence.
He was most dangerous when that devil was
awake, so she dared not look at him back.
Eagerly and low she replied.

'Yes, Richard, yes, yes, my king! The king
must have the king's sister, and Jehane go back
to the byre. Eagles do not mate with buzzards.'
Hereupon he snatched her up altogether and hid
her face in his breast.

'Never, never, never!' he swore to the rafters.
'As God lives and reigns, so live thou and so
reign, queen of me, my Picardy rose.'

She tried no more that night, fearing that his
love so keen-edged might make his will ride
rough. The watch-fires at Louviers trembled
and streamed up in the north. There was no
need for candles in the Dark Tower.

They rose up early to a fair dawn. The cloud-
wrack was blown off, leaving the sky a lake of
burnt yellow, pure, sweet, and cool. Thus the
world entered upon the summer of Saint Luke, to
a new-risen sun, to thin mists stealing off the
moor, to wet flowers hearted anew, to blue air,
and hope left for those who would go gleaning.
While Eustace Saint-Pol was snoring abed and
the Abbot Milo at his *Sursum Corda*, Richard
had Jehane by the hand. 'Come forth, my love;
we have the broad day before us and an empty
kingdom to roam in. Come, my red rose, let me
set you among the flowers.' What could she do
but harbour up her thoughts?

He took her afield, where flowers made the
earth still a singing-place, and gathered of these
to deck her bosom and hair. Of the harebells he
made knots, the ground-colour of her eyes; but
autumn loves the yellow, so she was stuck with
gold like a princess. She sat enthroned by his
command, this young girl in a high place, with

downcast eyes and a face all fire-colour, while he
worshipped her to his fancy. I believe he had no
after-thought; but she saw the dun smoke of the
fires at Louviers, and knew they would make
the night shudder again. Yet her sweetness,
patience, staid courtesy, humility, never failed
her; out of the deep wells of her soul she drew
them forth in a stream. Richard adored.
'Queen Jehane, Queen Jehane!' he cried out,
with his arms straightly round her — 'Was ever
man in the world blest so high since God said,
" Behold thy mother"? And so art thou
mother to me, O bride. Bride and queen as
thou shalt be.'

This was great invention. She put her hand
upon his head. 'My Richard, my Richard Yea-
and-Nay,' she said, as if pitying his wild heart.
The nickname jarred.

'Never call me that,' he told her. 'Leave that
to Bertran de Born, a fool's word to the fool who
made it.'

'If I could, if I could!' thought Jehane, and
sighed. There were tears in her eyes, also, as
she remembered what generosity in him must
be frozen up, and what glory of her own. But
she did not falter in what she had to do, while
he, too exalted to be pitied, began to sing a
Southern song —

Al' entrada del tems clair, eya !

When their hair commingled in their love,
when they were close together, there was little
distinguishing between them; he was more her
pair than Eustace her blood-brother, in stature and

shape, in hue and tincture of gold. Jehane you
know, but not Richard. Of him, son of a king,
heir of a king, if you wish some bodily sign, I will
say shortly that he was a very tall young man,
high-coloured and calm in the face, straight-nosed,
blue-eyed, spare of flesh, lithe, swift in movement.
He was at once bold and sleek, eager and cold
as ice — an odd combination, but not more odd
than the blend of Norman dog and Angevin cat
which had made him so.   Furtive he was not, yet
seeming to crouch for a spring; not savage, yet
primed for savagery; not cruel, yet quick on
the affront, and on the watch for it.   He was
neither a rogue nor a madman; and yet he was as
cunning as the one and as heedless as the other,
if that is a possible thing.   He was arrogant, but
his smile veiled the fault; you saw it best in a
sleepy look he had.   His blemishes were many,
his weaknesses two.   He trusted to his own force
too much, and despised everybody else in the
world.   Not that he thought them knaves; he
was certain they were fools.   And so most of
them were, no doubt, but not all.   The first flush
of him moved your admiration: great height,
great colour, the red and the yellow; his beard
which ran jutting to a point and gave his jaw the
clubbed look of a big cat's; his shut mouth, and
cold considering eyes; the eager set of his head,
his soft, padding motions — a leopard, a hunting
leopard, quick to strike, but quick to change
purpose.   This, then, was Richard Yea-and-Nay,
whom all women loved, and very few men.
These require to be trusted before they love;
and full trust Richard gave to no man, because

he could not believe him worth it. Women are
more generous givers, expecting not again.

Here was Jehane Saint-Pol, a girl of two-and-
twenty to his two-and-thirty, well born, well
formed, greatly desired among her peers, who,
having let her soul be stolen, was prepared to
cut it out of herself for his sake who took it,
and let it die. She was the creature of his love,
in and out by now the work of his hands. God
had given her a magnificent body, but Richard
had made it glow. God had made her soul a
fair room; but his love had filled it with light,
decked it with flowers and such artful furniture.
He, in fact, as she very well knew, had given
her the grace to deal queenly with herself. She
knew that she would have strength to deny him,
having learned the hardihood to give him her
soul. Fate had carried her too young into the
arms of the most glorious prince in the world.
Her brother, Eudo the Count, built castles on
that in his head. Now she was to tumble them
down. Her younger brother, Eustace, loved this
splendid Richard. Now she was to hurt him.
What was to become of herself? Mercy upon
her, I believe she never thought of that. His
honour was her necessity: the watch-fires in the
north told her the hour was at hand. The old
King was come up with a host to drive his son
to bed. Richard must go, and she woo him out.
Son of a king, heir of a king, he must go to the
king his father; and he knew he must go. Two
days' maddening delight, two nights' biting of nails,
miserable entreaty from Jehane, grown newly
pinched and grey in the face, and he owned it.

He said to her the last night, 'When I saw you first, my Queen of Snows, in the tribune at Vézelay, when the knights rode by for the melée, the green light from your eyes shot me, and wounded I cried out, " That maid or none ! " '

She bowed her head; but he went on. ' When they throned you queen of them all because you were so proud and still, and had such a high untroubled head; and when your sleeve was in my helm, and my heart in your lap, and men fallen to my spear were sent to kneel before you — what caused your cheek to burn and your eyes to shine so bright? '

She hid her face. ' Homage of the knights ! The love of me ! ' he cried; and then, ' Ah, Jehane of the Fair Girdle, when I took you from the pastures of Gisors, when I taught you love and learned from your young mouth what love might be, I was made man. But now you ask me to become dog.' And he swore yet again he could never leave her. But she smiled proudly, being in pain. ' Nay, my lord, but the man in you is awake, and not to leave you. You shall go because you are the king's son, and I shall pray for the new king.' So she beat him, and had him weeping terribly, his face in her lap. She wept no more, but dry-eyed kissed him, and dry-lipped went to bed. ' He said Yea that time,' records the Abbot Milo, ' but I never knew then what she paid for it. That was later.' He went next morning, and she saw him go.

c

CHAPTER II

BETIMES is best for an ugly business; your man of spirit will always rush what he loathes but yet must do. Count Richard of Poictou, having made up his mind and confessed himself overnight, must leave with the first cock of the morning, yet must take the sacrament. Before it was grey in the east he did so, fully armed in mail, with his red surcoat of leopards upon him, his sword girt, his spurs strapped on. Outside the chapel in the weeping mirk a squire held his shield, another his helm, a groom walked his horse. Milo the Abbot was celebrant, a snuffling boy served; the Count knelt before the housel-cloth haloed by the light of two thin candles. Hardly had the priest begun his *introibo* when Jehane Saint-Pol, who had been awake all night, stole in with a hood on her head, and holding herself very stiffly, knelt on the floor. She joined her hands and stuck them up before her, so that the tips of her fingers, pointing upwards as her thoughts would fly, were nearly level with her chin. Thus frozen in prayer she remained throughout the office; nor did she relax when at the elevation of the Host Richard bowed himself to the earth. It seemed as if she too, bearing between her hands her own heart, was lifting it up for sacrifice and for worship.

The Count was communicated. He was a very

18

religious man, who would sooner have gone without his sword than his Saviour upon any affairs.
Jehane saw him fed without a twitch of the lips.
She was in a great mood, a rapt and pillared saint;
but when mass was over and his thanksgiving to
make, she got up and hid herself away from him
in the shades. There she lurked darkling, and he,
lunging out, swept with his sword's point the very
edge of her gown. She did not hear him go, for
he trod like a cat; but she felt him touch her with
the sword, and shuddered once or twice. He went
out of the courtyard at a gallop.

While the abbot was reciting his own thanksgiving Jehane came out of her corner, minded to
speak with him. So much he divined, needing not
the beckoning look she sent him from her guarded
eyes. He sat himself down by the altar of Saint
Remy, and she knelt beside him.

'Well, my daughter?' says Milo.

'I think it is well,' she took him up.

The Abbot Milo, a red-faced, watery-eyed old
man, rheumy and weathered well, then opened his
mouth and spake such wisdom as he knew. He
held up his forefinger like a claw, and used it as
if describing signs and wonders in the air.

'Hearken, Madame Jehane,' he said. 'I say
that you have done well, and will maintain it.
That great prince, whom I love like my own son,
is not for you, nor for another. No, no. He is
married already.'

He hoped to startle her, the old rhetorician;
but he failed. Jehane was too dreary.

'He is married, my daughter,' he repeated;
'and to whom? Why, to himself. That man

from the birth has been a lonely soul. He can
never wed, as you understand it. You think him
your lover! Believe me, he is not. He is his
own lover. He is called. He has a destiny.
And what is that? you ask me.'

She did not, but rhetoric bade him suppose it.
'Salem is his destiny; Salem is his bride, the elect
lady in bonds. He will not wed Madame Alois
of France, nor you, nor any virgin in Christendom
until that spiritual wedlock is consummate. I
should not love him as I do if I did not believe it.
For why? Shall I call my own son apostate?
He is signed with the Cross, a married man, by
our Saviour!'

He leaned back in his chair, peering down at
her to see how she took it. She took it stilly,
and turned him a marble, storm-purged face, a
pair of eyes which seemed all black.

'What shall I do to be safe?' Her voice
sounded worn.

'Safe, my child?' He wondered. 'Bless me,
is not the Cross safety?'

'Not with him, father.'

This was perfectly true, though tainted with
scandal, he thought. The abbot, who was trained
to blink all such facts, had to learn that this girl
blinked none. True to his guidance, he blinked.

'Go home to your brother, my daughter; go
home to Saint-Pol-la-Marche. At the worst,
remember that there are always two arks for a
woman in flood-time, a convent and a bed.'

'I shall never choose a convent,' said Jehane.

'I think,' said the abbot, 'that you are perfectly
wise.'

I suppose the alternative struck a sudden terror into her; for the abbot abruptly records in his book that 'here her spirit seemed to flit out of her, and she began to tremble very much, and in vain to contend with tears. I had her all dissolved at my feet within a few moments. She was very young, and seemed lost.'

'Come, come,' he said, 'you have shown yourself a brave girl these two days. It is not every maid can sacrifice herself for a Count of Poictou, the eldest son of a king. Come, come, let us have no more of this.' He hoped, no doubt, to brace her by a roughness which was far from his nature; and it is possible that he succeeded in heading off a mutiny of the nerves. She was not violent under her despair, but went on crying very miserably, saying, 'Oh, what shall I do? what shall I do?'

'God knoweth,' says the abbot, 'this was a bad case; but I had a good thought for it.' He began to speak of Richard, of what he had done and what would live to do. 'They say that the strain of the fiend is in that race, my dear,' he told her. 'They say that Geoffrey Grey-Gown had intercourse with a demon. And certain it is that in Richard, as in all his brothers, that stinging grain lives in the blood. For testimony look at their cognisance of leopards, and advise yourself, whether any house in Christendom ever took that device but had known familiarly the devil in some shape? And look again at the deeds of these princes. What turned the young king to riot and death, and Geoffrey to rapine and death? What else will turn John Sansterre to treachery and death, or our tall Richard to violence and death?

Nothing else, nothing else. But before he dies you shall see him glorious ——'

'He is glorious already,' said Jehane, wiping her eyes.

'Keep him so, then,' said the abbot testily, who did not love to have his periods truncated.

'If I go back to Saint-Pol,' said Jehane, 'I shall fall in with Gilles de Gurdun, who has sworn to have me.'

'Well,' replied the abbot, 'why should he not? Does he receive the assurance of your brother the Count?'

Jehane shook her head. 'No, no. My brother wished me to be my lord Richard's. But Gilles needs no assurance. He will buy my marriage from the King of France. He is very sufficient.'

'Hath he substance? Hath he lands? Is he noble, then, Jehane?'

'He hath knighthood, a Church fief — oh, enough!'

'God forgive me if I did amiss,' writes the abbot here; 'but seeing her in a melting mood, dewy, soft, and adorable, I kissed that beautiful person, and she left the Chapel of Saint Remy somewhat comforted.'

Not only so, but the same day she left the Dark Tower with her brother Count Eustace, and rode towards Gisors and Saint-Pol-la-Marche. Nothing she could do could be shamefully done, because of her silence, and the high head upon which she carried it; yet the Count of Saint-Pol, when he heard her story, sitting bulky in his chair (like a stalled red bull), did his best to put shame upon her, that so he might cover his own bitterness. It was Eustace, a generous ardent youth in those days, who saved her from most of Eudo's wrath by drawing it upon himself.

The Count of Saint-Pol swore a great oath. 'By the teeth of God, Jehane,' he roared, 'I see how it is. He hath made thee a piece of ruin, and now runs wasting elsewhere.'

'You shall never say that of my sister, my lord,' cries Eustace, very red in the face, 'nor yet of the greatest knight in the world.'

'Why, you egg,' says the Count, 'what have you to do in this? Tell me the rights of it before you put me in the wrong. Is my house to be the sport of Anjou? Is that long son of pirates and the devil to batten on our pastures, tread under-foot, bruise and blacken, rout as he will, break hedge and away? By my father's soul, Eustace, I shall see her righted.' He turned to the still girl. 'You tell me that you sent him away? Where did you send him? Where did he go?'

'He went to the King of England at Louviers, and to the camp,' said Jehane. 'The King sent for him. I sent him not.'

'Who is there beside the King of England?'

'Madame Alois of France is there.'

The Count of Saint-Pol put his tongue in his cheek.

'Oho!' he said, 'Oho! That is how it stands? So she is to be cuckoo, hey?' He sat square and intent for a moment or two, working his mouth like a man who chews a straw. Then he slapped his big hand on his knee, and rose up. 'If I cannot spike this wheel of vice, trust me never. By my soul, a plot indeed. Oh, horrible, horrible

thief!' He turned gnashing upon his brother.
'Now, Eustace, what do you say to your greatest
knight in the world? And what now of your
sister, hey? Little fool, do you not catch the
measure of it now? Two honey years of Jehane
Saint-Pol, gossamer pledges of mouth and mouth,
of stealing fingers, kiss and clasp; but for the
French King's daughter — pish! the thing of
naught they have made her — the sacrament of
marriage, the treaty, the dowry-fee. Oh, heaven
and earth, Eustace, answer me if you can.'

All three were moved in their several ways:
the Count red and blinking, Eustace red and
trembling, Jehane white as a cloth, trembling also,
but very silent. The word was with the younger
man.

'I know nothing of all this, upon my word, my
lord,' he said, confused. 'I love Count Richard,
I love my sister. There may have been that
which, had I loved but one, I had condemned in
the other. I know not, but'—he saw Jehane's
marble face, and lifted his hand up—'by my hope,
I will never believe it. In love they came together,
my lord; in love, says Jehane, they have parted. I
have heard little of Madame Alois, but my thought
is, that kings and the sons of kings may marry
kings' daughters, yet not in the way of love.'

The Count fumed. 'You are a fool, I see,
and therefore not to my purpose. I must talk
with men. Stay you here, Eustace, and watch
over her till I return. Let none get at her, on
your dear life. There are those who — sniffing
rogues, climbers, boilers of their pots — keep them
out, Eustace, keep them out. As for you' — he

turned hectoring to the proud girl — 'As for you,
mistress, keep the house. You are not in the
market, you are spoilt goods. You shall go
where you should be. I am still lord of these
lands; there shall be no rebellion here. Keep
the house, I say. I return ere many days.' He
stamped out of the hall; they heard him next
rating the grooms at the gate.

Saint-Pol was a great house, a noble house, no
doubt of it. Its counts drew no limits in the
way of pedigree, but built themselves a fair temple
in that kind, with the Twelfth Apostle himself
for head of the corner. So far as estate went,
seeing their country was fruitful, compact, snugly
bounded between France and Normandy (owing
fealty to the first), they might have been sovereign
counts, like the house of Blois, like that of
Aquitaine, like that even of Anjou, which, from
nothing, had risen to be so high. More: by
marriage, by robbery on that great plan where
it ceases to be robbery and is called warfare, by
treaty and nice use of the balances, there was
no reason why kingship should not have been
theirs, or in their blood. Kingship, even now,
was not far off. They called the Marquess of
Montferrat cousin, and he (it was understood)
intended to be throned at Jerusalem. The
Emperor himself might call, and once (being
in liquor) did call Count Eudo of Saint-Pol
'cousin'; for the fact was so. You must understand that in the Gaul of that day things were
in this ticklish state, that a man (as they say)
was worth the scope of his sword: reiver yesterday, warrior to-morrow; yesterday wearing a

hemp collar, to-day a count's belt, and to-morrow, may be, a king's crown. You climbed in various ways, by the field, by the board, by the bed. A handsome daughter was nearly worth a stout son. Count Eudo reckoned himself stout enough, and reckoned Eustace was so; but the beauty of Jehane, that stately maid who might uphold a cornice, that still wonder of ivory and gold, was an emblement which he, the tenant, meant to profit by; and so for an hour (two years by the clock) he saw his profit fair. The infatuation of the girl for this man or that man was nothing; but the infatuation of the great Count of Poictou for her set Eudo's heart ablaze. God willing, Saint Maclou assisting, he might live to call Jehane ' My Lady Queen.' He shut his ears to report; there were those who called Richard a rake, and others who called him ' Yea-and-Nay '; that was Bertran de Born's name for him, and all Paris knew it. He shut his eyes to Richard's galling unconcern with himself and his dignity. Dignity of Saint-Pol! He would wait for his dignity. He shut his mind to Jehane's blown fame, to the threatenings of his dreadful Norman neighbour, Henry the old king, who had had an archbishop pole-axed like a steer; he dared the anger of his suzerain, in whose hands lay Jehane's marriage; a heady gambler, he staked the fortunes of his house upon this clinging of a girl to a wild prince. And now to tell himself that he deserved what he had got was but to feed his rage. Again he swore by God's teeth that he would have his way; and when he left his castle of Saint-Pol-la-Marche it was for Paris.

The head of his house, under the Emperor Henry, was there, Conrad of Montferrat, trying to negotiate the crown of Jerusalem. There must be a conference before the house of Saint-Pol could be let to fall. Surely the Marquess would never allow it! He must spike the wheel. Was not Alois of France within the degrees? She was sister to the French King: well, but what was Richard's mother? She had been wife to Louis, wife to Alois' father. Was this decency? What would the Pope say—an Italian? Was the Marquess Conrad an Italian for nothing? Was 'our cousin' the Emperor of no account, King of the Romans? The Pope Italian, the Marquess Italian, the Emperor on his throne, and God in His heaven—eh, eh! there should be a conference of these high powers. So, and with such whirl of question and answer, did the Count of Saint-Pol beat out to Paris.

But Jehane remained at Saint-Pol-la-Marche, praying much, going little abroad, seeing few persons. Then came (since rumour is a gadabout) Sir Gilles de Gurdun, as she knew he would, and knelt before her, and kissed her hand. Gilles was a square-shouldered, thick-set youth of the black Norman sort, ruddy, strong-jawed, small-eyed, low in the brow, bullet-headed. He was no taller than she, looked shorter, and had nothing to say. He had loved her since the time when she was an overgrown girl of twelve years, and he a squire about her father's house learning mannishness. The King of England had dubbed him a knight, but she had made him a man. She knew him to be a good one; as dull as a mud-flat, but honest,

wholesome, and of decent estate.   In a moment,
when he was come again, she saw that he was a
long lover who would treat her well.

'God help me, and him also,' she thought; 'it
may be that I shall need him before long.'

CHAPTER III

IN WHAT HARBOUR THEY FOUND THE

OLD LION

AT Evreux, across the heath, Count Richard found his company: the Viscount Adhémar of Limoges (called for the present the Good Viscount), the Count of Perigord, Sir Gaston of Béarn (who really loved him), the Bishop of Castres, and the Monk of Montauban (a singing-bird); some dozen of knights with their esquires, pages, and men-at-arms. He waited two days there for Abbot Milo to come up with last news of Jehane; then at the head of sixty spears he rode fleetly over the marshes towards Louviers. After his first, ' You are well met, my lords,' he had said very little, showing a cold humour; after a colloquy with Milo, which he had before he left his bed, he said nothing at all. Alone, as became one of his race, he rode ahead of his force; not even the chirping Monk (who remembered his brother Henry and often sighed for him) cared to risk a shot from his strong eyes. They were like blue stones, full of the cold glitter of their fire. It was at times like this, when a man stands naked confronting his purpose, that one saw the hag riding on the back of Anjou.

He was not thinking of it now, but the truth is that there had hardly been a time in his short life when he had not been his father's open enemy.

He could have told you that it had not been
always his fault, though he would never have told
you. But I say that what he, a youth of thirty,
had made of his inheritance was as nothing to
that elder's wasting of his. In moments of hot
rage Richard knew this, and justified himself; but
the melting hour came again when he heaped all
reproach upon himself, believing that but for such
and such he might have loved this rooted, terrible
old man who assuredly loved not him. Richard
was neither mule nor jade; he was open to per-
suasion on two sides. Compunction was one:
you could touch him on the heart and bring him
weeping to his knees; affection was another: if
he loved the petitioner he yielded handsomely.
Now, this time it was Jehane and not his conscience which had sent him to Louviers. First of
all Jehane had pleaded the Sepulchre, his old
father, filial obedience, and he had laughed at the
sweet fool. But when she, grown wiser, urged
him to pleasure her by treading on the heart she
had given him, he could not deny her. He was
converted, not convinced. So he rode alone, three
hundred yards from his lieges, reasoning out how
he could preserve his honour and yet yield. The
more he thought the less he liked it, but all the
more he felt necessity at his throat. And, as
always with him, when he thought he seemed as
if turned to stone. 'One way or another,' Milo
tells us, 'every man of the House of Anjou had
his unapproachable side, so accustomed were they
to the fortress-life.'

A broad plain, watered by many rivers, showed
the towers of Louviers and red roofs cinctured by

the greatest of them; short of the walls were the
ranked white tents, columned smoke, waggons,
with men and horses, as purposeless, little, and
busy as a swarm of bees. In the midst of this
array was a red pavilion with a standard at the
side, too heavy for the wind. All was set in the
clear sunless air of an autumn day in Normandy;
the hour, one short of noon. Richard reined up
for his company, on a little hill.

'The powers of England, my lords,' he said,
pointing with his hand. All stayed beside him.
Gaston of Béarn tweaked his black beard.

'Let us be done with the business, Richard,'
said this knight, 'before the irons can get out.'

'What!' cried the Count, 'shall a father smite
his son?' No one answered: in a moment he
was ashamed of himself. 'Before God,' he said,
'I mean no impiety. I will do what I have
undertaken as gently as may be. Come, gentlemen.' He rode on.

The camp was defended by fosse and bridge.
At the barbican all the Aquitanians except Richard dismounted, and all stayed about him while
a herald went forward to tell the King who was
come in. The King knew very well who it was,
but chose not to know it; he kept the herald
long enough to make his visitors chafe, then sent
word that the Count of Poictou would be received,
but alone. Claiming his right to ride in, Richard
followed the heralds at a foot's pace, alone, un-
greeted by any. At the mount of the standard
he got off his horse, found the ushers of the King's
door, and went swiftly to the entry of the pavilion
(which they held open for him), as though, like

some forest beast, he saw his prey.   There in the
entry he stiffened suddenly, and stiffly went down
on his two knees.   Midway of the great tent,
square and rugged before him, with working jaws
and restless little fired eyes, sat the old King his
father, hands on knees, between them a long bare
sword.   Beside him was his son John, thin and
flushed, and about, a circle of peers: two bishops
in purple, a pock-marked monk of Cluny, Bohun,
Grantmesnil, Drago de Merlou, and a few more.
On the ground was a secretary biting his pen.

The King looked his best on a throne, for his
upper part was his best.   It was, at least, the
mannish part.   With scanty red hair much
rubbed into disorder, a seamed red face, blotched
and shining; with a square jaw awry, the neck
and shoulders of a bull; with gnarled gross hands
at the end of arms long out of measure, a cruel
mouth and a nose like a bird's beak — his features
seemed to have been hacked coarsely out of wood
and as coarsely painted; but what might have
passed by such means for a man was transformed
by his burning eyes, with their fuel of pain, into
the similitude of a fallen angel.   The devil of
Anjou sat eating King Henry's eyes, and you
saw him at his meal.   It gave the man the look
of a wild boar easing his tusks against a tree,
horrible, yet content to be abhorred, splendid,
because so strong and lonely.   But the prospect
was not comfortable.   Little as he knew of his
father, Richard could make no mistake here.
The old King was in a picksome mood, fretted
by rage: angry that his son should kneel there,
more than angry that he had not knelt before.

The play began, like a farce. The King affected
not to see him, let him kneel on. Richard did
kneel on, as stiff as a rod. The King talked with
obscene jocosity, every snap betraying his humour,
to Prince John; he scandalised even his bishops,
he abashed even his barons. He infinitely de-
graded himself, yet seemed to wallow in disgrace.
So Richard's gorge (a tender organ) rose to hear
him. 'God, what wast Thou about, to let such
a hog be made?' he muttered, loud enough for at
least three people to hear. The King heard it
and was pleased; the Prince heard it, and with a
scared eye perceived that Bohun had heard it.
The King went grating on, John fidgeted;
Bohun, greatly daring, whispered in his master's
ear.

The King replied with a roar which all the
camp might have heard. 'Ha! Sacred Face, let
him kneel, Bohun. That is a new custom for
him, useful science for a man of his trade. All
men of the sword come to it sooner or later—
sooner or later, by God!'

Hereupon Richard, very deliberately, rose to
his feet and stepped forward to the throne. His
great height was a crowning abomination. The
King blinked up at him, showing his tushes.

'What now, sir?' he said.

'Later for me, sire, if kneeling is to be done
by soldiers,' said Richard. The King controlled
himself by swallowing.

'And yet, Richard,' he said, dry as dust, 'And
yet, Richard, you have knelt to the French lad
soon enough.'

'To my liege-lord, sire? Yes, it is true.'

D

'He is not your liege-lord, man,' roared the
King. 'I am your liege-lord, by heaven. I
gave and I can take away. Heed me now.'

'Fair sire,' says Richard, 'observe that I have
knelt to you. I am not here for any other reason,
and least of all to try conclusions of the voice. I
have come out of my lands with my company to
give you obedience. Be sure that they, on their
part, will pay you proper honour (as I do) if you
will let them.'

'You come from lands I have given you, as
Henry came, as Geoffrey came, to defy me,' said
the old man, trembling in his chair. 'What is
your obedience worth when I have measured
theirs: Henry's obedience! Geoffrey's obedience! Pish, man, what words you use.' He
got up and stamped about the tent like an irritable dwarf, crook-legged and long-armed, pricked,
maddened at every point. 'And you tell me of
your men, your lands, your company! Good
men all, a fair company, by the Rood of Grace!
Tell me now, Richard, have you Raimon of
Toulouse in that company? Have you Béziers?'

'No, sire,' said Richard, looking serenely down
at the working face.

'Nor ever will have,' snarled the King. 'Have
you the Knight of Béarn?'

'I have, sire.'

'Ill company, Richard. It is a white-faced,
lying beast, with a most goatish beard. Have
you your singing monk?'

'I have, sire.'

'Shameful company. Have you Adhémar of
Limoges?'

' Yes, sire.'

' Silly company.   Leave him with his women.
Have you your Abbot Milo ? '

' Yes.'

' Sick company.'   His head sank into his
breast; he found himself suddenly tired, even
of reviling, and had to sit down again.   Richard
felt a tide of pity; looking down at the huddled
old man, he held out his hand.

' Let us not quarrel, father,' he said; but that
brought up the King's head, like a call to arms.

' A last question, Richard.   Have you dared
bring here Bertran de Born ? '   He was on his
feet again for the reply, and the two men faced
each other.   Everybody knew how serious the
question was.   It sobered the Count, but drove
the pity out of him.

' Dare is not a word for Anjou, sire,' he
replied, picking his phrases; ' but Bertran is
not with me.'   Before the old man could break
again into savagery he went on to his main
purpose.   ' Sire, short speeches are best.   You
seek to draw my ill-humours, but you shall not
draw them.   As son and servant of your Grace
I came in, and so will go out.   As a son I have
knelt to the King my father, as servant I am
ready to obey him.   Let that marriage, designed
in the cradle by the French King and you, go on.
I will do my part if Madame Alois will do hers.'

Richard folded his arms; the King sat down
again.   A queer exchange of glances had passed
between his father and brother at the mention of
that lady's name.   Richard, who saw it, got the
feeling of some secret between them, the feeling of

being in a trap; but he said nothing.   The King
began his old harping.

'Attend to me now, Richard,' he said, with
much work of the eyebrows; 'if that ill-gotten
beast Bertran had been of your meinie our last
words had been said.   Beast!   He is a toothed
snake, that crawled into my boy's bed and bit
passion into him.   Lord Jesus, if ever again I
meet Bertran, help Thou me to redden his face!
But as it is, I am content.   Rest you here with me,
if so rough a lodging may content your nobility.
As for Madame Alois, she shall be sent for; but
I think I will not meet your bevy of joglars from
the south.   I have a proud stomach o' these days;
I doubt pastry from Languedoc would turn me
sour; and liking monks little enough as it is,
your throstle-cock of Montauban might cause
me to blaspheme.   See them entertained, Drago;
or better, let them entertain each other — with
singing games, holy God!   Go you, Bohun' —
and he turned — 'fetch in Madame Alois.'
Bohun went through a curtain behind him, and
the King sat in thought, biting his thumbs.

Madame Alois of France came out of the inner
tent, a slinking, thin girl, with the white and
tragic face of the fool in a comedy set in black
hair.   Richard thought she was mad by the way
she stared about her from one man to another;
but he went down on his knee in a moment.
Prince John turned stiff, the old King bent his
brows to watch Richard.   The lady, who was
dressed in black, and looked to be half fainting,
shrank in an odd way towards the wall, as if to
avoid a whip.   'Too long in England, poor soul,'

Richard thought; 'but why did she come from the King's tent?'

It was not a cheerful meeting, nor did the King show any desire to make it better. When by roundabout and furtive ways Madame Alois at last stood drooping by his chair, he began to talk to her in English, a language unknown to Richard, though familiar enough, he saw, to his father and brother. 'It seems to be his Grace's desire to make me ridiculous,' he went on to say to himself: 'what a dead-level of grim words! In English, it appears, you do not talk. You stab with the tongue.' In truth, there was no conversation. The King or the Prince spoke, and Madame Alois moistened her lips; she looked nowhere but at the old tyrant, not at his eyes, but above them, at his forehead, and with a trepidant gaze, like a watched hare's. 'The King has her in thrall, soul and body,' Richard considered. Then his knee began to ache, and he released it.

'Fair sire,' he began in his own tongue. Madame Alois gave a start, and 'Ha, Richard,' says the King, 'art thou still there, man?'

'Where else, my lord?' asked the son. The father looked at Alois.

'Deign to recognise in this baron, Madame,' he said, 'my son the Count of Poictou. Let him salute, Madame, that which he has sought from so far, and with such humility, pardieu; your white hand, Alois.' The strange girl quivered, then put her hand out. Richard, kissing it, found it horribly cold.

'Lady,' he said, 'I pray we may be better acquainted; but I must tell you that I have no

English. Let me hope that in this good land you may recover your French.' He got no answer from the lady, but, by heaven, he made his father angry.

'We hope, Richard, that you will teach Madame better things than that,' sniffed the old man, nosing about for battle.

'I pray that I may teach her no worse, my lord,' replied the other. 'You will perhaps allow that for a daughter of France the tongue may have its uses.'

'As English, Count, for the son of England!' cried his father; 'or for his wife, by the mass, if he is fit to have one.'

'Of that, sire, we must talk at your Grace's leisure,' said Richard slowly. 'Jesus!' he asked himself, 'will he put me to a block of ice? What is the matter with this woman?' The King put an end to his questions by dismissing Madame Alois, breaking up the assembly, and himself retiring. He was dreadfully fatigued, quite white and breathless. Richard saw him follow the lady through the inner curtain, and again was uncomfortably suspicious. But when his brother John made to slip in also he thought there must be an end of it. He tapped the young man on the shoulder.

'Brother, a word with you,' says he; and John came twittering back. The two were alone in the tent.

This John — Sansterre, Landlos, Lackland, so they variously called him — was a timid copy of his brother, a wry-necked reedy Richard with a sniff. Not so tall, yet more spare, with blue eyes

more pallid than his brother's, and protruding
where Richard's were inset, the difference lay
more in degree than kind. Richard was of heroic
build, but a well-knit, well-shaped hero; in John
the arms were too long, the head too small, the
brow too narrow. Richard's eyes were perhaps
too wide apart; no doubt John's were too near
together. Richard twitched his fingers when he
was moved, John bit his cheek. Richard stooped
from the neck, John from the shoulders. When
Richard threw up his head you saw the lion;
John at bay reminded you of a wolf in a corner.
John snarled at such times, Richard breathed
through his nose. John showed his teeth when
he was crossed, Richard when he was merry.
So many thousand points of unlikeness might be
named, all small: the Lord knows here are
enough. The Angevin cat-and-dog nature was
fairly divided between these two. Richard had
the sufficiency of the cat, John the dependence
of a dog; John had the cat's secretiveness,
Richard the dog's dash. At heart John was a
thief.

He feared and hated his brother; so when
Richard said, 'Brother, a word with you,' John
tried to disguise apprehension in disgust. The
result was a very sick smile.

'Willingly, dear brother, and the more so —— '
he began; but Richard cut him short.

'What under the light of the sky is the matter
with that lady?' he asked him.

John had been preparing for that. He raised
his eyebrows and splayed out both his hands.

'Can you ask? Eh, our Lord! Emotion — a

stranger in a strange land — an access of the
shudders — who knows women? So long from
France — dreadful of her brother — dreadful of
you — so many things! a silly mind — ah, my
brother!'

Richard checked him testily. 'Put a point,
put a point, you drown me in phrases; your
explanations explain nothing. One more word.
What in the devil's name is she doing in there?'
He had a short way. John began to stammer.

'A second father — a tender guardian ——'

'Pish!' said Count Richard, and turned to
leave the pavilion. Prince John slipped through
the curtains, and at that moment Richard heard
a little fretful cry within, not the cry of mortal
lady. 'What under heaven have they got in
there, this family?' he asked himself. Shrugging,
he went out into the fresh air.

The abbot notes that his lord and master came
running into his quarters, 'and tumbled upon me,
like a lover who finds his mistress after many days.
" Milo, Milo, Milo," he began to cry, three times
over, as if the name helped him, " Thou wilt live
to see a puddock upon the throne of England!"
Thus he strangely said.'

CHAPTER IV

WHEN the Count of Saint-Pol came to Paris he
found the going very delicate. For it is a delicate matter to confer in a king's capital, with a
king's allies, how best to throw obstacles in that
king's way. As a matter of fact he found that he
could do little or nothing in the business. King
Philip was in great feather concerning his sister's
arrival; the heralds were preparing to go out to
meet her. Nicholas d'Eu and the Baron of
Quercy were to accompany them; King Philip
thought Saint-Pol the very man to make a third,
but this did not suit the Count at all. He sought
out his kinsman the Marquess of Montferrat, a
heavy Italian, who gave him very little comfort.
All he could suggest was that his 'good cousin'
would do better to help him to the certain throne
of Jerusalem. 'What do you want with more
than one king in a family?' asked the Marquess.
Saint-Pol grew rather dry as he assured him that
one king would suffice, and that Anjou was nearer
than Jerusalem. He went on to hint at various
strange speculations rife concerning the history
of Madame Alois. 'If you want garbage, Eudo,'
said Montferrat to this, 'come not to me. But I
know a rat who might be of service.'

41

' The name of your rat, Marquess! It is all I ask.'

' Bertran de Born: who else ? ' said Montferrat. Now, Bertran de Born was the thorn in the flesh of Anjou, a rankling addition to their state whom they were never without. Saint-Pol knew his value very well, and decided to go down to see the man in his own country. So he would have gone, no doubt, had not his sovereign judged otherwise. Saint-Pol received commands to accompany the heralds to Louviers, so had to content himself with a messenger to the trobador and a letter which announced the extreme happiness of the great Count of Poictou. This, he knew, would draw the poison-bag.

The Frenchmen arrived at Louviers none too soon. As well mix fire and ice as Poictevin with Norman or Angevin with Angevin. The princes stalked about with claws out of velvet, the nobles bickered fiercely, and the men-at-arms did after their kind. There was open fighting. Gaston of Béarn picked a quarrel with John Botetort, and they fought it out with daggers in the fosse. Then Count Richard took one of his brother's goshawks and would not give it up. Over the long body of that bird half a score noblemen engaged with swords; the Count of Poictou himself accounted for six, and ended by pommelling his brother into a red jelly. There was a week or more of this, during which the old King hunted like a madman all day and revelled in gloomy vices all night. Richard saw little of him and little of the lady of France. She, a pale shade, flitted dismally out when evoked by the King, dismally in again at a nod from him.

Whenever she did appear Prince John hovered about, looking tormented; afterwards the pock-marked Cluniac might be heard lecturing her on theology and the soul's business in passionless monologue. It was very far from gay. As for her, Richard believed her melancholy mad; he himself grew fretful, irritable, most quarrelsome. Thus it was that he first plundered and then punched his brother.

After that Prince John disappeared for a little to nurse his sores, and Richard got within fair speaking distance of Madame Alois. In fact, she sent for him late one night when the King, as he knew, was away, munching the ashes of charred pleasure in some stews or other. He obeyed the summons with a half-shrug.

They received him with consternation. The distracted lady was in a chair, hugging herself; the Cluniac stood by, a mortified emblem; a scared woman or two fled behind the throne. Madame Alois, when she saw who the visitor was, began to shake.

'Oh, oh!' she said in a whisper, 'have you come to murder me, my lord?'

'Why, Madame,' Richard made haste to say, 'I would serve you any other way but that, and supposed I had the right. But I came because you sent for me.'

She passed her hand once or twice over her face, as if to brush cobwebs away; one of the women made a piteous appeal of the eyes to Richard, who took no notice of it; the monk said something to himself in a low voice, then to the Count, 'Madame is overwrought, my lord.'

'Yes, you rascal,' thought Richard; 'your
work.' Aloud he said, 'I hope her Grace will
give you leave to retire, sir.' Madame hereupon
waved her people away, and went on waving long
after they had gone. Thus she was alone with
her future lord. There was the wreck of fine
beauty about her drawn face, beauty of the black-
and-white, sheeted sort; but she looked as if
she walked with ghosts. Richard was very gentle
with her. He drew near, saying, 'I grieve to see
you thus, Madame'; but she stopped him with a
question —

'They seek to have you marry me?'

He smiled: 'Our masters desire it, Madame.'

'Are you very sure of that?'

'I am here,' he explained, 'because I am so
sure.'

'And you desire —— '

'I, Madame,' he said quickly and shortly,
'desire two things — the good of my country and
your good. If I desire anything else, God knows
it is to keep my promise.'

'What is your promise?'

'Madame,' said Richard, 'I bear the Cross on
my shoulder, as you see.'

'Why,' she said, fearfully regarding it, 'that is
God's work!'

She began to walk about the room quickly, and
to talk to herself. He could not catch properly
what she said. Religion came into it, and a
question of time. 'Now it should be done, now
it should be done!' and then, 'Hear, O thou
Shepherd of Israel!' and then with a wild look
into Richard's face — 'That was a strange thing to

do to a lady. They can never lay that to me!'
Afterwards she began to wring her hands, with a
cry of 'Fie, poison, poison, poison!' looking at
Richard all the time.

'This poor lady,' he told himself, 'is possessed
by a devil, therefore no wife for me, who have
devil enough and to spare.'

'What ails you, Madame?' he asked her.
'Tell me your grief, and upon my life I will
amend it if I can.'

'You cannot,' she said. 'Nothing can mend
it.'

'Then, with leave'—he went to the curtains—
'I will call your Grace's people. Our discussions
can be later; there is time enough.'

She would have stopped him had she dared, or
had the force; but literally she was spent. There
was just time to get the women in before she
tumbled. Richard, in his perplexity, determined
to wrangle out the matter with the King on the
morrow, cost what it might. So he did; and to
his high surprise the King reasoned instead of
railing. Madame Alois, he said, was weakly, un-
wholesome indeed. In his opinion she wanted,
what all young women want, a husband. She was
too much given to the cloister, she had visions,
she was feared to use the discipline, she ate
nothing, was more often on her knees than on
her feet. 'All this, my son,' said King Henry,
'you shall correct at your discretion. Humours,
vapours, qualms, fantasies — pouf! You can blow
them away with a kiss. Have you tried it? No?
Too cold? Nay, but you should.' And so on,
and so on. That day, none too soon, the French

ambassadors arrived, and Richard saw the Count of Saint-Pol among them.

He had never liked the Count of Saint-Pol; or perhaps it would be truer to say that he dis-liked him more than ordinary. But he belonged to, had even a tinge of, Jehane; some of her secret fragrance hung about him, he walked in some ray of her glory. It seemed to Richard, bothered, sick, fretted, a little disconcerted as he was now, that the Count of Saint-Pol had an air which none other of this people had. He greeted him therefore with more than usual affability, very much to Saint-Pol's concern. Richard ob-served this, and suddenly remembered that he was doing the man what the man must certainly believe to be a cruel wrong. '*Mort de Dieu!* What am I about?' his heart cried. 'I ought to be ashamed to look this fellow in the face, and here I am making a brother of him.'

'Saint-Pol,' he said immediately, 'I should like to speak with you. I owe you that.'

'Your Grace's servant,' said Eudo, with a stiff reverence, 'when and where you will.'

'Follow me,' said Richard, 'as soon as you have done with all this foppery.'   ·

In about an hour's time he was obeyed. After his fashion he took a straight plunge.

'Saint-Pol,' he said, 'I think you know where my heart is, whether here or elsewhere. I desire you to understand that in this case I am acting against my own will and judgment.'

The frankness of this lordly creature was un-mistakable, even to Saint-Pol.

'Hey, sire——,' he began spluttering, honesty in arms with rage. Richard took him up.

'If you doubt that, as you have my leave to do, I am ready to convince you. I will ride with you wherever you choose, and place myself at your discretion. Subject to this, mind you, that the award is final. Once more I will do it. Will you abide by that? Will you come with me?'

Saint-Pol cursed his fate. Here he was, tied to the French girl.

'My lord,' he said, 'I cannot obey you. My duty is to take Madame to Paris. That is my master's command.'

'Well,' said Richard, 'then I shall go alone. Once more I shall go. I am sick to death of this business.'

'My lord Richard,' cried Saint-Pol, 'I am no man to command you. Yet I say, Go. I know not what has passed between your Grace and my sister Jehane; but this I know very well. It will be a strange thing'—he laughed, not pleasantly—'a strange thing, I say, if you cannot bend that arbiter to your own way of thinking.'

Richard looked at him coldly.

'If I could do that, my friend,' he said, 'I should not suffer arbitration at all.'

'The proposition was not mine, my lord,' urged Saint-Pol.

'It could not be, sir,' Richard said sharply. 'I proposed it myself, because I consider that a lady has the right to dispose of her own person. She loved me once.'

'I believe that she is yours at this hour, sire.'

'That is what I propose to find out,' said Richard. 'Enough. What news have they in Paris?'

Saint-Pol could not help himself; he was
bursting with a budget he had received from
the south. 'They greatly admire a sirvente of
Bertran de Born's, sire.'

'What is the stuff of the sirvente?'

'It is a scandalous subject, sire. He calls it
the Sirvente of Kings, and speaks much evil of
your Order.' Richard laughed.

'I will warrant him to do that better than any
man alive, and allow him some reason for it. I
think I will go to see Bertran.'

'Ha, sire,' said Saint-Pol with meaning, 'he
will tell you many things, some good, and some
not so good.'

'Be sure he will,' said Richard. 'That is
Bertran's way.'

He would trust no one with his present reflec-
tions, and seek no outside strength against his
present temptations. He had always had his
way; it had seemed to come to him by right,
by the *droit de seigneur*, the natural law which
puts the necks of fools under the heels of strong
men. No need to consider of all that: he knew
that the thing desired lay to his hand; he could
make Jehane his again if he would, and neither
King of England nor King of France, nor Council of Westminster nor Diet of the Empire could
stop him — if he would. But that, he felt now,
was just what he would not. To beat her down
with torrents of love-cries; to have her trembling, cowed, drummed out of her wits by her
own heart-beats; to compel, to dominate, to tame,
when her young pride and young strength were
the things most beautiful in her: never, by the

Cross of Christ! That, I suppose, is as near to
true love as a man can get, to reverence in a
girl that which holds her apart. Richard got
so near precisely because he was less lover than
poet. You may doubt, if you choose (with Abbot
Milo), whether he had love in him. I doubt.
But certainly he was a poet. He saw Jehane
all glorious, and gave thanks for the sight. He
felt to touch heaven when he neared her; but
he did not covet her possession, at the moment.
Perhaps he felt that he did possess her: it is a
poet's way. So little, at any rate, did he covet,
that, having made up his mind what he would
do, he sent Gaston of Béarn to Saint-Pol-la-
Marche with a letter for Jehane, in which he
said: 'In two days I shall see you for the last
or for all time, as you will' — and then possessed himself in patience the appointed number of hours.

Gaston of Béarn, romantic figure in those grey
latitudes, pale, black-eyed, freakishly bearded,
dressed in bright green, rode his way singing,
announced himself to the lady as the Child of
Love; and when he saw her kissed her foot.

'Starry Wonder of the North,' he said, kneeling, 'I bring fuel to your ineffable fires. Our
King of Lovers and Lover among Kings is all
at your feet, sighing in this paper.' He seemed to
talk in capitals, with a flourish handed her the scroll.
He had the gratification to see her clap a hand to
her side directly she touched it; but no more. She
perused it with unwavering eyes in a stiff head.

'Farewell, sir,' she said then; 'I will prepare
for my lord.'

E

'And I, lady,' said Gaston, 'in consequence of
a vow I have vowed my saint, will await his coming in the forest, neither sleeping nor eating until
he has his enormous desires.   Farewell, lady.'

He went out backwards, to keep his promise.
The brown woodland was gay with him for a day
and a night; for he sang nearly all the time with
unflagging spirits.   But Jehane spent part of the
interval in the chapel, with her hands crossed upon
her fine bosom.   The God in her heart fought
with Him on the altar.   She said no prayers; but
when she left the place she sent a messenger for
Gilles de Gurdun, the blunt-nosed Norman knight
who loved her so much that he said nothing about
it.

This Gurdun, pricking through the woods, came
upon Gaston of Béarn, dazzling as a spring tree
and singing like an inspired machine.   He pulled
up at the wonderful sight, and scowled.   It is the
proper Norman greeting.   Gaston treated him as
part of the landscape, like the rest of it mournful,
but provocative of song.

'Give you good-day, beau sire,' said Gilles;
Gaston waved his hand and went on singing at
the top of his voice.   Then Gilles, who was
pressed, tried to pass ; and Gaston folded his arms.

'Ha, beef,' said he, 'none pass here but the
brave.'

'Out, parrot,' quoth Gilles, and plunged through
the wood.

Because of Gaston's vow there was no blood
shed at the moment, but he had hopes that he
might be released in time.   'There goes a dead
man,' was therefore his comment before he
resumed.

But Jehane, when she heard the horse, ran out to meet his rider. Her face was alight. 'Come in, come in,' she said, and took him by the hand. He followed her with a beating heart, neither daring nor knowing how to say anything. She led him into the little dark chapel.

'Gilles, Gilles,' she said panting, 'do you love me, Gilles?'

He was hoarse, could hardly speak for the crack in his throat. 'O God,' he said under his breath, 'O God, Jehane, how I love you!'

Here, because of a certain flicker in her eyes, he made forward; but she put out her two hands the length of her arms and fenced him off. 'No, no, Gilles, not yet.' Pain sharpened her voice. 'Listen first to me. I do not love you; but I am frightened. Some one is coming; you must be here to help me. I give myself to you — I will be yours — I must — there is no other way.'

She stopped; you could have heard the thudding of her heart.

'Give then,' said Gilles with a croak, and took her.

She felt herself engulfed in a sea of fire, but set her teeth and endured the burning of that death. The poor fellow did but kiss her once or twice, and kissed no closer than the Angevin; but the grace is one that goes by favour. Gilles, nevertheless, took primer seisin and was content. Afterwards, hand in hand, trembling each, the possessed and the possessing, they stood before the twinkling lamp which hinted at the Son of God, and waited what must happen.

In about half an hour's time Jehane heard the

long padding tread she knew so well, and took
a deep breath.   Next Gilles heard something.
    'One comes.   Who comes?' he said whisper-
ing.
    'Richard of Anjou.   I need you now.'
    'Do you want me to——?' Gilles honestly
thought he was to kill the Count.   She unde-
ceived him soon.
    'To kill Richard, Gilles?   Nay, man, he is
not for your killing.'   She gave a short laugh,
not very pleasant for her lover to hear.   But
Gilles, for all that, put hand to hilt.   The Count
of Poictou stooped at the entry and saw them
together.
    It wanted but that to blow the embers.   Some-
thing tigerish surged in him, some gust of
jealousy, some arrogant tide in the blood not
all clean.   He moved forward like a wind and
caught the girl up in his arms, lifted her off
her feet, smothered her cry.   'My Jehane, my
Jehane, who dares——?'   Gilles touched him
on the shoulder, and he turned like lightning with
Jehane held fast.   His breath came quick and
short through his nose: Gilles believed his last
hour at hand, but made the most of it.
    'What now, dog?' thus the lean Richard.
    'Set down the lady, my lord,' said doughty
Gilles.   'She is promised to me.'
    'Heart of God, what is this?'   He held back
his head, like a snake, that he might see what
he would strike at.   'Is it true, girl?'   Jehane
looked up from his shoulder, where she had
been hiding her face.   She could not speak, but
she nodded.

'It is true? Thou art promised?'

'I am promised, my lord,' said Jehane. 'Let me go.'

He put her down at once, between himself and Gurdun. Gurdun went to take up her hand again, but at a look from Richard forbore. The Count went on with his interrogatories, outwardly as calm as a field of snow.

'In whose name art thou promised to this knight, Jehane? In thy brother's?'

'No, lord. In my own.'

'Am I nothing?' She began to cry.

'Oh, oh!' she wailed, 'You are everything, everything in the world.'

He turned away from her, and stood facing the altar, with folded arms, considering. Gilles had the wit to be silent; the girl fought for breath. Richard, in fact, was touched to the heart, and capable of any sacrifice which could seem the equivalent of this. He must always lead, even in magnanimity; but it was a better thing than emulation moved him now. When he next turned with a calm, true face to Jehane there was not a shred of the Angevin in him; all was burnt away.

'What is the name of this knight, Jehane?' She told him, Gilles de Gurdun.

Then he said, 'Come hither, De Gurdun,' and Gilles knelt down before the son of his overlord. Jehane would have knelt to him too, but that he held her by the hand and would not suffer it.

'Now, Gilles, listen to what I shall tell you,' said Richard. 'There is no lady in the world more noble than this one, and no man living who

means more faithfully by her than I.   I will do
her will this day, and that speedily, lest the devil
be served.   Are you a true man, Gilles?'

'Lord,' said Gurdun, 'I try to be so.   Your
father made me a knight.   I have loved this lady
since she was twelve years old.'

'Are you a man of substance, my friend?'

'We have a good fief, my lord.   My father
holds of the Church of Rouen, and the Church
of the Duke.   I serve with a hundred spears
where I may, a *routier* if nothing better offer.'

'If I give you Jehane, what do you give
me?'

'Thanks, my good lord, and faith, and long
service.'

'Get up, Gilles,' said Richard.

Gilles kissed his knee, and rose.   Richard put
Jehane's hand into his and held the two together.

'God serve me as I shall serve you, Gilles, if
any harm come of this,' he said shrewdly, with
words that whistled in the air; and as Gilles
looked him squarely in the face, Richard ran an
eye over him.   Gilles was found honest.   Richard
kissed Jehane on the forehead, and went out without a look back.   At the edge of the wood he
found Gaston of Béarn sucking his fingers.

'There went by here,' said the gay youth, 'a
black knight with a face of a raw meat colour,
and the most villainous scowl ever you saw.   I
consider him to be dead already.'

'I have given him something which should
cure him of the scowl and justify his colour,'
answered him the Count.   'Moreover, I have
given him the chance of eternal life.'   Then with

a cry — ' Oh, Gaston, let us get to the South, see the sun fleck the roads, smell the oranges! Let us get to the South, man! It seems I have entertained an angel. And now that I have given her wings, and now that she is gone, I know how much I love her. Speed, Gaston! We will go to the South, see Bertran, and make some songs of good women and men in want!'

'Pardieu,' said Gaston. 'I am with you, Richard, for I am in want. I have eaten nothing for two days.'

So they rode out of the woods of Saint-Pol-la-Marche, and Richard began to sing songs of Jehane the Fair-Girdled; never truly her lover until he might love her no more.

CHAPTER V

DAY-LONG and night-long he sang of her, being now in the poetic mood, highly exalted, out of himself. The country took tints of Jehane, her shape, her fine nobility. The thrust hills of the Vexin were her breasts; the woods, being hot gold, her russet hair; in still green water he read the secrets of her eyes; in the milk of October dawns her calm brows had been dipped. The level light of the Beauce, so beneficent yet so austere, figured her soul. Fair-girdled was Touraine by Vienne and Loire; fair-girdled Jehane, who wore virgin candour about her loins and over her heart a shield of blue ice. As far southwards as Tours the dithyrambic prevailed; Richard was untiring in the hunt for analogues. Thence on to Poictiers, where the country (being his own) was perhaps more familiar; indeed, while he was climbing the grey peaks of Montagrier with his goal almost in sight, he turned scholiast and glossed his former raptures.

'You are not to tell me, Gaston,' he declared, 'that my Jehane has been untrue. She was never more wholly mine than when she gave herself to that other, never loved me more dearly. Such

power is given to women to lead this world. It is
the power of the Word, who cut Himself off and
made us His butchers in pure love. I shall do
my part. I shall wed the French girl, who in my
transports will never guess that in reality Jehane
will be in my arms.' Tears filled his eyes. 'For
we shall be wedded in the sight of heaven,' he
said sighing.

'Deus!' cried Gaston here, 'Such marriages
may be more to the taste of heaven than of men,
Richard. Man is a creature of sense.'

'He hath a spiritual part,' said Richard, 'so
rarely hidden that only the thin fingers of a girl
may get in to touch it. Then, being touched, he
knows that it is quick. Let me alone; I am not
all mud nor all devil. I shall do my duty, marry
the French girl, and love my golden Jehane until
I die.'

'That is the saying of a poet and king at once,'
said Gaston, and really believed it.

So they came at dusk to Autafort, a rock
castle on the confines of Perigord, held by Bertran de Born.

It looked, and was, a robber's hold, although it
had a poet for castellan. Its walls merely pro-
longed the precipices on which they were founded,
its towers but lifted the mountain spurs more
sharply to the sky. It dominated two watersheds,
was accessible only on one side, and then by a
ridgeway; from it the valley roads and rock-
strewn hillsides could be seen for many leagues.
Long before Richard was at the gate the Lord of
Autafort had had warning, and had peered down
upon his suzerain at his clambering. 'The crows

shall have Richard before Richard me,' said Bertran de Born ; so he had his bridge pulled up and portcullis let down, and Autafort showed a bald face to the newcomers.

Gaston grinned. 'Hospitality of Aquitaine! Hospitality of your duchy, Richard.'

'By my head,' said the Count, 'if I sleep under the stars I sleep at Autafort this night. But hear me charm this plotter.' He called at the top of his voice, 'Ha, Bertran! Come you down, man.' The surrounding hills echoed his cries, the jack-daws wheeled about the turrets; but presently came one and put his eye to the grille. Richard saw him.

'Is that you, then, Bertran?' he shouted. There was no answer, but the spyer was heard breathing hard at his vent.

'Come out of your earth, red fox,' Richard chid him. 'Show your grievous snout to the hills; do your snuffling abroad to the clear sky. I have whipped off the hounds; my father is not here. Will you let starve your liege-lord?'

At this the bolts were drawn, the bridge went down with a clatter, and Bertran de Born came out — a fine stout man, all in a pother, with a red, perplexed face, angry eyes, hair and beard cut in blocks, a body too big for his clothes — a man of hot blood, fumes and rages. Richard at sight of him, this unquiet sniffer of offences, this whirled about with stratagems, threw back his head and laughed long and loud.

'O thou plotter of thine own dis-ease! O rider of nightmares, what harm can I do thee? Not, believe me, a tithe of thy desert. Come

thou here straightly, Master Bertran, and take
what I shall give thee.'

'By God, Lord Richard——' said Bertran, and
boggled horribly; but the better man waited,
and in the end he came up sideways. Richard
swung from his horse, took his host by the shoulders, shook him well, and kissed him on both
cheeks. 'Spinner of mischief, red robber, singer
of the thoughts of God!' he said, 'I swear I love
thee through it all, Bertran, though I should do
better to wring thy neck. Now give us food and
drink and clean beds, for Gaston at least is a
dead man without them. Afterwards we will sing
songs.'

'Come in, come in, Richard,' said Bertran de
Born.

For a day or two Richard was bathed in golden
calm, hugging his darling thought, full of Jehane,
fearful to share her. Often he remembered it in
later life; it held a place and commanded a mood
which no hour of his wildest possession could out-
vie. The mountain air, still, but latently nimble,
the great mountains themselves dreaming in the
sunlight, the sailing birds, hinted a peace to his
soul whither his last conquest of his baser part
assured him he might soar. Now he could guess
(thought he) that quality in love which it borrows
from God and shares with the angels, ministers
of God, the steady burning of a flame keen and
hard. So on an afternoon of weather serene
beyond all belief of the North, mild, tired, softly
radiant, still as a summer noon; as he sat with
Bertran in a courtyard where were lemon-trees

and a fountain, and above the old white walls, and above the strutting pigeons, a square of blue, he began to speak of his affairs, of what he had done and of what was to do.

Bertran's was a grudging spirit: you shall hear the Abbot Milo upon that matter anon, than whom there are few better qualified to speak. He grudged Richard everything — his beauty, his knit and graceful body, his brain like a sword, his past exploits, his present content. What it was contented him he knew not altogether, though a letter from Saint-Pol had in part advised him; but he was sure he had wherewithal to discontent him. 'Foh! a juicy orange indeed,' he said to himself, 'but I can wring him dry.' If Richard hugged one thought, Bertran hugged another, and took it to bed with him o' nights. Now, there-fore, when Richard spoke of Jehane, Bertran said nothing, waiting his time; but when he went on to Madame Alois and his duty (which really col-oured all the former thought) Bertran made a grimace.

'Rascal,' says Richard, shamming rough, 'why do you make faces at me?'

Bertran began jerking about like the lid of a boiling pot, and presently sends a boy for his viol. At this, when it came, he snatched, and set to plucking a chord here and a chord there, grinning fearfully all the time.

'A *tenzon!* A *tenzon!* beau sire!' cries he. ' Now a *tenzon* between you and me!'

'Let it be so,' says Richard; 'have at you. I sing of the calm day, of the sweets of true love.'

'Accorded,' says the other. 'And I sing of

the sours of false love.   Do you set the mode,
prince of blood royal as you are.'

Richard took the viol without after-thought and
struck a few chords.   A great tenderness was in
his heart; he saw Duty and himself hand in hand
walking a long road by night; two large stars
beaconed the way; these were Jehane's eyes.   A
watcher or two stole into the upper gallery, leaned
on the parapet and listened, for both men were
renowned singers.   Richard began to sing of
green-eyed Jehane, who wore the gold girdle,
whose hair was red gold.   His song was —

> Li dous consire
> Quem don' Amors soven —

but I English it thus —

'That gentle thought which love will give
sometimes is like a plait of silk and gold, and so
is this song of mine to be; wherein you shall find
a red deep cry which cometh from the heart, and
a thin blue cry which is the cry of what is virgin
in my soul, and a golden long cry, the cry of the
King, and a cry clear as crystal and colder than a
white moon: and that is the cry of Jehane.'

Bertran, trembling, snatched at the viol.   'Mine
to sing, Richard, mine to sing!   Ha, love me no
more!'

> Cantar d' Amors non voilh,

he began —

'Your strands are warped and will not accord,
for love will warp any song.   It turneth the heart
of a man black, and the soul it eateth up.   At
fourteen goes the virgin first a-wallowing; and
soon the King croaks like a hog.   A plait!   Love

is a fetter of hot iron; so my song shall be iron-cruel like the bidding of Jehane. Say now, shall I set the song? The love-cry is the cry of a man who drags his way with his side torn; and the colour of it is dry red, like old blood; and the sound thereof maketh the hearers ache, so it quavers and shrills. For it cries only two things: sorrow and shame.'

He misconceived his adversary who thought to quell him by such vapours. Richard took the viol.

' Bertran, it is well seen that thou art pinched and have a torn side; but ask of thy itching fingers who graved the wound. Dry thou art, Bertran, for thy trough is dry; the husks prick thy gums, but there is no other meat. Well may the hearers' ears go aching; for thy cry, man, proceedeth from thy aching belly. But now I will set the song again, and tell thee of a lady girdled with fine gold. Beneath the girdle beats a red heart; but her spirit is like a spire of blue smoke, that comes from a fire, indeed, but strains up to heaven. Warmed by that fire, like that smoke I fly up; and so I lie among the stars with Jehane.'

Bertran's jaw was at work, mashing his tongue. 'Ah, Richard, is it so with thee? Wait now while I strike a blow.' He made the viol scream.

' What if I twist the song awry, and give thee good cause to limp the sorrowful way? What if for my aching belly I give thee an aching heart? Eh, if my fingers scratch my side, there are worse talons at thine. Watch for the Lion's claw, Richard, which tears not flesh but honour, and gives more pain than any knife. Pain! He is

King of Pain!   Mend that, then face sorrow and shame.'

Ending with a snap, he grinned more knowledge out of his red eyes than he pronounced with his mouth. His terrible excitement, the labour and sweat of it, set Richard's brows knitting. He stretched out his hand for the viol slowly; and his eyes were cold on Bertran, and never off him for a moment as he sang to this enemy, and judged him while he sang. The note was changed.

'The Lion is a royal beast, a king, whose son am I. We maul not each other in Anjou, save when the jackal from the South cometh snarling between. Then, when we see the unclean beast, saith one, "Faugh! is this your friend?" and the other, "Thou dost ill to say so." Then the blood may flow and the jackal get a meal. But here there is none to come licking blood. The prize is the White Roe of France, fed on the French lilies, and now in safe harbour. She shall lie by the Leopard, and the Lion rule the forest in peace because of the peace about him; and like a harvest moon above us, clear of the trees, will be Jehane.'

'Listen, Richard, I will be clearer yet,' came from between Bertran's teeth. He fairly ground them together. Having the viol, he struck but one note upon it, with such rudeness that the string broke. He threw the thing away and sang without it, leaning his hands on his knees, and craning forward that he might spit the words.

'This is the bite of the song: she is forsworn. Harbour? She kept harbour too long; she is mangled, she is torn. Touch not the Lion's prey, Leopard. You go hunting too late — for all but sorrow and shame.'

Richard stretched not his hand again ; his jaw dropped and most of the strong colour died down in his face. Turned to stone, stiff and immovable, he sat staring at the singer, while Bertran, biting his lip, still grinning and twitching with his late effort, watched him.

' Give me the truth, thou.' His voice was like an old man's, hollow.

' As God is in heaven that is the truth, Richard,' said Bertran de Born.

The Count's head went up, as when a hound yelps to the sky: laughter ensued, barking laughter — not mirth, not grief disguised, but mockery, the worst of all. One on the gallery nudged his fellow; that other shrugged him off. Richard stretched his long arms, his clenched fists to the dumb sky. ' Have I bent the knee to good issues or not? Have I abased my head? O clement prince! O judge in Israel! O father of kings! Hear now a parable of the Prodigal: Father, I have sinned against heaven and before thee, and thou art no more worthy to be called my father. O glutton! O filching dog!'

' By the torch of the Gospel, Count Richard, what I sang is true,' said Bertran, still tensely grinning, and now also wringing at his hang-nails. Richard, checked by the voice, turned blazing upon him.

' Why, thou school-boy rhymester, that is the only merit thou hast, and that not thine own! Thy japes are nought, thy tragics the mewing of

cats; but thy news, fellow, thy news is too rich
matter for thy sewer of a throat. Tragic? No,
it is worse: it is comic, O heaven! Heed you
now ——' In his bitter shame he began panto-
miming with his fingers : — ' Here are two persons,
father by the Grace of God, son by the grace of
the father. Saith father, " Son, thou art sprung
from kings; take this woman that is sprung from
kings, for I have no further use for her." Anon
cometh a white rag thinly from the inner tent —
mark her provenance. Son kneeleth down. " Wilt
thou have my son, cony?" saith father. " Yea,
dear heart," saith she. " 'Tis my counterpart, mark
you," saith father. " Better than nothing at all,"
saith she. Benevolent father, supple-kneed son,
convenient lady. Here is agreement. And thus
it ends.' Again he laughed outright at the steel-
blue face of the sky, then jumped in a flash from
his seat to the throat of Bertran. Bertran tumbled
backwards with a strangled cry, and Richard
pegged him to the ground.

'Thou yapping cur, Bertran,' he grated, ' thou
sick dog of my kennel, if this snarl of thine goes
true thou hast done a service to me and mine thou
knowest not of. There is little to do before I am
the richest man in Christendom. Why, dull rogue,
thou hast set me free ! ' He looked up exulting
from his work at the man's throat to shout this
word. ' But if it is not true, Bertran ' — he shook
him like a rat — ' if it is not true, I return, O
Bertran, and tear this false gullet out of its case,
and with thy speckled heart feed the crows of
Périgord.' Bertran had foam on his lips, but
Richard showed him no mercy. ' As it is, Ber·

F

tran,' he went on with his teeth on edge, 'I am minded to finish thee. But that I need something from thee I think I should do it. Tell me now whence came thy news. Tell me, Bertran, or thou art in hell in a moment.'

He had to let him up to win from him after a time that his informant was the Count of Saint-Pol. Little matter that this was untrue, the bringing in of his name set wild alarums clanging in Richard's head. It was only too likely to have been Saint-Pol's doing; there was obvious reason; but by the same token Saint-Pol might be a liar. He saw that he must by all means find Saint-Pol, and find him at once. He began to shout for Gaston. 'To horse, to horse, Gaston!' The court rang with his voice; to the clamour he made, which might betoken murder, arson, pillage, or the sin against the Holy Ghost, out came the vassals in a swarm. 'To horse, to horse, Béarnais! Where out of hell is Gaston of Béarn?' The devil of Anjou was loose in Autafort that day.

Gaston came delicately last, drawing his beard through his fist, to see Bertran de Born lie helpless in a lemon-bush hard by the wall. Richard, quite beyond himself, exploded with his story, and so was sobered. While Gaston made his comments, he, instead of listening, made comments of his own.

'Dear Lord Richard,' said Gaston reasonably, 'if you do not know Bertran by this time it is a strange thing and a pitiful thing. For it shows you without any wit. He was appointed, it would seem, to be the thorn in your rosebed of Anjou. What has he done since he was let be made but

set you all by the ears? What did he do by the
young King but miserably? What by Geoffrey?
Is there a man in the world he hates more than
the old King? Yes, there is one: you. Take
a token. The last time they two met was in this
very castle; and then the King your father kissed
him, and forgiving him Henry's death, gave him
back his Autafort; and Bertran too gave a kiss,
that love might abound. Judas, Judas! And
what did Judas next? Dear Richard, let us think
awhile, but not here. Let us go to Limoges and
think with the Viscount. But let us by all means
kill Bertran de Born first.'

During this speech, which had much to recommend it, Richard, as I have told you, did his thinking by himself. He always cooled as suddenly
as he boiled over; and now, warily regarding
the right hand and the left of this monstrous
fable, he saw that, though Saint-Pol might have
played fox in it, another must have played goat.
He could not fail to remember Louviers, and
certain horrid mysteries which had offended him
then with only vague disgust, as for matters which
were outside his own care. Now they all took
shape satyric, like hideous heads thrust out of the
dark to loll their tongues at him. To the shock
of his first dismay succeeded the onset of rage,
white and cold and deadly as a night frost. Eh,
but he would meet his teeth in some throat! But
he would go slowly to work, clear the ground and
stalk his prey. The leopard devises creeping
death. He made up his mind. Gaston he sent
to the South, to Angoulesme, to Périgord, to
Auvergne, to Cahors. The horn must be heard

at the head of every brown valley, the armed men shadow every white road. He himself went to his city of Poictiers.

Bertran de Born saw him go, and rubbed his hair till it stood like reeds shaken by the wind. Whether he loved mischief or not (and some say he breathed it); whether he had a grudge against Anjou not yet assuaged; whether he was in league with Prince John, or had indeed thought to do Prince Richard a service, let philosophers, experts of mankind, determine. If he had a turn for dramatics he had certainly indulged it now, and given himself strong meat for a new Sirvente of Kings. At least he was very busy after Richard's departure, himself preparing for a long journey to the South.

CHAPTER VI

COUNT RICHARD found time, while he was at
Poictiers awaiting the Aquitanian levies, to write
six letters to Jehane Saint-Pol. Of these some,
with their bearers, fell by the wayside. As luck
would have it, Jehane received but two, the first
and the last. The first said: ' I am in the way of
liberty, but by a red road. Have hopes of me.'
Jehane was long in answering. One may picture
the poor soul taking the dear and wicked thing
into the little chapel, laying it on the altar-stone
warm from her vest, restoring it after office done
to that haven whence she must banish its writer.
Fortified, she replied with, ' Alas, my lord, the
way of liberty leads not to me; nor can I serve
you otherwise than in bonds. I pray you, make
my yoke no heavier. — Your servant, in little ease,
Jehane.' This wistful unhappy letter gave him
heartache; he could scarcely keep himself at
home. Yet he must, being as yet sure of nothing.
He replied in a second and third, a fourth and a
fifth letter, which never reached her. The last
was sent when he had begun what he thought
fit to do at Tours, saying, ' I make war, but the
cause is righteous. Never misjudge me, Jehane.'
There were many reasons why she should not
answer this.

69

Returning to his deeds at Poictiers, I pick up the story from the Abbot Milo, whom he found there. The Count, you may judge, kept his own counsel. Milo was his confessor, but at this time Richard was not in a confessing humour; therefore Milo had to gather scandal as he could. There was very little difficulty about this. ' In the city of Tours,' he writes, 'in those middle days of Advent, it appears that rumour, still gadding, was adrift with names almost too high for the writing. There were many there who had no business; the Count of Blois, for instance, the Baron of Chateaudun, the fighting Bishop of Durham (I fear, a hireling shepherd), Geoffrey Talebot, Hugh of Saint-Circ. One reason of this was that King Henry was in England, not yet come to an agreement with the French King, nor likely to it if what we heard was true, yea, or a tenth part of it. God forbid that I should write what these ears heard; but this I will say. It was I who told the shocking tale to my lord Richard, adding also this hint, that his former friend was involved in it, Eudo Count of Saint-Pol. If you will believe me, not the tale of iniquity moved him; but he received it with shut mouth, and eyes fixed upon mine. But at the name of the Count of Saint-Pol he took a breath, at the mention of his part in the business he took a deep breath, and when he heard that this man was yet at Tours, he got up from his chair and struck the table with his closed fist. Knowing him as I did, I considered that the weather looked black for Saint-Pol.

'Next day Count Richard moved his hosts

out of the fields by Poictiers to the very bor-
ders of his country, and calling a halt at Saint-
Gilles and making snug against alarms, himself,
with my lord Gaston of Béarn, with the Dauphin of Auvergne also, and the Viscount of
Béziers, crossed the march into Touraine, and
so came to Tours about a week before Christmas, the weather being bright and frosty.'

It seems he did not take the abbot with him,
for the rest of the good man's record is full of
morality, a certain sign that facts failed him.
There may have been reasons; at any rate the
Count went into Tours in a trenchant humour,
with ears keen and wide for all shreds of report.
And he got enough and to spare. In the wet
market-place, on the flags of the great churchyard, by the pillars of the nave, in the hall, in
the chambers, in the inn-galleries; wherever men
met or women whispered in each other's necks,
there flew the names of Alois, King Philip's sister,
and of King Henry, Count Richard's father. Richard made short work, short and dry. It was in mid-
hall in the Bishop's palace, one day after dinner,
that he met and stopped the Count of Saint-Pol.

'What now, beau sire?' says the Count, out
of breath. Richard's eyes were alight. 'This,'
says he, 'that you lie in your throat.'

Count Eudo looked about him, and everywhere
saw the faces of men risen from the board intent
on him. 'Strange words, beau sire,' says he, very
white. Richard raised his voice till the metal
rang in it.

'But not strange doing, I think, on your part.
This has been going on, how long?'

Saint-Pol was stung. 'Ah, it becomes you
very ill to reproach me, my lord.'

'I think it becomes me excellently,' said Richard. 'You have lied for a vile purpose; you
have disgraced your name. You seek to drive
me by slander whither I may not go in honour.
You lie like a broker. You are a shameful
liar.'

No man could stand this from another, however great that other; and Saint-Pol was not
a coward. He looked up at his adversary, still
white, but steady.

'How then?' he asked him, 'how then if I
lie not, Count of Poictou? And how if you
know that I lie not?'

'Then,' said Richard, 'you use insult, which
is worse.'

Saint-Pol took off his glove of mail and flung
it with a clatter on the floor.

'Since it has come to this, my lord —— ' Richard spiked the glove with his sword, tossed it to
the hammer-beams of the roof, and caught it as
it fell.

'It shall come nearer, Count, I take it.' Thus
he finished the other's phrase, then stalked out
of the Bishop's house. It was then and there
that he wrote to Jehane that sixth letter, which
she received: 'I make war, but the cause is
righteous. Never misjudge me, Jehane.'

The end of it was a combat à outrance in the
meads by the Loire, with all Tours on the walls
to behold it. Richard was quite frank about the
part he proposed to himself. 'The man must
die,' he told the Dauphin of Auvergne, 'even

though he have spoken the truth.   As to that I am not sure, I am not yet informed.   But he is not fit to live on any ground.   By these slanders of his he has disgraced the name and outraged the honour of the most lovely lady in the world, whose truest misfortune is to be his sister; by the same token I must punish him for the dignity of the lady I am (at present) designed to wed. She is always the daughter of his liege-lord. What!'—he threw his head up —'Is not a daughter of France worth a broken back?'

' Tu-dieu, yes,' says the Dauphin; 'but it is a stoutish back, Richard.   It is a back which ranks high.   Kings clap it familiarly.   Conrad of Montferrat calls it a cousin's back.   The Emperor has embraced it at an Easter fair.'

' I would as soon break Conrad's back as his, Dauphin, believe me,' Richard replied; 'but Conrad has said nothing.   And there is another reason.'

' I have thought myself of a reason against it,' the Dauphin said quickly, yet with a flutter of timidity.   ' This man's name is Saint-Pol.'

Richard grew bleak in a moment.   ' That,' he said, ' is why I shall kill him.   He seeks to drive us to marriage.   Injurious beast!   His name is Pandarus.'   Then he left the Dauphin and shut himself up until the day of battle.

They had formed lists in the Loire meads: a red pavilion with leopards upon it for the Count of Poictou, a blue pavilion streaked with basilisks in silver for the Count of Saint-Pol.   The crowd was very great, for the city was full of people; in the tribune the King of England's throne was

left empty save for a drawn sword; but one sat
beside it as arbiter for the day of life and death,
and that was Prince John, Richard's brother, by
Richard summoned from Paris, and most un-
willingly there. Bishop Hugh of Durham sat
next him, and marvelled to see the sweat glisten
on his forehead on a day when all the world else
felt the north wind to their bones. 'Are you
suffering, dear lord?' 'Eh, Bishop Hugh, Bishop
Hugh, this is a mad day for me!' 'By God,'
thought Hugh of Durham, 'and so it might
prove, my man!'

They blew trumpets; and at the second sound-
ing Saint-Pol, the challenger, rode out on a big
grey horse, himself in a hauberk of chain mail with
a coif of the same, and a casque wherein three
grey heron's feathers. This was the badge of the
house: Jehane wore heron's feathers. He had a
blue surcoat and blue housings for his horse.
Behind him, esquire of honour, rode the young
Amadeus of Savoy, carrying his banner, a white
basilisk on a blue field. Saint-Pol was a burly man,
bearing his honours squarely on breast and back.

They sounded for the Count of Poictou, who
came presently out of his tent and lightly swung
himself into the saddle — a feat open to very few
men armed in mail. As he came cantering down
the long lists no man could fail to mark the size
and splendid ease he had; but some said, ' He is
younger by five years than Saint-Pol, and not so
stout a man.' He had a red plume above his
leopard crest, a white surcoat over his hauberk,
with three red leopards upon it. His shield was
of the same blazon, so also the housings of his

horse. The Dauphin of Auvergne carried his banner. The two men came together, saluted with ceremony, then turned with spears uplift to the tribune, the throned sword, the sweating prince beside it.

This one now rose up and caught at his chair, to give the signal. 'Oh, Richard of Anjou, do thou on the body of Saint-Pol what thy faith requires of thee; and do thou, Eudo, uphold the right thou hast, in the name of God in Trinity and of our Lady.' The Bishop of Tours blessed them both and the issue, they wheeled apart, and the battle began. It was short, three careers long. At the first shock Richard unhorsed his man; at the second he unhelmed him with a deep flesh-furrow in the cheek; at the third he drove down horse and man together and broke the Count's back. Saint-Pol never moved again.

The moment it was over, in the silence of all, Prince John came down from the tribune and fell upon Richard's neck. 'Oh, dearest brother,' cried he, 'what should I have done if the worst had befallen you? I cannot bear to think of it.'

'Oh, brother,' Richard said very quietly, 'I think you would have borne it very well. You would have married Madame Alois, and paid for a mass or two for me out of the dowry.'

This raking shot was heard by everybody. John grew red as fire. 'Why, what do you mean, Richard?' he stammered.

And Richard, 'Are my words so encumbered? Think them over, get them by heart. So doing, be pleased to ride with me to Paris.' At this the colour left John's face.

'Ah! To Paris?' He looked as if he saw death under a bush.

'That is where we must go,' said Richard, 'so soon as we have prayed for that poor blind worm on the ground, who now haply sees wherein he has offended.'

'Conrad of Montferrat, cousin of this dead, is there, Richard,' said the other with intention; but Richard laughed.

'In a very good hour we shall find him. I have to give him news of his cousin Saint-Pol. What is he there for?'

'It is in the matter of the kingdom of Jerusalem. He seeks Sibylla and that crown, and is like to get them.'

'I think not, John, I think not. We will fill his head with other thoughts; we will set it wanting mine. Your chance is a fair one yet, brother.'

Prince John laughed, but not comfortably. 'Your tongue bites, Richard.'

'Pooh,' says Richard, 'what else are you worth? I save my teeth'; and went his ways.

In Paris Richard repaired to the tower of his kinsman the Count of Angoulesme, but his brother to the Abbey of Saint-Germain. The Poictevin herald bore word to King Philip-Augustus on Richard's part; Prince John, as I suppose, bore his own word whither he had most need for it to go. It is believed that he contrived to see Madáme Alois in private; and if that great purple cape that held him in talk for nearly an hour by a windy corner of the Prè-aux-Clercs did not cover the back of Montferrat, then Gossip is a liar. Richard, for his part, took no account of John and his shifts; a wave of disgust for the creeping youth had filled the stronger man, and having got him into Paris there seemed nothing better to do with him than to let him alone. But that sensitive gorge of Richard's was one of his worst enemies: if he did not mean to hold the snake in the stick, he had better not have cleft the stick. As for John and his writhing, I am only half concerned with them; but let me tell you this. Whatever he did or did not sprang not from hatred of this or that man, but from fear, or from love of his own belly. Every prince of the house of Anjou loved inordinately some member of himself, some a noble member nobly, and others basely a base member. If John loved his belly, Richard loved his royal head: but enough. To be done with all this, Richard was summoned to the French King hot-foot, within a day or two of his coming; went immediately with his chaplain Anselm and other one or two, and was immediately received. He had, in fact, obeyed in such haste that he found two in the audience-chamber instead of one. With Philip of France was Conrad of Montferrat, a large, pale, ruminating Italian, full of bluster and thick blood. The French King was a youth, just the age of Jehane, of the thin, sharp, black-and-white mould into which had run the dregs of Capet. He was smooth-faced like a girl, and had no need to shave; his lips were very thin, set crooked in his face. So far as he was boy he loved and admired Richard, so far as he was Capet he distrusted him with all the rest of the world.

Richard knelt to his suzerain and was by him

caught up and kissed. Philip made him sit at his side on the throne. This put Montferrat, who was standing, sadly out of countenance, for he considered himself (as perhaps he was) the superior of any man uncrowned.

It seems that some news had drifted in on the west wind. 'Richard, oh, Richard!' the King began, half whimsical and half vexed, 'What have you been doing in Touraine?'

'Fair sire,' answered Richard, 'I have been doing what will, I fear, give pain to our cousin Montferrat. I have been breaking the back of the Count of Saint-Pol.' At this the Marquess, suffused with dark blood till he was colour of lead, broke out, pointing his finger as well as his words. As the bilge-water jets from a ketch when the hold is surcharged, so did the Marquess jet his expletives.

'Ha, sire! Ha, King of France! Now give me leave to break this brigand's back, who robs and reviles in one breath. Touch of the Gospel, is it to be borne?' Foaming with rage, he lunged forward a step or two, his hand upon his long sword. Richard slowly got up from the throne and stood his full height.

'Marquess, you use words I will not hear——'

King Philip broke in——'Fair lords, sweet lords——'; but Richard put his hand up, having a kingly way with him which even kings observed.

'Dear sire,'— his voice was level and cool — 'let me say my whole mind before the Marquess recovers his. The Count of Saint-Pol, for beastly reasons, spoke in my hearing either true things or false things concerning Madame Alois. If they

were true I was ready to die; if they were false I
hope he was. Believing them false, I had punished
one man for them before; but he had them from
Saint-Pol. Therefore I called Saint-Pol a liar,
and other proper things. This gave him occasion
to save his credit at the risk of his back. He
broke the one and I the other. Now I will hear
the Marquess.'

The Marquess tugged at his sword. 'And I,
Count of Poictou ——'; but King Philip held out
his sceptre, he too very much a king.

'And we, Count of Poictou,' he said, 'command
you by your loyalty to tell us what Saint-Pol dared
say of our sister Dame Alois.' Although his thin
boy's voice quavered, he seemed the more royal
for the human weakness. Richard was greatly
moved, thawed in a moment.

'God forgive me, Philip, but I cannot tell
thee ——' Pity broke up his tones.

The young king almost whimpered: 'Oh,
Richard, what is this?' But Richard turned
away his face. It was now the chance of the
great Italian.

'Now listen, King Philip,' he said, grim and
square, 'and listen you, Count of Poictou, whose
account is to be quieted presently. Of this
business I happen to know something. If it
serve not your honour I cannot help it. It
serves my murdered cousin's honour — therefore
listen.'

Richard's head was up. 'Peace, hound,' he
said, and the Marquess snarled like an old dog;
but Philip, with a quivering lip, put out his hand
till it touched Richard's shoulder. 'I must hear

it, Richard,' he said.   Richard put his arm round
the lad's neck: so the Marquess told his story.
At the end of it Richard dared look down into
Philip's marred eyes.   Then he kissed his forehead, and 'Oh, Philip,' says he, 'let him who is
hardy enough to tell this tale believe it, and let
us who hear it do as we must.   But now you
understand why I made an end of Saint-Pol, and
why, by heaven and earth, I will make an end of
this brass pot.'   He turned upon Montferrat with
his teeth bare.   'Conrad, Conrad, Conrad!' he
cried terribly, 'mark your goings about this
slippery world; for if when I get you alone I do
not send you quick into hell, may I go down myself beyond redemption of the Church!'

'That you will surely do, my lord,' says the
Marquess of Montferrat, greatly disturbed.

'If I get you there also I shall be reasonably
entertained for a short time,' Richard answered,
already cooled and ashamed of his heat.   Then
King Philip dismissed the Marquess, and as soon
as he was rid of him jumped into Richard's arms,
and cried his heart away.

Richard, who was fond of the youth, comforted
him as well as he was able, but on one point was
a rock.   He would not hear the word 'marriage'
until he had seen the lady.   'Oh, Richard, marry
her quick, marry her quick!   So we can face the
world,' the young King had blubbered, thinking
that course the simplest answer to the affront
upon his house.   It did not seem so simple to
the Count, or (rather) it seemed too simple by
half.   In his private mind he knew perfectly well
that he could not marry Madame Alois.   So, for

that matter, did King Philip by this time. 'I must see Alois, Philip, I must see her alone,' was all Richard had to say; and really it could not be gainsaid.

He went to her after proper warning, and saw the truth the moment he had view of her. Then also he knew that he had really seen it before. That white, furtive, creeping girl, from whose loose hair peered out a pair of haunted eyes; that drooped thing backing against the wall, feeling for it, flat against it, with open shocked mouth, astare but seeing nothing: the whole truth flared before him monstrously naked. He loathed the sight of her, but had to speak her smoothly.

'Princess——' he said, and came forward to touch her hand; but she slipped away from him, crouching to the wall. The torment of breath in her bosom was bad to see.

'Touch me not, Count of Poictou;' she whispered the words, and then moaned, 'O God, what will become of me?'

'Madame,' said Richard, rather dry, 'God may answer your question, since He knows all things, but certainly I cannot, unless you first tell me what has hitherto become of you.'

She steadied herself by the wall, her palms flat upon it, and leaned her body forward like one who searches in a dark place. Then, shaking her head, she let it fall to her breast. 'Is there any sorrow like my sorrow?' says she to herself, as though he had not been there.

Richard grew stern. 'So asked in His agony the Son of high God,' he reproved her. 'If you

G

dare ask Him that in His own words your sorrow
must be deep.'

She said, ' It is most deep.'

' But His,' said Richard, 'was bitter shame.'

She said, ' And mine is bitter.'

' But His was undeserved.' He spoke scorn;
so then she lifted up her head, and with eyes
most piteous searched his face. ' But mine,
Richard,' she said, 'but mine is deserved.'

' The hearing is pertinent,' said Richard. ' As
a son and man affianced it touches me pretty
close.'

Out of the hot and desperate struggle for
breath, sounds came from her, but no words.
But she ran forward blindly, and kneeling, caught
him by the knees; he could not but find pity in
his heart for the witless poor wretch, who seemed
to be fighting, not with regret nor for need of his
pity, but with some maggot in the brain which
drove her deeper into the fiery centre of the
storm. Richard did what he could. A religious
man himself, he pointed her to the Christ on the
wall; but she waved it out of sight, shook her
wild hair back, and clung to him still, asking
some unguessed mercy with her eyes and sobbing
breath. ' God help this tormented soul, for I
cannot,' he prayed; and said aloud, 'I will call
your women; let me go.' So he tried to undo
her hands, but she clenched her teeth together
and held on with frenzy, whining, grunting, like
some pounded animal. Dumbly they strove together for a little panting space of time.

' Ah, but you shall let me go,' he said then,
much distressed, and forcibly unknotted her mad

hands.   She fell back upon her heels, and looked up at him.   Such hopeless, grinning misery he had never seen on a face before.   He was certain now that she was out of her wits.

Yet once again she brushed her hands over her face, as he had seen her do before, like one who sweeps gossamers away on autumn mornings; and though she was all in a shiver and shake with the fever she had, she found her voice at last. ' Ah, thanks!   Ah, my thanks, O Christ my Saviour!' she sighed.   ' O sweet Saviour Christ, now I will tell him all the truth.'

If he had listened to her then it had been well for him.   But he did not.   The struggle had fretted him likewise; if she was mad he was maddened.   He got angry where he should have been most patient.   ' The truth, by heaven!' he snapped.   ' Ah, if I have not had enough of this truth!'   And so he left her shuddering.   As he went down the long corridor he heard shriek after shriek, and then the scurrying of many feet. Turning, he saw carried lights, women running. The sounds were muffled, they had her safe. Richard went to his house over the river, and slept for ten hours.

CHAPTER VII

OF THE CRACKLING OF THORNS UNDER POTS

JUST as no two pots will boil alike, so with men;
they seethe in trouble with a difference. With
one the grief is taken inly: this was Richard's
kind. The French King was feverish, the Marquess explosive, John of England all eyes and
alarms. So Richard's remedy for trouble was
action, Philip's counsel, the Marquess's a glut of
hatred, and John's plotting. The consequence
is, that in the present vexed state of things
Richard threw off his discontent with his bedclothes, and at once took the lead of the others,
because it could be done at once. He declared
open war against the King his father, despatching
heralds with the cartel the same day; he gave
King Philip to understand that the French power
might be for him or against him as seemed fitting,
but that no power in heaven or on earth would
engage him to marry Dame Alois. King Philip,
still clinging to his friend, made a treaty of alliance with him against Henry of England. That
done, sealed and delivered, Richard sent for his
brother John. 'Brother,' he said, 'I have declared war against my father, and Philip is to be
of our party. In his name and my own I am
to tell you that one of two things you must do.
You may stay in our lands or leave them; but if

you stay you must sign our treaty of alliance.'
Too definite for John, all this : he asked for time,
and Richard gave him till nightfall. At dusk he
sent for him again. John chose to stay in Paris.
Then Richard thought he would go home to
Poictou. The moment his back was turned
began various closetings of the magnates left
behind, with which I mean to fatigue the reader
as little as possible.

One such chamber-business I must record. To
Paris in the black February weather came pelting
the young Count Eustace, now by his brother's
death Count of Saint-Pol. Misfortune, they say,
makes of one a man or a saint. Of Eustace Saint-
Pol it had made a man. After his homage done,
this youth still kneeling, his hands still between
Philip's hands, looked fixedly into his sovereign's
face, and ' A boon, fair sire !' he said. ' A boon
to your new man !'

'What now, Saint-Pol?' asked King Philip.

'Sire,' he said, 'my sister's marriage is in you.
I beg you to give her to Messire Gilles de Gurdun,
a good knight of Normandy.'

' That is a poor marriage for her, Saint-Pol,'
said the King, considering, 'and a poor marriage
for me, by Saint Mary. Why should I enrich the
King of England, with whom I am at war? You
must give me reason for that.'

' I will give you this reason,' said young Saint-
Pol; 'it is because that devil who slew my brother
will have her else.'

King Philip said, ' Why, I can give her to
one who will hold her fast. Your Gurdun is a
Norman, you say? Well, but Count Richard in

a little while will have him under his hand; and
how are you served then?'

'I doubt, sire,' replied Saint-Pol. 'Moreover,
there is this, if it please you to hear it. When
the Count of Poictou repudiated (as he most
villainously did) my sister, he himself gave her
to Gurdun. But I fear him, lest seeing her any
other's he should take her again.'

'What is this, man?' asked King Philip.

'Sire, he writes letters to my sister that he is a
free man, and she keeps them by her and often
reads them in secret. So she was caught but
lately by my lady aunt, reading one in bed.'

The King's brow grew very black, for though
he knew that Richard would never marry Madame,
he did not choose (but resented) that any other
should know it. At this moment Montferrat
came in, and stood by his kinsman.

'Ah, sire,' said he, in those bloodhound tones
of his, 'give us leave to deal in this business with
free hands.'

'What would you do in it, Marquess?' asked
the King fretfully.

'Kill him, by God,' said the Marquess; and
young Saint-Pol added, 'Give us his life, O lord
King.'

King Philip thought. He was fresh from
making a treaty with Richard; but that was in
a war of requital only, and would be ended so
soon as the last drop had been drained from the
old King. What would follow the war? He
was by this time cooler towards Richard, very
much vexed at what he had just heard; he could
not help remembering that marriage with Alois

would have been the proper reply to scandalous report. Should he be able, when the war was done, to squeeze Richard into marriage or an equivalent in lands? He wondered, he doubted greatly. On the other hand, if he and Richard could crush old Henry, and Saint-Pol afterwards bruise Richard — why, what was Philip but a gainer?

Chewing the fringe of his mantle as he considered this and that, ' If I give Madame Jehane in marriage to your Gurdun,' he said dubiously, 'what will Gurdun do?'

Saint-Pol named the sum, a fair one.

' But what part will he take in the quarrel?' asked the King.

' He will take my part, as he is bound, sire.'

' Pest!' cried Philip, 'let us get at it. What is this part of yours?'

' The part of him who has a blood-feud, my lord,' said young Saint-Pol; and the Marquess said, ' That is my part also.'

' Have it according to your desires, my lords,' then said King Philip. ' I give you this marriage. Make it as speedily as may be, but let not Count Richard have news until it is done. There is a fire, I tell you, hidden in that tall man. Remember this too, Saint-Pol. You shall not make war on the side of England against Richard, for that will be against me. Your feud must wait its turn. For this present I have an account to settle in which Poictou is on my side. Marquess, you likewise are in my debt. See to it that you give my enemies no advantage.'

The Marquess and his cousin gave their words,

holding up the hilts of their swords before their faces.

Richard, in his city of Poictiers, was calmly forwarding his plans. His first act, since he now considered himself perfectly free, had been to send Gaston of Béarn with letters to Saint-Pol-la-Marche; his second, seeing no reason why he should wait for King Philip or any possible ally, to cross the frontier of Touraine in force. He took castle after castle in that rich land, clearing the way for the investiture of Tours, which was his first great objective.

I leave him at this employment and follow Gaston on his way to the North. It was early in March when that young man started, squally, dusty weather; but perfect trobador as he was, the nature of his errand warmed him; he composed a whole nosegay of scented songs in honour of Richard and the crocus-haired lady of the March who wore the broad girdle. Riding as he did through the realm of France, by Chateaudun, Chartres, and Pontoise, he narrowly missed Eustace of Saint-Pol, who was galloping the opposite way upon an errand dead opposed to his own. Gaston would have fought him, of course, but would have been killed to a certainty; for Saint-Pol rode as became his lordship, with a company, and the other was alone. He was spared any such mischance, however, and arrived in the highest spirits, with an *alba* (song of the dawn) for what he supposed to be Jehane's window. It shows what an eye he had for a lady's chamber that he was very nearly right. A lady did put her head out; not Jehane, but a rock-faced matron of vast proportions with grey hair plastered to her cheeks.

'Behold, behold the dawn, my tender heart!' breathed Gaston.

'Out, you cockerel,' said the old lady, and Gaston wooed her in vain. It appeared that she was an aunt, sworn to the service of the Count, and had Jehane safe in a tower under lock and key. Gaston retired into the woods to meditate. There he wrote five identic notes to the prisoner. The first he gave to a boy whom he found birds'-nesting. 'Take a turtle's nest, sweet boy,' said Gaston, 'to my lady Jehane; say it is first-fruits of the year, and win a silver piece. Beware of an old lady with a jaw like a flat-iron.' The second he gave to a woodman tying billets for the Castle ovens; the third a maid put in her placket, and he taught her the fourth by heart in a manner quite his own and very much to her taste. With the fifth he was most adroit. He demanded an interview with the duenna, whose name was Dame Gudule. She accorded. Gaston spilled his very soul out before her; he knelt to her, he kissed her large velvet feet. The lady was touched, I mean literally, for Gaston as he stooped fitted his fifth note into the braid of her ample skirt. The only one to arrive was the boy's in the bird's nest. The boy wanted his silver piece, and got it. So Jehane had another note to cherish.

But she had to answer it first. It said, ' *Vera Copia*. Ma mye, I set on to the burden you gave me, but it failed of breaking my back. I have punished some of the wicked, and have some still to punish. When this is done I shall come to you.

Wait for me. I regret your brother's death. He deserved it. The fight was fair. Learn of me from Gaston. — Richard of Anjou.' Her answer was leaping in her heart; she led the boy to the window.

'Look down, boy, and tell me what you can see.'

'*Dame!*' said the boy, 'I see the moat, and ducks on it.'

'Look again, dear, and tell me what you see.'

'I see an old fish on his back. He is dead.'

Jehane laughed quietly. 'He has been there many days. Tell the knight who sent you to stand thereabout, looking up. Tell him not to be there at any hour save that of mass, or vespers. Will you do this, dear boy?'

'Certain sure,' said the boy. Jehane gave him money and a kiss, then fastened herself to the window.

Gaston excelled in pantomime. Every day for a week he saw Jehane at her window, and enacted many strange plays. He showed her the old King stormy in his tent, the meagre white unrest of Alois, the outburst at Autafort and Bertran de Born with his tongue out; the meeting at Tours, the battle, the death of the Count her brother. He was admirable on Richard's love-desires. There could be no doubt at all about them. Pricked by his feats in this sort, Jehane overcame her reserve and turned her members into marionettes. She puffed her cheeks, hung her head, scowled upwards: there was Gilles de Gurdun to the life. She looped finger and thumb of the right hand and pierced them with the ring finger: ohè! her

fate.   Gaston in reply to this drew his sword and
ran a cypress-tree through the body.   Jehane shook
a sorrowful head, but he waved all such denials
away with a hand so expressive that Jehane broke
the window and leaned her body out.   Gaston
uttered a cheerful cry.

' Have no fear, lovely prisoner.   If that is his
intention he is gone.   I kill him.   It is arranged.'

' My brother Eustace is in Paris,' says Jehane
in a low but carrying voice, ' to get my marriage
from the King.'

' Again I say, fear nothing,' Gaston cried; but
Jehane strained out as far as she could.

' You must go away from here.   The window
is broken now, and they will find me out.   Take
a message to my lord.   If he is free indeed, he
knows me his in life or death.   I seek to do him
service.   Wed or unwed, what is that to me?
I am still Jehane.'

' Your name is Red Heart, and Golden Rose,
and Loiale Amye!   Farewell, Star of the North,'
said Gaston on his knees.   ' I seek this Gurdun of
yours.'

He found him after some days' perilous prowl-
ing of the Norman march.   Gilles had received
the summons of his Duke to be *vi et armis* at
Rouen; a little later Gaston might have met him
in the field of broad battle, but such delay was
not to his mind.   He met him instead in a woodland glade near Gisors, alone (by a great chance),
sword on thigh.

' Beef, thou diest,' said the Béarnais, peaking
his beard.   Gilles made no reply that can be
written, for what letters can shape a Norman

grunt? Perhaps 'Wauch!' comes nearest. They
fought on horseback, with swords, from noon to
sunset, and having hacked one another out of the
similitude of men, there was nothing left them to
do but swoon side by side on the sodden leaves.
In the morning Gaston, unclogging one eye, perceived that his enemy had gone. 'No matter,'
said the spent hero to himself. 'I will wait till
he comes back, and have at him again.'

He waited an unconscionable time, a month in
fact, during which he delighted to watch the shy
oncoming of a Northern spring, so different from
the sudden flooding of the South. He found the
wood-sorrel, he measured the crosiers of the brake,
and saw the blue mist of the hyacinth carpet the
glades. All this charmed him quite, until he
learned, by hazard, that the Sieur de Gurdun was
to be married to Dame Jehane Saint-Pol on Palm
Sunday in the church of Saint Sulpice of Gisors.
'God ha' mercy!' he thought, with a stab at the
heart; 'there is merely time.' He rode South on
the wind's wings.

CHAPTER VIII

Long before the pink flush on the almond
announced the earth a bride, on all Gaulish roads
had been heard the tramp of armed men, the ring
of steel on steel. This new war splintered Gaul.
Aquitaine held for Richard, who, though he had
quelled and afterwards governed that great duchy
with an iron whip, had made himself respected
there. So the Count of Provence sent him a
company, the Count of Toulouse and Dauphin
of Auvergne each brought a company; from
Périgord, from Bertram Count of Roussillon, from
Béarn, and (for reasons) from the wise King of
Navarre, came pikemen and slingers, and long-
bowmen, and knights with their esquires and
banner-bearers. The Duke of Burgundy and
Count of Champagne came from the east to fill
the battles of King Philip; in the west the
Countess of Brittany sent about the war-torch.
All the extremes of Gaul were in arms against the
red old Angevin who sat at her heart, who was
now still snarling in England, and sending message after secret message to his son John. That
same John, alone in Paris, headed no spears, partly
because he had none of his own, partly because he
dared not declare himself openly. He had taken a
side, driven by his vehement brother; for the first

93

time in his life he had put pen to parchment.
God knew (he thought) that was committal
enough. So he stayed in Paris, shifting his
body about to get comfort as the winds veered.
Nobody inquired of him, least of all his brother
Richard, who, beyond requiring his signature,
cared little what he did with his person. This
was characteristic of Richard. He would drive
a man into a high place and then forget him.
Reminded of his neglect, he would shrug and say,
'Yes. But he is a fool.' Insufficient answer: he
did not see or did not choose to see that there
are two sorts of fools. Stranded on his peak, one
man might be fool enough to stop there, another
to try a descent. Prince John (no fool either)
was of this second quality. How he tried to get
down, and where else he tried to go, will be made
clear in time. You and I must go to the war in
the west.

War showed Count Richard entered into his
birthright. As a strategist he was superb,. the
best of his time. What his eye took in his mind
snapped up — like a steel gin. And his eye was
the true soldier's eye, comprehending by signs,
investing with life what was tongueless else.
Over great stretches of barren country — that
limitless land of France — he could see massed
men on the move; creeping forward in snaky
columns, spread fanwise from clump to woody
clump; here camping snugly under the hill, there
lining the river bluffs with winged death; checked
here, helped there by a moraine — as well as you
or I may foresee the conduct of a chess-board.
He omitted nothing, judged times and seasons,

reckoned defences at their worth, knew all the fordable places by the lie of the land, timed cavalry and infantry to rendezvous, forestalled communications, provided not only for his own base, but against the enemy's. All this, of course, without maps, and very much against the systems of his neighbours. It was thus he had outwitted the heady barons of Aquitaine when little more than a lad, and had turned the hill forts into death-traps against their tenants. He had the secret of swift marching by night, of delivering assault upon assault, so that while you staggered under one blow you received another full. He could be as patient as Death, that inchmeal stalker of his prey; he could be as ruthless as the sea, and incredibly generous upon occasion. To the men he led he was a father, known and beloved as such; it was as a ruler they found him too lonely to be loved. In war he was the very footboy's friend. Personally, when the bat- tles joined, he was rash to a fault; but so blithe, so ready, and so gracefully strong, that to think of wounds upon so bright a surface was an impiety. No one did think of them: he seemed to play with danger as a cat with whirling leaves. ' I have seen him,' Milo writes somewhere, ' ride into a serry of knights, singing, throwing up and catching again his great sword Gaynpayn; then, all of a sudden, stiffen as with a gush of sap in his veins, dart his head forward, gather his horse together under him, and fling into the midst of them like a tiger into a herd of bulls. One saw nothing but tossing steel; yet Richard ever emerged, red but scatheless, on the further side.

Upon this man the brunt of war fell naturally: having begun, he did not hold his hand.   By the beginning of February he had laid his plans, by the end of it he had taken Saumur, cut Angers off from Tours, and turned all the valley of the Loire into a scorched cinder-bed.   In the early days of March he sat down before Tours with his siege-engines, petraries, mangonels, and towers, and daily battered at the walls, with intent to reduce it before the war was really afloat.   The city of Saint Martin was doomed; no help from Anjou could save it, for none could come that way.   Meantime the King his father had landed at Honfleur, assembled his Normans at Rouen, and was working his way warily down through the duchy, feeling for the French on his left, and for the Bretons on his right.   He never found the French ; they were far south of him, pushing through Orleans to join Richard at Le Mans. But the Countess of Brittany's men, under Hugh of Dinan, were sacking Avranches when old Henry heard the bad news from Touraine. That country and Maine were as the apple of his eye; yet he dared not leave Avranches fated behind him.   All he could do was to send Will- iam the Marshal with a small force into Anjou, while he himself spread out westward to give Hugh of Dinan battle and save Avranches, if that might be.   So it was that King Philip slipped in between him and Le Mans.   By this time Richard was master of Tours, and himself on the way to Le Mans, nosing the air for William the Marshal.   This was in the beginning of April.   Then on one and the same day he risked all he had won for the sake of a girl's proud face, and nearly lost his life into the bargain.

He had to cross the river Aune above La Flèche. That river, a sluggish but deep little stream, moves placidly among osiers on its way to swell the Loire. On either side the water-meadows stretch for three-quarters of a mile; low chalk-hills, fringed at the top, are ramparts to the sleepy valley. Creeping along the eastern spurs at dawn, Richard came in touch with his enemy, William the Marshal and his force of Normans and English. These had crossed the bridge at La Flèche, and came pricking now up the valley to save Le Mans. Heading them boldly, Richard threw out his archers like a waterspray over the flats, and while these checked the advance and had the van in confusion, thundered down the slopes with his knights, caught the Marshal on the flank, smote him hip and thigh, and swept the core of his army into the river. The Marshal's battle was thus destroyed; but the wedge had made too clean a cleft. Front and rear joined up and held; so Richard found himself in danger. The Viscount of Béziers, who led the rearguard, engaged the enemy, and pushed them slowly back towards the Aune; Richard wheeled his men and charged, to take them in the rear. His horse, stumbling on the rotten ground, fell badly and threw him: there were cries, 'Holà! Count Richard is down!' and some stayed to rescue and some pushed on. William the Marshal, on a white horse, came suddenly upon him as he lay. 'Mort de dieu!'

H

shrilled this good soldier, and threw up his spear
arm. 'God's feet, Marshal, kill one or other of
us!' said Richard lightly: he was pinned down
by his struggling beast. 'I leave you to the
devil, my lord Richard,' said the Marshal, and
drove his spear into the horse's chest. The
beast's death-plunge freed his master. Richard
jumped up: even on foot his head was level with
the rider's shield. 'Have at you now!' he cried;
but the Marshal shook his head, and rode after
his flying men. The day was with Poictou, Le
Mans must fall.

It fell, but not yet; nor did Richard see it fall.
Gaston of Béarn joined his master the next day.
'Hasten, hasten, fair lord!' he cried out as soon
as he saw him. Richard looked as if he had
never known the word.

'What news of Normandy, Gaston?'

'The English are through, Richard. The
country swarms with them. They hold Avranches,
and now are moving south.'

'They are too late,' said Richard. 'Tell me
what message you have from the Fair-Girdled.'

'Wed or unwed, she is yours. But she is kept
in a tower until Palm Sunday. Then they bring
her out and marry her to what remains of a black
Normandy pig. Not very much remains, but
(they tell me) enough for the purpose.'

'Spine of God,' said Richard, examining his
finger-nails.

'Swear by His heart, rather, my Count,' Gaston
said, 'for you have a red heart in your keeping.
Eh, eh, what a beautiful person is there! She
leaned her body out of the window — what a shape

that girdle confines! Bowered roses! Dian and
the Nymphs! Bosomed familiars of old Pan!
And what emerald fires! What molten hair!
The words came shortly from her, and brokenly,
as if her carved lips disdained such coarse uses!
Richard, her words were so: " Take a message to
my lord," quoth she. " I am his in life or death.
I seek to do him service. Wed or unwed, what
is that to me? I am still Jehane." Thus she —
but I? Well, well, my sword spake for me when
I carved that beef-bone bare.' The Béarnais
pulled his goatee, and looked at the ends of it for
split hairs. But Richard sat very still.

'Do you know, Gaston, whom you have seen?'
he said presently, in a trembling whisper.

'Perfectly well,' said the other. 'I have seen a
pale flower ripe for the sun.'

'You have seen the Countess of Poictou, Gaston,' said Richard, and took to his prayers.

Through these means, for the time, he was
held off his father's throat. But for Jehane and
her urgent affairs these two had grappled at Le
Mans. As it was, not Richard's hand was to fire
the cradle-city which had seen King Henry at the
breast. Before nightfall he had made his dispositions for a very risky business. He set aside the
Viscount of Béziers, Bertram Count of Roussillon,
Gaston of Béarn, to go with him, not because they
were the best men by any means, but so that he
might leave the best men in charge. These were
certainly the Dauphin, the Viscount of Limoges,
and the Count of Angoulesme, each of whom he
had proved as an enemy in his day. 'Gentlemen,'
he said to these three, 'I am about to go upon a

journey. Of you I shall require a little attention, certain patience, exact obedience. It will be necessary that you be before the walls of Le Mans in three days. Invest them, my lords, keep up your communications, and wait for the French King. Give no battle, offer no provocation, let hunger do your affair. I know where the King of England is, and shall be with you before him.' He went on to be more precise, but I omit the details. It was difficult for them to go wrong, but if the truth is to be known, he was in a mood which made him careless about that. He was free. He was going on insensate adventure; but he saw his road before him once again, like a long avenue of light, which Jehane made for him with a torch uplifted. Before it was day, armed from head to foot in chain mail, with a plain shield, and a double-bladed Norman axe in his saddle-bucket, he and his three companions set out on their journey. They rode leisurely, with loose reins and much turning in the saddle to talk, as if for a meet of the hounds.

Now was that vernal season of the year when winds are boon, the gentle rain never far off, the stars in heaven (like the flowers on earth) washed momently to a freshness which urges men to be pure. Riding day and night through the green breadth of France, though he had been plucked from the roaring pit of war, Richard (I know) went with a single aim before him — to see Jehane again. Nothing else in his heart, I say. Whatever purpose may have lurked in his mind, in heart he went clean, single in desire, chanting the canticles of Mary and the Virgin Saints. It was so.

He had been seethed in wicked doings from his
boyhood—I give him you no better than he was:
wild work in Poictou, the scour of hot blood;
devil's work in Touraine, riotous work in Paris,
tyrannous in Aquitaine. He had been blown
upon by every ill report; hatred against blood,
blasphemy against God's appointment, violence,
clamour, scandal against charitable dealing: all
these were laid to his name. He had behind him
a file of dead ancestors, cut-throats and worse.
He had faced unnameable sin and not blenched,
laughed where he should have wept, promised and
broken his promise; to be short, he had been a
creature of his house and time, too young acquainted with pride and too proud himself to deny
it. But now, with eyes alight like a boy's because
his heart was uplift, he was riding between the new-
budded woods, the melodies of a singing-boy on
his lips. and swaying before his heart's eye the
figure of a tall girl with green eyes and a sulky,
beautiful mouth. ' Lord, what is man?' cried the
Psalmist in dejection. ' Lord, what is man not?'
cry we, who know more of him.

His traverse took him four days and nights.
He rested at La Ferté, at Nogent-le-Rotrou, outside Dreux, and at Rosny. Here he stayed a day,
the Vigil of the Feast of Palms. He had it in
his mind not to see Jehane again until the very
moment when he might lose her.

CHAPTER IX

WILD WORK IN THE CHURCH OF GISORS

WHEN in March the chase is up, and the hunting wind searches out the fallow places of the earth, love also comes questing, desire is awake; man seeks maid, and maid seeks to be sought. If man or maid have loved already the case is worse; we hear love crying, but cannot tell where he is, how or with what honesty to let him in. All those ranging days Jehane — whether in bed cuddling her letters, or at the window of her tower, watching with brimmed eyes the pairing of the birds — showed a proud front of sufferance, while inly her heart played a wild tune. Not a crying girl, nor one capable of any easy utterance, she could do no more than stand still, and wonder why she was most glad when most wretched. She ought to have felt the taint, to love the man who had slain her brother; she might have known despair: she did neither. She sat or stood, or lay in her bed, and pressed to her heart with both hands the words that said, 'Never doubt me, Jehane,' or 'Ma mye, I shall come to you.' When he came, as he surely would, he would find her a wife — ah, let him come, let him come in his time, so only she saw him again!

March went out in dusty squalls, and April came in to the sound of the young lamb's bleat.

Willow-palm was golden in the hedges when the King of England's men filled Normandy, and Gilles de Gurdun, having been healed of his wounds, rode towards Rouen at the head of his levy. He went not without an understanding with Saint-Pol that he should have his sister on Palm Sunday in the church of Gisors. They could not marry at Saint-Pol-la-Marche, because Gilles was on his service and might not win so far; nor could they have married before he went, because of his ill-treatment at the hands of the Béarnais. Of this Gilles had made light. 'He got worse than he gave,' he told Saint-Pol. 'I left him dead in the wood.'

'Would you see Jehane, Gilles?' Saint-Pol had asked him before he went out. 'She is in her turret as meek as a mouse.'

'Time enough for that,' said Gilles quietly. 'She loves me not. But I, Eustace, love her so hot that I have fear of myself. I think I will not see her.'

'As you will,' said Saint-Pol. 'Farewell.'

In Gisors, then a walled town, trembling like a captive at the knees of a huge castle, there was a long grey church which called Saint Sulpice lord. It stood in a little square midway between the South Gate and the citadel, a narrow oblong place where they held the cattle market on Tuesdays, flagged and planted with pollard-limes. The west door of Saint Sulpice, resting on a stepped foundation, formed a solemn end to this humble space, and the great gable flanked by turrets threatened the huddled tenements of the craftsmen. On this morning of Palm Sunday the shaven crowns of the limes were budded gold and pink, the sky a fair sea-blue over Gisors, with a scurrying fleece of clouds like foam ; the poplars about the meadows were in their first flush, all the quicksets veiled in green. The town was early afoot, for the wedding party of the Sieur de Gurdun was to come in ; and Gurdun belonged to the Archbishop, and the Archbishop to the Duke. The bride also was reported unwilling, which added zest to the public appetite for her known beauty. Some knew for truth that she was the cast-off mistress of a very great man, driven into Gurdun's arms to dispose of scandal and of her. ' Eh, the minion ! ' said certain sniggering old women to whom this was told, ' she'll not find so soft a lap at Gurdun ! ' But others said, ' Gurdun is the Duke's, and will one day be the Duke's son's. What will Sieur Gilles do then with his straining wife ? You cannot keep your hawk on the cadge for ever — ah, nor hood her for ever ! ' And so on.

All this points to some public excitement. The town gate was opened full early, the booths about it did a great trade ; at a quarter before seven Sir Gilles de Gurdun rode in, with his father on his right hand, the prior of Rouen on his left, and half a dozen of his kindred, fair and solid men all. They were lightly armed, clothed in soft leather, without shields or any heavy war-furniture : old Gurdun a squarely built, red-faced man like his son, but with a bush of white hair all about his face, and eyebrows like curved snow-drifts ; the prior (old Gurdun's brother's son) with a big nose, long and pendulous ; Gilles' brother Bartholomew, and others whom it would be tedious to mention. Gilles himself looked well knit for the business in hand; all the old women agreed that he would make a masterful husband. They stabled their horses in the inn-yard, and went into the church porch to await the bride's party.

A trumpet at the gate announced her coming. She rode on a little ambling horse beside her brother Saint-Pol. With them were the portentous old lady, Dame Gudule, William des Barres, a very fine French knight, Nicholas d'Eu, and a young boy called Eloy de Mont-Luc, a cousin of Jehane's, to bear her train. The gossips at the gate called her a wooden bride; others said she was like a doll, a big doll; and others that they read in her eyes the scorn of death. She took no notice of anything or anybody, but looked straight before her and followed where she was led. This was straightway into the church by her brother, who had her by the hand and seemed in a great hurry. The marriage was to be made in the Lady Chapel, behind the high altar.

Twenty minutes later yet, or maybe a little less, there was another surging to the gate about the arrival of four knights, who came posting in, spattered with mud and the sweat and lather of their horses. They were quite unknown to the people of Gisors, but seen for great men, as indeed they were. Richard of Anjou was the first of them, a young man of inches incredible to Gisors. 'He had a face like King Arthur's of Britain,' says one: 'A red face, a tawny beard, eyes like stones.' Behind him were three abreast: Rous-

sillon, a grim, dark, heavy-eyed man, bearded like
a Turk; Béziers, sanguine and loose-limbed, a
man with a sharp tongue; Gaston of Béarn, airy
hunter of fine phrases, looking now like the prince
of a fairy-tale, with roving eyes all a-scare for
adventure.   The warders of the gate received
them with a flourish.   They knew nothing of
them, but were certain of their degree.

By preconcerted action they separated there.
Roussillon and Béziers sat like statues within the
gate, one on each side of the way, actually upon
the bridge; and so remained, the admired of all
the booths.   Gaston, like a yeoman-pricker in this
hunting of the roe, went with Richard to the edge
of the covert, that is, to the steps of Saint Sulpice,
and stood there holding his master's horse.   What
remained to be done was done with extreme swift-
ness.   Richard alone, craning his head forward,
stooping a little, swaying his scabbarded sword
in his hand, went with long soft strides into the
church.

At the entry he kneeled on one knee, and
looked about him from under his brows.   Three
or four masses were proceeding; out of the semi-
darkness shone the little twinkling lights, and
illuminated faintly the kneeling people, a priest's
vestment, a silver chalice.   But here was neither
marriage nor Jehane.   He got up presently, and
padded down the nave, kneeling to every altar
as he went.   Many an eye followed him as he
pushed on and past the curtain of the ambulatory.
They guessed him for the wedding, and so (God
knows) he was.   In the shadow of a great pillar
he stopped short, and again went down on his

knee; from here he could see the business in
train.

He saw Jehane at prayer, in green and white,
kneeling at her faldstool like a painted lady on an
altar tomb; he just saw the pure curve of her
cheek, the coiled masses of her hair, which seemed
to burn it. All the world with the lords thereof
was at his feet, but this treasure which he had
held and put away was denied him. By his own
act she was denied. He had said Yea, when Nay
had been the voice of heart and head, of honour
and love and reason at once; and now (close up
against her) he knew that he was to forbid his
own grant. He knew it, I say; but until he
saw her there he had not clearly known it. Go
on, I will show you the deeps of the man for good
or bad. Not lust of flesh, but of dominion,
ravened in him. This woman, this Jehane Saint-
Pol, this hot-haired slip of a girl was his. The
leopard had laid his paw upon her shoulder, the
mark was still there; he could not suffer any other
beast of the forest to touch that which he had
printed with his own mark, for himself.

Twi-form is the leopard; twi-natured was Richard of Anjou, dog and cat. Now here was all
cat. Not the wolf's lust, but the lion's jealous
rage spurred him to the act. He could see this
beautiful thing of flesh without any longing to
lick or tear; he could have seen the frail soul of
it, but half-born, sink back into the earth out of
sight; he could have killed Jehane or made her
as his mother to him. But he could not see one
other get that which was his. His by all heaven
she was. When Gurdun squared himself and

puffed his cheeks, and stood up; when Jehane, touched by Saint-Pol on the shoulder, shivered and left staring, and stood up in turn, swaying a little, and held out her thin hand; when the priest had the ring on his book, and the two hands, the red and the white, trembled to the touch — Richard rose from his knee and stole forward with his long, soft, crouching stride.

So softly he trod that the priest, old and blear-eyed as he was, saw him first: the others had heard nothing. With Jehane's hand in his own, the priest stopped and blinked. Who was this prowler, afoot when all else were on their knees? His jaw dropped; you saw that he was toothless. Inarticulate sounds, crackling and dry, came from his throat. Richard had stopped too, tense, quivering for a spring. The priest gave a prodigious sniff, turned to his book, looked up again: the crouching man was still there — but imminent. ' Wine of Jesus!' said the priest, and dropped Jehane's hand. Then she turned. She gave a short cry; the whole assembly started and huddled together as the mailed man made his spring.

It was done in a flash. From his crouched attitude he went, as it seemed, at one bound. That same shock drove Gilles de Gurdun back among his people, and the same found Jehane caged in a hoop of steel. So he affronting and she caught up stood together, for a moment. With one mailed hand he held her fast under the armpit, with the other he held a fidgety sword. His head was thrown back; through glimmering eyelids he watched them — as one

who says, What next? — breathing short through
his nose. It was the attitude of the snatching
lion, sudden, arrogant, shockingly swift; a gross
deed, done in a flash which was its wonderful
beauty. While the company was panting at the
shock—for barely a minute—he stood thus; and
Jehane, quiet under so fierce a hold, leaned not
upon him, but stood her own feet fairly, her calm
brows upon a level with his chin. Shameful if
it was, at that moment of rude conquest she had
no shame, and he no thought of shame.

Nor was there much time for thought at all.
Gurdun cried on the name of God and started
forward; at the same instant Saint-Pol made a
rush, and with him Des Barres. Richard, with
Jehane held close, went backwards on the way he
had come in. His long arm and long sword kept
his distance; he worked them like a scythe.
None tackled him there, though they followed
him up as dogs a boar in the forest; but old
Gurdun, the father, ran round the other way to
hold the west door. Richard, having gained the
nave and open country (as it were), went swiftly
down it, carrying Jehane with ease; he found the
strenuous old man before the door. 'Out of
my way, De Gurdun,' he cried in a high singing
voice, 'or I shall do that which I shall be sorry
for.'

'Bloody thief,' shouted old Gurdun, 'add murder
to the rest!' Richard stretched his sword arm
stiffly and swept him aside. He tumbled back;
the crowd received him — priests, choristers, peas-
ants, knights, all huddled together, baying like
dogs. Count Richard strode down the steps.

'Alavi! Alavia!' sang Gaston, 'this is a swift
marriage!' Richard, cooler than circumstances
warranted, set Jehane on his saddle, vaulted up
behind her, and as his pursuers were tumbling
down the steps, cantered over the flags into the
street. Roussillon and Béziers, holding the bridge,
saw him come. 'He has snatched his Sabine
woman,' said Béziers. 'Humph,' said Roussillon;
'now for beastly war.' Richard rode straight
between them at a hand-gallop; Gaston followed
close, cheering his beast like a maniac. Then the
iron pair turned inwards and rode out together,
taking the way he led them, the way of the Dark
Tower.

The wonder of Gisors was all dismay when it
was learned who this tall stranger was. The
Count of Poictou had ridden into his father's
country and robbed his father's man of his wife.
We are ruled by devils in Normandy, then!
There was no immediate pursuit. Saint-Pol knew
where to find him; but (as he told William des
Barres) it was useless to go there without some
force.

CHAPTER X

I CHRONICLE wild doings in this place, and have
no time for the sweets of love long denied. But
strange as the bridal had been, so the nuptials
were strange, one like the other played to a steel
undertone. When Richard had his Jehane, at
first he could not enjoy her. He rode away with
her like a storm; the way was long, the pace
furious. Not a word had passed between them,
at least not a reasoned word. Once or twice at
first he leaned forward over her shoulder and
set his cheek to her glowing cheek. Then she,
as if swayed by a tide, strained back to him, and
felt his kisses hot and eager, his few and pelting words, ' My bride — at last — my bride ! ' and
the pressure of his hand upon her heart. That
hand knows what tune the heart drummed out.
Mostly she sat up before him stiff as a sapling,
with eyes and ears wide for any hint of pursuit.
But he felt her tremble, and knew she would be
glad of him yet.

After all, they had six burning days for a
honeymoon, days which made those three who
with them held the tower wonder how such a
match could continue. Richard's love rushed
through him like a river in flood, that brims its
banks and carries down bridges by its turbid

III

mass; but hers was like the sea, unresting, ebbing, flowing, without aim or sure direction.   As
is usual with reserved persons, Jehane's transports, far from assuaging, tormented her, or
seemed a torment.   She loved uneasily, by hot
and cold fits; now melting, now dry, now fierce
in demand, next passionate in refusal.   To snatch
of love succeeded repulsion of love.   She would
fling herself headlong into Richard's arms, and
sob there, feverish; then, as suddenly, struggle
for release, as one who longs to hide herself, and
finding that refused, lie motionless like a woman
of wax.   Whether embraced or not, out of touch
with him she was desperate.   She could not bear
that, but sought (unknown to him) to have hold
of some part of him — the edge of his tunic, the
tip of his sword, his glove — something she must
have.   Without it she sat quivering, throbbing
all over, looking at him from under her brows
and biting her dumb lips.   If at such a time
as this some other addressed her the word (as,
to free her from her anguish, one would sometimes do), she would perhaps answer him, Yes
or No, but nothing more.   Usually she would
shake her head impatiently, as if all the world
and its affairs (like a cloud of flies) were buzzing about her, shutting out sound or sight of
her Richard.   Love like this, so deep, outwardly
still, inwardly ravening (because insatiable), is a
dreadful thing.   No one who saw Jehane with
Richard in those days could hope for the poor
girl's happiness.   As for him, he was more ex-
pansive, not at all tortured by love, master of
that as of everything else.   He teased her after

the first day, pinched her ear, held her by the chin. He used his strange powers against her; stole up on his noiseless feet, caught her hands behind her, held her fast, and pulled her back to be kissed. Once he lifted her up, a sure prisoner, to the top shelf of a cupboard, whence there was no escape but by the way she had gone. She stayed there quite silent, and when he opened the cupboard doors was found in the same tremulous, expectant state, her eyes still fixed upon him. Neither he nor she, publicly at least, discussed the past, the present or future; but it was known that he meant to make her his Countess as soon as he could reach Poic-tiers. To the onlookers, at any rate to one of them, it seemed that this could never be, and that she knew very well that the hours of this sharp, sweet, piercing intercourse were numbered. How could it last? How could she find either reason or courage to hope it? It seemed to Béziers, on the watch, that she was awaiting the end already. One is fretted to a rag by waiting. So Jehane dared not lose a moment of Richard, yet could enjoy not one, knowing that she must soon lose all.

Those six clear days of theirs had been wiselier spent upon the west road; but Richard's desire outmastered every thought. Having snatched Jehane from the very horns of the altar, he must hold her, make her his irrevocably at the first breathing place. Dealing with any but Normans, he had never had his six days. But the Norman people, as Abbot Milo says, 'slime-blooded, slow-bellies, are withal great eaters of beef, which breeds

I

in them, as well as a heaviness of motion, a certain slumbrous rage very dangerous to mankind. They crop grief after grief, chewing the cud of grievance; for when they are full of it they disgorge and regorge the abhorred sum, and have stuff for their spleens for many a year.' Even more than this smouldering nursed hate they love a punctilio; they walk by forms, whether the road is to a lady's heart or an enemy's throat. And so Saint-Pol found, and so Des Barres, Frenchmen both and fiery young men, who shook their fists in the faces of the Gurduns and the dust of such blockish hospitallers off their feet, when they saw the course affairs were to run. Gilles de Gurdun, if you will believe it, with the advice of his father and the countenance of his young brother Bartholomew, would not budge an inch towards the recovery of his wife or her ravisher's punishment until he had drawn out his injury fair on parchment. This he then proposed to carry to his Duke, old King Henry. 'Thus,' said the swart youth, 'I shall be within the law of my land, and gain the engines of the law on my side.' He seemed to think this important.

'With your accursed scruples,' cried Saint-Pol, smiting the table, 'you will gain nothing else. Within your country's law, blockhead! Why, my sister is within the Count's country by this time!'

'Oh, leave him, leave him, Eustace,' said Des Barres, 'and come with me. We shall meet him in the fair way yet, you and I together.' So the Frenchmen rode away, and Gilles, with his father and his parchments and his square forehead, went to Evreux, where King Henry then was. Kneeling before their Duke, expounding their grava-mens as if they were suing out a writ of *Mort d'Ancestor*, they very soon found out that he was no more a Norman than Saint-Pol. The old King made short work of their '*ut predictum ests*' and '*Quaesumus igiturs.*'

'Good sirs,' says he, knitting his brows, 'where is this lord who has done you so much injury?'

'My lord,' they report, 'he has her in his strong tower on the plain of Saint-André, some ten leagues from here.'

Then cries the old King, 'Smoke him out, you fools! What! a badger. Draw the thief.'

Then Gilles the elder flattened his lips together and afterwards pursed them. 'Lord,' he said, 'that we dare not do without your express com-mandment.'

'Why, why,' snaps the King, 'if I give it you, my solemn fools?'

Young Gilles stood up, a weighty youth. 'Lord Duke,' he said, 'this lord is the Count of Poictou, your son.' It had been a fine sight for sinful men to see the eyes of the old King strike fire at this word. His speech, they tell me, was terrible, glutted with rage.

'Ha, God!' he spluttered, cracking his fingers, 'so my Richard is the badger, ha? So then I have him, ha? If I do not draw him myself, by the Face!'

It is said that Longespée (a son of his by Madame Rosamund) and Geoffrey (another bastard), with Bohun and De Lacy and some more, tried to hinder him in this design, wherein (said they) he

set out to be a second Thyestes; but they might
as well have bandied words with destiny. 'War
is war,' said the foaming old man, 'whether with
a son or a grandmother you make it. Shall my
enemy range the field and I sit at home and lap
caudle? That is not the way of my house.' He
would by all means go that night, and called for
volunteers. His English barons, to their credit,
flatly refused either to entrap the son of their
master or to abandon the city at a time so criti-
cal. 'What, sire!' cried they, 'are private resent-
ments, like threadworms, to fret the dams of the
state? The floods are out, my lord King, and
brimming at the sluices. Be advised therefore.'

No wearer of the cap of Anjou was ever advised yet. I can hear in fancy the gnashing of
the old lion's fangs, in fancy see the foam he
churned at the corners of his mouth. He went
out with such men as he could gather in his haste,
nineteen of them in all. There were old Gilles
and young Gilles with their men; eight of the
King's own choosing, namely, Drago de Merlou,
Armand Taillefer, the Count of Ponthieu, Fulk
Perceforest, Fulk D'Oilly, Gilbert FitzReinfrid,
Ponce the bastard of Caen, and a butcher called
Rolf, to whom the King, mocking all chivalry,
gave the gilt spurs before he started. He did not
wear them long. The nineteenth was that great
king, bad man, and worse father, Henry Curtman-
tle himself.

It was a very dark night, without moon or
stars, a hot and still night wherein a man weather-
wise might smell the rain. The going upon the
moor was none too good in a good light; yet

they tell me that the old King went spurring over
brush and scrub, over tufted roots, through ridge
and hollow, with as much cheer as if the hunt was
up in Venvil Wood and himself a young man.
When his followers besought him to take heed,
all he would do was snap his fingers, the reins
dangling loose, and cry to the empty night, ' Hue,
Brock, hue!' as if he was baiting a badger. This
badger was the heir to his crown and dignity.

In the Dark Tower they heard him coming
three miles away. Roussillon was on the battlements, and came down to report horsemen on the
plain. 'Lights out,' said Richard, and gave Jehane
a kiss as he set her down. They blew out all the
lights, and stood two to each door ; no one spoke
any more. Jehane sat by the darkened fire with
a torch in her hand, ready to light it when she
was bid.

Thus when the Normans drew near they found
the tower true to its name, without a glimmer of
light. 'Let alone for that,' said the King, whose
grating voice they heard above all the others ;
' very soon we will have a fire.' He sent some
of his men to gather brushwood, ling, and dead
bracken ; meantime he began to beat at the door
with his axe, crying like a madman, ' Richard!
Richard! Thou graceless wretch, come out of thy
hold.'

Presently a little window-casement opened
above him ; Gaston of Béarn poked out his
head.

' Beau sire,' he says, ' what entertainment is
this for the Count your son?'

' No son of mine, by the Face!' cried the

King. 'Let that woman I have caged at home answer for him, who defies me for ever. Let me in, thou sickly dog.'

Gaston said, 'Beau sire, you shall come in if you will, and if you come in peace.'

Says the King, 'I will come in, by God, and as I will.'

'Foul request, King,' said Gaston, and shut the window.

'Have it as you will; it shall be foul by and by,' the King shouted to the night. He bid them fire the place.

To be short, they heaped a wood-stack before the door and set it ablaze. The crackling, the tossed flames, the leaping light, made the King drunk. He and his companions began capering about the fire with linked arms, hounding each other on with the cries of countrymen who draw a badger — 'Loo, loo, Vixen! Slip in, lass! Hue, Brock, hue, hue!' and similar gross noises, until for very shame Gilles and his kindred drew apart, saying to each other, 'We have let all hell loose, Legion and his minions.' So the two companies, the grievous and the aggrieved, were separate; and Richard, seeing this state of the case, took Roussillon and Béziers out by the other door, got behind the dancers, attacked suddenly, and drove three of them into the fire. 'There,' says the chronicler, 'the butcher Sir Rolf got a taste of his everlasting torments, there FitzReinfrid lay and charred; there Ponce of Caen, ill born, made a foul smoke as became him.' Turning to go in again, the three were confronted with the Norman segregates. Great work ensued by the light

of the fire. Gilles the elder was slain with an axe,
and if with an axe, then Richard slew him, for
he alone was so armed. Gilles the younger was
wounded in the thigh, but that was Roussillon's
work; his brother Bartholomew was killed by the
same terrific hitter; Béziers lost a finger of his
sword hand, and indeed the three barely got in
with their lives. The old King set up howling
like a wolf in famine at this loss; what comforted
him was that the fire had eaten up the southern
door and disclosed the entry of the tower —
Jehane holding up a torch, and before her Gaston, Richard, and Bertram of Roussillon, their
shields hiding their breasts.

'Lords,' said Richard, 'we await your leisures.'
None cared to attack: there was the fire to cross,
and in that narrow entry three desperate blades.
What could the old King do? He threatened
hell and death, he cursed his son more dreadfully,
and (you may take it) with far less reason, than
Almighty God cursed Sodom and Gomorrah,
cities of the plain; but Richard made no answer,
and when, quite beside himself, the old man
leaped the fire and came hideously on to the
swords, the points dropped at his son's direction.
Almost crying, the King turned to his followers.
'Taillefer, will you see me dishonoured? Where
is Ponthieu? Where is Drago?' So at last
they all attacked together, coming on with their
shields before them, in a phalanx. This was a
device that needs must fail; they could not drive
a wedge where they could not get in the point.
The three defending shields were locked in the
entry. Two men fell at the first assault, and

Richard's terrible axe crashed into Perceforest's skull and scattered his brains wide. Red and breathless work as it was, it was not long adoing. The King was dismayed at the killing of Perceforest, and dared risk no more lives at such long odds. 'Fire the other door, Drago,' he said grimly. 'We'll have the place down upon them.' The Normans were set to engage the three while others went to find fuel.

The Viscount of Béziers had had his hand dressed by Jehane, and was now able to take his turn. It was by a ruse of his that Richard got away without a life lost. With Jehane to help him, he got the horses trapped and housed. 'Now, Richard,' he said, 'listen to my proposals. I am going to open the north door and make away before they fire it. I shall have half of them after me as I reckon; but whereas I shall have a good start on a fresh horse, I doubt not of escape. Do you manage the rest: there will be three of you.'

Richard approved. 'Go, Raimon,' he said. 'We will join you on the edge of the plain.'

This was done. Jehane, when Béziers was ready, flung open the door. Out he shot like a bolt, and she shut it behind him. The old King got wind of him, spurred off with five or six at his heels, such as happened to be mounted. Richard fell back from the entry, got out his horse, and came forward. As he came he stooped and picked up Jehane, who, with a quick nestling movement, settled into his shield arm. Roussillon and Gaston in like manner got their horses; then at a signal they drove out of

the tower into the midst of the Normans. There
was a wild scuffle. Richard got a side blow on
the knee, but in return he caught Drago de
Merlou under the armpit and well-nigh cut him
in half. Taillefer and Gilles de Gurdun set upon
him together, and one of them wounded him in
the shoulder. But Taillefer got more than he
gave, for he fell almost as he delivered his blow,
and broke his jaw against a rock. As for
Gurdun, Richard hurtled full into him, bore him
backwards, and threw him also. Jehane safe in
arms, he rode over him where he lay. But lastly,
pcunding through the tussocks in the faint grey
light, he met his father charging full upon him,
intent to cut him off. 'Avoid me, father,' he
cried out. 'By God,' said the King, 'I will not.
I am for you, traitorous beast.' They came
together, and Richard heard the old man's breath
roaring like a foundered horse's. He held his
sword arm out stiffly to parry the blow. The
King's sword shivered and fell harmless as Richard
shot by him. Turning as he rode (to be sure he
had done him no more hurt), he saw the wicked
grey face of his father cursing him beyond redemption ; and that was the last living sight of it he
had.

They got clean away without the loss of a man
of theirs, reached the lands of the Count of
Perche, and there found a company of sixty
knights come out to look for Richard. With
them he rode down through Maine to Le Mans,
which had fallen, and now held the French King.
Richard's triumphant humour carried him strange
lengths. As they came near to the gates of Le

Mans, 'Now,' he said, 'they shall see me, like a pious knight, bear my holy banner before me.' He made Jehane stand up in the saddle in front of him; he held her there firmly by one long arm.   So he rode in the midst of his knights through the thronged streets to the church of Saint-Julien, Jehane Saint-Pol pillared before him like a saint.   The French king made much of him, and to Jehane was respectful.   Prince John was there, the Duke of Burgundy, the Dauphin of Auvergne, all the great men.   To Richard was given the Bishop's house; Jehane stayed with the Canonesses of Prémonstre.   But he saw her every day.

CHAPTER XI

WELL may the respectable Abbot Milo despond
over this affair. Hear him, and conceive how he
shook his head. 'O too great power of princes,'
he writes, 'lodged in a room too frail! O wagging
bladder that serves as cushion for a crown! O
swayed by idle breath, seeming god that yet is a
man, man driven by windy passion, that has yet
to ape the god's estate! Because Richard craved
this French girl, therefore he must take her, as it
were, from the lap of her mother. Because he
taught her his nobility, which is the mere wind in
a prince's nose, she taught him nobility again.
Then because a prince must not be less noble
than his nobles (but always *primus inter pares*),
he, seeing her nobly disposed, gave her over to a
man of her own choosing; and immediately after,
unable to bear it that a common person should
have what he had touched, took her away again,
doing slaughter to get her, to say nothing of outrage in the church. Last of all, as you are now
to hear, thinking that too much handling was dishonour to the thin vessel of her body, touched on
the generous spot, he made bad worse; he added
folly to force; he made a marriage where none
could be; he made immortal enmities, blocked up
appointed roads, and set himself to walk others

with a clog on his leg. Better far had she been a wanton of no account, a piece of dalliance, a pastime, a common delight! She was very much other than that. Dame Jehane was a good girl, a noble girl, a handsome girl of inches and bright blood; but by the Lord God of Israel (Who died on the Tree), these virtues cost her dear.'

All this, we may take it, is true; the pity is that the thing promised so fair. Those who had not known Jehane before were astonished at her capacity, discretion, and dignity. She had a part to play at Le Mans, where Richard kept his Easter, which would have taxed a wiser head. She moved warily, a poor thing of gauze, amid those great lights. King Philip had a tender nose; a very whiff of offence might have drawn blood. Prince John had a shrewd eye and an evil way of using it; he stroked women, but they seldom liked it, and never found good come of it. The Duke of Burgundy ate and drank too much. He resembled a sponge, when empty too rough a customer, when full too juicy. It was on one of the days when he was very full that, tilting at the ring, he won, or said he won, forty pounds of Richard. Empty, he claimed them, but Richard discerned a rasp in his manner of asking, and laughed at him. The Duke of Burgundy took this ill. He was never quite the same to Richard again; but he made great friends with Prince John.

With all these, and with their courtiers, who took complexion from their masters, Jehane had to hold the fair way. As a mistress who was to be a wife, the veiled familiarity with which she was treated was always preaching to her. How

dare she be a Countess who was of so little
account already? The poor girl felt herself
doomed beforehand. What king's mistress had
ever been his wife? And how could she be
Richard's wife, betrothed to Gilles de Gurdun?
Richard was much afield in these days, making
military dispositions against his coming absence
in Poictou. She saw him rarely; but in return
she saw his peers, and had to keep her head high
among the women of the French court. And so
she did until one day, as she was walking back
from mass with her ladies, she saw her brother
Saint-Pol on horseback, him and William des
Barres. Timidly she would have slipped by;
but Saint-Pol saw her, reined up his horse in the
middle of the street, and stared at her as if she
had been less than nothing to him. She felt her
knees fail her, she grew vividly red, but she kept
her way. After this terrible meeting she dared
not leave the convent.

Of course she was quite safe. Saint-Pol could
not do anything against the conqueror of Touraine, the ally of his master; but she felt tainted,
and had thoughts (not for the first time) of taking
the veil. One woman had already taken it; she
heard much concerning Madame Alois from the
Canonesses, how she had a little cell at Fontevrault among the nuns there, how she shivered
with cold in the hottest sun, how she shrieked o'
nights, how chattered to herself, and how she
used a cruel discipline. All these things working upon Jehane's mind made her love an agony.
Many and many a time when her royal lover
came to visit her she clung to him with tears,

imploring him to cast her off again; but the more she bewailed the more he pursued his end. In truth he was master by this time, and utterly misconceived her. Nothing she might say or do could stay him from his intent, which was to wed and afterwards crown her Countess of Poictou. This was to be done at Pentecost, as the only reparation he could make her.

Not even what befell on the way to Poictiers for this very thing could alter him. Again he misread her, or was too full of what he read in himself to read her at all. They left Le Mans a fortnight before Pentecost with a great train of lords and ladies, Richard looking like a young god, with the light of easy mastery shining in his eyes. She, poor girl, might have been going to the gallows — and before the end of the journey would thankfully have gone there; and no wonder. Listen to this.

Midway between Châtelherault and Poictiers is a sandy waste covered with scrub of juniper and wild plum, which contrives a living by some means between great bare rocks. It is a disconsolate place, believed to be the abode of devils and other damned spirits. Now, as they were riding over this desert, picking their way among the boulders at the discretion of their animals, it so happened that Richard and Jehane were in front by some forty paces. Riding so, presently Jehane gave a short gasping cry, and almost fell off her horse. She pointed with her hand, and ' Look, look, look!' she said in a dry whisper. There at a little distance from them was a leper, who sat scratching himself on a rock.

'Ride on, ride on, my heart,' said Richard;
but she, 'No, no, he is coming. We must wait.'
Her voice was full of despair.

The leper came jumping from rock to rock,
a horrible thing of rags and sores, with a loose
lower jaw, which his disease had fretted to dis-
location. He stood in their mid path, in full sun,
and plucking at his disastrous eyes, peered upon
the gay company. By this time all the riders were
clustered together before him, and he fingered
them out one after another — Richard, whom he
called the Red Count, Gaston, Béziers, Auvergne,
Limoges, Mercadet; but at Jehane he pointed
long, and in a voice between a croak and a clatter
(he had no palate), said thrice, 'Hail thou!'

She replied faintly, 'God be good to thee,
brother.' He kept his finger still upon her as he
spoke again: every one heard his words.

'Beware (he said) the Count's cap and the
Count's bed; for so sure as thou liest in either
thou art wife of a dead man, and of his killer.'
Jehane reeled, and Richard held her up.

'Begone, thou miserable,' he cried in his high
voice, 'lest I pity thee no more.' But the leper
was capering away over the rocks, hopping and
flapping his arms like an old raven. At a safe
distance he squatted down and watched them,
his chin on his bare knees.

This frightened Jehane so much that in the
refectory of a convent, where they stayed the
night, she could hardly see her victual for tears,
nor eat it for choking grief. She exhausted herself by entreaties. Milo says that she was heard
crying out at Richard night after night, conjur-

ing him by Christ on the Cross, and Mary at the
foot of the Cross, not to turn love into a stabbing
blade; but all to no purpose. He soothed and
petted her, he redoubled her honours, he com-
pelled her to love him ; and the more she agonised
the more he was confident he would right her.

Very definitely and with unexampled profusion
he provided for her household and estate as soon
as he was at home. Kings' daughters were among
her honourable women, at least, counts' daughters,
daughters of viscounts and castellans. She had
Lady Saill of Ventadorn, Lady Elis of Montfort, Lady Tibors, Lady Maent, Lady Beatrix, all
fully as noble, and two of them certainly more
beautiful than she. Lady Saill and Lady Elis
were the most lovely women of Aquitaine, Saill
with a face like a flame, Elis clear and cold as
spring water in the high rocks. He gave her a
chancellor of her seal, a steward of the household,
a bishop for chaplain. Viscount Ebles of Ventadorn was her champion, and Bertran de Born
(who had been doing secret mischief in the south,
as you will learn by and by), if you will believe
it, Bertran de Born was forgiven and made her
trobador. It was at a great Court of Love which
Richard caused to be held in the orchards
outside Poictiers, with pavilions and a Chastel
d'Amors, that Bertran came in and was forgiven
for the sake of his great singing. On a white
silk tribune before the castle sat Jehane, in a
red gown, upon her golden head a circlet of dull
silver, with the leaves and thorns which made
up the coronet of a countess. Richard bade sound
the silver trumpets, and his herald proclaim her

three times, to the north, to the east, and to the
south, as 'the most puissant and peerless princess,
Madame Jehane, by the grace of God Countess of
Poictou, Duchess of Aquitaine, consort of our illustrious dread lord Monsire Richard, Count and
Duke of the same.' Himself, gloriously attired in a
bliaut of white velvet and gold, with a purple cloak
over his shoulder, sustained in a *tenzon* with the
chief trobadors of Languedoc, that she was 'the
most pleasant lovely lady now on earth, or ever
known there since the days of Madame Dido,
Queen of Carthage, and Madame Cleopatra, Empress of Babylon'—unfortunate examples both, as
some thought.

Minstrels and poets of the greatest contended
with him; Saill had her champion in Guillem of
Cabestaing, Elis in Girault of Borneilh; the Dauphin of Auvergne sang of Tibors, and Peire Vidal
of Lady Maent. Towards the end came sideways
in that dishevelled red fox (whom nothing shamed),
Bertran de Born himself, looked askance at the
Count, puffed out his cheeks to give himself assurance, and began to sing of Jehane in a way that
brought tears to Richard's eyes. It was Bertran
who dubbed her with the name she ever afterwards went by throughout Poictou and the south,
the name of Bel Vezer. Richard at the end clipped
him in his arms, and with one arm still round his
wicked neck led him to the tribune where Jehane
sat blushing. ' Take him into your favour, Lady
Bel Vezer,' he said to her. ' Whatever his heart
may be, he hath a golden tongue.' Jehane, stooping, lent him her cheek, and Bertran fairly kissed
her whom he had sought to undo. Then turning,

K

fired with her favour, he let his shrill voice go spiring to heaven in her praise.

For these feats Bertran was appointed to her household, as I have said. He made no secret of his love for her, but sang of her night and day, and delighted Richard's generous heart. But indeed Jehane won the favour of most. If she was not so beautiful as Saill, she was more courteous, if not so pious as Elis, more the woman for that. There were many, misled by her petulant lips and watchful eyes, to call her sulky: these did not judge her silence favourably. They thought her cold, and so she was to all but one; their eyes might have told them what she was to him, and how when they met in love, to kiss or cling, their two souls burned together. And if she made a sweet lover, she promised to be a rare Countess. Her judgment was never at fault; she was noble, and her sedate gravity showed her to be so. She was no talker, and had great command over herself; but she was more pale than by ordinary, and her eyes were burning bright. The truth was, she was in a fever of apprehension, restless, doomed, miserable; devouringly in love, yet dreading to be loved. So, more and more evidently in pain, she walked her part through the blare of festival as Pentecost drew nigh.

'Upon that day,' to quote the mellifluous abbot, 'Upon that day when in leaping tongues the Spirit of God sat upon the heads of the Holy Apostles, and gave letters to the unlettered and to the speechless Its own nature, Count Richard wedded Dame Jehane, and afterwards crowned her Countess with his own hands.

'They put her, crying bitterly, into the Count's bed in the Castle of Poictiers on the evening of the same feast. Weeping also, but at a later day, I saw her crowned again at Angers with the Count's cap of Anjou. So to right her and himself Count Richard did both the greatest wrong of all.'

Much more pageantry followed the marriage. I admire Milo's account. 'He held a tournament after this, when the Count and the party of the castle maintained the field against all comers. There was great jousting for six days, I assure you; for I saw the whole of it. No English knights were there, nor any from Anjou; but a few French (without King Philip's goodwill), many Gascons and men of Toulouse and the Limousin; some from over the mountains, from Navarre, and Santiago, and Castile; there also came the Count of Champagne with his friends. King Sancho of Navarre was excessively friendly, with a gift of six white stallions, all housed, for Dame Jehane; nobody knew why or wherefore at the time, except Bertran de Born (O thief unrepentant!).

'Countess Jehane, with her ladies, being set in a great balcony of red and white roses, herself all in rose-coloured silk with a chaplet of purple flowers, the first day came Count Richard in green armour and a surcoat of the same embroidered with a naked man, a branch of yellow broom in his helm. None held up against him that day; the Duke of Burgundy fell and brake his collar-bone. The second day he drove into the mêlée suddenly, when there was a great press of spears, all in red with a flaming sun on his breast. He sat a blood-horse of Spain, bright chestnut colour and housed

in red.   Then, I tell you, we saw horses and men
sunder their loves.   The third day Pedro de
Vaqueiras, a knight from Santiago, encountered
him in his silver armour, when he rode a horse
white as the Holy Ghost.   By a chance blow the
Spaniard bore him back on to the crupper.   There
was a great shout, "The Count is down!   Look
to the castle, Poictou!"   Dame Jehane turned
colour of ash, for she remembered the leper's
prophecy, and knew that De Vaqueiras loved her.
But Richard recovered himself quickly, crying,
"Have at you again, Don Pedro."   So they
brought fresh spears, and down went De Vaqueiras
on his back, his horse upon him.   To be plain,
not Hector raging over the field with shouts for
Achilles, nor flamboyant Achilles spying after
Hector, nor Hannibal at Cannae, Roland in the
woody pass of Roncesvalles, nor the admired
Lancelot, nor Tristram dreadful in the Cornish
isle — not one of these heroes was more gloriously
mighty than Count Richard.   Like the war-horse
of Job (the prophet and afflicted man) he stamped
with his foot and said among the captains "ha
ha!"   His nostrils scented the battle from very
far off; he set on like the quarrell of a bow, and
gathering force as he went, came rocking into his
adversary like galley against galley.   With all
this he was gentle, had a pleasant laugh.   It was
good to be struck down by such a man, if it ever
can be good.   He bore away opposition as he
bore away the knights.'

   If one half of this were true, and no man in
steel could withstand him, how could circumstance, how could she, this slim and frightened

girl? Mad indeed with love and pride, quite beside herself, she forgot for once her tremors and
qualms. On the last day she fell panting upon
his breast; and he, a great lover, kissed her before them all, and lifted her high in his hands.
' Oyez, my lords!' he cried with a mighty voice,
' Is this a lovely wife I have won, or not?' They
answered him with a shout.

He took her a progress about his country afterwards. From Poictiers they went to Limoges,
thence westward to Angoulesme, and south to
Périgueux, to Bazas, to Cahors, Agen, even to
Dax, which is close to the country of the King
of Navarre. Wherever he led her she was hailed
with joy. Young girls met her with flowers in
their hands, wise men came kneeling, offering the
keys of their towns; the youth sang songs below
her balcony, the matrons made much of her and
asked her searching questions. They saw in her
a very superb and handsome Duchess, Jehane of
the Fair Girdle, now acclaimed in the soft sylla-
bles of Aquitaine as Bel Vezer. When they were
at Dax the wise King of Navarre sent ambassadors beseeching from them a visit to his city of
Pampluna; but Richard would not go. Then
they came back to Poictiers and shocking news.
This was of the death of King Henry of England, the old lion, ' dead (Milo is bold to say) in
his sin.'

CHAPTER XII

I MUST report what happened to the King of England when (like a falcon foiled in his stoop) he found himself outpaced and outgeneralled on the moor. Shaken off by those he sought to entrap, baited by the badger he hoped to draw, he took on something not to be shaken off, namely death, and had drawn from him what he would ill spare, namely the breath of his nostrils. To have done with all this eloquence, he caught a chill, which, working on a body shattered by rages and bad living, smouldered in him — a slow-eating fever which bit him to the bones, charred and shrivelled him up. In the clutches of this crawling disease he joined his forces with those of his Marshal, and marched to the relief of Le Mans, where the French King was taking his ease. Philip fired the place when he heard of his approach; so Henry got near enough to see the sky throbbing with red light, and over all a cloud of smoke blacker than his own despair. It is said that he had a fit of hard sobbing when he saw this dreadful sight. He would not suffer the host to approach the burning city, but took to his bed, turned his face to the tent-wall, and refused alike housel and meat. News, and of the worst, came fast. The French were at Châteaudun, the Countess of Brittany's men were threatening Anjou from the north; all Touraine with Saumur and a chain of border castles were subject to Richard his son. These things he heard without moving from his bed or opening his eyes.

After a week of this misery two of his lords, the Marshal, namely, and Bishop Hugh of Durham, came to his bedside and told him, 'Sire, here are come ambassadors from France speaking of a peace. How shall it be?'

'As you will,' said the King; 'only let me sleep.' He spoke drowsily, as if not really awake, but it is thought that he was more watchful than he chose to appear.

They held a hasty conference, Geoffrey his bastard, the Marshal, the Bishop: these and the French ambassadors. On the King's part they made but one request; and Geoffrey made that. The King was dying: let him be taken down to his castle of Chinon, not die in the fields like an old hunting dog. This was allowed. He took no sort of notice, let them do what they would with him, slept incessantly all the way to Chinon.

They brought him the parchments, sealed with his great seal; and he, quite broken, set his hand to them without so much as a curse on the robbery done his kingdom. But as the bearers were going out on tiptoe he suddenly sat up in bed. 'Hugh,' he grumbled, 'Bishop Hugh, come thou here.' The Bishop turned back eagerly, for those two had loved each other in their way, and knelt by his bed.

'Read me the signatures to these damned

things,' said the King; and Hugh rejoiced that he was better, yet feared to make him worse.

'Ah, dear sire,' he began to say; but 'Read, man,' said the old King, jerking his foot under the bedclothes. So Hugh the Bishop began to read them over, and the sick man listened with a shaky head, for by now the fever was running high.

'Philip the August, King of the Franks,' says the Bishop; and 'A dog's name,' the old King muttered in his throat. 'Sanchez, Catholic King of Navarre,' says Hugh; and 'Name of an owl,' King Henry. To the same ground-bass he treated the themes of the illustrious Duke of Burgundy, Henry Count of Champagne, and others of the French party. With these the Bishop would have stopped, but the King would have the whole. 'Nay, Hugh,' he said — and his teeth chattered as if it had been bitter cold — 'out with the name of my beloved son. So you shall see what joyful agreement there is in my house.' The Bishop read the name of Richard Count of Poictou, and the King grunted his 'Traitor from the womb,' as he had often done before.

'Who follows Richard?' he asked.

'Oh, our Lady, is he not enough, sire?' said the Bishop in fear. The old King sat bolt upright and steadied his head on his knees. 'Read,' he said again.

'I cannot read!' cried Hugh with a groan. The King said, 'You are a fool. Give me the parchment.'

He pored over it, with dim eyes almost out of his keeping, searching for the names at the top.

So he found what he had dreaded — 'John Count of Mortain.' Shaking fearfully, he began to point at the wall as if he saw the man before him. 'Jesu! Count by me, King by me, and Judas by me! Now, God, let me serve Thee as Thou deservest. Thou hast taken away all my sons. Now then the devil may have my soul, for Thou shalt never have it.' The death-rattle was heard in his throat, and Hugh sprang forward to help him: he was still stiffly upright, still looking (though with filmy eyes) at the wall, still trying to shape in words his wicked vaunts. No words came from him; his jaw dropped before his strong old body. They brought him the Sacrament; his soul rejected it—too clean food. Hugh and others about him, all in a sweat, got him down at last. They anointed him and said a few prayers, for they were in a desperate hurry when it came to the end. It was near midnight when he died, and at that hour, they terribly report, the wind sprang up and howled about the turrets of Chinon, as if all hell was out hunting for that which he had promised them. But, if the truth must be told, he had never kept his promises, and there is no reason to suppose that he kept that one either. Milo adds, 'So died this great, puissant, and terrible king, cursing his children, cursed in them, as they in him. All power was given over to him from his birth, save one only, power over himself. He was indeed a slave more wretched than those hinds, *glebæ ascriptitii*, whom at a distance he ruled in his lands: he was slave of his baser parts. With God he was always at war, and with God's elect. What of blessed

Thomas? Let Thomas answer on the Last Day.
I deny him none of his properties; he was open-
handed, open-minded, as bold as a lion. But his
vices ate him up. Peace be with the man; he was
a mighty king. He left a wife in prison, two
sons in arms against him, and many bastards.'

As soon as he was dead his people came about
like flies and despoiled the Castle of Chinon, the
bed where he lay (smiling grimly, as if death had
made him a cynic), his very body of the rings on
its fingers, the gold circlet, the Christ round his
neck. Such flagrancy was the penalty of death,
who had made himself too cheap in those days;
nor were there any left with him who might have
said, Honour my dead father, or dead master.
William the Marshal had gone to Rouen, afraid
of Richard; Geoffrey was half way to Angers after
treasure; the Bishop of Durham (for purposes)
had hastened off to Poictiers to be the first to hail
the new King. All that remained faithful in that
den of thieves were a couple of poor girls with
whom the old sinner had lately had to do. Seeing
he was left naked on his bed, one of these—
Nicolete her name was, from Harfleur — touched
the other on the shoulder — Kentish Mall they
called her — and said, 'They have robbed our
master of so much as a shirt to be buried in.
What shall we do?'

Mall said, ' If we are found with him we shall
be hanged, sure enough. Yet the old man was
kind to me.'

' And to me he was kind,' said Nicolete, ' God
wot.'

Then they looked at each other. ' Well?' said

Nicolete.   And Mall, 'What you do I will do.'
So they kissed together, knowing it was a gallows
matter, and went in to the dead body of the King.
They washed it tenderly, and anointed it, composed the hands and shut down the horrible sight-
less eyes, then put upon it the only shirt they
could find, which (being a boy's) was a very short
one.   Afterwards came the Chancellor, Stephen
of Turon, called up in a great hurry from a
merry-making, with one or two others, and took
some order in the affair.

The Chancellor knew perfectly well that King
Henry had desired to be buried in the church of
the nuns at Fontevrault.   There had been an old
prophecy that he should lie veiled among the
veiled women which had pleased him very much,
though it had often been his way to scoff at it.
But no one dared move him without the order of
the new King, whoever that might happen to be.
Who could tell when Anjou was claiming a
crown?   Messengers therefore were sent out hot-
foot to Count Richard at Poictiers, and to Count
John, who was supposed to be in Paris.   He, however, was at Tours with the French King, and
got the news first.

It caught him in the wind, so to put it.   Alain,
a Canon of Tours, came before him kneeling, and
told him.   'Lord Christ, Alain, what shall we
do?' says he, as white as a cheese-cloth.   They
fell talking of this or that, that might or might
never be done, when in burst King Philip, Saint-
Pol, Des Barres, and the purple-faced Duke of
Burgundy.   King Philip ran up to John and
clapped him on the back.

'King John! King John of England!' screamed
the young man, like a witch in the air; then Burgundy began his grumble of thunder.

'I stand for you, by God.   I am for you, man.'
But Saint-Pol knelt and touched his knee.

'Sire, do me right, and I become your man!'
So said Des Barres also.   Count John looked about
him and wrung his hands.

'Heh, my lords!   Heh, sirs!   What shall I do
now?'   He was liquid; fear and desire frittered
his heart to water.

They held a great debate, all talking at once,
except the subject of the bother.   He could only
bite his nails and look out of the window.   To
them, then, came creeping Alois of France, deadly
pale, habited in the grey weeds of a nun.   How she
got in, I know not; but they parted this way and
that before her, and so she came very close to John
in his chair, and touched him on the shoulder.
'What now, traitor?' she said hoarsely.   'Whom
next?   The sister betrayed; the father; and now
the brother and king?'

John shook.   'No, no, Alois, no no!' he said
in a whisper.   'Go to bed.   We think not of it.'
But she still stood looking at him, with a wry
smile on that face of hers, pinched with grief and
old before its time.   Saint-Pol stamped his foot.
'Whom shall we trust in Anjou?' he said to Des
Barres.   Des Barres shrugged.   The Duke of Burgundy grumbled something about 'd——d women,'
and King Philip ordered his sister to bed.   They
got her out of the room after a painful scene, and
fell to wrangling again, trying to screw some
resolution into the white prince whom they all

intended to use as a cat's-paw. About eight o'clock in the morning — they still at it — came a shatter of hoofs in the courtyard, which made Count John jump in his skin. A herald was announced.

Reeking he stood, and stood covered, in the presence of so much majesty.

'Speak, sir,' said King Philip; and 'Uncover before France, you dog,' said young Saint-Pol. The herald kept his cap where it was.

'I speak from England to the English. This is the command of my master, Richard King of the English, Duke of Normandy, Count of Anjou. Bid our brother, the illustrious Count of Mortain, attend us at Fontevrault with all speed for the obsequies of the King our father. And those who owe him obedience, let them come also.'

There was low murmuring in the chamber, which grew in volume, until at last Burgundy thundered out, 'England is here! Cut down that man.' But the herald stood his ground, and no one drew a sword. John dismissed him with a few smooth words; but he could not get rid of his friends so easily. Nor could they succeed with him. If Montferrat had been there they might have screwed him to the pitch. Montferrat had a clear course: any king of England who would help him to the throne of Jerusalem was the king of England he would serve. But Philip would not commit himself, and Burgundy waited on Philip. As for Saint-Pol, he was nothing but a sword or two and an unquenchable grudge. And forbidding in the background stood Alois, with reproach in her sunken eyes. The end of it was that Count John, after a while, rode out towards

Fontevrault with all the pomp he could muster.
Thither also, it is clear, went Madame Alois.

'I was with my master,' says Milo in his book,
'when they brought him the news.   He was not
long home from the South, had been hawking in
the meadows all day, and was now in great fettle,
sitting familiarly among his intimates, Jehane on
his knee.   Bertran de Born was in there singing
some free song, and the gentle Viscount of
Béziers, and Lady Elis of Montfort (who sat on a
cushion and played with Dame Jehane's hand),
and Gaston of Béarn, and (I think) Lady Tibors
of Vézelay.   Then came the usher suddenly into
the room with his wand, and by the door fell upon
one knee, a sort of state which Count Richard
had always disliked.   It made him testy.

' " Well, Gaucelm, well," he said ; " on your two
legs, my man, if you are to please me."

' " Lord   King ——— " Gaucelm   began,   then
stopped.   My lord bayed at him.

' " Oy Deus ! " he said in our tongue, below his
breath ; and Jehane slid off his knee and on to
her own.   So fell kneeling the whole company,
till Gaston of Béarn, more mad than most, sprang
up, shouting, " Hail, King of the English ! " and
better, " Hail, Count of Anjou ! "   We all began
on that cry ; but he stopped us with a poignant
look.

' " God have mercy on me : I am very wicked,"
he said, and covered up his face.   No one spoke.
Jehane bent herself far down and kissed his foot.

'Then he sent for the heralds, and in burst
Hugh Puiset, Bishop of Durham, with his flaming
face, outstripping all the others and decency at

once. By this time King Richard had recovered himself. He heard the tale without moving a feature, and gave a few short commands. The first was that the body of the dead King should be carried splendidly to Fontevrault; and the next that a pall should be set up in his private chapel here at Poictiers, and tall candles set lighted about it. So soon as this was done he left the chamber, all standing, and went alone to the chapel. He spent the night there on his knees, himself only with a few priests. He neither sent for Countess Jehane, nor did she presume to seek him. Her women tell me that she prayed all night before a Christ in her bed-chamber; and well she might, with a queen's crown in fair view. In two or three days' time King Richard pressed out, very early, for Fontevrault. I went with him, and so did Hugh of Durham, the Bishop of Poictiers, and the Dauphin of Auvergne. These, with the Chancellor of Poictou, the household servants and guards, were all we had with us. The Countess was to be ready upon word from him to go with her ladies and the court whithersoever he should appoint. Bertran de Born went away in the night, and King Richard never saw him again; but I shall have to speak of his last *tenzon*, and his last Sirvente of Kings, by heaven!

'Before he went King Richard kissed the Countess Jehane twice in the great hall. "Farewell, my queen," he said plainly, and, as some think, but not I, deliberately. "God be thy good friend. I shall see thee before many days." If the man was changed already, she was not at all changed. She was very grave, but not crying, and put up her face for his kisses as meek as any baby. She said nothing at all, but stood palely at the door with her women as King Richard rode over the bridge.

'For my part,' he concludes, 'when I consider the youth and fierce untutored blood of this noblest of his race; or when I remember their terrible names, Tortulf Forester, and Ingelger, Fulke the Black and Fulke the Red, and Geoffrey Greygown and Geoffrey the Fair, and that old Henry, the wickedest of all; their deeds also, how father warred upon his sons, and sons conspired against their fathers; how they hated righteous-ness and loved iniquity, and spurned monks and priests, and revelled in the shambles they had made: then I say to myself, Good Milo, how wouldst thou have received thy calling to be king and sovereign count? Wouldst thou have said, as Count John said, " Lord Christ, Alain, what shall we do?" Or rather, "God have mercy, I am very wicked." It is true that Count John was not called to those estates, and that King Richard was. But I choose sooner to think that each was confronted with his dead father, and not the emptied throne. In which case Count John thought of his safety and King Richard of his sin. Such musing is a windy business, suitable to old men. But I suppose that you who read are very young.'

CHAPTER XIII

HOW THEY MET AT FONTEVRAULT

COMMUNING with himself as he rode alone over the broomy downs, King Richard reined up shortly and sent back a messenger for Milo the Abbot; so Milo flogged his old mule. Directly he was level with his master, that master spoke in a quiet voice, like one who is prepared for the worst: 'Milo, what should a man do who has slain his own father? Is repentance possible for such a one?'

Milo looked up first at the blue sky, then about at the earth, all green and gold. He wrinkled close his eyes and let the sun play upon his face. The air was soft, the turf springy underfoot. He found it good to be there. 'Sire,' he said, 'it is a hard matter; yet there have been worse griefs than that in the world.'

'Name one, my friend,' says the King, whose eyes were fixed on the edge of the hill.

Milo said, 'There was a Father, my lord King Richard, who slew His own Son that the world might be the better. That was a terrible grief, I suppose.' The King was silent for a few paces; then he asked —

'And was the world much the better?'

'Beau sire,' replied Milo, 'not very much. But that was not God's fault; for it had, and still has, the chance of being the better for it.'

'And do you dare, Milo,' said the King, turning him a stern face, 'set my horrible offence
beside the Divine Sacrifice?'

'Not so, my lord King,' said Milo at large;
'but I draw this distinction. You are not so
guilty as you suppose; for in this world the
father maketh the son, both in the way of nature
and of precept. In heaven it is otherwise.
There the Son was from the beginning, co-
eternal with the Father, begotten but not made.
In the divine case there was pure sacrifice, and
no guilt at all. In the earthly case there was
much guilt, but as yet no sacrifice.'

'That guilt was mine, Milo,' said Richard with
a sob.

'Lord, I think not,' answered the old priest.
'You are what your fathers have made you. But
now mark me well: in doing sacrifice you can be
very greatly otherwise. Then if no more guilt
be upon you than hangs by the misfortunes of
tainted man, you can please Almighty God by
doing what you only among men can do, wholesome sacrifice.'

'Why, what sacrifice shall I do?' says the
King.

Milo stood up in his stirrups, greatly exalted in
the spirit.

'My lord,' he said, 'behold, it is for two years
that you have borne the sign of that sacrifice upon
you, but yet have done nothing of it. During
these years God's chosen seat hath lain dishonoured, become the wash-pot of the heathen.
The Holy Tree, stock beyond price, Rod of
Grace, figure of freedom, is in bonds. The

Sepulchre is ensepulchred; Antichrist reigns.
Lord, Lord,'— here the Abbot shook his lifted
finger, — 'how long shall this be? You ask me
of sin and sacrifice. Behold the way.'

King Richard jerked his head, then his horse's.
'Get back, Milo, and leave me,' he said curtly,
struck in the spurs, and galloped away over the
grey down.

The cavalcade halted at Thouars, and lay the
night in a convent of the Order of Savigny.
King Richard kept himself to himself, ate little,
spoke less. He prayed out the night, or most
of it, kneeling in his shirt in the sanctuary, with
his bare sword held before him like a cross. Next
morning he called up his household by the first
cock, had them out on the road before the sun,
and pushed forward with such haste that it was
one hour short of noon when they saw the great
church of the nuns of Fontevrault like a pile of
dim rock in their way.

At a mile's distance from the walls the King
got off his horse, and bid his squires strip him.
He ungirt his sword, took off helm and circlet,
cloak, blazoned surcoat, the girdle of his county.
Beggared so of all emblems of his grace, clad only
in hauberk of steel, bareheaded, without weapon,
and on foot, he walked among his mounted men
into the little town of Fontevrault. That which
he could not do off, his sovereign inches, sovereign eye, gait of mastery, prevailed over all other
robbery of his estate. The people bent their
knees as he passed; not a few — women with
babies in their shawls, lads and girls — caught at
his hand or hauberk's edge, to kiss it and get the

virtue out of him that is known to reside in a
king. When he came within sight of the church
he knelt and let his head sink down to his breast.
But his grief seemed to strike inwards like a
frost; he stiffened and got up, and went forward.
No one would have guessed him a penitent then,
who saw him mount the broad steps to meet his
brother. Before the shut doors of the abbey was
Count John, very splendid in a purple cloak, his
crown of a count upon his yellow hair. He stood
like a king among his peers, but flushed and restless, twiddling his fingers as kings do not twiddle
theirs.

Irresolution kept him where he was until Richard had topped the first flight of steps. But then
he came down to meet him in too much of a
hurry, tripping, blundering the degrees, nodding
and poking his head, with hands stretched out
and body bent, like his who supplicates what he
does not deserve.

'Hail, King of England, O hail!' he said,
wheedling, royally vested, royally above, yet
grovelling there to the prince below him. King
Richard stopped with his foot on the next step,
and let the Count come down.

'How lies he?' were his first words; the
other's face grew fearful.

'Eh, I know not,' he said, shuddering. 'I
have not seen him.' Now, he must have been
in Fontevrault for a day or more.

'Why not?' asked Richard; and John stretched
out his arms again.

'Oh, brother, I waited for you!' he cried, then
added lower, 'I could not face him alone.' This

was perfectly evident, or he would never have
said it.

'Pish!' said King Richard, 'that is no way
to mend matters. But it is written, " They shall
look on him whom they pierced." Come you
in.' He mounted the steps to his brother's
level; and men saw that he was nearly a hand
taller, though John was a fine tall man.

'With you, Richard, with you—but never
without you!' said John, in a hush, rolling his
eyes about. Richard, taking no notice, bid them
set open the doors. This was done: the chill
taint of the dark, of wax and damp and death
came out. John shivered, but King Richard
left him to shiver, and passed out of the sun
into the echoing nave. Lightly and fiercely he
went in, like a brave man who is fretful until
he meets his danger's face; and John caught
at his wrist, and went tiptoe after him. All the
rest, Poictevins and Frenchmen together, followed in a pack; then the two bishops vested.

At the far end of the church, beyond the
great Rood, they saw the candles flare about a
bier. Before that was a little white altar with a
priest saying his mass in a whisper. The high
altar was all dark, and behind a screen in the
north transept the nuns were singing the Office
for the Dead. King Richard pushed on quickly,
the others trooping behind. There in the midst
of all this chilly state, grim and sour-faced, as he
had always been, but now as unconcerned as all
the dead are, lay the empty majesty of England,
careless (as it seemed) of the full majesty; and
dead Anjou a stranger to the living.

It was not so altogether, if we are to believe
those who saw it. The hatred of the dead is a
fearful thing: of that which followed be God
the only judge, and I not even the reporter.
Milo saw it, and Milo (who got some comfort
out of it at last) shall tell you the tale; 'for I
know,' says he, 'that in the end the hidden
things are to be made plain, and even so, things
which then I guessed darkly have since been
opened out to my understanding. Behold!' he
goes on, 'I tell you a mystery. Lightly and
adventuring came King Richard to his dead
father, and Count John dragging behind him
like a load of care. Reverently he knelt him
down beside the bier, prayed for a little, then,
looking up, touched the grey old face. Before
God, I say, it was the act of a boy. But slowly,
slowly, we who watched quaking saw a black
stream well at the nostril of the dead, and slowly
drag a snake's way down the jaw: a sight to
shake those fraught with God — and what to
men in their trespasses? But while all the
others fell back gasping, or whispering their
prayers, scarce knowing what I was or did (save
that I loved King Richard), I whipt forward
with a handkerchief to cover the horror out of
sight. This I would have done, though all had
seen it; the King had seen it, and that white-
hearted traitor Count had seen it, and sprung
away with a wail, "O Christ! O Christ!" The
King stood up, and with his lifted hand stopped
me in the pious act. All held their breaths. I
saw the priest at the altar peer round the corner, his mouth making a ring. King Richard

was very pale and serious. He began to talk to his father, while the Count lay cowering on the pavement.

'"Thou thinkest me thy slayer, father," he said, "pointing at me the murder-sign. Well, I am content to take it; for be thou sure of this, that if that last war between us was rightfully begun it was rightfully ended. And of righteousness I think I am as good a judge as ever thou wert. Thy work is done, and mine is to do. If I may be as kingly as thou wert, I shall please thee yet; and if I fail in that I shall never blame thee, father. Now, Abbot Milo," he concluded, "cover the face." So I did, and Count John got up to his knees again, and looked at his brother.

'This was not the end. Madame Alois of France came into the church through the nuns' door, dressed all in grey, with a great grey hood on her head, and after her women in the same habit. She came hastily, with a quick shuffling motion of the feet, as if she was gliding; and by the bier she stood still, questing with her eyes from side to side, like a hunted thing. King Richard she saw, for he was standing up; but still she looked about and about. Now Count John was kneeling in the shadow, so she saw him last; but once meeting his deplorable eyes with her own she never left go again. Whatever she did (and it was much), or whatever said (and her mouth was pregnant), was with a fixed gaze on him.

'Being on the other side of the bier from him she watched, she put her arms over the dead body, as a priest at mass broods upon the Host he is making. And looking shrewdly at the Count,

" If the dead could speak, John," she said, "if the dead could speak, how think you it would report concerning you and me?"

'" Ha, Madame!" says Count John, shaking like a leafy tree, "what is this?" Madame Alois removed my handkerchief. The horror was still there.

'" He did me kindness," she said, looking wistfully at the empty face; "he tried to serve me this way and that way." She stroked it, then looked again at the Count. "But then you came, John; and you he loved above all. How have you served him, John, my bonny lad? Eh, Saviour!" She looked up on high — "Eh, Saviour, if the dead could speak!"

'No more than the dead could John speak; but King Richard answered her.

'" Madame," he said, "the dead hath spoken, and I have answered it. That is the kingly office, I think, to stand before God for the people. Let no other speak. All is said."

'" No, no, Richard," said Madame Alois, "all is not nearly said. So sure as I live in torment, you will rue it if you do not listen to me now."

'" Madame," replied the King, "I shall not listen. I require your silence. If I have it in me, I command it. I know what I have done."

'" You know nothing," said the lady, beginning to tremble. "You are a fool."

'" May be," said King Richard, with a little shrug, "but I am a king in Fontevrault."

' The Count of Mortain began to wag his head about and pluck at the morse of his cope. "Air, air!" he gasped; "I strangle! I suffocate!"

They carried him out of church to his lodging, and there bled him.

'" Once more, King Richard," said Madame, "will you hear the truth from me?"

'The king turned fiercely, saying, " Madame, I will hear nothing from you. My purpose is to take the Cross here in this church, and to set about our Lord's business as soon as may be. I urge you, therefore, to depart and, if you have time, to consider your soul's health — as I consider mine and my kingdom's."

'She began to cry, being overwrought with this terrible affair. " O Richard," she said, "forgive me my trespasses. I am most wretched."

'He stepped forward, and across the dead man kissed her on the forehead. " God knows, I forgive thee, Alois," he said.

'So then she went away with her people, and no long time afterwards took (as I believe) the whole vow in the convent of Fontevrault.' Thus Milo records a scene too high for me.

When they had buried the old King, Richard sent letters to his brother of France, reminding him of what they had both undertaken to do, namely, to redeem the Sepulchre and set up again in Jerusalem the True Cross. 'As for me,' he wrote, ' I do most earnestly purpose to set about that business as soon as I may ; and I require of you, sire and my brother, to witness my resumption of the Cross in this church of Fontevrault upon the feast of Monsire Saint John Baptist next coming. Let them also who are in your allegiance, the illustrious Duke of Burgundy, Conrad Marquess of Montferrat, and my cousin

Count Henry, be of your party and sharers with you in the new vow.' This done, he went to Chinon to secure his father's treasure, and then made preparations for his coronation as Count of Anjou, and for Jehane's coronation.

When she got his word that she was to meet him at Angers by a certain day there was no thought of disobedience; the pouting mouth meant no mutiny. It meant sickening fear. In Angers they crown the Count of Anjou with the red cap, and put upon his feet the red shoes. That would make Richard the Red Count indeed, whose cap and bed the leper had bid her beware. Beware she might, but how avoid? She knew Richard by this time for master. A year ago she had subjugated him in the Dark Tower; but since then he had handled her, moulded her, had but to nod and she served his will. With what heart of lead she came, come she did to await him in black Angers, steep and hardy little city of slate; and the meeting of the two brought tears to many eyes. She fell at his feet, clasped his knees, could not speak nor cease from looking up; and he, tall and kingly, stoops, lifts her, holds her upon his breast, strokes her face, kisses her eyes and sorrowful mouth. 'Child,' he says, 'art thou glad of me?' asking, as lovers love best to do, the things they know best already. 'O Richard! O Richard!' was all she could say, poor fond wretch; however, we go not by the sense of a bride's language, but by the passion that breaks it up. Every agony of self-reproach, of fear of him, of mistrust, of lurking fate, lay in those sobbed words, 'O Richard! O Richard!'

When he had her alone at night, and she had found her voice, she began to woo him and softly to beguile him with a hand to his chin, judging it a propitious time, while one of his held her head. All the arts of woman were hers that night, but his were the new purposes of a man. He had had a rude shock, was full of the sense of his sin; that grim old mocking face, grey among the candle-flames, was plain across the bed-chamber where they lay. To himself he made oath that he would sin no more. No, no: a king, he would do kingly. To her, clasped close in his arms, he gave kisses and sweet words. Alas, she wanted not the sugar of his tongue; she would have had him bitter, though it cost her dear. Lying there, lulled but not convinced, her sobs grew weaker. She cried herself to sleep, and he kissed her sleeping.

In the cathedral church of his fathers he did on, by the hands of the Archbishop, the red cap and girdle and shoes of Anjou; there he held up the leopard shield for all to see. There also upon the bent head of Jehane — she kneeling before him — he laid for a little while the same cap, then in its room a circlet of golden leaves. If he was sovereign Count, girt with the sword, then she was Countess of Anjou before her grudging world. What more was she? Wife of a dead man and his killer! The words stayed by her, and tinged the whole of her life.

CHAPTER XIV

MIRACLES, as a plain man, I hold to be the peculiar
of the Church. This chapter must be Milo's on
that ground, if there were no other. But there is
one strong other. Milo set the tune which caused
King Richard to dance. And a very good tune it
is — according to Milo. Therefore let him speak.
  'The office of Abbot,' he writes, 'is a solemn,
great office, being no less than that of spiritual
father to a family of men consecrate (as it is written, *Abba*, father); yet not on that account should
vainglory puff the cheeks of a pious man. God
knows that I am no boaster. He, therefore, will
not misjudge me, as certain others have done,
when I record in this place (for positive cause
and reason good) the exorbitant honours I received on the day of my lord Saint John Baptist
in this year of thankful redemption eleven hundred and eighty-nine. Forsooth, I myself, this
Milo of Saint Mary-of-the-Pine, was chosen to
preach in the church of the nuns of Fontevrault
before a congregation thus composed: — Two
kings (one crowned), one legate *a latere*, a reign-
ing duke (him of Burgundy, I mean), five cinctured counts, twice three bishops, abbots without
number; Jehane Countess of Anjou and wife to

the King of England, the Countess of Roussillon, the two Countesses of Angoulesme (the old and the young), Lady Elis of Montfort (reputed the most witty lady in Languedoc), thirteen pronounced poets, and the hairdresser of the King of France — to name no more. That sermon of mine — I shame not to report it — was found worthy the inscription in the Register of Fontevrault; and in the initial letter thereof, garlanded in gold work very beautiful to be seen, is the likeness of myself vested, with a mitre on my head, all done by that ingenious craftsman and faithful Christian man, Aristarchus of Byzantium, *suspirante deo.* There the curious may consult it, as indeed they do. I hope I know the demands of history upon proportion better than to write it all here. Briefly then, a second Peter, I stood up before that crowned assembly and was bold.

'What, I said, is Pharaoh but a noise? How else is Father Abraham but dusty in his cave? Duke Lot hath a monument less durable than his wicked wife's; and as for Noë, that great admiral, the waters of oblivion have him whom the waters of God might not drown. Conquered lies unconquered Agamemnon; how else lies Julius Cæsar? Nabuchodonosor, eater of grass, what is he? Kings pass, and their royal seat gathereth a little dust. Anon with a besom of feathers cometh Time the chamberlain, and scareth to his hiding-place the lizard on the wall. Think soberly, O ye kings! how your crowns are but yellow metal, and your purple robes the food of moths, and the sceptres of your power no better than hedge-twigs for the driving of rats. Round about your crystal orbs scurry the fleas at play in the night-time; in a little while the joints of your legs will grapple the degrees of your thrones with no more zest than an old bargeman's his greasy poop.

'At this King Philip said Tush, and fidgeted in his chair. He might have put me out of countenance, but that I saw King Richard clasp his knee and smile into the rafters, and knew by the peaking of his beard that I had pleased him.

' Thus by precept, by trope and flower of speech, I gaufred the edges of my discourse; then turning eastward with a cry, I grasped the pulpit firmly with one hand, the while I raised the other. Sorrow, I said, is more enduring than the pride of life, my lords, and to renounce than to heap riches. Behold the King of Sorrows! Behold the Man beggared! Ai, ai, my lords! is there to be no end to His sorrows, or shall He be stripped for ever? Yesterday He put off life itself, and to-day ye bid Him do away with the price of life. Yesterday He hung upon the Tree; and to-day ye hear it said, Down with the Tree; let Mahomet kindle his hearth with it. Let us be done, say you, with dead Lords and wooden stocks: we are kings, and our stocks golden. It is well said, my lords, after the fashion this world holds honourable. But I ask, did Job fear God for nought? But I say, consider the Maccabees. All your broad lands are not worth the rent of that little garden enclosed, where among ranked lilies sat Mary singing, God rest Thee, babe, I am Thy mother and daughter. You wag the head and an enemy dieth. You say, Come up, and some wretch getteth title to make others wretched. But

no power of life and member, no fountain of
earthly honour, no great breath nor acclamation
of trumpets, nor bearing of swords naked, nor
chrism, nor broad seal, nor homage, nor fealty
done, is worth that doom of the Lord to a man;
saying, I was naked (Christ is naked!) and ye
clothed Me; I was anhungered (Christ is hungry!)
and ye gave Me meat; I was in prison (so is
Christ!) and ye visited Me. Therefore again I
say unto you, Kings, by the spirit of the Lord
which is in me, Let us now go even unto Bethle-
hem. Awake, do on your panoplies, shake your
sceptres over the armied earth! So Hierusalem,
that bride among brides, that exalted virgin, that
elect lady crowned with stars, shall sit no longer
wasted in the brothel of the heathen: Amen!

'I said; and a great silence fell on all the
length and breadth of the church. King Richard
sat up stiff as a tree, staring at the Holy Rood as
though he had a vision of something at work.
King Philip of France, moody, was watching his
greater brother. Count John of Mortain had his
head sunk to his breast-bone, his thin hands not
at rest, but one finger picking ever at another.
Even the Duke of Burgundy, the burly eater,
was moved, as could be seen by the working of
his cheek-bones. Two nuns were carried out for
dead. All this I saw between my hands as I
knelt in prayer. But much more I saw: it seems
that I had called down testimony from on high.
I saw Countess Jehane, half-risen from her seat,
white in the face, open-mouthed, gaping at the
Cross. "Saviour, the Rood! the Rood!" she
cried out, choking, then fell back and lay quite

still.	Many rose to their feet, some dropped to their knees; all looked.

' We saw the great painted Christ on the Rood stoop His head forward thrice.	At the first and second times, amid cries of wonder, men looked to see whither He bent His head.	But at the third time all with one consent fell upon their faces, except only Richard King of England.	He, indeed, rose up and stood to his full height.	I saw his blue eyes shine like sapphires as he began to speak to the Christ.	Though he spoke measuredly and low, you could mark the exultation singing behind his tones.

' " Ah, now, my Lord God," said he, " I perceive that Thou hast singled me out of all these peers for a work of Thine; which is a thing so glorious for me that, if I glory in it, I am justified, since the work is glorious.	I take it upon me, my Lord, and shall not falter in it nor be slow.	Enough said: Thou askest not words of me.	Now let me go, that the work may begin." After which, very devoutly kneeling, he signed to the Archbishop of Tours, who sat in the sedilia of the sanctuary, to affix the Cross to his shoulder.	Which was done, and afterwards to most of the company then present — to King Philip, to the Duke of Burgundy, to Henry Count of Champagne, Bertram Count of Roussillon, and Raymond Count of Toulouse; to many bishops; also to James d'Avesnes, William des Barres, and to Eustace Count of Saint-Pol, the brother of Countess Jehane.	But Count John took no Cross, nor did Geoffrey the bastard of Anjou.	Afterwards, I believe, these two worked the

French King into a fury because Richard should
have taken upon him the chief place in this
miraculous adventure.   The Duke of Burgundy
was not at all pleased either.   But everybody
else knew that it was to King Richard the Holy
Rood had pointed; and he knew it himself, and
events proved it so.

' But that night after supper he and King
Philip kissed each other, and swore brotherhood
on their sword-hilts before all the peers.   I am
not one to deny generous moments to that politic
prince ; this I consider to have been one, evoked
certainly by the nobility of King Richard.   That
appointed champion's exaltation still burned in
him; he was fiercely excited, his eyes were bright
with fever of fire.   " Hey, Philip," he laughed,
" now you and I must cross the sea !   And you
a bad sailor, Philip ! "

' " 'Tis so, indeed, Richard," says King Philip,
looking rather foolish.   King Richard clapped
him on the shoulder.   " A stout heart, my Philip,"
he says, " is betokened by your high stomach.
That shall stand us in a good stead in Palestine."
Then it was that King Philip kissed him, and
him King Richard again.

' He was in great heart that day, full to the
neck with hope and adventure.   I would like to
see the man or woman to have denied him anything.   At times like these he was (I do not seek
to disguise it) a frank lover.   *Non omnia possumus
omnes;* if any man think he must have been
Galahad the Bloodless Knight because he had
been singled out by the questing Rood, he knows
little how high ventures foment rich blood.   Lan-

M

celot he never was, to love broadcast; but Tristram, rather, lover of one woman.   Hope, pride, knowledge of his force, ran tingling in him; perhaps he saw her fairer than any woman could have been; perhaps he saw her rosy through his sanguine eyes.   He clipped her in his arms in full hall that night in a way that made her rosy enough.   Not that she denied him: good heaven, who was she to do that?   There as he had her close upon his breast he kissed her a dozen times, and " Jehane, wilt thou fare with me to England?" he asked her fondly, "or must I leave thee peaking here, my Countess of Anjou?"

'She would have had her own answer ready to that, good soul, but that the leper gave her another.   In a low, urgent voice she answered, " Ah, sweet lord, I must never leave thee now "— as if to ask, Was there need?   So he went on talking to her, lover talk, teasing talk, to see what she would say; and all the while Jehane stood very near him, with her face held between his two hands as closely as wine is held by a cup.   To whatever he chose to say, and in whatever fashion, whether strokingly (as to a beloved child), or gruffly (in sport) as one speaks to a pet dog, she replied in very meek manner, eyeing him intently, " Yea, Richard," or " Nay, Richard," agreeing with him always.   This he observed. " They call me Yea-and-Nay, dear girl," he said, "and thou hast learned it of them.   But I warn thee, Jehane, *ma mie*, I am in a mood of Yea this night.   Therefore deny me not."

'" Lord, I shall never deny thee," says Jehane, red as a rose.   And reason enough!   I remembered the words; for while she said them, it is certain she was praying how best she might make herself a liar, like Saint Peter.

'Pretty matters! on the faith I profess. And if a man, who is king of men, may not play with his young wife, I know not who may play with her. That is my answer to King Philip Augustus, who fretted and chafed at this harmless performance. As for Saint-Pol, who ground his teeth over it, I would have a different answer for him.'

I have given Milo his full tether; but there are things to say which he knew nothing about. Richard was changed, for all his wild mood of that night; nor was Jehane slow to perceive it. Perhaps, indeed, she was too quick, with her wit oversharpened by her uneasy conscience. But that night she saw, or thought she saw this in Richard: that whereas the righting of her had been his only concern before the day of the bowing Rood, now he had another concern. And the next day, when at dawn he left her and was with his Council until dinner, she knew it for sure. After dinner (which he scarcely ate) he rose and visited King Philip. With him, the Legate and the Archbishops, he remained till late at night. Day succeeded day in this manner. The French King, the Duke, and their trains went to Paris. Then came Guy of Lusignan, King (and no king) of Jerusalem, for help. Richard promised him his, not because he liked him any better than the Marquess (who kept him out), but because Guy's title seemed to him a good one. At bottom Richard was as deliberate as a pair of scales;

and just now was acting the perfect king, the
very touchstone of justice.   Through all this
time of great doings Jehane stayed quaking at
home, sitting strangely among her women — a
countess who knew she was none, a queen by
nature who dreaded to be queen by law.   Yet
one thing she dreaded more.   She was in a
horrible pass.   Wife of a dead man and his
killer!   Why, what should she do?   She dared
not go on playing wife to the champion of
heaven, and yet she dared not leave him lest she
should be snatched into the arms of his assassin.
On which horn should she impale her poor heart?
She tried to wring prayers out of it, she tried to
moisten her aching eyes with the dew of tears.
Slowly, by agony of effort, she approached her
bosom to the steel.   One night Richard came
to her, and she drove herself to speak.   He came,
and she fenced him off.

'Richard, O Richard, touch me not!'

'God on the Cross, what is this?'

'Touch me not, touch me never; but never
leave me!'

'O my pale rose!   O fair-girdled!'   She stood
up, white as her gown, transfigured, very serious.

'I am not thy wife, Richard; I am no man's
wife.   No, but I am thy slave, bound to thee by
a curse, held from thee by thy high calling.   I
dare not leave thee, my Richard, nor dare stay
by thee so close, lest ruin come of it.'

Richard watched her, frowning.   He was much
moved, but thought of what she said.

'Ruin, Jehane, ruin?'

'Ruin of thy venture, my knight of God!   Ah,

chosen, elect, comrade of the Rood, gossip of Jesus
Christ, duke dedicate ! '   She was hued like flame
as the great thoughts leaped in her.   ' Ah, my
Christian King, it is so little a thing I ask of thee,
to set me apart !   What am I to thee, whose bride
is the virgin city, the holy place ?   What is Jehane,
a poor thing handed about, to vex heaven, or be a
stumbling-block in the way of the Cross ?   Put me
away, Richard, let me go; have done with me,
sweet lord.'   And then swiftly she ran and clasped
his knees : ' But ask me not to leave thee — no, but
I dare not indeed ! '   Her tears streamed freely
now.   When Richard with a cry snatched her up,
she lay weeping like a lost child in his arms.

He laid her on the bed, worn frail by the strife
she had endured; she had no strength to open her
eyes, but moved her lips to thank him for his pains.
At first she turned her head from side to side,
seeking a cool place on the pillow ; later she fell
into a heavy, drugged sleep.   He watched her till
it was nearly light, brooding over her unconscious
face.   No thoughts of a king were his, I think;
but once more he lapped them in that young girl's
bosom, and let them sway, ebb and flow, with it.

On the flow, great with her theme, he saw her
inspired, standing with her torch of flame to point
his road.   A splintry way leads to the Cross, where
even kings consecrate must tear their feet.   If he
knew himself, as at such naked hours he must, he
knew whither his heart was set.   He was to lead
the armies of Christendom, because no other man
could do it.   Had he any other pure and stern
desire but that ?   None.   If he could win back
the Sepulchre, new plant the Holy Cross, set a

Christian king on the throne below Golgotha,
keep word with God Who had bowed to him
from the Rood, give the heathen sword for sword,
and hold the armed world like a spear in his hand,
to shake as he shook — God of all power and
might, was this not worthy his heart?

His heart and Jehane's! The flowing bosom
ebbed, and drained him of all but pity. He saw
her like a dead flower, wan, bruised, thrown away.
Robbery! He had stolen her by force. He
clenched his two hands about his knèe and shook
himself to and fro. Thief! Damned thief!
Had he made her amends? He groaned. Not
yet. Should she not be crowned? She prayed
that she might not be. She meant that; all her
soul came sobbing to her lips as she prayed him.
He could not deny her that prayer. If she would
not mount his throne, she should not — he was
King. But that other bidding: Touch me not,
she said. He looked at her sleeping; her bosom
filled and lifted his hand. God have no mercy on
him if he denied her that either. ' So take Thou,
God, my heart's desire, if I give her not hers.'
Then he stooped and kissed her forehead; she
opened her eyes and smiled feebly, half awake.

He was not a man, I say it again, at the mercy
of women's lure. Milo was right; he was Tristram,
not Galahad nor Lancelot; a man of cold appetite,
a man whose head was master, touched rarely, and
then stirred only to certain deeps. So far as he
could love woman born he loved Jehane, saw
her exceedingly lovely, loved her proud remote
spirit, her nobility, her sobriety. He saw her
bodily perfections too, how splendid a person,

how sumptuous in hue and light. Admiring, taking glory in these, yet he required the sting of another man's hand upon her to seize her for himself. For purposes of policy, for ends which seemed to him good, he could have lived with Jehane as a brother with a sister: one thing provided, Let no other man touch.

Now this policy was imperative, this end God said was good. Jehane implored with tears, Christ called from the Cross; so King Richard fell upon his knees and kissed the girl's forehead. When he left her that morning he sought out Milo and confessed his sins. Shriven he arose, to do what remained in the west before he could be crowned in Rouen, and crowned in Westminster.

CHAPTER XV

LAST *TENZON* OF BERTRAN DE BORN

I WISH to be done with Bertran de Born, that lagging fox; but the dogs of my art must make a backward cast if they are to kill him in the open. I beg the reader, then, to remember that when Richard left him half-throttled in his own house, and when he had recovered wind enough to stir his gall, he made preparations for a long journey to the South. In that scandal concerning Alois of France he believed he had stuff which might wreck Count Richard more disastrously than Count Richard could wreck him. He hoped to raise the South, and thither he went, his own dung-fly, buzzing over the offal he had blown; and the first point he headed for was Pampluna across the Pyrenees. It is folly to dig into the mind of a man diseased by malice; better treat such like sour ground, burn with lime (or let God burn) and abide the event in faith. If of all men in the world Bertran hated Richard of Anjou, it was not because Richard had misused him, but because he had used him too lightly. Richard, offended with Bertran, gave him a flick on the ear and sent him to the devil with his japes. He did no more because he valued him no more. He thought him a perverse rascal, glorious poet, ill-conditioned vassal, untimely parasite of his father's

realm. He knew he had caused endless mischief,
but he could not hate such a cork on a waterspray. Now, it fretted Bertran to white heat that
he should be despised by a great man. It seemed
that at last he could do him considerable harm.
He could embroil him with two kings, France
and England, and induce a third to harass him
from the South. So he crossed the mountains
and went into Navarre.

Over those stony ridges and bare fields Don
Sancho was king, the seventh of his name; and
he kept his state in the city of Pampluna. Reputed the wisest prince of his day, it is certain
that he had need to be so, such neighbours as he
had. West of him was Santiago, south of him
Castile. These two urgent kings, edging (as it
were) on the same bench with him, made his seat
a shifty comfort. No sooner had he warmed
himself a place than he was hoist to a cold one.
In front of him, over against the sun, he saw
Philip of France pinched to the same degree
between England and Burgundy, eager to stretch
his extremities since he could not broaden his
sides. Don Sancho had no call to love France;
but he feared England greatly — the horrible old
brindled Lion, and Richard, offspring of the
Lion and the Pard, Richard the Leopard, who
made more songs and fought more quarrels out
than any Christian prince. Here were quodlibets
for Don Sancho's logic. In appearance he was
a pale vexed man, with anxious eyes and a thin
beard, at which (in his troubles) he plucked as
often as he could afford the hairs. Next to his
bleached lands he loved minstrels and physicians.

Averrhoes was often at his court; so were Guillem of Cabestaing and Peire Vidal. He knew
and went so far as to love Bertran de Born.
Perhaps he was not too good a Christian, certainly he was a very hungry one; and kings, with
the rest of the world, are to be judged by their
necessities, not their professions. So much will
suffice, I hope, concerning Don Sancho the
Wise.

In those days which saw Count Richard's back
turned on Autafort, and Saint-Pol's broken at
Tours, Bertran de Born came to Pampluna, asking to be received by the King of Navarre. Don
Sancho was glad to see him.

' Now, Bertran,' says he, ' you shall give me
news of poets and the food of poets. All the talk
here is of bad debts.'

' Oy, sire,' says Bertran, ' what can I tell you ?
The land is in flames, the women have streaked
faces, far and wide travels the torch of war.'

' I am sorry to hear it,' says King Sancho, ' and
trust that you have not brought one of those
torches with you.'

Bertran shook his head; interruptions worried
him, for he lived maddeningly, like a man that
has a drumming in his ear.

' Sire,' he said, ' there is a new strife between
the Count of Poictou, " Yea-and-Nay," and the
French King on this account: the Count repudi-
ates Madame Alois.'

' Now, why does he do that, Bertran ? ' cried
King Sancho, opening his eyes wide.

' Sire, it is because he pretends that his father,
the old King, has done him dishonour. Says the

Count, Madame Alois might be my stepmother, never my wife.'

'Deus!' said the King. 'Bertran, is this the truth?'

That was a question for which Bertran was fully prepared. He always had it put, and always gave the same answer. 'As I am a Christian, sire,' he said, 'the Gospel is no truer.'

To which King Sancho replied, 'I do most devoutly believe in the Holy Gospel, whatever any Arabian may say to the contrary. But is it for this, pray, that you propose to light candles of war in Navarre?'

'Ah,' said Bertran, with his hand scratching in his vest, 'I light no candles, my lord; but I counsel you to light them.'

'Phew!' said King Sancho, and stuck his arms out; 'on whose account, Bertran, on whose account?'

Bertran replied savagely, 'On account of Dame Alois slandered, of her brother France deceived in his hope, of the English King strangely accused, of his son John (a hopeful prince, Benjamin of a second Israel), and of Queen Eleanor of England, of whose kindred your Grace is.'

'Deus! Oy, Deus!' cried King Sancho, pale with amazement, 'and are all these thrones in arms, lighting candles against Count Richard?'

'It is so indeed, sire,' says Bertran; and King Sancho frowned, with this comment — 'There seems little chivalry here, take it as you will.' Next he inquired, where was the Count of Poictou?

Bertran was ready. 'He rages his lands, sire, like a leopard caged. Now and again he raids

the marches, harries France or Anjou, and with-
draws.'

'And the King his father, Bertran, where is he?
Far off, I hope.'

'He,' said Bertran, 'is in Normandy with a
host, seeking the head of his son Richard on a
charger.'

'The great man that he is!' cried Don Sancho.
Bertran could not contain himself.

'Great or not, he is to pay his debts!   The old
rascal stag is rotten with fever.'

I suppose Don Sancho was not called Wise for
nothing.   At any rate he sat for a while considering the man before him.   Then he asked, where
was King Philip?

'Sire,' replied Bertran, 'he is in his city of
Paris, comforting Dame Alois, and assembling
his estates for Count Richard's flank.'

'And Prince John?'

'Oh, sire, he has friends.   He waits.   Watch
for him presently.'

King Sancho frowned his forehead into furrows,
and allowed himself a hair or two of his beard.
'We will think of it, Bertran,' he said presently.
'Yes, we will think of it, after our own fashion.
God rest you, Bertran, pray go refresh yourself.'
So he dismissed him.

When he was alone he went on frowning, and
between whiles tapped his teeth with his beard-
comb.   He knew that Bertran had not come
lying for nothing to Pampluna; he must find
out on whose account he was lying, and upon
what rock of truth (if any at all) he had built
up his lies.   Was it because he hated the father,

or because he hated the son? Or because he
served Prince John? Let that alone for a
moment. This story of Alois: it must be, he
thought, either true or false, but was no invention
of Bertran's. Whichever it was, King Philip
would make war upon King Henry, not upon
Richard; since, wanting timber, you cut at the
trunk, not at the branches. He believed Bertran
so far, that the Count of Poictou was in his
country, and King Henry with a host in his.
War between Philip and the Count was a foolishness. Peace between the Count and King Henry
was another. Don Sancho believed (since he
believed in God) that old King Henry was at
death's door; and he saw above all things that, if
the scandal was reasonably founded, there would
be a bachelor prince spoiling for wedlock. On all
grounds, therefore, he decided to write privily to
his kinswoman, Queen Eleanor of England.

And so he did, to a very different tune
from that imagined by Bertran, the letter which
follows : —

'Madame (Sister and Aunt),' he wrote, 'this
day has brought tidings to my private ear whereat
in part I mourn with you, and rejoice in part, as a
wise physician who, hearing of some great lover in
the article of death, knows that he has both the
wit and the remedy to work his cure. Madame,
with a hand upon my heart I may certify the flow
of my blood for the causes, serious and horrific,
which have led to strife between your exalted lord
and most dear consort in Christ Jesus, my lord
Henry the pious King of England (whom God
assoil) and his august neighbour of France. But,

Madame (Sister and Aunt), it is no less my comfort
to affirm that the estate of your noble son, the
Count of Poictou, no less moves my anguish.
What, Madame! So fierce a youth and so
strenuous, widowed of his hopeful bed! The
face of Paris with the fate of Menelaus! The
sweet accomplishments of King David (chief of
trobadors) and the ignominy of the husband of
Bathsheba! You see that my eloquence burns
me up; and verily, Madame (Sister and Aunt),
the hot coal of the wrath of your son has touched
my mouth, so that at the last I speak with my
tongue.

'I ask myself, Madame, why do not the virgins
of Christendom arise and offer their unrifled zones
to his noble fingers? Sister and Aunt, there is
one at least, in Navarre, who so arises. I offer
my child Berengère, called by trobadors (because
of her chaste seclusion) Frozen Heart, to be
thawed in the sun of your son. I offer, moreover, my great fiefs of Oliocastro, Cingovilas,
Monte Negro, and Sierra Alba as far as Agreda;
and a dowry also of 60,000 marks in gold of
Byzance, to be numbered by three bishops, one
each of our choosing, and the third to be chosen
by our lord and ghostly father the Pope. And
I offer to you, Madame (Sister and Aunt), the
devotion of a brother and nephew, the right hand
of concord, and the kiss of peace. I pray God
daily to preserve your Celsitude. — From our
court of Pampluna, etc. Under the Privy Signet
of the King himself — Sanchius Navarrensium
Rex, Sapiens, Pater Patriæ, Pius, Catholicus.'

This done, and means taken for sure despatch,

he sends for the virgin in question, and embracing her with one arm, holds her close to his knee.

'My child,' he says, 'you are to be wedded to the greatest prince now on life, the pattern of chivalry, the mirror of manly beauty, heir to a great throne. What do you say to this?'

The virgin kept her eyes down; a very faint flush of rose troubled her cheek.

'I am in your hands, sire,' she said, whereupon Don Sancho enfolded her.

'You are in my arms, dear child,' he testified. 'Your lord will be King of England, Duke of Normandy and Aquitaine, Count of Anjou, Poictou, and Maine, and lord of some island in the western sea whose name I have forgotten. He is also the subject of prophecy, which (as the Arabians know very well) declares that he will rule such an empire as Alexander never saw, nor the mighty Charles dreamed of. Does this please you, my child?'

'He is a very great lord,' said Berengère, 'and will be a great king. I hope to serve him faithfully.'

'By Saint James, and so you shall!' cried the happy Don Sancho. 'Go, my child, and say your prayers. You will have something to pray about at last.'

She was the only daughter he had left, exorbitantly loved; a little creature too much brocaded to move, cold as snow, pious as a virgin enclosed, with small regular features like a fairy queen's. She had a narrow mind, and small heart for meeting tribulation, which, indeed, she seemed

never likely to know. Sometimes, being in her
robes of state, crusted with gems, crowned, coifed,
ringed, she looked like nothing so much as a
stiff doll-goddess set in glass over an altar. It
was thus she showed her best, when with fixed
eyes and a frigid smile she stood above the
court, an unapproachable glittering star set in
the clear sky of a night to give men hopes of
an ordered heaven. It was thus Bertran de
Born had seen her, when for a time his hot
and wrong heart was at rest, and he could look
on a creature of this world without desire to
mar it. Half in mockery, half in love, he called
her Frozen Heart. Later on, you remember, he
called Jehane Bel Vezer. He was the nicknamer
of Europe in his day.

So now, or almost so, he saw her new come
from her father's side — a little flushed, but very
much the great small lady, ma dame Berengère
of Navarre.

'The sun shines upon my Frozen Heart,' said
Bertran. She gave him her hand to kiss.

'No heart of yours am I, Bertran,' she said;
'but chosen for a king.'

'A king, lady! Whom then?'

She answered, 'A king to be. My lord Richard of Poictou.'

He clacked his tongue on his palate, and
bolted this pill as best he could. Bad was best.
He saw himself made newly so great a fool that
he dared not think of it. If he had known at
that time of Richard's dealing with Jehane
Saint-Pol, you may be sure he would have
squirted some venom. But he knew nothing

at all about it; and as to the other affair, even
he dared not speak.

'A great lord, a hot lord, a very strenuous
lord!' he said in jerks. It was all there was
to say.

'He is a prince who might claim a lady's
love, I suppose,' said Berengère, with considering looks.

'Ho ho! And so he has!' cried Bertran.
'I assure your Grace he is no novice. Many
he has claimed, and many have claimed him.
Shall I number them?'

'I beg that you will not,' she said, stiffening
herself. So Bertran grinned his rage. But he
had one thing to say.

'This much I will tell you, Princess. The
name I give him is Yea-and-Nay: beware of it.
He is ever of two minds: hot head and cold
heart, flaming heart and chilled head. He will
be for God and the enemy of God; will expect
heaven and tamper with hell. With rage he
will go up, laughing come down. Ho! He
will be for you and against you; eager, slow;
a wooer, a scorner; a singer of madrigals, ah,
and a croaker afterwards. There is no stability
in him, neither length of love nor of hate, no
bottom, little faith.' Berengère rose.

'You vex yourself, Bertran, and me also,' she said.
'It is ill talking between a prince and his friend.'

'Am I not your friend then, my lady?' he
asked her with bitterness.

'You cannot be the friend of a prince, Bertran,'
said Berengère calmly. His muttered 'O God,
the true word!' sufficed him for thought all his

N

road from Navarre. He went, as you know already, to Poictiers, where Richard was making festival with Jehane.

But when, unhappy liar, he found out the truth, it came too late to be of service to his designs. Don Sancho, he learned, was beforehand with him even there, fully informed of the outrage at Gisors and the marriage at Poictiers, with very clear views of the worth of each performance. Bertran, gnashing his teeth, took up the service of the man he loathed; gnashing his teeth, he let Richard kiss him in the lists and shower favours upon him. When presents of stallions came from Navarre he began to see what Don Sancho was about. Any meeting of Richard and that profound schemer would have been Bertran's ruin. So when Richard was King, he judged it time to be off.

'Now here,' says Abbot Milo, dealing with the same topics, 'I make an end of Bertran de Born, who did enough mischief in his life to give three kings wretchedness — the young King Henry, and the old King Henry, and the new King Richard. If he was not the thorn of Anjou, whose thorn was he? Some time afterwards he died alone and miserable, having seen (as he thought) all his plots miscarry, the object of his hatred do the better for his evil designs, and the object of his love the better without them. He was cast off. His peers were at the Holy War, his enemy on a throne. There had arisen a generation which shrugged at his eld, and remained one which still thought him a misgoverned youth. Great poet he was, great thief, and a silly fool. So there's an end of him: let him be.'

CHAPTER XVI

It was in the gules of August, we read, that King
Richard set out for his duchy and kingdom, on
horseback, riding alone, splendid in red and gold;
Countess Jehane in a litter; his true brother and
his half-brother, his bishops, his chancellor, and
his friends with him, each according to his degree.
They went by Alençon, Lisieux, and Pont l'Evêque
to Rouen; and there they found the Queen-Mother,
an unquenchable spirit. One of Richard's first
acts had been to free her from the fortress in
which, for ten years or more, the old King had
kept her. There were no prison-traces upon her
when she met her son, and fixed her son's mistress
with a calculating eye. A low-browed, swarthy
woman, heavily built, with the wreck of great
beauty upon her, having fingers like the talons of
a bird and a trap-mouth; it was not hard to see
that into the rocky mortice where Richard had
been cast there went some grains of flint from her.
She had slow, deliberate movements of the body,
but a darting mind; she was a most passionate
woman, but frugal of her passion, eking it out to
cover long designs. Whether she loved or hated
— and she could glow with either lust until she
seemed incandescent — she went slowly to work.
The quicker she saw, the slower she was reducing

sight into possession.   With all this, like her son
Richard, she was capable of strong revulsions.
Thus she had loved, then hated King Henry;
thus she was to spurn, then to cling to Jehane.

At Rouen she did her best to crush the young
girl to the pavement with her intolerable flat-
lidded eyes.   When Jehane saw her stand on the
steps of the church amidst the pomp of Normandy
and England — three archbishops by her, William Marshal, William Longchamp, the earls, the
baronage, the knights, heralds, blowers of trumpets; when at her example all this glory of Church
and State bent the knee to Richard of Anjou, and
he, kneeling in turn, kissed his mother's hand,
then rose and to the others gave his to be kissed;
when he, vowed to her, pledged to her, known of
her more secretly than of any, passed through the
blare of horns alone into the soaring nave — Jehane shivered and crossed herself, faltered a little,
and might have fallen.   Her King was doing by
her as she had prayed him; but the scrutiny of
the Queen-Mother had been a dry gloss to the
text.   She had been able to bear her forsaking
with a purer heart, but for the narrow eyes that
witnessed it and gleamed.   One of her ladies,
Magdalène Coucy, put an arm about her; so
Countess Jehane stiffened and jerked up her head,
and after that walked with no more faltering.   If
she had seen, as Milo saw, Gilles de Gurdun
glowering at her from a corner, it might have
gone hard with her.   But she did not.

They crowned Richard Duke of Normandy,
and to him came all the barons of the duchy one
by one, to do him homage.   And first the Arch-

bishop of Rouen, in whose allegiance was that same
Sir Gilles. But Gilles knew very well that there
could be no fealty from him to this robber of a
duke. Gilles had seen Jehane; and when he could
bear the sight no more for fear his eyes should
bleed, he went and walked about the streets to
cool his head. He swore by all the saints in
the calendar of Rouen — and these are many —
that he would close this account. Let him be
torn apart by horses, he would kill the man who
had stolen his wife and killed his father and
brother, were he duke, king, or Emperor of the
West. Meantime, in the church that golden-
haired duke, set high on the throne of Normandy,
received between his hands the hands of the
Normans; and in a stall of the choir Jehane
prayed fervently for him, with her arms enfolding
her bosom.

Gilles was seen again at Harfleur, when the
King embarked for England. He had a hood over
his head; but Milo knew him by the little steady
eyes and bar of black above. When the great
painted sails bellied to the off-shore wind and
the dragon-standard of England pointed the
sea-way northward into the haze, Milo saw Gilles
standing on the mole, a little apart from his friends,
watching the galley which took Jehane out of
reach.

If Milo found the Normans like ginger in the
mouth, it is not to be supposed that the English
suited him any better. He calls them 'fog-
stewed,' says that they ate too much, and were
as proud of that as of everything else they did.

Luckily, he had very little to do with them, though not much less, perhaps, than his master. Dry facts content him : how the King disembarked at Southampton and took horse ; how he rode through forests to Winchester ; how there he was met by the bishop, heard mass in the minster, and departed for Guildford ; thence again, how through wood and heath they came to Westminster ' and a fair church set in meadows by a broad stream ' — to tell this rapidly contents him. But once in London the story begins to concentrate. It is clear there was danger for Jehane. King Richard, it seems, caused her to be lodged ' in a place of nuns over the river, in a place which is called in English Lamehithe.'

This was quite true; danger there was, as Richard saw, who knew his mother. But he did not then know how quick with danger the times were. The Queen-Mother had upon her the letter of Don Sancho the Wise, and to her the politics of Europe were an open book. One holy war succeeded another, and one king; but what king that might be depended neither upon holiness nor war so much as on the way each was used. Marriage with Navarre might push Anjou across the mountains; the holy war might lift it across the sea. Who was the ' yellow-haired King of the West' whom they of the East foretold, if not her goodly son ? Should God be thwarted by a——? She hesitated not for a word, but I hesitate.

If the Queen-Mother was afraid of anything in the world, it was of the devil in the race she had mothered. It had thwarted her in their father, but it cowed her in her sons. Most of all, I think,

in Richard she feared it, because Richard could be
so cold. A flamy devil as in young Henry, or a
brimstone devil as in Geoffrey of Brittany, or a
spitfire devil as was John's — with these she could
cope, her lord had had them all. But in Richard
she was shy of the bleak isolation, the self-sufficing,
the hard, chill core. She dreaded it, yet it drew
her; she was tempted to beat vainly at it for the
passion's sake; and so in this case she dared to
do. She would cheerfully have killed the minion,
but she dared the King first.

When she opened to him the matter of Don
Sancho's letter, none knew better than Richard
that the matter might have been good. Yet he
would have nothing to say to it. 'Madame,' his
words were, 'this is an idle letter, if not imperti-
nent. Don Sancho knows very well that I am
married already.'

'Eh, sire! Eh, Richard!' said the Queen-
Mother, 'then he knows more than I.'

'I think not, Madame,' the King replied, 'since
I have this moment informed you.'

The Queen swallowed this; then said, 'This
wife of yours, Richard, who is not Duchess of
Normandy, will not be Queen, I doubt?' *

Richard's face grew haggard; for the moment
he looked old. 'Such again is the fact, Madame.'

'But —— ' the Queen began. Richard looked
at her, so she ended there.

Afterwards she talked with the Archbishop of
Canterbury, with the Marshal, with Longchamp of
Ely, and her son John. All these worthies were
pulling different ways, each trying to get the rope
to himself. With that rope John hoped to hang

his brother yet. 'Dearest Madame,' he said, 'Richard cannot marry in Navarre even if he were willing. Once he has been betrothed, and has broken plight; once he saw his mistress betrothed, and broke her plight. Now he is wedded, or says that he is. Suppose that you get him to break this wedlock, will you give him another woman to deceive? There is no more faithless beast in the world than Richard.'

'Your words prove that there is one at least,' said the Queen-Mother with heat. 'You speak very ill, my son.'

Said John, 'And he does very ill, by the Bread!'

William Marshal interposed. 'I have seen much of the Countess of Anjou, Madame,' said this honest gentleman. 'Let me tell your Grace that she is a most exalted lady.' He would have said more had the Queen-Mother endured it, but she cried out upon him.

'Anjou! Who dares put her up there?'

'Madame,' said William, 'it was my lord the King.' The Queen fumed.

Then the Archbishop said, 'She is nobly born, of the house of Saint-Pol. I understand that she has a clear mind.'

'More,' cried the Marshal, 'she has a clear heart!'

'If she had nothing clear about her I have that which would bleach her white enough,' said the Queen-Mother; and Longchamp, who had said nothing at all, grinned.

In the event, the Queen one day took to her barge, crossed the river, and confronted the girl who stood between England and Navarre.

Jehane, who was sitting with her ladies at needlework, was not so scared as they were. Like the nymphs of the hunting Maid they all clustered about her, showing the Queen-Mother how tall she was and how nobly figured. She flushed a little and breathed a little faster; but making her reverence she recovered herself, and stood with that curious look on her face, half surprise, half discontent, which made men call her the sulky fair. So the Queen-Mother read the look.

'No pouting with me, mistress,' she said. 'Send these women away. It is with you I have to deal.'

'Do we deal singly, Madame?' said Jehane. 'Then my ladies shall seek for yours the comforts of a discomfortable lodging. I am sorry I have no better.' The Queen-Mother nodded her people out of the room; so she and Jehane were left alone together.

'Mistress,' said the Queen-Mother, 'what is this between you and my son? Playing and kissing are to be left below the degrees of a throne. Let there be no more of it. Do you dare, are you so hardy in the eyes, as to look up to a kingly seat, or measure your head for a king's crown?'

Jehane had plenty of spirit, which a very little of this sort of talk would have fanned into a flame; but she had irony too.

'Madame, alas!' she said, with a hint of shrugging; 'if I have worn the Count's cap I know the measure of my head.'

The Queen-Mother took her by the wrist. 'My girl,' said she, 'you know very well that you

are no Countess at all in my son's right, but are
what one of your nurture should not be. And
you shall understand that I am a plain-dealer in
such affairs when they concern this realm, and
have bled little heifers like you whiter than veal
and as cold as most of the dead; and will do it
again if need be.'

Jehane did not flinch nor turn her eyes from
considering her whitening wrist.

'Oh, Madame,' she says, 'you will never bleed
me; I am quite sure of that. Alas, it would be
well if you could, without offence.'

'Why, whom should I offend then?' the Queen
said, sniffing — 'your ladyship?'

'A greater,' said Jehane.

'You think the King would be offended?'

'Madame,' Jehane said, 'he could be offended;
but so would you be.'

The Queen-Mother tightened hold. 'I am not
easily offended, mistress,' she said, and smiled
rather bleakly.

Jehane also smiled, but with patience, not trying
to get free her wrist.

'My blood would offend you. You dare not
bleed me.'

'Death in life!' the Queen cried, 'is there any
but the King to stop me now?'

'Madame,' Jehane answered, 'there is the
spoken word against you, the spirit of prophecy.'

Then her jailer saw that Jehane's eyes were
green, and very steady. This checked her.

'Who speaks? Who prophesies?'

Jehane told her, 'The leper in a desert place,
saying, " Beware the Count's cap and the Count's

bed; for so sure as thou liest in either thou art wife of a dead man and of his killer."'

The Queen-Mother, a very religious woman, took this saying soberly. She dropped Jehane's wrist, stared at and about her, looked up, looked down; then said, ' Tell me more of this, my girl.'

' Hey, Madame,' said Jehane, ' I will gladly tell you the whole. The saying of the leper was very dreadful to me, for I thought, here is a man punished by God indeed, but so near death as to be likely familiar with the secrets of death. Such a one cannot be a liar, nor would he speak idly who has so little time left to pray in. Therefore I urged my lord Richard by his good love for me to forgo his purpose of wedding me in Poictiers. But he would not listen, but said that, as he had stolen me from my betrothed, it comported not with his honour to dishonour me. So he wedded me, and fulfilled both terms of the leper's prophecy. Then I saw myself in peril, and was not at all comforted by the advice of certain nuns, which was that, although I had lain in the Count's bed, I had not lain, but had knelt, in the Count's cap; and that therefore the terms were not fulfilled. I thought that foolishness, and still think so. But this is my own thought. I have never rightly been in either as the leper intended, for I do not think the marriage a good one. If I am no wife, then, God pity me, I have done a great sin; but I am no Countess of Anjou. So I give the prophet the lie. On the other hand, if I am put away by my lord the King that he may make a good marriage, I shall be claimed again by the man to whom I was betrothed before, and so the doom be in danger of fulfilment. For, look now, Madame, the leper said, " Wife of a dead man and his killer "; and there is none so sure to kill the King as Sir Gilles de Gurdun. Alas, alas, Madame, to what a strait am I come, who sought no one's hurt! I have considered night and day what it were best to do since the King, at my prayer, left me; and now my judgment is this. I must be with the King, though not the King's *mie;* because so surely as he sends me away, so surely will Gilles de Gurdun have me.'

She stopped, out of breath, feeling some shame to have spoken so much. The Queen-Mother came to her at once, with her hands out. 'By my soul, Jehane,' she said, 'you are a good woman. Never leave my son.'

'I never mean to leave him,' said Jehane. 'That is my punishment, and (I think) his also.'

'His punishment, my child?'

'Why, Madame,' said Jehane, 'you think that the King must wed.'

'Yes, yes.'

'And to wed, he must put me away.'

'Yes, yes, child.'

'Therefore, although he loves me, he may never have his dear desire; and although I love him, I may give him no comfort. Yet we can never leave each other for fear of the leper's prophecy; but he must always long and I grieve. That, I think, is punishment for a man and woman.'

The Queen-Mother sobbed. 'Terrible punishment for a little pleasant sin! Yet I doubt'— she said, politic through all—'yet I doubt my

son, being a fierce lover, will have his way with
thee.'

Jehane shook her head. 'No means,' she said,
drawing in her breath, 'no means, Madame. I
have his life to think of.' Here, pitying herself,
she turned away her face. The Queen-Mother
came suddenly and kissed her. They cried
together, Jehane and the flinty old shrew of
Aquitaine.

A pact was made, and sealed with kisses, between these two women who loved King Richard,
that Jehane should do her best to further the
Navarrese match. Circumstance was her friend
in this pious robbery of herself: Richard, who
stood so deep engaged in honour to God Almighty,
could get no money.

Busy as he was with one shift after another to
redeem his credit, busy also pushing on his coronation, he yet continued to see his mistress most
days, either walking with her in the garden of the
nuns' house where she lodged, or sitting by her
within doors. At these snatched moments there
was a beautiful equality between them; the girl
no longer subject to the man, the man more master of himself for being less master of her. As
often as not he sat on the floor at her feet while
she worked at those age-long tapestries which her
generation loved; leaning his head back to her
knee, he would so lie and search her face, and
wonder to himself what the world to come could
have more fair to show than this calm treasurer
of lovely flesh. This was, at the time, her chief
glory, that with all her riches — fragrant allure,
soft warmth, the delicacy, nice luxury of her

every part, the glow, the tincture, the throbbing fire — she could keep a strong hand upon herself; sway herself modestly; have so much and give so little; be so apt for a bridal, and yet without a sigh play the nun! 'If she, being devirginate through me, can cry herself virgin again — then cannot I, by the King of Heaven?' This was Richard's day-thought, a very mannish thought; for women do not consider their own beauties so closely, see no divinity in themselves, and find a man to be a glorious fool to think one of them more desirable than another. He never spoke this thought, but worshipped her silently for the most part; and she, reading the homage of his upturned face, steeled herself against the sweet flattery, held her peace, and in her fierce proud mind made endless plots against his.

In silence their souls conversed upon a theme never mentioned between them. His restless quest of her face taught him much, disposed him; she, with all the good guile of women to her hand, waited, judging the time. Then one day as they sat together in a window she suddenly slipped away from his hand, dropped to her knees, and began to pray.

For a while he let her alone, finding the act as lovely as she. But presently he stooped his face till it almost touched her cheek, and 'Tell me thy prayer, dear heart! Let me pray also!' he whispered.

'I pray for my lord the King,' she said. 'Let me pray.' But as he insisted, urging, leaning to her, she drew her head back and lifted to his view her face, blanched with pure patience.

'O King Christ,' she prayed, 'take from my soiled hand this sacrifice!'

She prayed to Christ, but looked at Richard. He dared speak for Christ.

'What sacrifice, my child?'

'I give Thee the hero who has lain upon my breast; I give Thee the marriage-bed, the cap of the Count. I give Thee the kisses, the clinging together, the vows, the long bliss where none may speak. I give Thee the language of love, the strife, the after-calm, the assurance, the hope and the promise. But I keep, Lord, the memory of love as a hostage of Thine.'

King Richard, breathless now, looked in her face. It was that of a mild angel, steadfast, grave, hued like fire, acquainted with grief. 'O God-fraught! O saint in the battle! O dipped in the flame! Jehane, Jehane, Jehane! Quicken me!' So he cried in anguish of spirit.

'Quicken thee, Richard?' she said. 'Nay, but thou art quick, my King. The Cross hath made thee quick; thou hast given more than I.'

'I will give all by thy direction,' he said, 'for I know that thou wilt save my honour.'

'Trust me there,' said Jehane, and let him kiss her cheek.

She got a great hold upon him by these means. Quick with the Holy Ghost or not, there was no doubting the quickness of his mind. Here Jehane's wit had not played her false; he read her whole meaning; she never let go the footing she had gained, but in all her commerce with him walked a saint, a maid ravished only by a great thought. Visibly to him she stood symbol of belief, sacramental, the fire on the altar, the fine shy spirit of love lurking (like a rock-flower) at the Cross's foot. And so this fire with which she led him, like the torch she had held up to show him his earlier way, lifted her; and so she became indeed what she signified.

She stood very near the Queen-Mother when Richard was crowned and anointed King of the English, unearthly pure, with eyes like stars, robed in dull red, crowned herself with silver. All those about her, marking the respect which the old Queen paid her, scarce dared lift their eyes to her face. The tall King, stripped to the shirt, was anointed, then robed, then crowned; afterwards sat with orb and sceptre to receive homage. Jehane came in her turn to kneel before him. But her work had been done. That icy stream in the blood, which is cause and proof at once of the kingly isolation, was doubly in Richard, first of that name. He beheld her kneeling at his knee, knew her and knew her not. She with her cold lips kissed his cold hand. That day had love, by her own desire, been frozen; and that which was to awaken it was itself numb in sleep.

On the third of September they crowned him King, and found that he was to be King indeed. On the same day the citizens of London killed all the Jews they could find; and Richard banished his brother John from his dominions in England and France for three years and three days.

CHAPTER XVII

I SUPPOSE that the present relations of King
Richard and the Countess of Poictou (as she chose
to call herself now) were as singular as could sub-
sist between a strong man and beautiful woman,
both in love. I am not to extenuate or explain,
but say once for all to the curious that she was
never again to him (nor had been since that day
at Fontevrault) what a sister might not have been.
Yet, with all that, it was evident to the world at
large that he was a lover, and she mistress of his
mind. Not only implicitly so, as witnessed their
long intercourse of the eyes, their quick glances,
stealthy watching of each other, the little tender
acts (as the giving or receiving of a flower), the
brooding silences, the praying at the same time
or place; but explicitly he pronounced himself her
knight. All his songs were of her; he wrote to
her many times a day, and she answered his letters
by her page, and kept the latest of them always
within her vest, over against her heart. She
allowed herself more scope than he, trusting herself further: it is known that she treasured dis-
carded things of his, and went so far as to wear
(she, the Fair-Girdled!) a studded belt of his made
to fit her. She was never without this rude
monument of her former grace. But this was

o   193

the sum-total of their bodily intercourse, apart from speech. Of their spiritual ecstasies I have no warrant to speak, though I believe these were very innocent. She would not dare, nor he care, to indulge in so laxative a joy.

He conversed with her freely upon all affairs of moment; there was no constraint on either side. He was even merry in her company, and astonishingly frank. Singular man! the Navarrese marriage was a common subject of their talk; she spoke of it with serious mockery and he with mock seriousness. From Richard it was, 'Countess Jehane, when the chalk-faced Spaniard reigns you must mend your manners.' And she might say, 'Beau sire, Madame Berengère will never like your songs unless you sing of her.' All this served the girl's private ends. Gradually and gradually she led him to see that thing as fixed. She did it, as it were, on tiptoe, for she knew what a shyer he was; but luckily for her schemes, the Queen-Mother trusted her to the bottom, said nothing and allowed nothing to be said.

Meantime the affairs of the Crusade conspired with Jehane to drive Richard once more to church. If he got little money in England, where abbeys were rich in corn but poor in pelf, and the barons had been so prompt to rob each other that they could not be robbed by the King, — he got less in Gaul, eaten up by war for a hundred years. You cannot bleed a stuck pig, as King Richard found. England was empty of money. He got men enough; from one motive or another every English knight was willing to rifle the East.

He had ships enough. But of what use ships and men if there was no food for them nor money to buy it? He tried to borrow, he tried to beg, he tried what in a less glorious cause a plain man would call stealing. King Richard came not of a squeamish race, and would have sold anything to any buyer, pawned his crown or taken another man's to get the worth of a company's pay out of it. Fines, escheats, reliefs, forfeitures, wardships, marriages — he heaped exaction on exaction, with mighty little result. When his mind was set he was inexorable, insatiable, without scruple. What he got only sharpened his appetite for more. King Tancred of Sicily owed the dowry of Richard's sister Joan. He swore he would wring that out of him to the last doit. He offered the city of London to the highest bidder, and lamented the slaughter of the Jews when the tenders were few. Here was a position to be in! His Englishmen lay rotting in Southampton town, his ships in Southampton water. His Normans and Poictevins were over-ripe; he as dry as an unpinched pear. He saw, to his infinite vexation, his honour again in pawn, and no means of redeeming it. Jehane, with tears in her voice, plied the Navarrese marriage with more passion than she would ever have allowed herself to urge her own. Richard said he would think of it. 'Now I have him half-way,' Jehane told the Queen-Mother. He was driven the other half by his banished brother John.

Prince John, bundled out of the country within a week of the coronation, went to Paris and a

pocketful of mischief in which to put his hand.
King Philip, who should have been preparing for
the East, was listening to counsels much more to
his liking. Conrad of Montferrat was there, with
large white fingers explaining on the table, and a
large white face set as lightly as a mouse-trap.
His Italian mind, with that strange capacity for
subserving business with passion, had a task of
election here. The Marquess knew that Richard
would sooner help the devil than him to Jerusalem;
not only·on this account, but on every conceivable
account did he hate Richard. If he could embroil
the two leaders of the Crusade, there was his affair:
Philip would need him. In Paris also was Saint-
Pol, fizzling with mischief, and behind him, where-
ever he went, stalked Gilles de Gurdun, murder in
his heart. The massive Norman was a fine foil
to the Count: they were the two poles of hatred.
The Duke of Burgundy was not there, but Conrad
knew that he could be counted. Richard owed
him (so he said) forty pounds; besides, Richard
had called him a sponge — and it was true. There,
lastly, was Des Barres, that fine Frenchman, ready
to hate anybody who was not French, and most
ready to hate Richard, who had broken up the
Gisors wedding and put, single-handed, all the
guests to shame. Now, this was a company after
Prince John's own heart. Standing next to the
English throne, he was an excellent footstool; he
felt the delicate position, he was flattered at every
turn. The Marquess found him most useful, not
only because he was on better terms with Philip
than himself could hope to be, but because he
understood him better. John knew that there

were two tender spots in that moody King, and
he knew which was the tenderer, pardieu! So
Conrad's gross finger, guided by John's, probed
the raw of Philip's self-esteem, and found a rankling wound, very proud flesh. Oh, intolerable
affront to the House of Capet, that a tall Angevin
robber should take up and throw away a daughter
of France, and then whistle you to a war in the
East! Prince John, you perceive, knew where to
rub in the salt.

The storm broke when King Richard was again
at Chinon. King Philip sent messengers — William des Barres, the Bishop of Beauvais, and
Stephen of Meaux — about the homage due to
him for Normandy and all the French fiefs. So
far well; King Richard was very urbane, as bland
as such an incisive dealer could be. He would
do homage for Normandy, Anjou, and the rest on
such and such a day. 'But,' he added quietly, 'I
attach the condition that it be done at Vézelay,
when I am there with my army for the East, and
he with his army.'

The ambassadors demurred, talking among
themselves: Richard sat on immovable, his hands
on his knees. Presently the Bishop of Beauvais,
better soldier than priest, stood out from his fellows
and made this remarkable speech: —

'Beau sire, our lord the august King takes it
very ill that you have so long delayed the marriage agreed upon solemnly between your Grace
and Madame Alois his sister. Therefore ——'
Milo (who was present) says that he saw his master narrow his eyes so much that he seemed to
have none at all, but 'sockets and blank balls in

them, like statues.' The Bishop of Beauvais, appar-
ently, did not observe it. ' Therefore,' he went on,
orotund, ' our lord the King desires that the marriage may be celebrated before he sets out for
Acre and the blessed work in those parts. Other
matters there are for settlement, such as the title
of the most illustrious Marquess of Montferrat to
the holy throne, in which my master is persuaded
your Grace will conform to his desires. This and
other matters a many.'

The King got up. ' Too many matters, Bishop
of Beauvais,' he said, ' for my appetite, which is
poor just now. There is no debate. Say this to
your master, I pay homage where it is due. If
by his own act he prove that it is not due, I will
not be blamed. As to the Marquess, I will never
get a kingdom for him, and I marvel that King
Philip can make no better choice than of a man
whose only title is rape, and can get no better ally
than the slanderer of his sister. And upon the
subject of that unhappy lady, I tell you this upon
the Holy Gospels, that I will marry King Philip
himself before I will marry her ; and so much he
very well knows. I am upon the point to depart
in the fulfilment of my vows. Let your master
please himself. He is a bad sailor, he tells me.
Am I to think him a bad soldier? And if so, in
such a cause, what sort of a Christian, what sort
of a king, am I to think him ? '

The Bishop, his diplomacy at an end, grew
very red. He had nothing to say. Des Barres
must needs put in his word.

' Bethink you, fair sire,' he says : ' the Marquess
is of my kindred.'

'Oh, I do think, Des Barres,' the King answered him; 'and I am very sorry for you. But
I am not answerable for the trespasses of your
ancestry.'

Des Barres glared about him, as if he hoped to
find a reply among the joists.

'My lord,' he began again, 'it is laid in charge
upon us to speak the mind of France. Our
master is greatly put about in his sister's affair,
and not he only, but his allies with him. Among
whom, sire, you must be pleased to reckon my
lord John of Mortain.'

He had done better to leave John out; Richard's
eyes burnt him, and his voice cut. 'Let my brother
John have her, who knows her rights and wrongs.
As for you, Des Barres, take back to your master
your windy conversation, and this also, that I allow
no man to dictate marriages to me.' So said, he
broke up the audience, and would see no more
of the ambassadors. They, in two or three days,
departed with what grace they had in them.

The immediate effect of this, you may perhaps
expect, was to drive Richard all the road to
Navarre. He was profoundly offended, so much
so that not Jehane herself dared speak to him.
As he always did when his heart mastered his head,
he acted now alone and at once. In the heart we
choose to seat rage of all sorts, the purest and the
most base, the most fervent and the most cold.
It so happened that there was business for our
King in Gascony, congenial business. Guillem de
Chisi, a vassal of his, had been robbing pilgrims,
so Guillem was to be hanged. Richard went
swift-foot to Cahors, hanged Guillem in front of

his own gatehouse, then wrote letters to Pampluna inviting King Sancho to a conference
'upon many affairs touching Almighty God and
ourselves.' Thus he put it, and King Sancho
needed no accents to the vowels. The wise man
set out with a great train, his virgin with him.

The day of his expectation, King Richard heard
mass in a most unchristian frame of mind. There
was no *Sursum Corda* for him ; but he knelt like
a stone image, inert and cold from breast to back-
bone ; said nothing, moved not. How differently
do men and women stand at the gate of sorrows !
Not far off him knelt Countess Jehane, who in
her hands again (it may be said) held up her
bleeding heart. The luxury of this strange sacrifice made the girl glow like a fire opal ; she was
in a fierce ecstasy, her lips parted, eyes half-shut ;
she breathed short, she panted. There is no
moralising over these things : love is a hearty
feeder, and thrives on a fast-day as well as on a
gaudy. By fasting come visions, tremors, swoon-
ings and such like, dainty perversions of sense.
But part of Jehane's exaltation, you must know,
came of another spur. She had a sure and certain hope ; she knew what she knew, though no
other even guessed it. With that to carry she
could lift up her head. No woman in the world
need grudge the usurper of place while she may
go on, carrying her title below the heart. More
of this presently. Two hours before noon, in that
clear October weather, over the brown hills came
a company of knights on white destriers, with
their pennons flying and white cloaks over theil

mail, the outriders of Navarre. They were met
in the meadow of the Charterhouse and escorted
to their quarters, which were on the right of the
King's pavilion. That same pavilion was of
purple silk, worked over with gold leopards the
size of life. It had two standards beside it, the
dragon of the English, the leopards of Anjou.
The pavilion of King Sancho was of green silk
with silver emblems — a heart, a castle, a stag;
Saint George, Saint Michael, Saint James the
Great, and Saint Martin with his split cloak — a
shining place before whose door stood twenty
ladies in white, their hair let loose, to receive
Madame Berengère and minister to her. Chief
among these was Countess Jehane. King Richard
was not in his own pavilion, but would greet his
brother king in the hall of the citadel.

So in due time, after three soundings on the
silver trumpets and much curious ceremony of
bread and salt, came Don Sancho the Wise in a
meinie of his peers, very noble on a roan horse;
and Dame Berengère his daughter in a wine-
coloured litter, with her ladies about her on
ambling palfreys, the colour of burnt grass. When
they took this little princess out of her silken cage
the first face she looked for and the first she
saw was that of Jehane Saint-Pol, who received
her courteously.

Jehane always wore sumptuous clothing, being
aware, no doubt, that her person justified the dis-
play. For this time she had dressed herself in
silver brocade, let her bosom go bare, and brought
the strong golden plaits round about in her
favourite fashion. Upon her head she had a

coronet of silver flowers, in her neck a blue jewel. All the colour she had lay in her hue of faint rose, in her hair like corn in the sun, in her eyes of green, in her deep red lips. But her height, free build, and liberal curves marked her out of a bevy that glowed in a more Southern fashion. She had to stoop overmuch to kiss Berengère's hand; and this made the little Spaniard bite her lip.

Berengère herself was like a bell, in a stiff dress of crimson sewn with great pearls in leaf and scroll-work. From the waist upwards she was the handle of the bell. This immoderation of her clothes, the fright she was in — so nervous at first that she could hardly stand — became her very ill. She was quite white in the face, with solemn black eyes, glazed and expressionless; her little hands stuck out from her sides like a puppet's. Handsome as no doubt she was, she looked a doll beside the tall Jehane, who could have dandled her comfortably on her knee. She spoke no language but her own, and that not the *langue d'oc*, but a blurred dialect of it, rougher even than Gascon. Conversation was very difficult on these terms. At first the Princess was shy; then (when she grew curious and forgot her qualms) Jehane was shy. Berengère fingered the jewel in the other's neck, turned it about, wanted to know whence it had come, whose gift it was, etc., etc. Jehane blushed to report it the gift of a friend; whereupon the Princess looked her up and down in a way that made her hot all over.

But when it came to the time of meeting King Richard, Berengère's nervous fears came crowding back; the poor little creature began to shake, clung to Jehane. 'How tall is the king, how tall is he? Taller than you?' she asked, looking up at the Picard girl.

'Oh, yes, Madame, he is taller than I.'

'They say he is cruel. Did you — do you think him cruel?'

'Madame, no, no.'

'He is a poet, they say. Has he made many songs of me?'

Jehane murmured her doubts, exquisitely confused.

'Fifty poets,' continued nestling Berengère, 'have made songs of me. There is a wreath of songs. They call me Frozen Heart: do you know why? They say I am too proud to love a poet. But if the poet is a king! I have a certain fear just now. I think I will——' She took Jehane's arm — 'No! no!' She drew away. 'You are too tall — I will never take your arm — I am ashamed. I beg you to go before me. Lead the way.'

So Jehane went first of all the ladies who led the Queen to the King.

King Richard, who himself loved to go splendidly, sat upon his throne in the citadel looking like a statue of gold and ivory. Upon his head was a crown of gold, he had a long tunic of white velvet, round his shoulders a great cope of figured gold brocade, work of Genoa, and very curious. His face and hands were paler than their wont was, his eyes frosty blue, like a winter sea that is made bright, not warm, by the sun. He sat up stiffly, hands on knees; and all about him stood the lords and prelates of the most

sumptuous court in the West. King Sancho the
Wise was ready to stoop all his wisdom and
burden of years before such superb state as this;
but the moment his procession entered the hall
Richard went down from his daïs to meet it,
kissed him on the cheek, asked how he did, and
set the careworn man at his ease. As for Berengère, he took from her of both cheeks, held her
small hand, spoke in her own language honourable and cheerful words, drove a little colour into
her face, screwed a word or two out of her.
Afterwards there was high mass, sung by the
Archbishop of Auch, and a great banquet, served
in the cloister-garth of the Charterhouse under a
red canopy, because the hall of the citadel was
too small.

At this feast King Richard played a great part
— cheerful, easy of approach, making phrases like
swords, giving and taking the talk without any
advantage of his rank. His jokes had a bite in
them, as when he said of Bertran that the best
proof of the excellence of his verses was that he
had undoubtedly made them himself; or of Averrhoes, the Arabian physician and infidel philosopher, that the man equalised his harms by poi-
soning with his drugs the bodies of those whose
minds had been tainted by his heresies. But he
was the first to set the laugh against himself, and
had a flash of Dame Berengère's fine teeth before
he had been ten minutes at table.

After dinner the Kings and their ministers
went into debate; and then it seemed that
Richard had got up from his meat perverse. He
would only talk of one thing, namely, sixty thou-

sand gold besants. On this he harped maddeningly, with calculations of how much victual the
sum would buy, of the weight in ounces, of its
content in sacks in a barn, of the mileage of the
coins set edge to edge, and so on, and so on.
Don Sancho sat winking and fidgeting in his
chair, and talked of his illustrious daughter.

'Milled edges they should have, these besants,'
says King Richard, 'whereof, allowing (say) three
hundred and fifty to a piece, we have a surprising
total of'—here he figured on the table, and
King Sancho pursued his drift until Richard
brought his hand slamming down—'of one-and-
twenty million ridges of gold upon the treasure!'
he concluded with a waggish look. Agreement
was as hard as to prolong parallels to a point.
Yet this went on for some two hours, until, worn
frail by such futilities, the Navarrese chancellor
plumply asked his brother of England if King
Richard would marry. 'Marry!' cried he, when
they brought him down the question, 'yes, I am
all for marrying. I will marry one-and-twenty
million milled edges, our Saviour!' They reported
to King Sancho the substance of these words, and
asked him if such and such would be the dowry
of his lady daughter.

'Ask King Richard if he will have her with
that in hand and the territories demarked,' said
Don Sancho.

This was done. Richard grew grave, made no
more jokes. He turned to Milo, who happened
to be near him.

'Where is the little lady?' he asked him.
Milo looked out of the window.

' My lord,' he said, 'she is in the orchard at
this moment; and I think the Countess is with
her.'   Richard blenched, as if he had been struck
with a whip.   Collecting himself, he turned and
looked down through the window to the leafy
orchard below.   He looked long, and saw (as
Milo had seen) the two girls, the tall and the
little, the crimson and the white, standing near
together in the shade.   Jehane had her head bent,
for Berengère had hold of the jewel in her bosom.
Then Berengère put her arms round the other's
neck and leaned her head where the jewel lay.
Jehane stooped her head lower and lower, cheek
touched cheek.   At this King Richard turned
about; despair set hard was on his face.   He said
in a dry voice, ' Tell the King I will do it.'

In the tedious negotiations of the next few days
it was arranged that the Princess should await the
Queen-Mother at Bayonne, and sail with her and
the fleet to Sicily.   There King Richard would
meet and marry her.   What had passed between
her and Jehane in the orchard, who knows?   They
kissed at parting; but Jehane neither told Richard,
nor did he ask her, why Berengère had lain her
cheek upon her bosom, or why herself had stooped
so low her head.   Women's ways!

So Red Heart made her sacrifice, and Frozen
Heart suffered the Sun; and he they called later
Lion-Heart went out to fight Saladin, and less
open foes than he.

BOOK II

THE BOOK OF NAY

CHAPTER I

THE CHAPTER CALLED MATE-GRIFON

DIFFERING from the Mantuan as much in sort as
degree, I sing less the arms than the man, less the
panoply of some Christian king offended than the
heart of one in its urgent private transports ; less
treaties than the agony of treating, less personages
than persons, the actors rather than the scene.
Arms pass like the fashion of them, to-day or to-
morrow they will be gone; but men live, their
secret springs what they have always been. How
the two Kings, then, smeared over their strifes at
Vézelay ; how John of Mortain was left biting his
nails, and Alois weeping at the foot of a cross;
how Christian armies like dusty snakes dragged
their lengths down the white shores of Rhone, and
how some took ship at Marseilles, and some saved
their stomachs at the cost of their shoes; of King
Richard's royal galley *Trenchemer*, a red ship with
a red bridge, and the dragon at the mast; of the
shields that made her bulwarks terrible ; of who
went adventurous and who remained; of a fleet
that lay upon the waters like a flock of sea-gulls —
countless, now at rest, now beating the sea into
spumy wrath; of what way they made, qualms
they suffered, prayers they said in their extremity,
vows they made and afterwards broke, thoughts
they had and afterwards were ashamed of — of

these and all such things I must be silent if I am
to make a good end to my history.   It shall be
enough for you that the red ship held King
Richard, and King Richard his own thoughts,
and that never far from him, in a ship called *Li
Chastel Orgoilous*, sat Jehane with certain women
of hers, nursing her hope and a new and fearful
wonder she had.   Prayer sits well in women, and
age-long watching: one imagines that Jehane never
left the poop through those long white days, those
burning nights; but could always be seen or felt,
a still figure sitting apart, elbow on knee, chin
in hand — like a Norn reading fate in the starred
web of the night.   In the dark watches, when the
ships lay drifting under the stars, or lurched forward as the surges drove them on, and the tink-
ling of the water against the side was all the
sound, some woman's voice (not Jehane's) would
be heard singing faint and far off, some little
shrill and winding prayer.

> Saincte Catherine,
> Vélà la nuict qui gagne !

they would hear, and hang upon the cadence.   At
such times Richard, stretched upon his lion-skin,
would raise himself, and lift up his face to the
immense, and with his noble voice make the darkness tremble as he sang —

> Domna, dels angels regina,
> Domna, roza ses espina,
> Domna, joves enfantina,
> Domna, estela marina,
> De las autras plus luzens !

But so soon as his voice filled the night, the
woman's faltered and died; and he, holding on
for a stave or more, would stop on a note that
had a wailing fall, and the lapping of the waves or
cry of hidden birds take up the rule again. This
did not often obtain. Mostly he watched out the
night, sleeping little, talking none, but revolving
in his mind the great deeds to do. By day he
was master of the fleet, an admirable seaman
who, knowing nothing of ships' business before
he embarked, dared not confess so much to himself. Richard must be leader if he was to be
undertaker at all. So he led his fleet from his
first hour with it, and brought it safely into the
roadstead.

They made Messina prosperously, a white city
cooped within walls, with turrets and belfries and
shining domes, stooping sharply to the violet sea.
King Philip with his legions was to have come by
land as far as Genoa, and was not expected yet
awhile. Nor was there any sign of the Queen-
Mother, of Berengère, or of the convoy from
Navarre.

A landing was made in the early morning.
Before the Sicilians were well awake Richard's
army was in camp, the camp entrenched, and a
most salutary gallows set up just outside it, with a
thief upon it as a warning to his brothers of Sicily.
So far good. The next thing was an embassy to
King Tancred, the Sicilian King, which demanded
(1) the person of Queen Joan (Richard's sister),
(2) her dowry, (3) a golden table twelve foot long,
(4) a silk tent, and (5) a hundred galleys fitted out

for two years. This despatched, Richard entertained himself with his hawks and dogs, and with
short excursions into Calabria. On one of these
he went to visit the saintly Abbot Joachim, at once
prophet and philosopher and man of cool sense;
and on another to kill wild boars. When he came
back in October from the second of these, he found
matters going rather ill.

King Tancred avoided seeing him, sent no
tables, nor ships, nor dowry. He did send Queen
Joan, and Queen Joan's bed; moreover, because
she had been Queen of Sicily, he sent a sack of
gold coins for her entertainment; but he did not
propose to go any further. Richard, seeing what
sort of courses his plans were likely to take, crossed
once more into Calabria, attacked a fortified town
which the Sicilians had settled, turned the settlers
out, and established his sister there with Jehane,
her shipload of ladies, and a strong garrison.
Then he returned to Messina.

Certainly, he saw, his camp there could be of
no long tenure. The Grifons, as they called the
inhabitants, were about it like hornets; not a day
passed without the murder of some man of his, or
an ambush which cost him a score. Thieving was
a courtesy, raiding an amenity in a Grifon, it
appeared. Richard, hoping yet for the dowry
and a peaceful departing, had laid a strict command
that no harm should be done to any one of them
unless he should be caught bloody-handed. 'Well
and good!' writes Milo; 'but this meant to say
that no man might scratch himself for fear he
should kill a louse.' Nature could not endure
such a direction, so Richard then (whose own

temper was none of the longest) let himself go,
fell upon a party of these brigands, put half to
the sword and hanged the other half in rows before the landward gate of Messina. You will say
that this did not advance his treaty with King
Tancred; but in a sense it did. When the Mes-
senians came out of their gates to attack him in
open field, it was found and reported by Gaston
of Béarn, who drove them in with loss, that William des Barres and the Count of Saint-Pol had
been with them, each heading a company of
knights. Richard flew into a royal, and an
Angevin, rage. He swore by God's back that
he would bring the walls flat; and so he did.
'This is the work of that little pale devil of
France, then,' he said. 'A likely beginning, by
my soul! Now let me see if I can bring two
kings to reason at once.'

He used the argument of the long arm. Bringing up his engines from the ships, he pounded the
walls of Messina to such purpose that he could
have walked in barefoot in two or three places.
King Tancred came in person to sue for peace;
but Richard wanted more than dowry by this
time. 'The peace you shall have,' he said, 'is the
peace of God which passeth understanding, and
for which, I take it, you are not yet ready, unless
you bring hither with you Philip of France.' This
the unfortunate Tancred really could not do; but
he did bring proxies of Philip's. Saint-Pol came,
Des Barres, and the Bishop of Beauvais with his
russet, soldier's face. King Richard sat considering these worthy men.

'Ah, now, Saint-Pol, you are playing a good

part in this Christian adventure, I think!' he broke out after a time.   Saint-Pol squared his jaw.   'If I had caught you in your late sally, my friend,' Richard went on, 'I should have hanged you on a tree, knight or no knight. Why, fool, do you think your shameful brother worth so much treachery?   With him before your eyes can you do no better? I hope so. Get you back, and tell King Philip this: He and I are vowed to honesty; but if he breaks faith again, I have that in me which shall break him.   As for you, Bishop of Beauvais'—one saw the old war-priest blink —'I know nothing of your part in this business, and am willing to think charitably. If you, an old man, have any of the grace of God left in you, bestow some of it on your master. Teach him to serve God as you serve Him, Beauvais. I will try to be content with that.' He turned to Des Barres, the finest soldier of the three. 'William,' he said more gently, for he really liked the man, 'I hope to meet you in a better field, and side by side. But if face to face again, William,' and he lifted his hand, 'beware of me.'

None of them had a word to say, but with troubled faces left the presence; which shows (to some men's thinking) that Richard's strength lay in his cause. That was not the opinion of Des Barres, nor is it mine. Meeting them afterwards, when he made a pact of friendship and alliance with Tancred, and renewed that which he had had with Philip, he showed them a perfectly open countenance. Nevertheless, he took possession of Messina, as he had said he would, and built a great tower upon the wall, which he called Mate-Grifon.

Then he sent for his sister and Jehane, and kept
a royal Christmas in the conquered city.
Trouble was not over. There were constant
strifes between nation and nation, man and man.
Winter storms delayed the Queen-Mother; Richard fretted and fumed at the wasting of his force,
but saw not the worst of the matter. If vice was
eating his army, jealousy was eating Philip's sour
little heart, and rage that of Saint-Pol. Saint-
Pol, with Gurdun to back him, had determined
to kill the English King; with them went, or was
ready to go, Des Barres. He was not such a
steady hater by any means. Some men seek
temptation, others fall under it; Des Barres was
of this kind.

Of temptation there was a plenty, since Richard
was the most fearless of men. When he had forgiven an injury it did not exist for him any more.
He was glad to see Des Barres, glad to play, talk,
grumble, or swear with him — a most excellent
enemy. One day, idling home from a hawking
match, he got tilting with the Frenchman, with
reeds for lances. Neither seemed in earnest until
Richard's horse slipped on a loose stone and threw
him. This was near the gate. You should have
seen the change in Des Barres. 'Hue! Hue!
Passavant!' he yelled, possessed with the devil
of destruction; and came pounding at Richard as
if he would ride over him. At the battle-cry a
swarm of fellows—Frenchmen and Brabanters—
came out and about with pikes. Richard was on
his feet by that time, perfectly advised what was
astir. He was alone, but he had a sword. This
he drew, and took a stride or two towards Des

Barres, who had pulled up short of him, and was panting. The pikemen, who might have hacked him to pieces, paused for another word. A second of time passed without it, and Richard knew he was safe. He went up to Des Barres.

'Learn, Des Barres,' he said, 'that I allow no cries about my head save those for Saint George.'

'Sire,' said Des Barres, 'I am no man of yours.'

'It is truly said,' replied Richard, 'but I will dub you one'; and he smote him with the flat of his sword across the cheek. The blood leapt after the sword.

'Soul of a virgin!' cried Des Barres, white as cloth, except for the broad weal on his face.

'Your soul against mine, graceless dog,' said the King. 'Another word and I pull you down.' Just then who should come riding out of the gate but Gilles de Gurdun, armed cap-a-pie?

'Here, my lord,' said Des Barres, clearing his throat, 'comes a gentleman who has sought your Grace with better cause than mine.'

'Who is your gentleman?' Richard asked him.

'It is De Gurdun, sire, a Norman knight whose name should be familiar.'

'I know him perfectly,' said Richard. He turned to one of the bystanders, saying, 'Fetch that gentleman to me.' The man ran nimbly to meet De Gurdun.

Des Barres, watching narrowly, saw Gilles start, saw him look, almost saw the bracing of his nerves. What exactly followed was curious. Gilles moved

his horse forward slowly. King Richard, standing
in leather doublet and plumed cap, waited for him,
his arms folded. Des Barres on horseback, an
enemy; the bystanders, tattered, savage, high-fed
men, enemies also; in front the most implacable
enemy of all.

When De Gurdun was within spear-reach he
stopped his horse and sat looking at the King.
Richard returned the look; it was an eyeing
match, soon over. Gurdun swung off the horse,
threw the rein to a soldier, and tried footing it.
The steady duel of the eyes continued until Gilles
was actually within sword's distance. Here he
stopped once more; finally gave a queer little
grunt, and went down on one knee. Des Barres
sighed as he eased his heart. The tension had
been terrible.

Richard said, ' De Gurdun, stand up and answer
me. You seek my life, as I understand. Is it
so ? '

Sir Gilles began to stammer. 'No man has
loved the law — no knight ever loved lady —— '
and so on; but Richard cut him short.

' Answer me, man,' he said, in a voice which
was nearly as dry as his father's, 'do you wish for
my life ? '

' King,' said Gilles, his great emotion lending
him dignity, 'if I do, is it a strange matter ?
You have had my father's and brother's. You
have mine in your hand. You corrupted and
then stole my beloved. Are these no griefs ? '

Richard grew impatient; he could never bear
waiting.

' Do you wish my life ? ' he asked again. Gilles

was overwrought. 'By God on high, but I do wish it!' he cried out, almost whimpering.

King Richard threw down his sword. 'Take it then, you fool,' he said. 'You talk too much.'

A silence fell upon the party, so profound that the cicala in the dry hedge shrilled to pierce the ear. Richard stood like a stock, with Des Barres gaping at him. Gurdun was all of a tremble, but swung his sword about in his sword-hand. After a while he took a deep breath, a fumbling step forward; and Des Barres, leaning out over the saddle, caught him by the surcoat.

'Drop that man, Des Barres,' said Richard, without moving his eyes from the Norman. Des Barres obeyed; and as the silence resumed Gilles began twitching his sword again. When a lizard rustled in the grass a man started as if shot.

Gilles gave over first, threw his sword away with a sob. 'God ha' mercy, I cannot! I cannot!' he fretted, and stood blinking the tears from his eyes. Richard picked up his weapon and returned it to him. 'You are brave enough, my friend,' he said, 'for better work. Go and do better in Syria.'

'There is no better work for me, sir,' said Gurdun, 'unless you can justify yourself.'

'I never justify myself,' said Richard. 'Give me my sword.' De Gurdun gave it him. Richard sheathed it, went to his horse, mounted, rode away at walking pace. Nobody moved till he was out of sight. Then said Des Barres with a high oath, 'I could serve that King if he would let me.'

'God damn him,' said Gilles de Gurdun for his part.

It was near the end of January when they sighted over sea the painted sails of the Queen-Mother's galley. Her fleet anchored in the roads, and the lady came ashore. She had two interviews, one with her son, one with Jehane. But she did not choose to see her daughter, Queen Joan, a very handsome, free lady.

'Marriage!' cried King Richard, when this was broached. 'This is no time to talk of marriage. I have waited six months, and now the lady must wait a while, other six if needs be. We leave this accursed island in two days. Between my friends and my enemies I have fought the length and breadth of it twice over. Am I to spend my whole host killing Christians? A little more inactivity, good mother, and I shall be in league with the Soldan against Philip. Bring the lady to Acre, and I will marry her there.'

'No, no, Richard,' said the Queen-Mother; 'I am needed in England. I cannot come.'

'Then let Joan take her,' said the King.

The Queen-Mother, knowing him very well, tried him no further. She sent for Jehane, and held her close in talk for nearly an hour.

'Never leave my son, Jehane,' was the string she harped on. 'Never leave him for good or ill weather. Mated or unmated, never leave him.'

'Never in life, Madame,' said Jehane, then bit her lip lest she should utter what her mind was full of. But the Queen-Mother had no eyes.

'Pray for him,' she said; and Jehane, 'I pray hourly, Madame.' Then the Queen kissed her on both cheeks, and in such kindness they parted.

CHAPTER II

MILO the abbot writes, 'When the spring airs,
moving warmly over the earth, ruffled the surface
of the deep, and that to a tune so winning that
there was no thought of the treachery below, we
took to the ships and steered a course south-east
by south. This was in the quindenes of Easter.
The two queens (if I may call them so, of whom
one had been and one hoped to be of that estate),
Joan and Berengère, went in a great ship which
they call a dromond, a heavy-timbered ship carrying a crowd of sail. With them, by request of
Madame Berengère, went Countess Jehane, not
by any request of her own. The King himself
led her aboard, and by the hand into the state
pavilion on the poop.

'" Madame," he said to his affianced, " I bring
you your desired mate. Use her as you would
use me, for if I have a friend upon earth it is she."

'" Oh, sire," says Berengère, " I am acquainted
with this lady. She has nothing to fear from me."

'Queen Joan said nothing, being afraid of her
brother. So Madame Jehane kissed the hands
of the pair of queens, meekly kneeling to each in
turn; and so far as I know she did them faithful
service through all the mischances of a voyage

whereon every woman and every other man was
horribly sick.

'Having made the Pharos in favourable weather,
and kept Mount Gibello and the wild Calabrian
coast upon our lee (as is fitting), we stood out for
the straight course over the immense waste of
water. Now was no more land to be seen at
either hand; but the sky fitted close upon the
edges of the sea like a dome of glass on a man's
forehead. There was neither cover from the sun
nor hiding-place from the prying concourse of the
stars; the wind came searchingly, the waters
stirred beneath it, or, being driven, heaped themselves up into towers of ruin. The cordage
flacked, the strong ribs creaked; like a beast over-
burdened the whole ship groaned, wallowing in a
sea-trough without breath to climb. So we endured for many days, a straggling host of men,
ordinarily capable, powerless now beneath that
dumb tyrant the sky. Where else could be our
refuge? We all looked to King Richard—by
day to his royal ensign, by night to the great wax
candle which he always had lighted and stuck in a
lantern. His commands were shouted from ship
to ship over two miles or more of sea; if any
strayed or dropped behind we lay-to that he
might come up. But very often, after a day's idle
rolling, we knew that the sea had claimed some
boatload of our poor souls, and went on. The
galleys kept touch with the dromonds, enclosing
them (as it were) within the cusps of a new moon,
and so driving them forward. To see this light
of our King's moving, now fast, now slow, now up,
now down, restlessly over the field of the night,

was to remember the God of the Israelites, who
(for their sakes and ours) became a pillar of fire
at that season, and transformed himself into a tall
cloud in the daytime. Busy as it was, this point
of light, it only figured the unresting spirit of the
King, careful of all these children of his, ordering
the hosts of the Lord.

'Storms drove us at length on to the island of
Crete, where Minos once had his kingly habitation,
and his wife died of pleasure. Again they drove
us, more unfortunately, out of our course upon the
inhospitable coasts of Rhodes, where the salt wind
suffers no trees to live, nor safe anchorage to be,
nor shelter from the ravage of the sea. In this
vexed place there was no sign of land but a long
line of surf beating upon a rocky shore, the mist
of spray and blown sand, spars of drowned ships,
innumerable anxious flocks of birds. Here was
no roadstead for us; yet here, but for the signal
providence of heaven, we had likely all have
perished (as many did perish), miserably failing at
once of purpose, the sacraments of Christ, and
reasonable beds. The fleet was scattered wide,
no ship could see his neighbour; we called on the
King, on the Saviour, on the Father of all. But
deep answered to deep, and the prayer of so many
Christians, as it appeared, skilled little to change
the eternal purposes of God.

'Then one inspired among us climbed up to
the masthead, having in his teeth a piece of the
True Cross set in a silver heart; and called aloud
to the wild weather, "Save, Lord, we perish!"
as was said of old by very sacred persons. To
which palpable truth so urgently declared an

answer was vouchsafed, not indeed according to our full desires, yet (doubtless) level with our deserts. The wind veered to the north ; and though it abated nothing of its force, preserved us from the teeth of the rocks. Before it now, under bare poles, without need of oars, we drove to the southward; and while a little light still endured descried a great mountainous and naked coast rising out of the heaped waters, which we knew to be the land of Cyprus. Off the western face of this dark shore, in a little shelter at last, we lay-to and tossed all night. Next day in fairer weather, hoisting sail, we made a good haven defended by stout sea-walls, a mole and two lighthouses : these were of a city called Limasol. Upon my galley, at least, there was one who sang *Lauda Sion*, whose tune before had been *Adhæsit pavimento*, when he rested tired eyes upon the clustered spires of a white city, smokeless and asleep in the early morning light.'

So far without weariness I hope Milo may have conducted the reader. In relation to the sea you may take him for an expert in the terrors he describes. Not so in Cyprus. War tempts him to prolixity, to classical allusion, even to hexameters of astonishingly loose joints. Every stroke of his hero's sword-arm seems to him of weight. No doubt it was, once ; but not in a chronicle of this sort, where the Cypriote gests must take a lowly place among others fair and foul of this King-errant. Let me put Milo on the shelf for a little, and abridge.

I tell you then that the Emperor of Cyprus, by name Isaac, was a thin-faced man with high cheek·

bones. A Greek of the Greeks, he undervalued what he had never seen, precisely for that reason. When heralds went up to Nikosia to announce the coming-in of King Richard, Isaac mumbled his lips. 'Prutt!' he said, 'I am the Emperor. What have I to do with your kings?' Richard showed him that with one king he had plenty to do, by assaulting Limasol and putting armies to flight in the plains about Nikosia. Shall I sing the battle of the fifty against five thousand; tell how King Richard with precisely half a hundred knights came cantering against the sun and a host, as gay and debonair as to a driving of stags? They say that he himself led the charge, covered in a wonderful silken surcoat, colour of a bullfinch's breast, and wrought upon in black and white heraldry. They say that at the sight of the pensils a-flutter, at the sound of the hunting-horns, the Grifons let fly a shaft a-piece; then threw down their bows and scattered. But the knights caught them. Isaac was on a hill to watch the battle. 'Who is that marvellous tall knight who seems to be swimming among my horse?' 'Splendour, it is Rikardos, King of the West,' they told him, 'reputed a fierce swimmer.' 'He drowns, he drowns!' cried the Emperor, as the red plumes were whelmed in black. 'Nay, but he dives rather, Majesty.' He heard the death-shouts, he saw white faces turned his way; then the mass was cleft asunder, blown off and dispersed like the sparks from a smithy. The thing was of little moment in a time of much; there was no fighting left in the Cypriotes after that sunny morning's work. Nikosia fell, and

the Emperor Isaac, in silver chains, heard from
his prison-house the shouts which welcomed the
Emperor Richard. These things were accom-
plished by the first week in May. Then came
Guy of Lusignan with bad news of Acre and
worse of himself. Philip was before the town,
Montferrat with him. Montferrat had the Archduke's of Austria as well as French support; with
these worthies, and the ravished wife of old King
Baldwin for title-deed, he claimed the throne of
Jerusalem; and King Guy of Lusignan (but for
the name of the thing) was of no account at all.
Guy said that the siege of Acre was a foppery.
King Philip was ill, or thought he was; Montferrat was treating with Saladin; the French
knights openly visited the Saracen women; and
the Duke of Burgundy got drunk. 'What else
could he get, poor fool?' asked Richard; then
said, 'But I promise you this: Montferrat shall
never be King of Jerusalem while I live—not
because I love you, my friend, but because I love
the law. I shall come as soon as I can to Acre,
when I have done here the things which must be
done.' He meant his marriage.

Little Madame Berengère was lodged, as became her, in the Emperor's palace at Limasol,
having with her Queen Joan of Sicily, and among
her women the young fair lady Jehane, none too
fair, poor girl, by this time. Berengère herself,
who was not very intelligent, remarked her, and
gave her the cold shoulder. As day swallowed
up day, and Richard, at his affairs, gave her no
thought, or at least no sign, Jehane's condition
became an abominable eyesore to the Queen-

Q

designate; so Queen Joan plucked up her courage to the point, and seeking out her brother, let
him know that she had tidings for his private ear.

'I do not admit that I have such an ear,' said
Richard. 'It is no part of a king's baggage.
Yet by all means name your tidings, my sister.'

'Dear sire,' said Joan, 'it appears that you
have sown a seed, and must look before long for
the harvest.' The King laughed.

'God knows, I have sown enough seeds. But
mostly they come up tares, I am apt to find. My
harvesting is of little worth. What now, sister?'

'Beau sire,' says the Queen, 'I know not how
you will take it. Your bonamy, the Picardy lady,
is with child, and not so far from her time neither.
My sister Berengère is greatly offended.'

King Richard began to tremble; but whether
from the ague which was never long out of him,
or from joy, or from trouble, who knows?

'Oh, sister,' he said, 'Oh, sister, are you very
sure of this?'

'I was sure of it,' replied the lady, 'the moment
I saw her in the autumn at Messina. But now
your question is not worth the asking.'

The King abruptly left his sister and went over
to the Queen's side of the palace. Berengère was
sitting upon a balcony, all her ladies with her; but
Jehane a little apart. When the King was announced all rose to their feet. He looked neither
right nor left of him, but fixedly at Jehane, with a
high bright flush upon his sharp face and fever
sparks in his eyes. To these signals Jehane,
because of her great exaltation, flew the answering
flags. Richard touched Berengère's hand with

the hair on his lip: to Jehane he said, 'Come, ma mye,' and led her out of the balcony. This was not as it should have been; but Richard, used to his way, took it, and Richard moved could move bigger mountains than those of ceremony. He lunged forward along the corridors, Jehane following as she might, led by the hand, but not against her will. No doubt she was with child, no doubt she was glorious on that account. She was a very proud girl.

Alone, those two who had loved so fondly gazed each at the work wrought upon the other without a word said, the King all luminous with love, and she all dewy. If soul spoke to soul ever in this world, said Richard's soul, 'O Vase, that bearest the pledge of my love!' and hers, 'O Strong Wine, that brimmest in my cup!'

He came forward and embraced her with his arm. He felt her heart beat, he guessed her pride; he felt her thrill, he knew his own defeat. He felt her so strong and salient under his hand — so strong, so full-budded, so hopeful of fruit — that despair of her loss seized him again, terrible rage. He sickened, while in her the warm blood leaped. He wanted everything; she, nothing in the world. He, the king of men, was the bond; she, the cast-off minion, she, this Jehane Saint-Pol, was the free. So God, making war upon the great, rights the balances of this world.

But he was extraordinarily gentle with her; he gripped himself and throttled the animal close. Gaining grace as he went, his heart throve upon its own blood. Balm was shed on his burning face, he sucked peace as it fell. Then he, too, discerned the God near by; to him, too, came with beating wings the pure young Love, that best of all, which hath no needs save them of spending.

His voice was hushed to a boy's murmur.

' Jehane, ma mye, is it true?'

' I am the mother of a son,' she said.

' Give God the glory!'

But she said, ' He hath given it to me.' Her face was turned to where God might be: Richard, looking down, kissed her on the mouth. Tremblingly they kissed and long, not as young lovers, but as spouse and spouse, drinking their common joy.

After a while his present troubles came thronging back, and he said bitterly: ' Ah, child, thou art widowed of me while yet we both live. Yet it was in thy power to be mother of a king.'

Said she, leaning her head on his breast, ' Every woman that beareth a child is mother of a king; but not every woman's child hath a king to his father. Thus it is with me, Richard, who am doubly blessed.'

' Ah, God!' he cried, poignantly concerned, ' Ah God, Jehane, see what trammels I have enmeshed us in, thee in one net and me in another! So that neither can I help thee, being roped down to this work, nor thou thyself, trapped by my fault. How shall I do? Lo, my sin, my sin! I cried Yea; and now cometh God, and, Nay, King Richard, He saith. The sin is mine, and the burden of the sin is thine. Is this a horrible thing?'

Jehane smiled up in his face. ' And dost thou

think it, Richard, a burden so grievous,' she said,
'to be mother of thy son? Dost thou think that
the world can be harsh to me after that; or that
in the life to come there will be no remembrance
to make the long days sweet?' She looked very
proudly upon him, smiling all the time; she put
her hands up and crowned his head with them.
'Oh, my dear life, my pride and my master,' said
Jehane, 'let all come to me that must come now;
I am rich above all my desires, and my lowliness
has been of no account with God. Now let me
go, blessing His name.'

He would not let her go, but still looked earnestly down at her, struggling with himself against
himself.

'I must be married, Jehane,' says he presently.
And she, 'In a good hour, my lord.'

'It is an accursed hour,' he said; 'nothing but
ill can come of it.'

'Lord,' said she, 'thou art vowed to this
work.'

'I know it very well,' he replied; 'but a man
does as he can.'

'You, my King Richard, do as you will,' said
Jehane. So he kissed her and let her go.

Among the multitudinous affairs now heaped
upon him—business of his new empire and his
old, business of Guy's, business of the war, business of marriage—he set first and foremost this
business of Jehane's. He removed her from the
Queen's house, gave her house and household of
her own. It was in Limasol, a pleasant place over-
looking the sea and the ships, a square white house
set deep in myrtle woods and oleanders. Once

more the ' Countess of Poictou ' had her seneschal,
chaplain, ladies of honour.   That done, he fixed
Saint Pancras' day for his marriage, had the ships
got out, furnished, and appointed for sea.   The
night before Saint Pancras he sent for Abbot Milo
in a hurry.   Milo found him walking about his
room, taking long, carefully accurate strides from
flagstone to flagstone.

He continued this feverish devotion for some
minutes after his confessor's coming-in; and
seeing him deep in thought, the good man stood
patient by the doorway.   So presently Richard
seemed aware of him, stopped in mid walk, and
looking at him, said —

' Milo, continence is, I suppose, of all virtues
the most excellent ? '   Milo prepared to expati-
ate.

' Undoubtedly, sire, it is so, because of all
virtues the least comfortable.   Saint Chrysostom,
indeed, goes so far as to declare——'; but
Richard broke in.

' And therefore, Milo, it is urged upon the
clergy by the ordinances of many honourable
popes and patriarchs ? '

' *Distinguo*, sire,' said Milo, ' *distinguo*.   There
are other reasons.   It is written, So run that ye
may obtain.   Now, no man can run after the
prize we seek if he carrieth a woman on his back.
And that for two reasons: first, because she
is so much dead weight; and second, because a
woman is so made that, if her bearer did achieve
the reward, she would immediately claim a share
in it.   But that is no part of the divine plan, as I
understand it.'

'Let us talk of the laity, Milo,' said the King, abstractedly. ' If one of them set up for a runner, should he not be a virgin ? '

' Lord,' replied the abbot, 'if he can.   But that is not so convenient.'

' How not so ? ' asked King Richard.

' My lord,' Milo said, 'if all the laity were virgins there would soon be no laity at all, and then there would be no priests — a state of affairs not provided for by the Holy Church.   Moreover, the laity have a kingdom in this world ; but the religious not of this world.   Now, this world is too excellent a good place not to be peopled ; and God hath appointed a pleasant way.'

Said the King, ' A way of sorrow and shame.'

' Not so, sire,' said Milo, ' but a way of honour. And if I rejoice that the same way is before your Grace, I am not alone in happiness.'

' A king's business,' said Richard, ' is to govern himself wisely (having paid his debts), and his people wisely.   It may be that he should get heirs if none are.   But if heirs there be, then what is his business with more ?   Why should his son be better king than his brother, for example ? '

' Lord,' Milo admonished, 'a king who is sure of himself will make sure of his issue.   That too is a king's business.'

Said Richard moodily, ' Who is sure of himself ? '   He turned away his head, bidding Milo a good night.   As the abbot made his reverence he added, ' I am to be married to-morrow.'

' I devoutly hope so,' said the good man.   ' And then your Grace will have a surer hope than in your Grace's brother.'

'Get you to bed, Milo,' Richard said, 'and let me be alone.'

Married he was, so far as the Church could provide, in the Basilica of Limasol, with the Bishop of Salisbury to celebrate. Vassals of his, and allies, great lords of three realms, bishops and noble knights filled the church and saw the rites done. High above them afterwards, before the altar, he sat crowned and vested in purple, holding in his right hand the sceptre of his power, and the orb of his dominion in his left hand. Then Berengère, daughter of Navarre, kneeling before him, was by him thrice crowned: Queen of England, Empress of Cyprus, Duchess of Normandy. But she never got upon her little dark head the red cap of Anjou which had covered up Jehane's gold hair. Jehane was neither at the church nor at the great feast that followed. She, on Richard's bidding, was in her ship, *Li Chastel Orgoilous*, whose head swayed to the running tide.

But a great feast was held, at which Queen Berengère sat by the King in a gold chair, and was served on knees by the chief officers of the household, the kingdom, and the duchy. Also, after dinner, full and free homage was done her— a desperate long ceremony. The little lady had great dignity; and if they found her stiff, it is to be hoped they remembered her very young. But although everybody saw that Richard was in the clutches of his ague throughout these performances, so much so that when he was not talking his teeth chattered in his head, and his hand spilt the wine on its way to the mouth — none were

prepared for what was to come, unless such intimates as Gaston of Béarn or Mercadet, his Gascon captain, may have known it. At the close of
the homage-giving he rose up in his throne, threw
back his purple robe, and showed to all beholders
the wrinkled mail beneath it. He was, in fact, in
chain-armour from shoulders to feet. For a moment all looked open-mouthed. He drew his
sword with a great gesture, and held it on high.

'Peers and noble vassals,' he called out in
measured tones (in which, nevertheless, deep
down the shaking fit could be discerned, vibrat-
ing the music), 'the work calls us; Acre is in
peril. Kings, who are servants of the King of
Kings, put by their private concerns; queens,
who bow to one throne only, to that bow with
haste. Now, you of the Cross, who follows me
to win the Cross? The ships are ready, my
lords. Shall we go?'

The great hall was struck dumb. Queen
Berengère, only half understanding, looked scared
about her. One could not but pity the extin-
guishment of her poor little great affairs. Queen
Joan grew very red. She had the spirit of her
family, was angry, fiercely whispered in her
brother's ear. He barely heard her; he shook
her words from his ears, stamped on the pavement.

'Never, never! I am for the Cross! Lord
Jesus, behold thy knight! The work is ready,
shall I not do it? I call Yea! for this turn.
Ha, Anjou! To the ships, to the ships!'

His sword flickered in the air; there followed
it, leaping after the beam, a great swish of steel,
soon a forest of swords.

'Ha, Richard! Ha, Anjou! Ha, Saint George!'
So they made the rafters volley; and so headlong
after King Richard tumbled out into the dusk
and sought the ships. The new Queen was crying miserably on the daïs, Queen Joan tapping
her foot beside her. Late at night they also put
out to sea. On his knees, facing the shrouded
East, King Richard spent his wedding night, with
his bare sword for his partner.

CHAPTER III

AFTER they had lost the harbour of Limasol, from that hasty dark hour of setting out, the fleet sailed (it seemed) under new stars and encountered a new strange air. All night they toiled at the oars; and in the morning, very early, every eye was turned to the fired East, where, in the sea-haze, lay the sacred places clothed (like the Sacrament) in that gauzy veil. First of them *Trenchemer* steered, the King's red galley, in whose prow, stiff and hieratic as a figurehead, was the King himself, watching for a sign. The great ships rolled and plunged, the tide came racing by them, blue-green water lipped with foam, carrying upon it unknown weeds, golden fruit floating, wreckage unfamiliar, a dead fish scarlet-rayed, a basket strangely wrought — drifting heralds of a country of dreams. About noon, when mass had been said upon his galley, King Richard was seen to throw up his arms and stretch them wide; the shout followed the sign — 'Terra Sancta! Terra Sancta!' they heard him cry. Voice after voice, tongue after tongue, took up the word and lifted it from ship to ship. All fell upon their knees, save the rowers. A dim coast, veiled in violet, lifted before their eyes — mountain ranges, great hollows, clouded places, so far and silent, so mysteriously wrapt, full of awe, no one could speak, no one had

235

thought to speak, but must look and search and wonder. A quick flight of shore birds, flashing creatures that twittered as they swept by, broke the spell. This then was a land where living things abode; it was not only of the sacred dead. They drew nearer, their hearts comforted.

They saw Margat, a lonely tower high on a split rock; they saw Tortosa, with a haven in the sea; Tripolis, a very white city; Neplyn. Botron they saw, with a great terraced castle; afterwards Beyrout, cedars about its skirt. Mountains rose up nearer to the sound of the surf; they saw Lebanon capped with cloud-wreaths, then snowy Hermon gleaming in the sun. They saw Mount Tabor with a grey head, and two mountains like spires which stood separate and apart. Tyre they passed, and Sidon, rich cities set in the sand, then Scandalion; at length after a long night of watching a soft hill showed, covered with verdure and glossy dark woods, Carmel, shaped like a woman's breast. Making this hallowed mount, in the plain beyond they saw Acre, many-towered; and all about it the tents of the Christian hosts, and before it in the blue waters of the bay ships riding at anchor, more numerous than the sea-birds that haunt Monte Gibello or swim sentinel about its base. Trumpets from the shore answered to their trumpets; they heard a wild tattoo of drums within the walls. On even keels in the motionless tide the ships took up their moorings; and King Richard, throwing the end of his cloak over his shoulder, jumped off the gunwale of *Trenchemer*, and waded breast-deep to shore. He was the first of his realm to touch this storied Syrian earth.

Now for affairs. The meeting of the Kings was cordial, or seemed so. King Philip came out of his pavilion to meet his royal brother, and Richard, kissing him, asked him how he did. 'Very vilely, Richard,' said the young man. 'I think there is a sword in my head. The glaring sun flattens me by day, and all night I shiver.'

'Fever, my poor coz,' said Richard, with a kind hand upon his shoulder. Philip burst out with his symptoms, wailing like a child: 'The devil bites me. I vomit black. My skin is as dry as a snake's. Yesterday they bled me three ounces.' Richard walked back with him among the tents, conversing cheerfully, and for a few days held his old ascendancy over Philip; but only for a few. Other of the leaders he saw: some gave him no welcome. The Marquess of Montferrat kept his quarters, the Duke of Burgundy was in bed. The Archduke of Austria, Luitpold, a hairy man with light red eyelashes, professed great civility; but Richard had a bad way with strangers. Not being receptive, he took no pains to pretend that he was. The Archduke made long speeches, Richard short replies; the Archduke made longer speeches, Richard no replies. Then the Archduke grew very red, and Richard nearly yawned. This was at the English King's formal reception by the leaders of the Crusade. With the Grand Master of the Temple he got on better, liking the looks of the man. He did not observe Saint-Pol on King Philip's left hand; but there he was, flushed, excited, and tensely observant of his enemy. That same night, when they held a council of war, there was seen a smoulder of that

fire which you might have decently supposed put
out.   King Philip came down in a mighty hurry,
and sat himself in the throne; Montferrat, Burgundy, and others of that faction serried round
about him.   The English and Angevin chiefs
were furious, and the Archduke halted between
two opinions.   By the time (lateish) when King
Richard was announced Gaston of Béarn and
young Saint-Pol had their swords half out.   But
Richard came and stood in the doorway, a magnificent leisurely figure.   All his party rose up.
Richard waited, watching.   The Archduke (who
really had not seen him before) rose with
apologies; then the French followed suit, singly,
one here and one there.   There only remained
seated King Philip and the Marquess of Montferrat.   Still Richard waited by the door; presently, in a quiet voice, he said to the usher, ' Take
your wand, usher, to that paralytic over there.
Tell him that he shall use it, or I will.'   The
message was delivered: at an angry nod from
King Philip the Marquess got darkly up, and
Richard came into the hall with King Guy of
Jerusalem.   These two sat down one on each
side of France; and so the council began.

It was hopeless from the outset — a *posse* of
hornets droned into fury by the Archduke.   While
he talked the rest maddened, longing for each
other's blood, failing that of Luitpold.   Richard,
who as yet had no plans of his own, took no
interest whatever in plans.   He acted throughout
as if the Marquess was not there, and as if he
wished with all his heart that the Archduke was
not there.   On his part, the Marquess would have

given nearly all he owned to have behaved so to
Guy of Lusignan set over him; but the Marquess
had not that art of lazy scorn which belongs to
the royal among beasts: he glowered, he was
sulky. Meantime the Archduke buzzed his age-
long periods, and Richard (clasping his knee)
looked at the ceiling. At last he sighed profoundly, and 'God of heaven and earth!' escaped
him. King Philip burst into a guffaw — his first
for many a day — and broke up the assembly.
Richard had himself rowed out to Jehane in her
ship.

He had no business there, though his business
was innocent enough; but she could not tell him
so now. The girl was dejected, ill, and very
nervous about herself. Moreover, she had suffered from sea-sickness. She could not hide her
comfort to have him; so he took her up and
kissed her as of old, and ended by settling her
on his knee. There she cried, quietly but freely.
He stayed with her till she slept; then went back
to the shore and walked about the trenches, thinking out the business before him. The dawn light
found him at it. In a day or two, having got his
tackle ashore, he began the assault upon a plan
of his own, without reference to any other princi-
pality or power at all. By this time King Philip
lay heaped in his bed, and had had his distem-
pered brain wrought upon by Montferrat and his
kind, Saint-Pol, Des Barres, and their kind.

Richard had with him Poictevins and Angevins, men of Provence and Languedoc, Normans
and English, Scots and Welshry, black Genoese,

Sicilians, Pisans, and Grifons from Cyprus. The
Count of Champagne had his Flemings to hand;
the Templars and the Hospitallers served him
gladly. It was an agglomerate, a horde, not an
army, and nobody but he could have wielded it.
He, by the virtue in him, had them all at his nod.
The English, who love to be commanded, hauled
stones for him all day, though he had not a word
of their language. The swart, praying Italians
raved themselves hoarse whenever he came into
their lines; even the Cypriotes, sullen and timor-
ous creatures, whom no power among themselves
could have driven to the walls, fixed the great
petraries and mangonels, and ran grinning into
the trap of death for this tawny-haired hero who
stood singing, bareheaded, within bow-shot of the
Turks, and laughed like a boy when some fellow
slipped on to his back upon the dry grass. He
was everywhere, day after day — in the trenches,
on the towers, teaching the bowmen their business, crying ' Mort de Dieu!' when a mangonel
did its work, and some flung rock made the wall
to fly; he crouched under the tortoise-screens
with the miners, took a mattock himself as indif-
ferently as an arbalest or a cross-bow. He could
do everything, and have (if not a word) a cheerful
grin for every man who did his duty. As it was
evident that he knew what such duty should
be, and could have done it better himself, men
sweated to win his praise. He was nearly killed
on a scaling-ladder, too early put up, or too long
left so. Three arrows struck him, and the
defenders, calling on Allah, rolled an enormous
boulder to the edge of the wall, which must have

crushed him out of recognition on the Last Day.
'Garde, sire!' 'Domna del Ciel!' came the
cries from below; but 'Lady Virgin!' growled a
shockhead from Bocton-under-Bleane, and pulled
his King bodily off the ladder. The poor fellow
was shot in the throat at the next moment; the
stone fell harmless. King Richard took up his
dead Englishman in his arms and carried him
to the trenches. He did no more fighting until
he had seen him buried, and ordained a mass
for him. Things of those sort tempted men to
love him.

The siege lasted ten days or more with varying
successes. Day and night in the city they heard
the drums beat to arms, the cries of the Sheiks,
and more piercing, drawn-out cries than theirs.
To the nightly shrilled pronouncement of the
greatness of God came as answer the Christian's
wailing prayer, 'Save us, Holy Sepulchre!' The
King of France had an engine which he called
The Bad Neighbour, and did well with it until
the Turks provided a Bad Kinsman, much bigger,
which put the Neighbour to shame, and finally
burned him. King Richard had a belfry, and the
Count of Flanders could throw stones with his
sling from the trenches into the market-place; at
any rate he said he could, and they all believed
him. The Christians caused the Accursed Tower
to totter; they made a breach below the Tower
of Flies, in a most horrible part of the haven.
Mine and countermine, Richard on the north side
worked night and day, denying himself rest, food,
reasonable care, for a week forgetful of Jehane
and her hope. The weather grew stiflingly hot,

R

night and day there was no breath of wind; the whole country reeked of death and abomination. Once, indeed, a gate was set fire to and rushed. The Christians saw before them for the first time the ghostly winding way of a street, where blind pale houses heeled to each other, six feet apart. There was a breathless fight in that pent way, a strangling, throttled business; Richard with his peers of Normandy, swaying banners, the crashing sound of steel on steel, the splash of split polls: but it could not be carried. The Turks, surging down on them, a wall of men, bodily forced them out. There was no room to swing an axe, no space for a horse to fall, least of all for draught of the bow. Richard cried the retreat; they could not turn, so walked backwards fighting, and the Turks repaired the gate. Acre did not fall by the sword, but by starvation rather, and the diligent negotiations of Saladin with our King. Richard's terms were, Restore the True Cross, empty us Acre of men-at-arms, leave two thousand hostages. This was accepted at last. The Kings rode into Acre on the twelfth of July with their hosts, and the hollow-eyed courtesans watched them furtively from upper windows. They knew their harvest was to reap.

Harvest with them was seed-time with others. It was seed-time with the Archduke. King Richard set up his household in the Castle (with a good lodging for Jehane in the Street of the Camel); King Philip, miserably ill, went to the house of the Templars; with him, sedulously his friend, the Marquess of Montferrat. But Luitpold of Austria proposed himself for the Castle, and Richard

endured him as well as he could. But then
Luitpold went further. He set up his banner on
the tower, side by side with Richard's Dragon,
meaning no offence at all. Now King Richard's
way was a short way. He had found the Archduke a burdensome ass, but no more. The world
was full of such; one must take them as part
of the general economy of Providence. But he
knew his own worth perfectly well, and his own
standing in the host; so when they told him
where the Austrian's flag flew, he said, ' Take it
down.' They took it down. Luitpold grew red,
made a long speech in German at which Richard
frowned, and another (shorter) in Latin, at which
he laughed. Luitpold put up his flag again;
again Richard said, ' Take it down.' Luitpold
was so angry that he made no speeches at all; he
ran up his flag a third time. When King Richard
was told, he laughed, and on this occasion said,
' Throw it away.' Gaston of Béarn, more viva-
cious than discreet, did so with ignominious de-
tail. That day there was a council of the great
estates, at which King Philip presided in a furred
gown; for though the weather was suffocating his
fever kept him chill to the bones. To the Marquess, pale with his old grudge, was now added
the Archduke, flaming with his new one. The
mottled Duke of Burgundy blinked approval of
all grudges, and young Saint-Pol poured fire into
the fire. Richard was not present, nor any of his
faction; they, because they had not been adver-
tised, he, because he was in the Street of the
Camel at the knees of Jehane the Fair.

The Archduke began on the instant. ' By

God, my lords,' he said, 'is there in the world
a beast more flagrant than the King of England
not killed already?' The Marquess showed
the white rims of his eyes — 'Injurious, desperate, bloody villain,' was his commentary; and
Saint-Pol lifted up his hand to his master for
leave to speak mischief. But King Philip said
fretfully, 'Well, well, we can all speak of something, I suppose. He scorns me, he has
always scorned me. He refuses me homage, he
shamed my sister; and now he takes the lead
of me.'

The Marquess kept muttering to the table,
'Hopeless villain, hopeless villain!' and the Archduke, after staring about him for sympathy,
claimed attention, if not that; for he brought his
fist down with a thump.

'By thunder, but I kill him!' he said deep in
his throat. Saint-Pol came running and kissed
his knee, to Luitpold's great surprise.

Philip shivered in his furs. 'I must go home,'
he fretted; 'I am smitten to death. I must die
in France.'

'Where is the King of England?' asked the
Marquess, knowing perfectly well.

'Evil light upon him,' cried Saint-Pol, 'he is
in my sister's house. Between them they give
me a nephew.'

'Oho!' Montferrat said. 'Is that it? Why,
then, we know where to strike him quickest. We
should make Navarre of our party.'

'He has done that himself, by all accounts,'
said the Duke of Burgundy, wide-awake.

The Archduke, returning to his new lodgings
in the Bishop's house, sent for his astrologers and
asked them, Could he kill the King of England?
' My lord,' said they, ' you cannot.'
' How is that ? ' he asked.
' Lord,' they told him, ' by our arts we discover
that he will live for a hundred years.'
' It is very remarkable,' said the Archduke.
' What sort of years will they be ? '
' Lord,' said the astrologers, ' they are divers in
complexion ; but many of them are red.'
' I will provide that they be,' said the Arch-
duke. ' Go away.'

The Marquess sought no astrologers, but instead the Street of the Camel and Jehane's house.
He observed this with great care, watching from
an entry to see how King Richard would come
out, whether attended or not. He observed more
than the house, for much more was forced upon
him. Human garbage filled the close ways of
Acre, men and women marred by themselves or
a hideous begetting, hairless persons and snug
little chamberers, botch-faces, scald-heads, minions
of many sorts, silent-footed Arabians as shameless
as dogs, Greeks, pimps and panders, abominable
women. Murder was swiftly and secretly done.
Montferrat from his entry saw the manner of it.
A Norman knight called Hamon le Rotrou came
out of an infamous house in the dusk, and stepped
into the Street of the Camel with his cloak delicately round him. Fine as he was, he was insanely
a lover of the vile thing he had left; for he knelt
down in the street to kiss her well-worn doorstep.
He knelt under the light of a small lamp, and out

of the shadow behind him stepped catfoot a tall
thin man, white from head to foot, who, saying
'All hail, master,' stabbed Hamon deep in the
side. Hamon jerked up his head, tottered, fell
without more than a tired man's sigh sideways
into the arms of his killer. This one eased his
fall as tenderly as if he was upholding a girl, let
him down into the kennel, drew him thence by
the shoulders into the dark, and himself vanished.
Montferrat swore softly to himself, 'That was
neatly done. I must find out who this expert
may be.' He went away full of it, having forgotten his housed enemy.

There was a Sheik Moffadin in the jail, one of
the Soldan's hostages for the return of the True
Cross. The Marquess went to see him.

'Who of your people,' he asked, 'is very tall
and light-footed, robes him from head to foot in
white linen, and kills quietly, as if he loved the
dead, with an " All hail, master " ? '

'We call him an Assassin in our language,'
the Sheik replied; 'but he is not of our people
by any means. He is a servant of the Old Man
who dwells on Lebanon.'

'What old man is this, Moffadin ? '

'I can tell you no more of him,' said the Sheik,
'save that he is master of many such men, who
serve him faithfully and in silence. But he hates
the Soldan, and the Soldan him.'

'How do they serve him, by killing ? '

'Yes. They kill whomsoever he points out, and
so receive (or think to receive) a crown in Paradise.'

'Is this old man's name Death, by our Saviour ? '
cried the Marquess.

The Sheik answered, 'His name is Sinan.
But the name of Death would suit him very
well.'

'Where should I get speech with some of his
servants?' the Marquess inquired; adding, 'For
my life is in danger. I have enemies who are
irksome to me.'

'By the Tower of Flies you will find them,'
said the Sheik, 'and late at night. There are
always some of his people walking there. Seek
out such a man as you have seen, and without
fear accost him after his fashion, kissing him and
saying, "Ah, Ali. Ah, Abdallah, servant of Ali."'

'I am very much obliged to you, Moffadin,'
said the Marquess.

That same night Jehane was in pain, and King
Richard dared not leave her, nor the physicians
either. And in the morning early she was delivered of a child, a strong boy, and then lay
back and slept profoundly. Richard set two
black women to fan the flies off her without
stopping once under pain of death; and having
seen to the proper care of the child and other
things, returned alone through the blanching
streets, glorifying and praising God.

CHAPTER IV

In the church of Saint Lazarus of the Knights, on Lammas Day, the son of Richard and Jehane was made a Christian by the Abbot of Poictiers. Gossips were the Count of Champagne, the Earl of Leicester, and (by proxy) the Queen-Mother. He was named Fulke.

At the moment of anointing the church-bell was rung; and at that moment Gilles de Gurdun spat upon the pavement outside. Saint-Pol said to him, 'We must do better than that, Gilles.'

And Gilles, 'I pray God may spit him out.'

'Oh, He!' said Saint-Pol with a bitter laugh; 'He helps those who are helpful of themselves.'

'I cannot help myself, Eustace,' said Gurdun. 'I have tried. I had him unarmed before me at Messina, and he looked me down, and I could not do it.'

'Have at his back, then.'

'I hope it may not come to that, said Gilles; 'and yet it may, if it must.'

'Come with me to-night to the Tower of Flies,' said Saint-Pol. 'Here is my shameful sister brought out of church. I cannot stay.'

'I stay,' said Gilles de Gurdun. King Richard came out of church, and Jehane, and the child carried on a shield.

248

Jehane, who had much ado to walk without falling, saw not Gilles; but Gilles saw her, and the red in his face took a tinge of black. While she was before him he gaped at her, with a dry tongue clacking in his mouth, consumed by a dreadful despair; but when she had passed by, swaying in her weakness, barely able to hold up her lovely head, he lifted his face to the white sky, and looked unwinking at the sun, wondering where else an equal cruelty could abide. In this golden king, as cruel as the sun, and as swift, and as splendid! Ah, dastard, dastard! At the minute Gilles could have leapt at him and mauled the great shoulders with a dog's weapons. There was no solace for him but to bite. So he dashed his forearm into his face, and sluiced his teeth in that.

But King Richard of the high head mounted his horse in the churchyard, and rode among the people before Jehane's bearers to the Street of the Camel. Squires of his threw silver coins among the crowds who filled the ways.

Within the house, he laid her on her bed, and held up the child before her, high in the air. He was in that great mood where nothing could resist him. She, faint and fragrant on the bed, so frail as to seem transparent, a disembodied sprite, smiled because she felt at ease, as the feeble do when they first lie down.

'Lo, Fulke of Anjou!' sang Richard — 'Fulke, son of Richard, the son of Henry, the son of Geoffrey, the son of Fulke! Fulke, my son Fulke, I will make thee a knight even now!' He held the babe in one hand, with the free hand drew his long sword.   The flat blade touched the nodding little head.

'Rise up, Sir Fulke of Anjou, true knight of thine house, Sieur de Cuigny when I have thee home again.   By the Face!' he cried shortly, as if remembering something, 'we must get him the badge: a switch of wild broom!'

'Dear lord, sweet lord,' murmured Jehane, faint in bed, nearly gone: but he raved on.

'When I lay, even as thou, Fulke, naked by my mother, my father sent for a branch of the broom, and stuck it in the pillow against I could carry it. And shalt thou go without it, boy?   Art not thou of the broom-bearers?'   He put the child into the nurse's arm and went to the door.   He called for Gaston of Béarn, for the Dauphin of Auvergne, for Mercadet, for the devil.   The Bishop of Salisbury came running in.   'Bishop,' said King Richard, 'you must serve me to-day.   You must take ship, my friend, with speed; you must go to Bordeaux, thence a-horseback to the moor above Angers.   Pluck me a branch of the wild broom and return.   I must have it, I tell you; so go.   Haste, Bishop.   God be with you.'

The Bishop began to splutter.   'Hey, sire——!'

'Never call me that again, Bishop, if your ship is within sight by sunset,' he said.   'Call me rather the Prince of the Devils.   See my chancellor, take my ring to him, omit nothing.   Off with you, and back with all speed.'

'Ha, sire, look you now,' cried the desperate bishop, 'there will be no broom before next Easter. Here we are at Lammas.'

'There will be a miracle,' said Richard; 'I am

sure of it. Go.' Fairly pushing him from the
door, he returned to find Jehane in a dead faint.
This set him raving a new tune. He fell upon his
knees incontinent, raised her in his arms, carried
her about, kissed her all over, cried upon the saints
and God, did every extravagance under the
sun, omitted the one wise thing of letting in the
physicians. Abbot Milo at last, coming in, saved
Jehane from him for the deeper purposes of God.

The Count of Saint-Pol, going to the Castle, to
the Queen's side, found the Marquess with her.
She also lay white and twisting on a couch, crisping and uncrisping her little hands. Montferrat
stood at her head; three of her ladies knelt about
her, whispering in her own tongue, proffering
orange water, sweetmeats, a feather whisk. Saint-
Pol knelt in her view.

'Madame, how is it with your Grace?' he said.
The little lady quivered, but took no notice.

'Madame,' said Saint-Pol again, 'I am a peer
of France, but a knight before all. I am come to
serve your Grace with my manhood. I pray you
speak to me.' The Marquess folded his arms;
his large white face was a sight to see.

Queen Berengère's palms were bleeding a little
where her nails had broken the skin. She was
quite white; but her eyes, burning black, had no
pupils. When Saint-Pol spoke for the second
time she shook beyond all control and threw her
head about. Also she spoke.

'I suffer, I suffer horribly. It is cruel beyond
understanding or knowledge that a girl should
suffer as I suffer. Where is God? Where is
Mary? Where are the angels?'

'Dearest Madame, dearest Madame,' said the cooing women, and one stroked her face. But the Queen shook the hand off, and went wailing on, saying more than she could have meant.

'Is it good usage of the daughter of a king, Lord Jesus? Is this the way of marriage, that the bride be left on her wedding day?' She jumped up on her couch and took hold of her bosom in the sight of men. 'She hath given him a child! He is with her now. Am I not fit for children? Shall there never be milk? Oh, oh, here is more shame than I can bear!' She hid her face in her hands, and rocked herself about.

Montferrat (really moved) said low to Saint-Pol: 'Are we knights to suffer these wrongs to be?' Said Saint-Pol with a sob in his voice, 'Ah, God, mend it!'

'He will,' said Montferrat, 'if we help to mend.'

This reminded Saint-Pol of his own words to De Gurdun; so he made haste to throw himself before the Queen, that he might still be pure in his devotion. 'My lady Berengère,' he said ardently, 'take me for your soldier. I am a bad man, but surely not so bad as this. Let me fight him for you.'

The Queen shook her head, impatient. 'Hey! What can you do against so glorious a man? He is the greatest in the world.'

'Ha, domeneddio!' said the Marquess with a snort. 'I have that which will abate such glory. Dearest Madame, we go to pray for your health.' He kissed her hand, and drew away with him Saint-Pol, who was trembling under the thoughts that fired him.

'Oh, my soul, Marquess!' said the youth, when they were in the glare of day again. 'What shall we do to mend this wretchedness?' The Marquess looked shrewdly.

'End the wretch who wrought it.'

'Do we go clean to that, Marquess? Have we no back-thoughts of our own?'

'The work is clean enough. You come to-night to the Tower of Flies?'

'Yes, yes, I will come,' said Saint-Pol.

'I shall have one with me,' the Marquess went on, 'who will be of service, mind you.'

'Ah,' said Saint-Pol, 'and so shall I.'

The Marquess stroked his nose. 'Hum,' he said, advising, 'who might your man be, Saint-Pol?'

'One,' said Eustace, 'who has reason to hate Richard as much as that poor lady in there.'

'Who is that?'

'My sister Jehane's lover.'

'By the visible Host,' said Montferrat, 'we shall be a loving company, all told.' So they parted for the time.

The Tower of Flies stands apart from the city on a spit of sand which splays out into two flanges, and so embraces in two hooks a lagoon of scummy ooze, of weeds and garbage, of all the waste and silt of a slack water. In front of it only is the tidal sea, which there flows languidly with a half-foot rise; on the other is the causeway running up to the city wall. Above and all about this dead marsh you hear day and night the buzzing of innumerable great flies, and in the daytime see them hanging like gauze in the thick air. They

say the reason is that anciently the pagans sacri-
ficed hecatombs hereabout to the idols they worshipped; but another (more likely) is that the
lagoon is a dead slack, and stinks abominably.
All dead things thrown from the city walls come
floating thither, and there stay rotting.   The flies
get what they can, sharing with the creatures of
land and sea; for great fish feed there; and at
night the jackals and hyænas come down, and
bicker over what they can drag out.   But more
than once or twice the sharks drag them in, and
have fresh meat, if their brother sharks allow it.
However all this may be, the place has a dreadful
name, a dreadful smell, and a dreadful sound, what
with the humming of flies and dull rippling of the
sharks.   These can seldom be seen, since the water
is too thick; but you can tell their movements by
the long oily waves (like the heads of large arrows)
which their fins throw behind them as they quest
from carcase to carcase down there in the ooze.

Thither in the murk of night came Montferrat
in a black cloak, holding his nose, but made feverish through his ears by the veiled chorus of the
flies.   By the starshine and glow of the putrid
water he saw a tall man in a white robe, who
stood at the extreme edge of the spit and looked
at the sharks.   Montferrat hid his guards behind
the Tower, crossed himself, drew his sword to hack
a way through the monstrous flies, and so came
swishing forward, like a man who mows a swathe.

The tall man saw him, but did not move.
The Marquess came quite close.

'What are you looking at, my friend?' he
asked, in the Arabian tongue.

'I am looking at the sharks, which have a new corpse in there,' said the man. 'See what a turmoil there is in the water. There must be six monsters together in that swirl. See, see, there speeds another!'

The Marquess turned sick. 'God help, I cannot look,' he said.

'Why,' said the Arabian, 'It is a dead man they fight over.'

'May be, may be,' said the Marquess. 'You, my friend, are very familiar with death. So am I; nor do I fear living man. But these great fish terrify me.'

'You are a fool,' returned the other. 'They seek only their meat. But you and I, and our like, seek nicer things than that. We have our souls to feed; and the soul of a man is a free eater, of stranger appetite than a shark.'

The Marquess looked at the flies. 'O God, Arabian, let us go away from this place! Is there no rest from the flies?'

'None at all,' said the Arabian; 'for thousands have been slain here; and the flies also must be fed.'

'Pah, horrible!' said the Marquess, all in a sweat. The Arabian turned; but his face was hidden, with a horrible appearance, as if a hooded cloak stood up by itself and a voice proceeded from a fleshless garb. 'You, Marquess of Montferrat,' it said, 'what do you want with me by the Tower of Flies?'

The Marquess remembered his needs. 'I want the death of a man,' he said; 'but not here, O Christ.'

'Who sent you?' asked the Arabian.

'The Sheik Moffadin, a captive, in the name of Ali, and of Abdallah, servant of Ali.' So the Marquess, and would have kissed the man, but that he saw no face under the hood, and dared not kiss emptiness.

'Come with me,' said the Arabian.

An hour later the Marquess came into the Tower of Flies, shaking. He found Saint-Pol there, the Archduke of Austria, and Gilles de Gurdun. There were no greetings.

'Where is your man, Marquess?' asked Saint-Pol of the pale Italian.

'He is out yonder looking at the sharks,' said the Marquess, in a whisper; 'but he will serve us if we dare use him.' He struck at the flies weaving about his head. 'This is a horrible place, Saint-Pol,' he said, staring. Saint-Pol shrugged.

'The deed we compass, dear Marquess, is none of the choicest, remember,' said he. The Marquess then saw that Austria's broad leather back was covered with flies. This quickened his loathing.

'By our Saviour,' he said, 'one must hate a man very much to talk against him here.'

'Do you hate enough?' asked Saint-Pol.

The Marquess stared about him. He saw the Archduke peacefully twiddle his thumbs. He saw De Gurdun, who stood moodily, looking at the floor.

'Oh, content you,' Saint-Pol answered him. 'That man hates more than you or I. And with more reason.'

'What are your reasons, Eustace?' asked Montferrat, still in a whisper.

'I hate him,' said Saint-Pol, 'for my brother's sake, whose back he broke; for my sister's sake, whose heart he must break before he has done with her; for my house's sake, to which (in Eudo's person) he gave the lie; because he is of Anjou, cruel as a cat and savage as a dog; because he is a ruthless, swift, treacherous, secret, unconscionable beast. Are these enough reasons for you?'

'By God, Eustace,' said the breathless Montferrat, 'I cannot think it. Not here!'

'Then,' said Saint-Pol, 'I hate him for Berengère's sweet sake. That is a good and clean hatred, I believe. That wasted lady, writhing white on a bed, moved me to pure pity. If I loved her before I will love her now with whole service, not daring belie my knighthood. I love that queen and intend to serve her. I have never seen such pitiful beauty before. What! Is the man insatiate? Shall he have everything? He shall have nothing. That will serve for me, I hope. Now, Marquess, it is your turn.'

The Marquess struck out at the flies. 'I hate him,' he said, 'because, before the King of France, he called me a liar and threatened me with ignominious death.' He gasped here, and looked round him to see what effect he had made. Saint-Pol's eyes (green-grey like his sister's) were upon him, rather coldly; Gurdun's on the floor still. The Archduke was scratching in his beard; and the chorus of flies swelled and shrilled. The Marquess needed alliances.

'Eh, my friends,' he said, almost praying, 'will this not serve me?'

Said Saint-Pol, 'Marquess, listen to this man. Speak, Gilles.'

Gilles looked up. 'I have tried to kill him. I had my chance fair. I could not do it. I shall try again, for the law is on my side. To you, lords, I shall say nothing, for I am a man ashamed to speak of what I desire to do, not yet certain whether I can accomplish it. This I say, the man is my liege lord, but a thief for all that. I loved my Lady Jehane when she was twelve years old and I a page in her father's house. I have never loved any other woman, and never shall. There are no other women. She gave herself to me for good reason, and he himself gave her into my hand for good reason. And then he robbed me of her on my wedding day, and has slain my father and young brother to keep her. He has given her a child: enough of this. Dastard! I will follow and follow until I dare to strike. Then I will kill him. Let me alone.' Gilles, red and gloomy, had to jerk the words out: he was no speaker. The Marquess had a fierce eye.

'Ha, De Gurdun,' he said, 'we need thee, good knight. But come out of this accursed fly-roost, and we shall show thee a better way than thine. It is the flies that make thee afraid.'

'Eh, damn the flies,' said Gilles. 'They will never disturb me. They do but seek their meat.'

'They disturb me horribly,' said the Marquess, with Italian candour.

Saint-Pol laughed. 'I told you that I could bring you in a man,' he said. 'Now, Marquess, you have our two clean reasons.   What is yours?'

'I have given you mine,' said Montferrat, shifting his feet. 'He called me a liar.'

'It lacks cogency,' said Saint-Pol. 'One must have clean reasons in an unclean place.' The Marquess broke out into blasphemy.

'May hell scorch us all if I have no reasons! What! Has he not kept me from my kingdom? Guy of Lusignan will be king by his means. What is Philip against Richard? What am I? What is the Archduke?' He had forgotten that the Archduke was there.

'By Beelzebub, the god of this place,' said that deep-voiced hairy man, 'you shall see what the Archduke is when you want him. But I am no murderer. I am going home. I know what is due to a prince, and from a prince.'

'Do as you please, my lord,' said Saint-Pol; 'but our schemes are like to be endangered by such goings.'

'I have so little liking for your schemes, to be plain with you,' replied the Archduke, 'that they may fail and fail again for me. How I deal with the King of England, who has insulted me beyond hope, is a matter for him and me to determine.'

'Cousin,' said Montferrat, 'you desert me.'

'Cousin again,' said the Archduke, 'do you wonder?' And so he walked out.

'Punctilious boar!' cried Saint-Pol in a fume, 'who can only get his tushes in one way! Now, Marquess, what are we to do?'

The Marquess smiled darkly, and tapped his nose. 'I have my business in good train. I have

an ancient friend on Lebanon. Stand in with me,
the pair of you, and I have all done smoothly.'
   'You hire?' asked Saint-Pol, drily.   Then he
shrugged — 'Oh, but we may trust you!'
   'Per la Madonna!' said the Marquess.
   'What will you do, Gilles?' Saint-Pol asked
the Norman.   'Will you leave it to the Marquess
of Montferrat?'
   'I will not,' said Gilles.   'I follow King Rich-
ard from point to point.   I hire nobody.'
   The Marquess's hands went up, desperate of such
folly.   'You only with me, my Eustace!' he said.
   Saint-Pol looked up.   'I differ from either.   I
have a finer plan than either.   You are satisfied
with a sword-stroke in the back ——'
   'By my soul, it shall not be in the back!' cried
De Gurdun.   Saint-Pol shrugged again.
   'That is the Marquess's way.   But what matter?
You want to see him down.   So do I, by heaven,
but in hell, not on the earth.   I will see him
tormented.   I will see him ashamed.   I will
wreck his hopes.   I will make him a mockery
of all kings, drag his high spirit through the mud
of disastrousness.   Pouf!   Do you think him all
flesh?   He is finer stuff than that.   What he
makes others I seek to make him — soiled, defiled,
a blown rag.   There is work to be done in that
kind here and at home.   King Philip will see to
one; I stay with the host.'
   'It is a good plan,' said the Marquess; 'I
admire it exceedingly.   But steel is safer for a
common man.   I go to Lebanon, for my part,
to my friends there.   But I think we are in agreement.'

Before they went away, they cut their arms with a dagger, and mingled their blood. The Marquess wrapped his wound deep in his cloak to keep the flies from it. Across the silence of the night, as they made their way into the city, came the cry of the watchman from a belfry: 'Save us, Holy Sepulchre!' It floated from tower to tower, from land far out to sea. Jehane, dry in her hot bed, heard it; Richard, on his knees in an oratory, heard it, crossed himself, and repeated the words. Queen Berengère moaned in her sleep; the Duke of Burgundy snored; and the Arabian spat into the lagoon.

CHAPTER V

SINCE the Soldan broke his pledges, King Richard swore that he would keep his. So he had
all the two thousand hostages killed, except
the Sheik Moffadin, whom the Marquess had
enlarged. He has been blamed for this, and I (if
it were my business) should blame him too. He
asked no counsel, and allowed no comment: by
this time he was absolute over the armies in Acre.
If I am to say anything upon the red business it
shall be this, that he knew very well where his
danger lay. It was his friends, not his enemies,
he had reason to fear; and upon these the effect
of what he did was instantaneous, and perhaps
well-timed. The Count of Flanders had died of
the camp-sickness; King Philip was stricken to
the bones with the same crawling disease. Nothing now could keep Philip away from France.
Acre was full of rumours, meetings of kings and
princes, spies, racing messengers. Who should
stay and who go was the matter of debate.
Philip meant to go: his friend, Prince John of
England, had been writing to him. Flanders
must be occupied, and Flanders, near England,
was nearer yet to Normandy. The Marquess
also meant to go — to Sidon for Lebanon. He

had things to do up there on Richard's and his own account, as you shall hear. But the Archduke chose to stay in Acre — and so on.

King Richard heard of each of these hasty discussions with a shrug, and only put his hand down when they were all concluded. He said that unless French hostages were left in his keeping for the fulfilment of covenants, he should know what to do.

'And what is that, King of England?' asked Philip.

'What becomes me,' was the short answer, given in full hall before the magnates. They looked at each other and askance at the sanguine-hued King, who drove them all huddling before him by mere magnanimity. What could they do but leave hostages? They left Burgundy, Beauvais, and Henry of Champagne — one friend, one enemy, and one blockhead. Now you see a reason for drawing the sword upon the wretched Turks. If Richard had planted, they, poor devils, had to water.

So King Philip went home, and the Marquess to Sidon for Lebanon; and Richard, knowing full well that they meant him ill here and at home, turned his face towards Jerusalem.

When the time came for ordering the goings of his host, he grew very nervous about what he must leave behind him in Acre. Whether he was a good man or not, a good husband, a good lover or not, he was passionately a father. In every surge and cry of his wild heart he showed this. The heart is a generous inn, keeps open house, grows wide to meet all comers. The company is divers. In King Richard's heart sat three guests: Christ and His lost Cross, Jehane and her lost honour, and little Fulke upon her breast. Christ was a dumb guest, but the most eloquent still. There had been no nods from Him since the great day of Fontevrault; but Richard watched Him daily and held himself bound to be His footboy. See these desperate shifts of the greathearted man! Here were his two other guests: little Fulke, who claimed everything, and still Jehane, who claimed nothing; and outside the door stood Berengère, crisping and uncrisping her small hands. To serve Christ he had married the Queen; to serve the Queen he had put away Jehane; to honour Jehane (who had given him her honour) he had abjured the Queen. Now lastly, he prayed Christ to save him Fulke, his first and only son. 'My Saviour Christ,' he prayed on his last night at Acre, 'let Thine honour be the first end of this adventure. But if honour come to Thee, my Lord, through me, let honour stay with me and my son through Thee. I cannot think I do amiss to ask so much. One other thing I ask before I go out. Watch over these treasures of mine that I leave in pawn, for I know very well that I shall get no more of them.' Then he kissed the mother and the child, comforting them, and went out, not trusting himself to look back at the house.

He had made the defences of Acre as good as he knew, which was very good indeed. He had bettered the harbour; he left ships in it, established a post between it and Beyrout, between

Beyrout and Cyprus. He sent Guy of Lusignan to be his regent in that island, Emperor if he chose. He left Abbot Milo to comfort Jehane, the Viscount of Béziers to rule the town and garrison. Shriven, fortified with the Sacrament, he spent his last night in Acre on the 21st of August. Next morning, as soon as it was day, he led his army out on its march to Jerusalem.

Joppa was his immediate object, to which place a road ran between the mountains and the sea, never far from either. He had little or no transport, nor could expect food by the way, for Saladin had seen to that. The ships had to work down level with him, with reserves of men and stores; and even so the thing had an ugly look. The mountains of Ephraim, not very lofty, were covered with a thick growth of holm-oak: excellent cover, wherein, as he knew quite well, the Saracens could move as he moved, choose their time, and attack him on front, rear, or left flank, wherever chance offered. It was a journey of peril, harassing, slow, and without glory.

For six weeks he led and held a running battle, wherein the powers of earth and air, the powers of Mahomet, and dark forces within his own lines all strove against him. He met them alone, with a blank face, eyes bare, teeth hard-set. Whatever provocation was offered from without or within, he would not attack, nor let his friends attack, until the enemy was in his hand. You, who know what longanimity may be and how hard a thing to come at, may admire him for this.

Directly the Christians were over the brook Belus, their difficulties were upon them. The

way was through a pebbly waste of beach and
salt-grass, and a sea-scrub of grey bushes. A mile
to their left the rocks began, spurs of the mountains; the shrubs became stunted trees; the
rocks climbed, the trees with them; then the
forest rose, first sparsely, then thick and dark;
lastly, into the deep blue of the sky soared the
toothed ridges, grey, scarred, and splintry.
Scurrying horsemen, on beasts incredibly sure
of foot, hung on the edge of these fastnesses,
yelling, whirling their lances, white-clad, swarthy
and hoarse. They came by fifties, or in clouds
they came, swept by like a windstorm, and were
gone. And in each shrill and terrible rush some
stragglers, be sure, would call upon Christ in vain.
Or sometimes great companies of Mamelukes in
mail, massed companies in blocks of men, stood
covered by their bowmen as if offering battle. If
the Christians opened out to attack (as at first
they did), or some party of knights, more adventurous than another, pricked forward at a canter,
and hastening as their hearts grew high cried at
last the charge, ' Passavant!' or ' Sauve Anjou!'
out of the wood with cries would come the black
cavalry, sweep up behind our men, and cut off
one company or another. And if so by day, by
night there was no long peace under the large
stars. Desperate stampedes, the scattering of
camp-fires, trampling, grunting in the dark;
ghostly horsemen looming and vanishing suddenly in the half-light; and in the lull the queru-
lous howling of wild beasts disappointed.

To their full days succeeded their empty days,
when they were alone with the desert and the sun.

Then hunger and thirst assailed them, serpents
bit them, stinging flies drove men mad, the sand
burnt their feet through steel and leather.   They
lost more this way than by Saracen ambush, and
lost more hearts than men.   This was a time for
private grudges to awaken.   Hatred feeds on such
dry meat.   In the empty watches of the night, in
the blistering daytime, under the white sky or the
deep violet, Des Barres remembered his struck face,
De Gurdun his stolen wife, Saint-Pol his dead
brother, and the Duke of Burgundy his forty pounds.

It must be said that Richard stretched his
authority as far as it would go.   His direct aim
was to reach Joppa with speed, and thence to
strike inward over the hills to the Holy City.   It
was against sense to attack this enemy hugging
the woody heights; but as time went on, as he
lost men and heard the muttering of those who
saw them go, he understood that if he could tempt
Saladin into close battle upon chosen ground it
would be well.   This was a difficult matter, for
though (as he knew) the Saracen army followed
him in the woods, it kept well out of sight.   None
but the light horsemen showed near at hand, and
their tactics were to sting like wasps, and fly —
never to join battle.   At last, in the swamp of
Arsûf, where the Dead River splays over broad
marshes, and goes in a swamp to the sea-edge, he
saw his chance, and took it.

Here a feint, carried out by Gaston of Béarn
with great spirit, brought Saladin into the open.
The Christians continued their toilsome march,
Saladin attacked their rear; and for six hours or
more that rearguard fought a retreating battle,

meeting shock after shock, striking no blow, while the centre and the van watched them. This was one of the tensest days of Richard's iron rule. De Charron, commanding the rear, sent imploring messengers — 'For Christ's love let us charge, sire, we can bear no more of this.' He was answered, 'Let them come on again.' Then Saint-Pol, seeing one of the chances of his life, was in open mutiny of the tongue. 'Are we sheep, then?' Thus he to the French with Burgundy. 'Is the King a drover of cattle? Where is the chivalry of France?' Even Richard's friends grew fretful: Champagne tossing his head, muttering curses to himself, Gaston of Béarn pale and serious, chewing his beard. Two more wild assaults the rearguard took stiffly, at the third they broke in two places, but repelled the Turks. Richard, watching like a hawk, saw his opportunity. He sent down a message to the Duke of Burgundy, to Saint-Pol and De Charron — 'Hold them yet once more; at six blasts of my trumpet, charge' The Duke of Burgundy, block though he was, was prepared to obey. About him came buzzing Saint-Pol and his friends: 'Impossible, my lord Duke, we cannot keep in our men. Attack, attack.' Saladin was then coming on, one of his thunderous charges. 'God strike blind those French mules!' cried Richard. 'They are out!' This was true: from left to centre the Christian bowmen were out, the knights pricking after them to the charge. Richard cursed them from his heart. 'Sound trumpets!' he shouted, 'we must let go.' They sounded; they ran forward: the English first, then the Normans, Poictevins, men of Anjou

and Pisa, black Genoese — but the left had moved
before them, and made doubtful Richard's échelon.
They knelt, pulled bowstrings to the ear. The
sky grew dun as the long shafts flew; the oncoming tide of men flickered and tossed like a broken
sea, and the Soldan's green banner dipped like a
reed in it. A second time the blast of arrows,
like a gust of death, smote them flat: Richard's
voice rang sharply out — ' Passavant, chivalers !
Sauve Anjou ! ' — and a young Poictevin knight,
stooping low in his saddle, went rocking down
the line with words for Henry of Champagne,
who ruled the centre. The archers ran back
and crouched; Richard and his chivalry on the
extreme right moved out, the next company
after him, and the next, and the next, company
following company, until, in échelon, all the long
fluttering array galloped over the marsh, over-
lapped and enfolded the Saracen hordes in their
bright embrace. A frenzied cry from some emir
by the standard gave notice of the danger; the
bodyguard about the Soldan were seen urging him.
Saladin gave some hasty order as he rode off;
Richard saw it, and tasted the bitterness of folly.
' By God, we shall lose him — oh, bemused hog
of Burgundy ! ' He sent a man flying to the
Duke; but it was too late. Saladin gained the
woods, and with him his bodyguard, the flower
of his state.

The Mamelukes also turned to fly. To right,
to left, the mad horsemen drove — the black, the
plumed, the Nubians in yellow, the Turcomans
with spotted skins over their mail, the men of
Syria, knighthood of Egypt — trampling under-

foot their own kind. But the steel chain held
most of these; the knights had bound horse to
horse: wide on the left the Templars and Hospitallers fanned out and swept all stragglers into
the net. So within hoops of iron, as it were,
the slaughter began, silent, breathless, wet work.
Here James d'Avesnes was killed, a good knight;
and here Des Barres went down in a huddle of
black men, and had infallibly perished but that
King Richard himself with his axe dug him out.
'Your pardon, King of the World,' sobbed Des
Barres, kissing his enemy's knee. 'Pooh,' says
Richard, 'we are all kings here. Take my sword
and get crowns'; and so he turned again into
battle, and Des Barres pressed after him. That
was the beginning of a firm friendship between
the two. Des Barres eschewed the counsels of
Saint-Pol from that day.

But there was treachery still awake and about.
When the rout was begun Richard reined up for
a minute, to breathe his horse and watch the way
of the field. He sat apart from his friends, seeing
the lines ride by. All in a moment inexplicably,
as when in a race of the tide comes a sudden
thwart gust of wind and changes the face of the
day, there was a scurry, a babble of voices, the
stampede of men fighting to kill: the Turks with
Christians on their backs came trampling, struggling together. A sword glinted close to Richard — 'Death to the Angevin devil!' he heard,
and turning received in mid shield De Gurdun's
sword. At the same moment a knight ran full
tilt into the assailant, knocked him off his horse,
and himself reeled, powerless to strike. This

was Des Barres, paying his debts. The King smiled grimly to see the wholesome treachery, and Gurdun's dismay at it. 'Gilles, Gilles,' says he, 'be sure you get me alone in the world when next you strike at my back. Now get you up, Norman, and fight a flying enemy, if you please. I will await your return.' De Gurdun saluted, but avoided his lord's face, and rode after the Turks. Des Barres stood, deep-breathing, by the King.

'Will he come back, sire?' asked the French knight.

'Not he,' said Richard; 'he is ashamed of himself.' He added, 'That is a very honest man, to whom I have done a wrong. But listen to this, Des Barres; if I had not wronged him, I was so placed that I should have injured a most holy innocent soul. Let be. I shall meet De Gurdun again. He may have me yet if he do not tire.'

He had been speaking as if to himself so far, but now turned his hawk-eyes upon Des Barres. 'Tell me now,' he said, 'who gave the order to the rear to charge, against my order?'

'Sire,' replied Des Barres, 'it was the Duke of Burgundy.'

'You do not understand me,' said Richard. 'It came through the Duke of Burgundy's windpipe. But who put it into his thick head?'

Des Barres looked troubled. 'Ah, sire, must I answer you?'

Considering him, King Richard said, 'No, Des Barres, you need not. For now I know who it was. Well, he has lost me my game, and won a part of his, I doubt.' Then he rode off, bidding Des Barres sound the recall.

'Of the pagans that day,' writes Milo by hearsay,
'we made hecatombs two score five: yet the King
my master took no pleasure of that, as I gather,
deeming that he should have had Saladin's head in
a bag. Also we gained a clear road to Joppa.' So
they did; but Joppa was a heap of stones.

They held a great council there. Richard put
out his views. There were two things to be done:
repair Joppa and march at once on Jerusalem,
there to find and have again at Saladin; or pursue
the coast road to Ascalon and raise the siege of
that city. 'I, my lords, am for Ascalon,' Richard
said. 'It is the key of Egypt. While the Soldan
holds us cooped up in Ascalon he can get his
pack-mules through. If we relieve it, after the
battery we have done him we can hold Jerusalem
at our whim. What do you say to this, Duke of
Burgundy?'

In the natural order of things the Duke would
have said nothing. But he had been filled to the
neck by Saint-Pol. Richard being for Ascalon,
the key of Egypt, the Duke declared himself for
Jerusalem, 'the key,' as he rather flatly said, 'of
the world.' To this Richard contented himself
with replying, that a key was little worth unless
you could open the door with it. All the French
stood by their leader, except Des Barres. He,
with Richard's party, leaned to the King's side.
But the Duke of Burgundy would not budge, sat
like a lump. He would not go to Ascalon, and
none of his battle should go. Richard cursed all
Frenchmen, but gave in. The truth was, he dared
not leave Saint-Pol behind him.

They repaired the walls and towers of Joppa, garrisoned the place. Then late in the autumn (truthfully, too late) they struck inland over a rolling grass country towards Blanchegarde, a white castle on a green hill. Moving slowly and cautiously, they pushed on to Ramleh, thence to Bêtenoble, which is actually within two days' march of Jerusalem. The month was October, mellow autumn weather. King Richard, moved by the sacred influences, the level peace of the fair land, filled day and night with the thought that he was on the threshold of that soil which bore the very footmarks of our blessed Saviour — King Richard, I say, was in great heart. He had been against the enterprise thus to do; he would have approached from Ascalon; the enterprise was folly. But it was glorious folly, for which a man might well die. He was ready to die, though he hoped and believed that he should not. Saladin, once bitten, would be shy: he had been badly bitten at Arsûf. Then came the Bishop of Beauvais with Burgundy to his tent — Saint-Pol stayed behind — with speeches, saying that the winter season was at hand; that it would be more prudent to withdraw to Joppa, or even to go down to Ascalon. Ascalon needed succours, it seemed. Richard's heart stood still at this treachery; then he blazed out in fury. 'Are we hare or hounds, by heaven? Do you presume ——?' He mastered himself. 'What part, pray, does Almighty God take in these pastimes of yours?'

The Duke of Burgundy looked heavily at the Bishop. The Bishop said, 'Sire, Ascalon is besieged.'

T

Said Richard, ' You old fool, do you not know
the Soldan better than that? Or do you put him
on a parity with this Duke? It was under siege
three weeks ago, as you remember perfectly well.'

The Duke still looked at the Bishop. Driven
again to say something, the latter began — ' Sire,
your words are injurious; but I have spoken
advisedly. The Count of Saint-Pol —— '

' Ah,' said Richard, ' the Count of Saint-Pol?
Now I begin to understand you. Please to fetch
in your Count of Saint-Pol.'

Saint-Pol was sent for, and he came, darkly
smiling, respectful, but aware. King Richard held
his voice, but not his hand, on the curb. The
hand shook a little.

' Saint-Pol,' he said, ' the Duke of Burgundy
refers me to the Bishop, the Bishop to you. This
seems the order of command in King Philip's host.
Between the three of you I conceive to lie the
honour of France. Now observe me. Three weeks
ago I was for Ascalon, and you for Jerusalem. Now
that I have brought you within two days of your
desire — two days, observe — you are for Ascalon,
and I for Jerusalem. What is the meaning of
this?'

' Sire,' said Saint-Pol, reasonably, ' it means that
we believe the Holy City impregnable at this
season, or untenable; and Ascalon still pregnable.'

The King put a hand to the table. ' It means
nothing of the sort, man. You do not believe
Ascalon can be taken. It is eight days' journey,
and was in straits a month ago. You make me
ashamed of the men I am forced to lead. What

faith have you? What religion? The faith of
your sick master the Runagate! The religion of
your white Marquess of Montferrat! And I had
taken you for men. Foh! you are rats.'

This was dreadful hearing: Saint-Pol bit his
lip, but made no other answer.

'Sire,' said the Bishop with heat, 'my manhood
has never been reproached before. When you
carried war into my country in the King your
father's time, I met you in a hauberk of mail. If
I met your Grace, judge if I should fear the Soldan. It is my devout hope to kiss the Holy
Sepulchre and touch the Holy Cross, but before
I die, not afterwards.'

'Pish!' said King Richard.

'Sire,' Beauvais ventured again, 'our master
King Philip set us over his host as foster-fathers
of his children. We dare not imperil so many
lives unadvisedly.'

'Unadvisedly!' the King thundered at him,
red to the roots of his hair.

'I withdraw the word, sire,' said the Bishop in
a hurry; 'yet it is the mature opinion of us all
that we should seek the coast for winter-quarters,
not the high lands. We claim, at least, the duty
of choosing for those whose guardians we are.'

If Richard had been himself of two years earlier
he would have killed then and there a second
Count of Saint-Pol; and for a pulse or two the
young man saw his death bright in the King's
eyes. That the angry man commanded himself
is, I think, to his credit. As it was, he did what
he had certainly never done before: he tried to
reason with the Duke of Burgundy.

'Duke of Burgundy,' he said, leaning over his chair and talking low, 'you are no Frenchman, and the more of a man on that account. You and I have had our differences. I have blamed you, and you me. But I have never found you a laggard when there was work for the sword or adventure for the heart. Now, of all adventures in the world the highest in which a man may engage is here. Across those hills lies the city of God, of which (I suppose) no soul among us might, unhelped, dare hope the sight, much less the touch, least of all the redemption. I tell you, Duke of Burgundy, there is that within me (not my own) which will lead you thither with profit, glory and honour. Will you trust me? So far as I have gone along with you I have done reasonably well. Did I scatter the heathen at Arsûf? No thanks to you, Burgundy, but I did. Did I hold a safe course to Joppa? Have I then brought you so near, and myself so near, for nothing at all? If I have been a fool in my day, I am not a fool now. I speak what I know. With this host I can save the city. Without the best of it, I can do nothing. What do you say, my lord? Will you let Beauvais take his Frenchmen to dishonour, and you and your Burgundians play for honour with me? The prize is great, the reward sure, here or in heaven. What do you say, Duke of Burgundy?'

His voice shook by now, and all the bystanders watched without breath the heavy, brooding, mottled man over against him. He, faithful to his nature, looked at the Bishop of Beauvais. But Beauvais was looking at his ring.

'What do you say, my lord?' again asked King Richard.

The Duke of Burgundy was troubled: he blinked, looking at Saint-Pol. But Saint-Pol was looking at the tent-roof.

'Be pleased to look at me,' said Richard; and the man did look, working under his wrongs.

'By God, Richard,' said the Duke of Burgundy, 'you owe me forty pound!'

King Richard laughed till he was helpless.

'It may be, it may well be,' he gasped between the throes of his mirth. 'O lump of clay! O wonderful half-man! O most expressive river-horse! You shall be paid and sent about your business. Archbishop, be pleased to pay this man his bill. I will content you, Burgundy, with money; but I will be damned before I take you to Jerusalem. My lords,' he said, altering voice and look in a moment, 'I will conduct you to the ships. Since I am not strong enough for Jerusalem I will go to Ascalon. But you! By the living God, you shall go back to France.' He dismissed them all, and next day broke up his camp.

But before that, very early in the morning, after a night spent with his head in his hands, he rode out with Gaston and Des Barres to a hill which they call Montjoy, because from there the pilgrims, tending south, see first among the folded hills Jerusalem itself lie like a dove in a nest. The moon was low and cold, the sun not up; but the heavens and earth were full of shadowless light; every hill-top, every black rock upon it stood sharply cut out, as with a knife. King Richard rode silently, his face covered in a great

hood; neither man with him dared speak, but
kept the distance due. So they skirted hill after
hill, wound in and out of the deep valleys, until
at last Gaston pricked forward and touched
his master on the arm. Richard started, not
turned.

'Montjoy, dear master,' said Gaston.

There before them, as out of a cup, rose a dark
conical hill with streamers of white light behind
and, as might be, leaping from it. 'The light
shines on Jerusalem,' said Gaston: Richard, looking up at the glory, uncovered his head. Sharp
against the light stood a single man on Montjoy,
who faced the full sun. They who saw him there
were still deep in shade.

'Gaston and Des Barres,' said King Richard,
when they had reached the foot of the wet hill,
'stay you here. Let me go on alone.'

Gaston demurred. 'The hill is manned, sire.
Beware an ambush. You have enemies close by.'
He hinted at Saint-Pol.

'I have only one enemy that I fear, Gaston,'
said the King; 'and he rides my horse. Do as I
tell you.'

They obeyed; so he went under their anxious
eyes. Slowly he toiled up the bridle-path which
the feet of many pilgrims had worn into the turf;
slowly they saw him dip from the head downwards into the splendour of the dawn. But when
horse and man were bathed full in light, those
two below touched each other and held hands;
for they saw him hoist his great shield from his
shoulder and hold it before his face. So as he
stayed, screening himself from what he sought

but dared not touch, the solitary watcher turned, and came near him, and spoke.

'Why does the great King cover his face?' said Gilles de Gurdun; 'and why does he, of his own will, keep the light of God from him? Is he at the edge of his dominion? Hath he touched the limit of his power? Then I am stronger than my Duke; for I see the towers shine in the sun; I see the Mount of Olives, Calvary also, and the holy temple of God. I see the Church of the Sepulchre, the battlements and great gates of the city. Look, my lord King. See that which you desire, that you may take it. Fulke of Anjou was King of Jerusalem; and shall not Richard be a king? What is lacking? What is amiss? For kings may desire that which they see, and take that which they desire, though other men go cursing and naked.'

Said King Richard from behind his shield, 'Is that you, Gurdun, my enemy?'

'I am that man,' said Gilles, 'and bolder than you are, since I can look unoffended upon the place where our Lord God suffered as a man. Suffering, it seems, maketh me sib with God.'

'I will never look upon the city, though I have risked all for the sake of it,' said Richard; 'for now I know that it was no design of God's to allow me to take it, although it was certainly His desire that I should come into this country. Perhaps He thought me other than now I am. I will not look. For if I look upon it I shall lead my men up against it; and then they will be cut off and destroyed, since we are too few. I will never see what I cannot save.'

Said Gilles between his teeth, 'You robber, you have seen my wife, and cannot save her now' Richard laughed softly.

'God bless her,' he said, 'she is my true wife, and will be saved sure enough. Yet I will tell you this, Gurdun. If she was not mine she should be yours; and what is more, she may be so yet.'

'You speak idly,' said Gurdun, 'of things which no man knows.'

'Ah,' said the King, 'but I do know them. Leave me: I wish to pray.'

Gilles moved off, and sat himself on the edge of the hill looking towards Jerusalem. If Richard prayed, it was with the heart, for his lips never opened. But I believe that his heart, in this hour of clear defeat, was turned to stone. He took his joys with riot, his triumphs calmly; his griefs he shut in a trap. Such a nature as his, I suppose, respects no persons. Whether God beat him, or his enemy, he would take it the same way. All that Gilles heard him say aloud was this: 'What I have done I have done: deliver us from evil.' He bade no farewell to his hope, he asked no greeting for his altered way. When he had turned his back upon the sacred places he lowered his shield; and then rode down the hill into the cold shadow of the valley.

If he was changed, or if his soul, naked of hope, was stricken bleak, so was the road he had to go. That day he broke up his camp and fared for Ascalon and the sea. Stormy weather set in, the rains overtook him; he was quagged, blighted with fever, lost his way, his men, his men's love.

Camp-sickness came and spread like a fungus. Men, rotten through to the brain, died shrieking, and as they shrieked they cursed his name. One, a Poictevin named Rolf, whom he knew well, turned away his blackened face when Richard came to visit him.

'Ah, Rolf,' said the King,'dost thou turn away from me, man?'

'I do that, by our Lord,' said Rolf,'since by these deeds of thine my wife and children will starve, or she become a whore.'

'As God lives,' said Richard, 'I will see to it.'

'I do not think He can be living any more,' said Rolf,'if He lets thee live, King Richard.' Richard went away. The time dragged, the rain fell pitilessly, without end. He found rivers in floods, fords roaring torrents, all ways choked. At every turn the Duke of Burgundy and Saint-Pol worked against him.

Also he found Ascalon in ruins, but grimly set about rebuilding it. This took him all the winter, because the French (judging, perhaps, that they had done their affair) took to the ships and sailed back to Acre. There they heard, what came more slowly to King Richard, strange news of the Marquess of Montferrat, and terrible news of Jehane Saint-Pol.

CHAPTER VI

THE CHAPTER CALLED CLYTEMNESTRA

At Acre, by the time September was set, the sun had put all the air to the sword, so that the city lay stifled, stinking in its own vice; and the nights were worse than the days. Then was the great harvest of the flies, when men died so quickly that there was no time to bury them. So also mothers saw their children flag or felt their force grow thin: one or another swooned suddenly and woke no more; or a woman found a dead child at the breast, or a child whimpered to find his mother so cold. At this time, while Jehane lay panting in bed, awake hour by hour and fretting over what she should do when the fountains of her milk should be dry, and this little Fulke, royal glutton, crave without getting of her—she heard the women set there to fan her talking to each other in drowsy murmurs, believing that she slept. By now she knew their speech.

Said one between the slow passes of the fans, 'Giafar ibn Mulk hath come into the city secretly.' And the other, 'Then we have a thief the more.'

'Peace,' said the first, 'thou grudger. He is one of my lovers, and telleth me whatsoever I seek to know. He is come in from Lebanon; so much, and more, I know already.'

'What ill report doth he bring of his master?'

asked the second, a lazy girl, whose name was
Misra, as the first was called Fanoum.

Fanoum answered, 'Very ill report of the Melek'
— that was King Richard's name here — 'but it
is according to the desires of the Marquess.'

'Ohè!' said Misra, 'we must tell this sleeper.
She is moon of the Melek.'

'Thou art a fool to think me a fool,'• said
Fanoum. 'Why, then, shall I be one to turn the
horn of a mad cow, to pierce my own thigh? Let
the Franks kill each other, what have we but
gain? They are dogs alike.'

Misra said, 'Hearken thou, O Fanoum, the
Melek is no dog. Nay, he is more than a man.
He is the yellow-haired King of the West, rid-
ing a white horse, who was foretold by various
prophets, that he should come up against the
Sultan. That I know.'

'Then he will have more than a man's death,'
said Fanoum. 'The Marquess goeth with Giafar
to Lebanon, to see the Old Man of Musse, whom
he serveth. The Melek must die, for of all men
living or dead the Marquess hateth him.'

'Oh, King of Kings!' said Misra, with a little
sob, 'and thou wilt stand by, thou sorrowful,
while the Marquess kills the Melek!'

Fanoum answered, 'Certainly I will; for any
of our lord's people can kill the Marquess; but
it needeth the guile of the Old Man to kill the
Melek. Let the wolf slay the lion while he sleep-
eth: anon cometh the shepherd and slayeth the
gorged wolf. That is good sense.'

'Well,' said Misra, 'it may be so. But I am
sorry for his favourite here. There are no daugh-

ters of Ali so goodly as this one.   The Melek is
a wise lover of women.'

'Let be for that,' replied Fanoum comfortably;
'the Old Man of Musse is a wiser.   He will come
and have her, and we do well enough in Lebanon.'

They would have said more, had Jehane needed
any more.   But it seemed to her that she knew
enough.   There was danger brewing for King
Richard, whom she, faithless wretch, had let go
without her.   As she thought of the leper, of her
promise to the Queen-Mother, of Richard tower-
ing but to fall, her heart grew cold in her bosom,
then filled with fire and throbbed as if to burst.
It is extraordinary, however, how soon she saw
her way clear, and on how small a knowledge.
Who this Old Man might be, who lived on Lebanon and was most wise in the matter of women,
she could have no guess; but she was quite sure
of him, was certain that he was wise.   She knew
something of the Marquess, her cousin.   Any ally
of his must be a murdermonger.   A wise lover of
women, the Old Man of Musse, who dwelt on
Lebanon!   Wiser than Richard!   And she more
goodly than the daughters of Ali!   Who were the
daughters of Ali?   Beautiful women?   What did
it matter if she excelled them?   God knew these
things; but Jehane knew that she must go to market with the Old Man of Musse.   So much she
calmly revolved in her mind as she lay her length,
with shut eyes, in her bed.

With the first cranny of light she had herself
dressed by her sulky, sleepy women, and went
abroad.   There were very few to see her, none

to dare her any harm, so well as she was known.
Two eunuchs at a wicked door spat as she passed;
she saw the feet of a murdered man sticking out
of a drain, the scurry of a little troop of rats.
Mostly, the dogs of the city had it to themselves.
No women were about, but here and there a
guarded light betrayed sin still awake, and here
and there a bell, calling the faithful to church,
sounded a homely note of peace. The morning
was desperately close, without a waft of air. She
found the Abbot Milo at his lodging, in the act
of setting off to mass at the church of Saint
Martha. The sight of her wild face stopped
him.

'No time to lose, my child,' he said, when he
had heard her. 'We must go to the Queen: it
is due to her. Saviour of mankind!' he cried
with flacking arms, 'for what wast Thou content
to lay down Thy life!' They hurried out together
just as the sun broke upon the tiles of the domed
churches, and Acre began to creep out of bed.

The Queen was not yet risen, but sent them
word that she would receive the abbot, 'but on
no account Madame de Saint-Pol.' Jehane pushed
off the insult just as she pushed her hot hair from
her face. She had no thoughts to spare for herself. The abbot went into the Queen's house.

Berengère looked very drowned, he thought,
in her great bed. One saw a sharp white oval
floating in the black clouds which were her
hair. She looked younger than any bride could
be, childish, a child ill of a fever, wilful, queru-
lous, miserable. All the time she listened to
what Milo had to say her lips twitched, and

her fingers plucked gold threads out of the cherubim on the coverlet.

'Kill the King of England? Kill my lord' Montferrat? Eh, they cannot kill him! Oh, oh, oh!'—she moaned shudderingly—'I would that they could! Then perhaps I should sleep o' nights.' Her strained eyes pierced him for an answer. What answer could he give?

'My news is authentic, Madame. I came at once, as my duty was, to your Grace, as to the proper person——' Here she sat right up in her bed, wide-eyed, all alight.

'Yes, yes, I am the proper person. I will do it, if no other can. Virgin Mary!'—she stretched her arms out, like one crucified—'Look at me. Am I worthy of this?' If she addressed the Virgin Mary her invitation was pointedly to the abbot, a less proper spectator. He did look, however, and pitied her deeply; at her lips dry with hatred, which should have been freshly kissed, at her drawn cheeks, into her amazed young heart: eh, God, he knew her loveworthy once, and now most pitiful. He had nothing to say; she went on breathless, gathering speed.

'He has spurned me whom he chose. He has left me on my wedding day. I have never seen him alone—do you heed me? never, never once. Ah, now, he has chosen for his minion: let her save him if she can. What have I to do with him? I am the daughter of a king; and what is he to me, who treats me so? If I am not to be mother of England, I am still daughter of Navarre. Let him die, let them kill him: what else can serve me now?' She fell back, and lay staring up at him. In every word she said there was sickening justice: what could Milo do? In his private mind he confirmed a suspicion — being still loyal to his King — that one and the same thing may be at one and the same time all black and all white. He did his best to put this strange case.

'Madame,' he said, 'I cannot excuse our lord the King, nor will I; but I can defend that noble lady whose only faults are her beauty and strong heart.' Mentioning Jehane's beauty, he saw the Queen look quickly at him, her first intelligent look. 'Yes, Madame, her beauty, and the love she has been taught to give our lord. The King married her, uncanonically, it is true; but who was she to hold up church law before his face? Well, then she, by her own pure act, caused herself to be put away by the King, abjuring thus his kingly seat. Hey, but it is so, that by her own prayers, her proper pleading, her proper tears, she worked against her proper honour, and against the child in her womb. What more could she do? What more could any wife, any mother, than that? Ah, say that you hate her without stint, would you have her die? Why, no! for what pain can be worse than to live as she lives? My lady, she prevailed against the King; but she could not prevail against her own holy nature working upon the King's great heart. No! When the King found out that she was to be mother of his child, he loved her so well that, though he must respect her prayers, he must needs respect her person also. The King thought within himself, " I have promised Madame de Saint-Pol that I will never strive with her in love; and I will not. Now must I promise Almighty God that, in her life, I will not strive so at all." Alas, Madame, and alas! Here the King was too strong for the girl; here her own nobility rose up against her. Pity her, not blame her; and for the King — I dare to say it — find pity as well as blame. All those who love his high heart, his crowned head, find pity for him in theirs. For many there are who do better, having no occasion to do as ill; but there can be none who mean better, for none have such great motions.'

Milo might have spared his breath. The Queen had heard one phrase of all his speech, and during the rest had pondered that. When he had done, she said, 'Fetch me in this lady. I would speak with her.'

'Breast shall touch breast here,' said Milo to himself, full of hope, 'and mouth meet mouth. Courage, old heart.'

When the tall girl was brought in Queen Berengère did not look at her, nor make any response to her deep reverence; but bade her fetch a mirror from the table. In this she looked at herself steadily for some time, smoothing and coiling back her hair, arranging her neck-covering so as to show something of her bosom, and so on. She sent Jehane for boxes of unguent, her colour-boxes, brush for the eyebrows, powder for the face. Finally she had brought to her a little crown of diamonds, and set it in her hair. After patting her head and turning it about and about, she put the glass down and made a long survey of Jehane.

'They do well,' she said, 'who call you sulky:

you have a sulky mouth. I allow your shape;
but there are reasons for that. You are very tall;
you have a long throat. Green eyes are my
detestation — fie, turn them from me. Your hair
is wonderful, and your skin. I suppose women
of the North are so commonly. Come nearer.'
Jehane obeying, the Queen touched her neck,
then her cheek. 'Show me your teeth,' she said.
' They are strong and good, but much larger than
mine. Your hands are big, and so are your ears;
you do well to cover them. Let me see your
foot.' She peeped over the edge of the bed;
Jehane put her foot out. ' It is not so large as I
expected,' said the Queen, ' but much larger than
mine.' Then she sighed and threw herself back.
' You are certainly a very tall girl. And twenty-
three years old? I am not twenty yet, and have
had fifty lovers. The Abbot of Poictiers said you
were beautiful. Do you think yourself so ? '
     ' It is not my part to think of it, Madame,'
said Jehane, holding herself rather stiffly.
     ' You mean that you know it too well,' said
Berengère. ' I suppose it is true. You have a
fine colour and a fine person — but that is a
woman's. Now look at me carefully, and say
how you find me. Put your hand here, and here,
and here. Touch my hair; look well at my eyes.
My hair reaches to my knees when I stand up,
to the floor when I sit down. I am a king's
daughter. Do you not think me beautiful ? '
     ' Yes, Madame. Oh, Madame —— ! ' Jehane,
trembling before her visions, could hardly stand
still; but the Queen (who had no visions now the
mirror was put by) went plaining on.

'When I was in my father's court his poets
called me Frozen Heart, because I was cold in
loving. Messire Bertran de Born loved me, and
so did my cousin the Count of Provence, and the
Count of Orange, and Raimbaut, and Gaucelm,
and Ebles of Ventadorn. Now I have found one
colder than ever I was, and I am burning. Are
you a great lover of the King?'

At this question, put so quietly, Jehane grew
grave. It took her above her sense of dangers,
being in itself a dignity. 'I love the King so
well, Queen Berengère,' she said, 'that I think I
shall make him hate me in time.'

'Folly,' snapped the Queen, 'or guile. You
would spur him. Is it true what the Abbot Milo
told me?'

'I know not what he has told you,' said Jehane;
'but it is true that I have not dared let the King
love me, and now dare least of all.'

The Queen clenched her hands and teeth.
'You devil,' she said, 'how I hate you. You
reject what I long for, and he loathes me for your
sake. You a creature of nought, and I a king's
daughter.'

From the nostrils of Jehane the breath came
fluttering and quick; in her splendid bosom
stirred a storm that, if she had chosen to let it
loose, could have shrivelled this little prickly leaf:
but she replied nothing to the Queen's hatred.
Instead, with eyes fixed in vacancy, and one hand
upon her neck, she spoke her own purpose and
lifted the talk to high matters.

'I touch not again your King and mine, O
Queen. But I go to save him.'

'Woman,' said Berengère, 'do you dare tell
me this? Are my miseries nothing to you?
Have you not worked woe enough?'

Jehane suddenly threw her hair back, fell upon
her knees, lifted her chin. 'Madame, Madame,
Madame! I must save him if I die. I implore
your pardon — I must go!'

'Why, what can you do against Montferrat?'
The Queen shivered a little: Jehane looked
fixedly at her, solemn as a dying nun.

'You say that I am handsome,' she said, then
stopped. Then in a very low voice —'Well, I
will do what I can.' She hung her golden
head.

The Queen, after a moment of shock, laughed
cruelly. 'I suppose I could not wish you anything worse than that. I hate you above all
people in the world, mother of a bastard. Oh, it
will be enough punishment. Go, you hot snake;
leave me.'

Jehane rose to her feet, bowed her head and
went out. Next moment the Queen must have
whipped out of bed, for she caught her before she
could shut the door, and clung to her neck, sobbing desperately. 'O God, Jehane, save Richard!
Have mercy on me, I am most wretched.' Now
the other seemed to be queen.

'My girl,' said Jehane, ' I will do what I promised.' She kissed the scorching forehead, and
went away with Milo to find Giafar ibn Mulk.

To get at him it was necessary to put the girl
Fanoum to the question. This was done. Giafar
ibn Mulk, enticed into the house, proved to be a
young man of prudence and resource. He could

not, he said, conduct them to his master, because
he had been told to conduct the Marquess; but
an equally sure guide could be found, and there
were no objections to his delaying his own illustrious convoy for a week or more. Further than
that he could not go, nor did the near prospect of
death, which the abbot exhibited to him, prove
any inducement to the alteration of his mind.
'Death?' he said, when the implements of that
were before him. 'If I am to die, I am to die:
not twice it happens to a man. But I recommend
to these priests the expediency of first finding El
Safy.' As this was to be their guide up Lebanon,
those priests agreed. El Safy also agreed, when
they had him. A galley was got ready for sea;
the provisional Grand Master of the Temple
wrote a commendatory letter to his 'beloved
friend in the one God, Sinan, Lord of the
Assassins, *Vetus de Monte*'; and then, in two
days' time, Milo the abbot, Jehane with her little
Fulke, a few women, and El Safy (their master in
the affair), left Acre for Tortosa, whence they
must climb on mule-back to Lebanon.

CHAPTER VII

FROM the haven at Acre to the bill of Tortosa is
two days' sailing with a fair wind. Thence, climbing the mountains, you reach Musse in four days
more, if the passes are open. If they are shut
you do not reach it at all. High on Lebanon,
above the frozen gorge where Orontes and Leon-
tes, rivers of Syria, separate in their courses;
above the terrace of cedars, above Shurky the
clouded mountain, lies a deep green valley senti-
nelled on all sides by snow peaks and by the
fortresses upon their tops. In the midst of that,
among cedars and lines of cypress trees, is the
white palace of the Lord of the Assassins, as big
as a town. A man may climb from pass to pass
of Lebanon without striking upon the place;
sighting it from some dangerous crag, he may
yet never approach it. None visit the Old Man
of Musse but those who court Death in one of
his shapes; and to such he never denies it. Dazzling snow-curtains, black hanging-woods, sheer
walls of granite, frame it in: looking up on all
sides you see the soaring pikes; and deep under
a coffer-lid of blue it lies, greener than an emerald,
a valley of easy sleep. There in the great chambers young men lie dreaming of women, and sleek

293

boys stand about the doorways with cups of mad-
ness held close to their breasts.   They are eaters
and drinkers of hemp, these people, which causes
them to sleep much and wake up mad.   Then,
when the Old Man calls one or another and says,
Go down the mountains into the cities of the sea-
board, and when thou seest such-a-one, kiss him
and strike deep — he goes out then and there with
fixed eyeballs, and never turns them about until
he finds whom he seeks, nor ever shuts them
until his work is done.   This is the custom of
Musse in the enclosed valley of Lebanon.

Thither on mules from Tortosa came El Safy,
leading the Abbot Milo and Jehane, and brought
them easily through all the defiles to that castle
on a spur which is called Mont-Ferrand, but in
the language of the Saracens, Bārin.   From that
height they looked down upon the domes and
gardens of Musse, and knew that half their work
was done.

What immediately followed was due to the
insistence of El Safy, who said that if Jehane was
not suitably attired and veiled she would fail of
her mission.   Jehane did not like this.

'It is not the custom of our women to be
veiled, El Safy,' she said, 'except at the hour
when they are to be married.'

'And it is not the custom of our men,' replied
the Assassin, 'to choose unveiled women.   And
this for obvious reasons.'

'What are your reasons, my son?' asked the
abbot.

'I will tell you,' said El Safy.   'If a man
should come to our master with a veiled woman,

saying, My lord, I have here a woman faced like
the moon, and more melting than the peach that
drops from the wall, the Old Man would straightway conceive what manner of beauty this was, and
picture it more glorious than the truth could ever
be; and then the reality would climb up to meet
his imagining. But otherwise if he saw her bare-
faced before him; for eyesight is destructive to
mind-sight if it precede it. The eye must be
servant. So then he, dreaming of the veiled
treasure, weds her and finds that she is just what
was predicted of her by the merchant. For
women and other delights, as we understand the
affair, are according to our zest; and our zest
is a thing of the mind's devising, added unto
desire as the edge of a sword is superadded to
the sword. So the fair woman must certainly be
veiled.'

'The saying hath meat in it,' said the abbot;
'but here is no question of merchants, nor of
marriage, pardieu.'

'If there is no question of marriage, of what is
there question in this company?' asked El Safy.
'Let me tell you that two questions only concern
the Old Man of Musse.'

Jehane, who had stood pouting, with a very
high head, throughout this little colloquy, said
nothing; but now she allowed El Safy his way.
So she was dressed.

They put on her a purple vest, thickly embroidered with gold and pearls, underdrawers of
scarlet silk, and gauze trousers (such as Eastern
women wear) of many folds. Her hair was
plaited and braided with pearls, a broad silk

girdle tied about her waist. Over all was put
a thick white veil, heavily fringed with gold.
Round her ankles they put anklets of gold,
with little bells on them which tinkled as she
walked; last, scarlet slippers. They would have
painted her face and eyebrows, but that El Safy
decided that this was not at all necessary. When
all was done she turned to one of her women and
demanded her baby. El Safy, to Milo's surprise,
made no demur. Then they put her in a gold
cage on a mule's back, and so let her down by a
steep path into the region of birds and flowering
trees. There was very little conversation, except
when the abbot hit his foot against a rock. In
the valley they passed through a thick cedar
grove, and so came to the first of four gates of
approach.

Half a score handsome boys, bare-legged and
in very short white tunics, led them from hall to
hall, even to the innermost, where the Old Man
kept his state. The first hall was of cedar painted
red; the second was of green wood, with a fountain in the middle; the third was deep blue, and
the fourth colour of fire. But the next hall,
which was long and very lofty, was white like
snow, except for the floor, which had a blood-
red carpet; and there, on a white throne, sat
the Old Man of Musse, himself as blanched as
a swan, robed all in white, white-bearded; and
about him his Assassins as colourless as he.

The ten boys knelt down and crossed their
arms upon their bosoms; El Safy fell flat upon
his face, and crawling so, like a worm, came at
length to the steps of the throne. The Old Man

let him lie while he blinked solemnly before him. Not the Pope himself, as Milo had once seen him, hoar with sanctity, looked more remotely, more awfully pure than this king of murder, snowy upon his blood-red field. What gave closer mystery was that the light came strange and milky through agate windows, and that when the Old Man spoke it was in a dry, whispering voice which, with the sound of a murmur in the forest, was in tune with the silence of all the rest. El Safy stood up, and was rigid. There ensued a passionless flow of question and answer. The Old Man murmured to the roof, scarcely moving his lips; El Safy answered by rote, not moving any other muscles but his jaw's. As for the Assassins, they stayed squat against the walls, as if they had been dead men, buried sitting.

At a sign from El Safy the abbot with veiled Jehane came down the hall, and stood before the white spectre on his throne. Jehane saw that this was really a man. There was a faint tinge of red at his nostrils, his eyes were yellowish and very bright, his nails coloured red. The shape of his head was that of an old bird. She judged him bald under his high cap; but his beard came below his breast-bone. When he opened his mouth to speak she observed that his teeth were the whitest part of him, and his lips rather grey. He did not seem to look at her, but said to the abbot, ' Tell me why you have come into my country, being a Frank and a Christian dog; and why you have brought with you this fair woman.'

' My lord,' said the abbot, after clearing his throat, ' we are lovers and servants of the great

king whom you call the Melek Richard, a lion
indeed in the paths of the Moslems, who makes
bitter war upon your enemy the Soldan; and in
defence of him we are come. For it appears that
a servant of your lordship's, called Giafar ibn Mulk,
is now in Acre, which is King Richard's good town,
conspiring with the Marquess the death of our
lord.'

'It is the first I have heard of it,' said the Old
Man. 'He was sent for a different purpose, but
his hand is otherwise free. What else have you
to say?'

'Why, this, my lord,' said the abbot, 'that our
lord the King has too many enemies not declared,
who compass his destruction while he compasses
their soul's health. This is so shameful that we
think it no time for the King's lovers to be asleep.
Therefore I, with this woman, who, of all persons
living in the world, is most dear to him (as he
to her), have come to warn your lordship of the
Marquess his abominable design, in the sure hope
that your lordship will lend it no favour. King
Richard, we believe, is besieging the Holy City,
and therefore (no doubt) hath the countenance of
Almighty God. But if the devil (who loves the
Marquess, and is sure to have him) may reckon
your lordship also upon his side, we doubt that he
may prevail.'

'And do you also think,' asked the Old Man,
scarcely audible, 'That the Melek Richard will
thank you for these precautions of yours?'

'My lord,' said Milo, 'we seek not his thanks,
nor his good opinion, but his safety.

'It is one thing to seek safety,' said the Old

Man, 'but another thing to find or keep it. Get you back to the doorway.'

So they did, and the lord of the place sat for a long time in a stare, not moving hand or foot. Now it happened that the child in Jehane's arm woke up, and began to stretch itself, and whimper, and nozzle about for food. Jehane tried to hush it by rocking herself to and fro gently on one foot. The abbot, horrified, frowned and shook his head; but Jehane, who knew but one lord now Richard was away, took no notice. Presently young Fulke set up a howl which sounded piercing in that still place. Milo began to say his prayers; but no one moved except Jehane, whose course, to her own mind, was clear. She put the great veil back over her head, and bared her beauty; she unfastened the purple vest, and bared her bosom. This she gave to the child's searching mouth. The free gesture, the bent head, the unconscious doing, made the act as lovely as the person. Fulke murmured his joy, and Jehane looking presently up saw the Old Man's solemn eyes blinking at her. This did not disconcert her very much, for she thought, ' If he is correctly reported he has seen a mother before now.'

It might seem that he had or had not: his action reads either way. After three minutes' blinking he sent an old Assassin (not El Safy) down the hall to the door.

' Thus,' he reported, 'saith the Old Man of Musse, Lord of the Assassins. Tell the Sheik of the Nazarenes that the Marquess of Montferrat shall come up and go down, and after that come up no more. Also, let the Sheik depart in peace

and with all speed, lest I repent and put him suddenly to death.   As for the fair woman, she must
remain among my ladies, and become my dutiful
wife, as a ransom price.'

The abbot, as one thunderstruck, raised his
hands on high. ' O sack of sin !' he groaned, ' O
dross for the melting-pot! O unspeakable sacrifice!'   But Jehane, gravely smiling, checked him.
' Why, Lord Abbot, is any sacrifice too great for
King Richard?' she asked, gently reproving him.
' Nay, go, my father; I shall do very well.   I am
not at all afraid.   Now do what I shall tell you.
Kiss the hand of my lord Richard from me when
you see him, bidding him remember the vows we
made to each other on the day at Fontevrault
when he took up the Cross, and again before the
lifted Host at Cahors.   And to my lady Queen
Berengère say this, that from this day forth I am
wife of a man, and stand not between her bed and
the King, as God knows I have never meant to
stand.   Kiss me now, my father, and pray dili-
gently for me.'   He tells us that he did, and
records the day long ago when he had first kissed
the poor girl in the chapel of the Dark Tower,
the day when, as she hoped, she had taught her
great lover to tread upon her heart.

At this time a great black, the chief of the
eunuchs, came and touched her on the shoulder.
'Whither now, friend?' said Jehane.   He pointed
the way, being a deaf-mute.   ' Lead,' said she; ' I
will follow.'   And so she did.

She turned no more her head, nor did she go
with it lowered, but carried it cheerfully, as if her
business was good.   The black led her by many

winding ways to a garden filled with orange-trees, and across this to a bronze door. There stood two more blacks on guard, with naked swords in their hands. The eunuch struck twice on the lintel. The door was opened from within, and they entered. An old lady dressed in black came to meet them; to her the eunuch handed Jehane, made a reverence, and retired. They shut the bronze doors. What more? After the bath, and putting on of habits more sumptuous than she had ever heard tell of, she was taken by slaves into the Hall of Felicity. There, among the heavy-eyed languid women, Jehane sat herself staidly down, and suckled her child.

CHAPTER VIII

THE Marquess of Montferrat travelled splendidly
from Acre to Sidon with six galleys in his convoy.
So many, indeed, did not suffice him; for at Sidon
he took off his favourite wife with her women,
eunuchs and janissaries, and thus with twelve ships
came to Tripolis. Thence by the Aleppo road he
went to Karak of the Knights, thence again, after
a rest of two days, he started — he, the knights
and esquires of his body in cloth of gold, with
scarlet housings for the mules, litters for his
womenkind; with his poets, his jongleurs, his
priest, his Turcopoles and favourites; all this gaudy
company, for the great ascent of Mont-Ferrand.

His mind was to impress the Old Man of
Musse, but it fell out otherwise. The Old Man
was not easily impressed, because he was so
accustomed to impressing. You do not prophesy
to prophets, or shake priests with miracles. When
he reached the top of Mont-Ferrand he was met
by a grave old Sheik, who informed him quietly
that he must remain there. The Marquess was
very angry, the Sheik very grave. The Marquess
stormed, and talked of armed hosts. ' Look up,
my lord,' said the Sheik. The mountain-ridges
were lined with bowmen; in the hanging-woods

302

he saw the gleam of spears; between them and the sky, on all sides as far as one could see, gloomed the frozen peaks. The Marquess felt a sinking. He arose chastened on the morrow, and negotiations were resumed on the altered footing. Finally, he begged for but three persons, without whose company he said he could not do. He must have his chaplain, his fool, and his barber. Impossible, the Sheik said; adding that if they were so necessary to the Marquess he might 'for the present' remain with them at Mont-Ferrand. In that case, however, he would not see the Lord of the Assassins.

'But that, very honourable sir,' said the Marquess, with ill-concealed impatience, 'is the simple object of my journey.'

'So it was reported,' the Sheik observed. 'It is for you to consider. For my own part I should say that these persons cannot be indispensable for a short visit.'

'I can give his lordship a week,' said the Marquess.

'My master,' replied the Sheik, 'may give you an hour, but considers that half that time should be ample. To be sure, there is the waiting for audience, which is always wearisome.'

'My friend,' the Marquess said, opening his eyes, 'I am the King-elect of Jerusalem.'

'I know nothing of such things,' replied the Sheik. 'I think we had better go down.' Three only went down: the Sheik, the Marquess, and Giafar ibn Mulk.

When at last they were in the garden-valley, and better still had reached the third of the halls of degree, they were met by the chief of the eunuchs, who told them his master was in the harem, and could not be disturbed. The Marquess, who so far had been all smiles and interest, was now greatly annoyed; but there was no help for that. In the blue court he must needs wait for nearly three hours. By the time he was ushered into the milky light of the audience chamber he was faint with rage and apprehension; he was dazzled, he stumbled over the blood-red carpet, arrived fainting at the throne. There he stayed, tongue-cloven, while the colourless Lord of Assassins blinked inscrutably upon him, with eyes so narrow that he could not tell whether he so much as saw him; and the adepts, rigid by the tribune-wall, stared at their own knees.

'What do you need of me, Marquess of Montferrat?' asked the old hierarch in his most remote voice. The Marquess gulped some dignity into himself.

'Excellent sir,' he said, 'I seek the amity of one king to another, alliance in a common good cause, the giving and receiving of benefits, and similar courtesies.'

These propositions were written down on tablets, and carefully scrutinized by the Old Man of Musse, who said at last —

'Let us take these considerations in order. Of what kings do you propound the amity?'

'Of yourself, sir,' replied the Marquess, 'and of myself.'

'I am not a king,' said Sinan, 'and had not heard that you were one either.'

'I am King-elect of Jerusalem,' the Marquess

replied with stiffness. The Old Man raised his wrinkled forehead.

'Well,' he said, 'let us get on. What is your common good cause?'

'Eh, eh,' said the Marquess, brightening, 'it is the cause of righteous punishment. I strike at your enemy the Soldan through his friend King Richard.' The Old Man pondered him.

'Do you strike, Marquess?' he asked at length.

'Sir,' the Marquess made haste to answer, 'your question is just. It so happens that I cannot strike King Richard because I cannot reach him. I admit it: I am quite frank. But you can strike him, I believe. In so doing, let me observe, you will deal a mortal blow at Saladin, who loves him, and makes treaties with him to your detriment and the scandal of Christendom.'

'Do you speak of the scandal of Christendom?' asked Sinan, twinkling.

'Alas, I must,' said the Marquess, very mournful.

'The cause is near to your heart, I see, Marquess.'

'It is in it,' replied the Marquess. The Old Man considered him afresh; then inquired where the Melek might be found.

The Marquess told him. 'We believe he is at Ascalon, separate from the Duke of Burgundy.'

'Giafar ibn Mulk and Cogia Hassan,' said the Old Man, as if talking in his sleep, 'come hither.' The two young men rose from the wall and fell upon their faces before the throne. Their master spoke to them in the tone of one ordering a meal.

'Return with the Marquess to the coast by the

x

way of Emesa and Baalbek; and when you are within sight of Sidon, strike. One of you will be burned alive. I think it will be Giafar. Let the other return speedily with a token. The audience is finished.'

The Old Man closed his eyes. At a touch from another the two prostrate Assassins crept up and kissed his foot, then rose, waiting for the Marquess. He, pale as death, saw, felt, heard nothing. At another sign a man put his hand on either shoulder.

' Ha, Jesus-God!' grunted the Marquess, as the sweat dripped off him.

' Stop bleating, silly sheep, you will awaken the Master,' said Giafar in a quick whisper. They led him away, and the Old Man slept in peace.

The Marquess saw nothing of his people at Mont-Ferrand, for (to begin with) they were not there, and (secondly) he was led another way. By the desolate crag of Masyaf, where a fortress, hung (as it seems) in mid-air, watches the valleys like a little cloud; through fields of snow, by terraces cut in the ice where the sheer rises and drops a thousand feet either way; so to Emesa, a mountain village huddled in perpetual shadows; thence down to Baalbek, and by foaming river-gorges into the sun and sight of the dimpling sea: thus they led the doomed Italian. He by this time knew the end was coming, and had braced himself to meet it stolidly.

The towers of Sidon rose chastely white above the violet; they saw the golden sands rimmed with foam; they saw the ships. Going down a lane, luxuriant with flowers and scented shrubs, where steep cactus hedges shut out the furrowed fields and olive gardens, and the cicalas made hissing music, Giafar ibn Mulk broke the silence of the three men.

'Is it time?' he asked of his brother, without turning his head.

'Not yet,' Cogia replied. The Marquess prayed vehemently, but with shut lips.

They reached an open moor, where there were rocks covered with cistus and wild vine. Here the air was very sweet and pure, the sun pleasant. The Marquess's ass grew frisky, pricked up his ears and brayed. Giafar ibn Mulk edged up close, and put his arm round the Marquess's neck.

'The signal is a good one,' he said. 'Strike, Cogia.'

Cogia drove his knife in up to the heft. The Marquess coughed. Giafar lifted him from his ass, quite dead.

'Now,' says he, 'go thou back, Cogia. I will stay here. For so the Old Man plainly desired.'

'I think with you,' said Cogia. 'Give me the token.' So they cut off the Marquess's right hand, and Cogia, after shaking it, put it in his vest. When he was well upon his way to the mountain road, Giafar sat down on a bank of violets, ate some bread and dates, then went to sleep in the sun. So afterwards he was found by a picket of soldiers from Sidon, who also found all of their lord but his right hand. They took Giafar ibn Mulk and burned him alive.

The Old Man of Musse was extremely kind to
Jehane, who pleased him so well that he was
seldom out of her company. He thought Fulke
a fine little boy, as he could hardly fail to be,
owning such parents. All the liberty that was
possible to the favourite of such a great prince
she had. One day, about six weeks after she had
first come into the valley, he sent for her. When
she had come in and made her reverence he drew
her near to his throne, put his arm round her, and
kissed her. He observed with satisfaction that
she was looking very well.

'My child,' he said kindly, 'I have news which
I am sure will please you. Very much of the
Marquess of Montferrat is by this time lying dis-
integrate in a vault.'

Jehane's green eyes faltered for a moment as
she gazed into his wise old face.

'Sir,' she asked, by habit, 'is this true?'

'It is quite true,' said the Old Man. 'In proof
of it regard his hand, which one of my Assassins,
the survivor, has brought me.' He drew from
his bosom a pale hand, and would have laid it in
Jehane's lap if she had let him. As she would
not, he placed it beside him on the floor. Pur-
suing his discourse, he said—

'I might fairly claim my reward for that. And
so I should if I had not got it already.'

Again Jehane pondered him gravely. 'What
reward more have you, sire?'

The Old Man, smiling very wisely, pressed her
waist. Jehane thought.

'Why, what will you do with me now, sire?'
she inquired. 'Will you kill me?'

'Can you ask?' said the Old Man. Then he
went on more seriously to say that he supposed
the life of King Richard to be safe for the immediate future, but that he foresaw great difficulties in his way before he could be snug at home.
'The Marquess of Montferrat was by no means
his only enemy,' he told her. 'The Melek suffers,
what all great men suffer, from the envy of others
who are too obviously fools for him to suppose
them human creatures. But there is nothing a
fool dislikes so much as to behold his own folly;
and as your Melek is a looking-glass for these
kind, you may depend upon it they will smudge
him if they can. He is the bravest man in the
world, and one of the best rulers; but he has no
discretion. He is too absolute and loves too little.'

Jehane opened her eyes very wide. 'Why, do
you know my lord, sire?' she asked. The Old
Man took her hand.

'There are very few personages in the world of
whom I do not know something,' he said; 'and I
tell you that there are terms to the Melek's gov-
ernment. A man cannot say Yea and Nay as he
chooses without paying the price. The debt on
either hand mounts up. He may choose with
whom he will settle — those he has favoured or
those he has denied. As a rule one finds the
former more insatiable. Let him then beware of
his brother.'

Jehane leaned towards him, pleading with eyes
and mouth. 'Oh, sire,' she said, trembling at the
lips, 'if you have any regard for me, tell me when
any danger threatens King Richard. For then I
must leave you.'

'Why, that is as it may be,' said her master;
'but I will let you know what I think good for
you to know, and that must content you.'

Jehane's beauty, enhanced as it was now by the
sumptuous attire which she loved and by her
bodily well-being, was great, and her modesty
greater; but her heart was the greatest thing she
had. She raised her eyes again to the twinkling
eyes of her possessor, and kept them there for
a few steady seconds, while she turned over his
words in her mind. Then she looked down, saying, 'I will certainly stay with you till my lord's
danger is at hand. It is a good air for my baby.'

'It is good for all manner of things,' said the
Old Man; 'and remarkably good for you, my
Garden of Exhaustless Pleasure. And I will
see to it that it continues to water the roses
in your cheeks, beautiful child.' Jehane folded
her hands.

'You will do as you choose, my lord,' said she,
'I doubt not.'

'Be quite sure of it, dear child,' said the Old
Man.

Then he sent her back into the harem.

CHAPTER IX

'CONSIDER with anxious care the marrow of
your master when he is fortunate,' writes Milo
of Poictiers: 'if it lasts him, he is a slow spender
of his force; but on that account all the more
dangerous in adversity, having the deeper funds.
By this I would be understood to imply that the
devil of Anjou, turned to fighting uses in King
Richard's latter years, found him a habitable
fortalice.' With the best reasons in life for the
reflection, he might have said it more simply;
for it is simply true. Deserted by his allies,
balked of his great aspiration, within a day's
march of the temple of God, yet as far from
that as from his castle of Chinon; eaten with
fever; having death, lost purpose, murmurings,
fed envy reproach, upon his conscience — he
yet fought his way through sullen leagues of
mud to Ascalon; besieged it, drove his enemy
out, regained it. Thence, pushing quickly south,
he surprised Darum, and put the garrison to the
sword. By this act he cut Saladin in two, and
drove such a wedge into the body of his empire
as might leave either lung of it at his mercy.
The time seemed, indeed, ripe for negotiation.
Saladin sent his brother down from Jerusa-

lem with presents of hawks; Richard, sitting
in armed state at Darum, received him affably.
There was still a chance that treaty might win
for Jesus Christ what the sword had not won.

Then, as if in mockery of the greatness of men,
came ill news apace. The Frenchmen, back in
Acre, heard tell of Montferrat's doings and un-
doing. Pretty work of this sort perturbed the
allies. The Duke of Burgundy charged Saladin
with the murder; Saint-Pol loudly charged King
Richard, and the Duke's death, coming timely,
left him in the field. He made the most of his
chance, wrote to the Emperor, to King Philip,
to his cousin the Archduke of Austria (at home
by now), of this last shameful deed of the red
Angevin. He even sent messengers to Richard
himself with open letters of accusal. Richard
laughed, but for all that broke off negotiations
with Saladin until he could prove Saint-Pol
as great a liar as he himself knew him to be.
Then rose up again the question of the Crown
of Jerusalem. The Count of Champagne took
ship and came to Darum to beg it of Richard.
He too brought news with him. The Duke of
Burgundy was dead of an apoplexy. 'It seems
that God is still faintly on my side,' said Richard. 'There went out a sooty candle.'

The next words gave his boast the lie. 'Beau
sire,' said Count Henry, 'I grieve to tell you
something more. Before I left Acre I saw the
Abbot Milo.'

Richard had grey streaks in his face. 'Ah,'
he says hoarsely, 'go on, cousin.' The young
man stammered.

'Beau sire, God strikes in divers places, but always finds out the joints of our harness.'

'Go on,' says King Richard, sitting very still.

'Dear sire, my cousin, the Abbot Milo went out of Acre three weeks before the death of the Marquess. With him also went Madame Jehane; but he returned without her. This is all I know, though it is not all that the abbot knows.'

At the mention of her name the King took a sharp breath, as you or I do when quick pain strikes us. To the rest he listened without a sign; and asked at the end, 'Where is Milo?'

'He is at Acre, sire,' says the Count; 'and in prison.'

'Who put him there?'

'Myself, sire.'

'You did wrong, Count. Get you back to Acre and bring him to me.' Champagne went away.

Great trouble, as you know, always made Richard dumb; the grief struck inwards and congealed. He became more than ever his own councillor, the worst in the world. Lucky for the Abbot Milo that he was in bonds; but now you see why he penned the aphorism with which I began this chapter.

After that short, stabbing flash across his face, he shut down misery in a vice. The rest of his talk with the Count might have been held with a groom. Henry of Champagne, knowing the man, left him the moment he got the word; and King Richard sat down by the table, and for three

hours never stirred.   He was literally motionless.
Straightly rigid, a little grey about the face, white
at the cheek-bones; his clenched hand stiff on
the board, white also at the knuckles; his eyes
fixed on the door — men came in, knelt and said
their say, then encountering his blank eyes bent
their heads and backed out quietly.   If he thought,
none may learn his thought; if he felt, none may
touch the place ; if he prayed, let those who are
able imagine his prayers.   What Jehane had been
to him this book may have shadowed out: this
only I say, that he knew, from the very first hint
of the fact, why she had gone out with Milo and
sent Milo home alone.   The Queen knew, because
Jehane had told her; but he knew with no telling
at all.   She had gone away to save him from
herself.   Needing him not, because she so loved
him, it was her beauty which was hungry for his
desire.   Not daring to mar her beauty, she had
sought to hide it.   Greater love hath none than
this.   If he thought of that it should have soft-
ened him.   He did not think of it : he knew it.
    At the end of his grim vigil he got up and
went out of his house.   He was served with his
horse, his esquires came at call to the routine of
garrison days and nights.   He rode round the
walls, out at one of the gates, on a sharp canter of
reconnaissance in the hills.   Perhaps he spoke
more shortly than usual, and more drily; there
may have been a dead quality in his voice, usually
so salient.   There was no other sign.   At supper
he sat before them all, ate and drank at his wont.
Once only he startled the hallful of them.   He
dropped his great gold cup, and it split.

But as day followed night, all men saw the
change in him, Christians and Saracens alike.
A spirit of quiet savagery seemed to possess
him; the cunning, with the mad interludes, of a
devil.   He set patient traps for the Saracens in
the hills, and slaughtered all he took.   One day
he fell upon a great caravan of camels coming
from Babylon to Jerusalem, and having cut the
escort to pieces, slew also the merchants and trav-
ellers.   He seemed to give the sword the more
heartily in that he sought it for himself, but could
never get it.   No doubt he deserved to get it.
He performed deeds of impossible foolhardy gal-
lantry, the deeds of a knight-errant; rode solitary,
made single-handed rescues, suffered himself to
be cut off from his posts, and then with a handful
of knights, or alone, indeed, carved his way back
to Darum.   Des Barres, the Earl of Leicester and
the Grand Master, never left his side; Gaston of
Béarn used to sleep at the foot of his bed and
creep about after him like a cat; but this terrible
mood of his wore them out.   Then, at last, the
Count of Champagne came back with Milo and
more bad news.   Joppa was in sore straits, again
besieged; the Bishop of Sarum was returned from
the West, having a branch of dead broom in his
hand and stories of a throttled kingdom on his
lips.

   Before any other Richard had Milo alone.
The good abbot is very reticent about the interview in his book.   What he omits is more sig-
nificant than what he says.   'I found my master,'
he writes, 'sitting up in his bed in his *hauberk of
mail*.   They told me he had eaten nothing for

two days, yet vomited continually. He had killed five hundred Saracens meantime. I suppose he knew who I was. " Tell me, my good man," he said (strange address !), " the name of the person to whom Madame d'Anjou took you."

' I said, " Sire, we went to the Lord of the Assassins, whom they call Old Man of Musse."

' " Why did you go, monk ? " he asked, and felt about for his sword, but could not find it. Yet it was close by. I said, " Sire, because of a report which had reached the ears of Madame that the Marquess and the Old Man were in league to have you murdered." To this he made no reply, except to call me a fool. Later he asked, " How died the Marquess ? "

' " Sire," I answered, " most miserably. He went up Lebanon to see the Old Man, and came presently down again with two of the Assassins in his company, but none of his train. These persons, being near his city of Sidon, at a signal agreed upon stabbed him with their long knives, then cut off his right hand and despatched it to the Old Man by one of them. The other stayed by the corpse, and was so found peacefully sleeping, and burned."

' The King said nothing, but gave me money and a little jewel he used to wear, as if I had done him a service. Then he nodded a dismissal, and I, wondering, left him. He did not speak to me again for many weeks.'

You may collect that Richard was very ill. He was. The disease of his mind fed fat upon the disease of his body, and from the spoils of the

feast savagery reared its clotted head. Syrian
mothers still quell their children with the name of
Melek Richard, a reminiscence of the dreadful
time when he was without ruth or rest. He spoke
of his purposes to none, listened to none. The
Bishop of Sarum had come in with a budget of
disastrous news: Count John had England under
his heel, Philip of France had entered Normandy
in force, the lords of Aquitaine were in revolt.
If God had no use for him in the East, here was
work to do in the West. But had He none?
What of Joppa, shuddering under the sword?
What of Acre, where the French army wallowed
in sloth, with two queens at its mercy and Saint-
Pol in the mercy-seat? What, indeed, of Jehane?

Nobody breathed her name; yet night and day
the image of her floated, half-hid in scarlet clouds,
before King Richard. These clouds, a torn regi-
ment, raced across his vision, like cavalry broken,
in mad retreat. Out of the tumbled mass two
hands would throw up, white, long, thin hands,
Jehane's hands drowned in frothy blood. Then,
in his waking dream, when he drove in the spurs
and started to save, the colours changed, black
swam over the blood; and one hand only would
stay, held up warningly, saying, ' Forbear, I am
separate, fenced, set apart.' Thus it was always:
menace, wicked endeavour, shipwreck, ruin; always so, her agony and denial, his wrath and
defeat.

But this was wholesome torment. There was
other not so purgatorial — damned torment. That
was when the sudden thought of her possession by
another man, of his own robbery, his own impo-

tence to regain, came upon him in a surging flood
and made his neck swell with the rage of a beast.
And no crouching to spring, no flash through the
air, no snatching here. Here was no Gilles de
Gurdun to deal with. Only the beast's resource
was his, who had the beast's desire without his
power. At such times of obsession he lashed up
and down his chamber or the flat roof of his house,
all the tragic quest of a leopard in a cage making
blank his desperate hunting eyes. 'Lord, Lord,
Lord, how long can this endure?' Alas, the cage
was wider than any room, and stronger by virtue
of his own fashioning of the locks. But to do him
justice, Jehane's grave face would sail like a moon
among the storm-clouds sooner or later, and humble
him to the dust.

Sometimes, mostly at dawn, when a cool wind
stole through the trees, he saw the trail of events
more clearly, and knew whom to blame and whom
to praise. Generous as he was through and
through, at these times he did not spare the whip.
But the image he set up before whom to scourge
himself was Jehane Saint-Pol, that pure cold saint,
offering up her proud body for his needs; and so
sure as he did that he desired her, and so sure as
he desired he raged that he had been robbed.
Robber as he owned himself, now he had been
robbed. So the old black strife began again.
Many and many a dawn, as he thought of these
things, he went out alone into the shadowless
places of the land, to the quiet lapping sea, to the
gardens, or to the housetop fronting the new-born
day, with prayer throbbing for utterance, but a
tongue too dry to pray. Despair seized on him,

and he led his men out to death-dealing, that so haply he might find death for himself. The time wore to early summer, while he was nightly visited by the thought of his sin, and daily winning more stuff for repentance. Then, one morning, instead of going out singly to battle with his own soul, he went in to the Abbot Milo. What follows shall be told in his own words.

' The King came to me very early in the morning of Saints Primus and Felician, while I yet lay in my bed. " Milo, Milo," said he, "what must I do to be saved?" He was very white and wild, shaking all over. I said, " Dear Master, save thy people. On all sides they cry to thee — from England, from Normandy, from Anjou, from Joppa also, and Acre. There is no lack of entreaty." He shook his head. " Here," he said, " I can do no more. God is against me, the work too holy for such a wretch." " Lord," I said, "we are all wretches, Heaven save us! If your Grace is held off God's inheritance, you can at least hold others from your own. Here, may be, you took a charge too heavy; but there, at home, the charge was laid upon you. Renouncing here, you shall gain there. It cannot be otherwise." I believed in what I said; but he gripped the caps of his knees and rocked himself about. " They have beaten me, Milo. Saint-Pol, Burgundy, Beauvais — I am bayed by curs. What am I, Milo?" " Sire," I said, "your father's son. As they bayed the old lion, so they bay the young." He gaped at me, open-mouthed. " By God. Milo," he said, " I bayed him myself, and believed that he deserved it." " Lord," I answered, "who

am I to judge a great king? For my part 1
never believed that monstrous sin was upon him."
Here he jumped up. "I am going home, Milo,"
he said; "I am going home. I am going to my
father's tomb. I will do penance there, and serve
my people, and live clean. Look now, Milo,
shrive me if thou hast the power, for my need
is great." The thought was blessed to him. He
confessed his sins then and there, all a huddle of
them, weeping so bitterly that I should have wept
myself had I not been ready rather to laugh and
crack my fingers to see the breaking up of his
long and deadly frost. Before I shrived him,
moreover, I dared to speak of Madame Jehane,
how he had now lost her for ever, and why; how
she was now at last a man's wife, and that by her
own deliberate will; and how also he must do
his duty by the Queen. To all of which he gave
heed and promises of quiet endurance. Then I
shrived him, and that very morning gave him
the Lord's sacred body in the Church of the
Sepulchre. I believed him sane; and so for a
long time he was, as he testified by deeds of
incredible valour.'

It was not long after this that the fleet put out
to sea, shaping course for Acre. Message after
message came in from beleaguered Joppa; but
King Richard paid little heed to them, pending
the issue of new treating with Saladin. He certainly sailed with a single eye on Acre. But
Joppa lay on his course, and it is probable, he
being what he was, that the sight of no means to
do great deeds made great deeds done. When his
red galley sighted Joppa, standing in for the pur-

pose, all seemed over with the doomed city. This, no doubt (since his mood was hot), urged him to one of those impossible acts, 'incredible deeds of valour,' as Milo calls them, for which his name lives, while those of many better kings are forgotten.

The country about Joppa slopes sharply to the sea, and gives little or no shelter for ships; but so quick is the slope that a galley may ride under the very walls of the town and take in provision from the seaward windows. On the landward side it is dangerously placed, seeing that the stoop of the country runs from the mountains to it. The few outlying forts, the stone bridge over the river, cannot be held against a resolute foe. When King Richard's fleet drew near enough to see, it was plain what had been done. The Saracens had carried the outworks; they held the bridge. At leisure they had broached the walls and swarmed in. The flag on the citadel still flew; battle or carnage was raging in the streets all about it. Its fall was a matter of hours.

Now King Richard stood on the poop of his galley, watching all this. He saw a man come running down the mole chased by half a dozen horsemen in yellow, a priest by the look of him; you could see the gleam of his tonsure as he plunged. For so he did, plunged into the sea and swam for his life. The pursuers drew up on the verge and shot at him with their long bows. They were of Saladin's bodyguard, fine marksmen who should never have missed him. But the priest swam like a fish, and they did miss him. King Richard himself hooked him out by the gown,

Y

and then clipped him in his arms like a lover.
'Oh, brave priest! Oh, hardy heart!' he cried,
full of the man's bravery. 'Give him room there.
Let him cough up the salt. By my soul, barons,
I wish that any draught of wine may be so glorious
sweet.'

The priest sat up and told his tale. The city
was a shambles; every man, woman, or child had
been put to the sword. Only the citadel held
out; there was no time to lose. No time was
lost; for King Richard, in his tunic and breeches
as he was, in his deck shoes, without a helm, unmailed in any part, snatched up shield and axe.
'Who follows Anjou?' he called out, then plunged
into the sea. Des Barres immediately followed him,
then Gaston of Béarn (with a yell) and the Earl
of Leicester neck and neck; then the Bishop
of Salisbury, a stout-hearted prince, Auvergne,
Limoges, and Mercadet. These eight were all
the men in authority that *Trenchemer* held, except
some clerks, fat men who loved not water. But
as soon as the other ships saw what was afoot, a
man here and there followed his King. The rest
rowed closer to the shore and engaged the Saracen horsemen with their archers. Long before
any men could be got off the eight were on dry
land, and had found a way into the sacked city.

How they did what they did the God of Battles
knows best; but that they did it is certain. All
accounts of the fray agree, Bohadin with Vinsauf,
Moslem and Christian alike. What pent rage,
what storm curbed up short, what gall, what mor-
tification, what smoulder of resentment, bit into
King Richard, we may guess who know him.

Such it was as to nerve his arm, nerve his following to be his lovers, make him unassailable, make a devil of him. Not a devil. of blind fury, but a cold devil who could devise a scope for his malice, choose how to do his stabbing work wiseliest. Inside the town gate they took up close order, wedgewise, linked and riveted; a shield before, shields beside, Richard with his double-axe for the wedge's beak. They took the steep street at a brisk pace, turning neither right nor left, but heading always for the citadel, boring through and trampling down what met them. This at first was not very much, only at one corner a company of Nubian spears came pelting down a lane, hoping to cut them off by a flank movement. Richard stopped his wedge; the blacks buffeted into their shields with a shock that scattered and tossed them up like spray. The wedge held firm; red work for axe and swords while it lasted. They killed most of the Nubians, drove bodily through the rabble at their heels; then into the square of the citadel they came. It was packed with a shrieking horde, whose drums made the day a hell, whose great banners wagged and rocked like osiers in a flood-water. They were trying to fire the citadel, and some were swarming the walls from others' backs. The square was like a whirlpool in the sea, a sea of tense faces whose waves were surging men and the flying wrack their gonfanons.

King Richard saw how matters lay in this horrible hive; these men could not fight so close. Cavalry can do nothing in a dense mass of foot, bowmen cannot shoot confined; spearmen against swords are little worth, javelins sped once. So much he saw, and also the straining crowd, the lifted, threatening arms, the stretched necks about the citadel. 'O Lord, the heathen are come into Thine inheritance. At the word, sirs, cleave a way.' And then he cried above the infernal riot, 'Save, Holy Sepulchre! Save, Saint George!' and the wedge drove into the thick of them.

This work was butcher's work, like sawing through live flesh. Too much blood in the business: after a while the haft of the King's axe got rotten with it, and at a certain last blow gave way and bent like a pulpy stock. He helped himself to a beheaded Mameluke's scimitar, and did his affair with that. Once, twice, thrice, and four times they furrowed that swarm of men; nothing broke their line. Richard himself was only cut in the feet, where he trod on mailed bodies or broken swords; the others (being themselves in mail) were without scathe. They held the square until the Count of Champagne came up with knights and Pisan arbalestiers, and then the day was won. They drove out the invaders; on the Templars' house they ran up the English dragon-flag. King Richard rested himself.

Two days later a pitched battle was fought on the slopes above Joppa. Saladin met Richard for the last time, and the Melek worsted him. Our King with fifteen knights played the wedge again when his enemy was packed to his taste; and this time (being known) with less carnage. But the left wing of the invading army re-entered the town, the garrison had a panic. Richard wheeled and scoured them out at the other end; so they perished in the sea. Men say, who saw him, that

he did it alone. So terrible a name he had with
the Saracens, this may very well be. There had
never been seen, said they, such a fighter before.
Like sheep they huddled at his sight, and like
sheep his onset scattered them. 'Let God arise,'
says Milo with a shaking pen: 'and lo! He
arose. O lion in the path, who shall stand up
against thee?'

He drove Saladin into the hills, and set him
manning once more the watch-towers of Jerusalem. But he had reached his limit; sickness
fastened on him, and on the ebb of his fury came
lagging old despair. For a week he lay in his
bed delirious, babbling breathless foolish things of
Jehane and the Dark Tower, of the broomy downs
by Poictiers, the hills of Languedoc, of Henry his
handsome brother, of Bertran de Born and the
falcon at Le Puy. Then followed a pleasant
thing. Saladin, the noble foe, heard of it, and
sent Saphadin his brother to visit him. They
brought the great Emir into the tent of his
great enemy.

'O God of the Christians!' cried he with tears,
'what is this work of thine, to make such a mirror of thy might, and then to shatter the glass?'
He kissed King Richard's burning forehead, then
stood facing the standers-by.

'I tell you, my lords, there has been no such
king as this in our country. My brother the
Sultan would rather lose Jerusalem than have
such a man to die.'

At this Richard opened his eyes. 'Eh, Saphadin, my friend,' he says, 'death is not mine yet,
nor Jerusalem either. Make me a truce with my

brother Saladin for three years. Then with the
grace of God I will come and fight him again.
But for this time I am spent.'

'Are you wounded, dear sire?' asked Saphadin.

'Wounded?' said the King in a whisper.
'Yes, wounded in the soul, and in the heart —
sick, sick, sick.'

Saphadin, kneeling down, kissed his ring.
'May the God whom in secret we both worship,
the God of Gods, do well by you, my brother.'
So he said, and Richard nodded and smiled at
him kindly.

When peace was made they carried him to his
ship. The fleet went to Acre.

CHAPTER X

THE CHAPTER CALLED BONDS

KING RICHARD sent for his sister Joan of Sicily
on the morrow of his coming to Acre, and thus
addressed her: 'Let me hear now, sister, the truth
of what passed when the Queen saw Madame
d'Anjou.'

'Madame d'Anjou!' cried Joan, who (as you
know) had plenty of spirit; 'I think you rob the
Queen of a title there.'

'I cannot rob her of what she never had,' said
King Richard; 'but I will repeat my question if
you do not remember it.'

'No need, sire,' replied the lady, and told him
all she knew. She added, 'Sire and my brother,
if I may dare to say so, I think the Queen has a
grief. Madame Jehane made no pretensions — I
hope I do her full justice — but remember that
the Queen made none either. You took her of
your royal will; she was conscious of the honour.
But of what you gave you took away more than
half. The Queen loves you, Richard; she is a
most miserable lady, yet there is time still. Make
a wife of your queen, brother Richard, and all
will be well. For what other reason in the world
did Madame Jehane what she did? For love of
an old man whom she had never seen, do you
think?'

The King's brow grew dark red. He spoke deliberately. ' I will never make her my wife. I will never willingly see her again. I should sin against religion or honour if I did either. I will never do that. Let her go to her own country.'

' Sire, sire,' said Joan, ' how is she to do that ? '

' As she will,' says the King; ' but, for my part of it, with every proper accompaniment.'

' Sire, the dowry —— '

' I return it, every groat.'

' The affront —— '

' The affront is offered. I prevent a greater affront.'

' Is this fixed, Richard ? '

' Irrevocably.'

' She loves you, sire ! '

' She loves ill. Get up on your feet.'

' Sire, I beseech you pity her.'

' I pity her deeply. I think I pity everybody with whom I have had to deal. I do not choose to have any more pitiful persons about me. Fare you well, sister. Go, lest I pity you.' She pleaded.

' Ah, sire ! '

' The audience is at an end,' said the King; and the Queen of Sicily rose to take leave.

He kept his word, never saw Berengère again but once, and that was not yet. What remained for him to do in Syria he did, patched up a truce with Saladin, saw to Henry of Champagne's election, to Guy of Lusignan's establishment; dealt out such rewards and punishments as lay in his power, sent the two queens with a convoy

to Marseilles. Then, two years from his hopeful
entry into Acre as a conqueror, he left it a defeated
man. He had won every battle he had fought
and taken every city he had invested. His allies
had beaten him, not the heathen.

They were to beat him again, with help. The
very skies took their part. He was beset by
storms from the day he launched on the deep,
separated from his convoy, driven from one shore
to another, fatally delayed. His enemies had
time to gather at home: Eustace of Saint-Pol,
Beauvais, Philip of France; and behind all these
was John of Mortain, moving heaven and earth
and them to get him a realm. By a providence,
as he thought it, Richard put into Corsica under
stress of weather, and there heard how the land
lay in Gaul. Philip had won over Raymond of
Toulouse, Saint-Pol heading a joint-army of theirs
was near Marseilles, ready to destroy him. King
Richard was to walk into a trap. By this time,
you must know, he had no more to his power
than the galley he rode in, and three others. He
had no Des Barres, no Gaston, no Béziers; he
had not even Mercadet his captain, and no
thought where they might be. The trap would
have caught him fast.

'Pretty work,' he said, 'pretty work. But I
will better it.' He put about, and steered round
Sicily for the coast of Dalmatia; here was caught
again by furious gales, lost three ships out of the
four he had, and finally sought haven at Gazara,
a little fishing village on that empty shore. His
intention was to travel home by way of Germany
and the Low Countries, and so land in England

while his brother John was still in France. Either
he had forgotten, or did not care to remember,
that all this country was a fief of the Archduke
Luitpold's. He knew, of course, that Luitpold
hated him, but not that he held him guilty of
Montferrat's murder. Suspecting no great difficulty, he sent up messengers to the lord of Gazara
for a safe-conduct for certain merchants, pilgrims. This man was an Austrian knight called
Gunther.

'Who are your pilgrims?' Gunther asked; and
was told, Master Hugh, a merchant of Alost, he
and his servants.

'What manner of a merchant?' was Gunther's
next question.

'My lord,' they said, who had seen him, 'a fine
man, tall as a tree, and strong and straight, having
keen blue eyes, and a reddish beard on his chin,
as the men of Flanders do not use.'

Gunther said, 'Let me see this merchant,' and
went down to the inn where King Richard was.

Now Richard was sitting by the fire, warming
himself. When Gunther came in, furred and
portly, he did not rise up; which was unfortunate
in a pretended merchant.

'Are you Master Hugh of Alost?' Gunther
asked, looking him over.

'That is the name I bear,' said Richard. 'And
who are you, my friend?'

The Austrian stammered. 'Hey, thou dear
God, I am Lord Gunther of this castle and town!'
he said, raising his voice. Then the King got up
to make a reverence, and in so doing betrayed his
stature.

' I should have guessed it, sir, by your gentle-
ness in coming to visit me here. I ask your
pardon.' Thus the King, while Gunther wondered.

' You are a very tall merchant, Hugh,' says he.
' Do they make your sort in Alost?' King
Richard laughed.

' It is the only advantage I have of your lordship. For the rest, my countrywomen make
straight men, I think.'

' Were you bred in Alost, Master Hugh?' asked
Gunther suspiciously; and again Richard laughed
as he said, ' Ah, you must ask my mother, Lord
Gunther.'

' Lightning!' was the Austrian's thought; 'here
is a pretty easy merchant.'

He raised some little difficulties, vexations of
routine, which King Richard persistently laughed
at, while doing his best to fulfil them. Gunther
did not relish this. He named the Archduke as
his overlord, hard upon strangers. Richard let it
slip that he did not greatly esteem the Archduke.
However, in the end he got his safe-conduct, and
all would have been well if, on leaving Gazara, he
had not overpaid the bill.

Overpay is not the word: he drowned the bill.
In a hurry for the road, the innkeeper fretted him.
' Reckoning, landlord!' he cried, with one foot
in the stirrup: 'how the devil am I to reckon
half-way up a horse? Here, reckon yourself, my
man, and content you with these.' He threw a
fistful of gold besants on the flags, turned his
horse sharply and cantered out of the yard.
' Colossal man!' gasped the innkeeper. ' King or

devil, but no merchant under the sun.' So the news spread abroad, and Gunther puffed his cheeks over it. A six-foot-two man, a monstrous leisurely merchant, who rose not to the lord of a castle and town, who did not wait for his lordship's humour, but found laughable matter in his own; who was taller than the Archduke and thought his Grace a dull dog; who made a Danaë of his landlord! Was this man Jove? Who could think the Archduke a dull dog except an Emperor, or, perhaps, a great king? A king: stay now. There were wandering kings abroad. How if Richard of England had lost his way? Here he slapped his thigh: but this must be Richard of England — what other king was so tall? And in that case, O thunder in the sky, he had let slip his Archduke's deadly enemy! He howled for his lanzknechts, his boots, helmet, great sword; he set off at once, and riding by forest ways, cut off the merchant in a day and a night. He ran him to earth in the small wooden inn of a small wooden village high up in the Carinthian Alps, Blomau by name, which lies in a forest clearing on the road to Gratz.

King Richard was drinking sour beer in the kitchen, and not liking it. The lanzknechts surrounded the house; Gunther with two of them behind him came clattering in. Glad of the diversion, Richard looked up.

'Ha, here is Lord Gunther again,' said he. 'Better than beer.'

'King Richard of England,' said the Austrian, white by nature, heat, and his feelings, 'I make you my prisoner.'

'So it seems,' replied the King; 'sit down, Gunther. I offer you beer and a most indifferent cheese.'

But Gunther would by no means sit down in the presence of an anointed king for one bidding.

'Ah, sire, it is proper that I should stand before you,' he said huskily, greatly excited.

'It is not at all proper when I tell you to be seated,' returned King Richard. So Gunther sat down and wiped his head, Richard finished his beer; and then they went to sleep on the floor. Early in the morning the prisoner woke up his gaoler.

'Come, Gunther,' he says, 'we had better take the road.'

'I am ready, sire,' says Gunther, manifestly unready. He rose and shook himself.

'Lead, then,' Richard said.

'I follow you, sire.'

'Lead, you white dog,' said the King, and showed his teeth for a moment. The Austrian obeyed. One of Richard's few attendants, a Norman called Martin Vaux, adopted for his own salvation the simple expedient of staying behind; and Gunther was in far too exalted a mood to notice such a trifle. When he and his troop had rounded the forest road, Martin Vaux rounded it also, but in the opposite direction. He was rather a fool, though not fool enough to go to prison if he could help it. Being a seaman by grace, he smelt for his element, and by grace found it after not many days. More of him presently.

Archduke Luitpold was in his good town of
Gratz when news was brought him, and the man.
'Du lieber Gott!' he crowed. 'Ach, mein Gun-
ther!' and embraced his vassal.

His fiery little eyes burned red, as Mars when
he flickers; but he was a gentleman. He took
Richard's proffered hand, and after some fumbling
about, kissed it.

'Ha, sire!' came the words, deeply exultant,
from his big throat. 'Now we are on more equal
terms, it appears.'

'I agree with you, Luitpold,' said the King;
and then, even as the Archduke was wetting his
lips for the purpose, he added, 'But I hope you
will not stretch your privilege so far as to make
me a speech.'

Austria swallowed hard. 'Sire, it would take
many speeches to wipe out the provocations I have
received at your hands. All the speeches in the
councils of the world could not excuse the deaths
of my second cousin the Count of Saint-Pol and
of my first cousin the Marquess of Montferrat.'

'That is true,' replied Richard, 'but neither
could they restore them to life.'

'Sire, sire!' cried the Archduke, 'upon my
soul I believe you guilty of the Marquess's
death.'

'I assumed that you did,' was the King's answer; 'and your protestation adds no weight to
my theory, but otherwise.'

'Do you admit it, King Richard?' The Archduke, an amazed man, looked foolish. His mouth
fell open and his hair stuck out; this gave him
the appearance of a perturbed eagle in a bush.

'I am far from denying it,' says Richard. 'I never deny any charges, and never make any unless I am prepared to pursue them; which is not the case at present.'

'I must keep you in safe hold, sire,' the Archduke said. 'I must communicate with my lord the Roman Emperor.'

'You are in your right, Luitpold,' said King Richard.

The end of the day's work was that the King of England was lodged in a high tower, some sixty feet above the town wall.

Now consider the acts of Martin Vaux, smelling for the sea. In a little time he did better than that, for he saw it from the top of a high mountain, shining far off in the haze, and then had nothing to do but follow down a river-bed, which brought him duly to Trieste. Thence he got a passage to Venice, where the wineshops were too good or too many for him. He talked of his misfortunes, of his broken shoes, of Austrian beer, of his exalted master, of his extreme ingenuity and capacity for all kinds of faithful service. Now Venice was, as it is now, a place *colluvies gentium*. Gaunt, lonely Arabs stalked the narrow streets, or dreamed motionless by the walls of the quay. The city was full of strayed Crusaders, disastrous broken blades, of renegade Christians, renegade Moslems, adaptable Jews, of pilgrims, and chafferers of relics from the holy places. Martin's story spread like the plague, but not (unhappily) to any advantage of King Richard imperturbable in his tower. Martin Vaux then, having drunk up the charity

of Venice, shipped for Ancona.   There too he
met with attentions, for there he met a country-
man of his, the Sieur Gilles de Gurdun, a Norman knight.

When Sir Gilles heard that King Richard was
in prison, but that Jehane was not with him, he
grew very red.   That he had never learned of her
deeds at Acre need not surprise you.   He had
not heard because he had not been to Acre with
the French host, but instead had gone pilgrim to
Jerusalem, and thence with Lusignan to Cyprus.
So now he took Martin Vaux by the windpipe
and shook him till his eyes stared like agate balls.
' Tell me where Madame Jehane is, you clot, or I
finish what I have begun,' he said terribly.   But
Martin could tell him no more, for he was quite
dead.   It was proper, even in Ancona, to be
moving after that; and Gilles was very ready to
move.   The hunger and thirst for Jehane, which
had never left him for long, came aching back
to such a pitch that he felt he must now find
her, see her, touch her, or die.   The King was
her only clue; he must hunt him out wherever he
might be.   One of two things had occurred:
either Richard had tired of her, or he had lost her
by mischance of travel.   There was a third possible thing, that the Queen had had her murdered.
He put that from him, being sure she was not
dead.   ' Death,' said Gilles, ' is great, but not
great enough to have Jehane in her beauty.'   He
really believed this.   So he came back to his two
positions.   If the King had tired of her, he would
not scruple (being as he was) to admit as much
to Gilles.   If he had lost her, he was safe in

prison; and Gilles knew that with time he could find her. But he must be sure. He thought of another thing. 'If he is in prison, in chains, he might be stabbed with certain ease.' His heart exulted at the hot thought.

It was not hard to follow back on Martin's dallying footsteps. He traced him to Venice, to Trieste, up the mountains as far as Blomau. There he lost him, and shot very wide of the mark. In fact, the slow-witted young man went to Vienna on a false rumour — but it boots not recount his wanderings. Six months after he left Ancona, ragged, hatless, unkempt, hungry, he came within sight of the strong towers of Gratz; and as he went limping by the town ditch he heard a clear, high voice singing —

> Li dous consire
> Quem don' Amors soven —

and knew that he had run down his man.

One other, crouching under the wall, most intent watcher, saw him stop as if hit, clap his hand to his shock-head, then listen, brooding, working his jaws from side to side. The voice stayed; Gilles turned and slowly went his way back. He limped under the gateway into the town, and the croucher by the wall peered at him between the meshes of her dishevelled hair.

z

CHAPTER XI

THE CHAPTER CALLED *A LATERE*

THE Old Man of Musse, Lord of all the Assassins, descendant of Ali, Fulness of Light, Master of them that eat hemp, and many things beside, wedded Jehane and made her his principal wife. He valued in her, apart from her bodily perfections, her discretion, obedience, good sense, and that extraordinary sort of pride which makes its possessor humble, so inset it is; too proud, you may say, to give pride a thought. Esteeming her at this price, it is not remarkable if she came to be his only wife.

This was the manner of her life. When her husband left her, which was very early in the morning, she generally slept for an hour, then rose and went to the bath. Her boy was brought to her in the pavilion of the Garden of Fountains; she spent two hours or more with him, teaching him his prayers, the honour of his father, love and duty to his mother, respect for the long purposes of God. At ten o'clock she broke her fast, and afterwards her women sat with her at needlework; and one would sing, or one tell a good tale; or, leave being given, they would gossip among themselves, with a look ever at her for approval or (what rarely happened) disapproval. There was not a soul among her slaves who did not love her,

338

nor one who did not fear her. She talked no
more than she had ever done, but she judged no
less. Many times a day the Old Man sent for
her, or sometimes came to her room, to discuss
his affairs. He never found her out of humour,
dull, perverse, or otherwise than well-disposed to
all his desires. Far from that, every Friday he
gave thanks in the mosque for the gift of such an
admirable wife — grave, discreet, pious, amorous,
chaste, obedient, nimble, complaisant, and most
beautiful, as he hereby declared that he found her.
Being a man of the greatest possible experience,
this was high praise; nor had he been slow in
making up his mind that she was to be trusted.
He was about to prove his deed as good as his
opinion.

Word was brought her on a day, as she sat in
the harem with her boy on her knee, singing to
herself and him some winding song of France,
that this redoubtable lord of hers was waiting to
see her in her chamber. She put the child down
and followed the eunuch. Entering the room
where the Old Man sat, she knelt down, as was
customary, and kissed his knee. He touched
her bent head. 'Rise up, my child,' says he, 'sit
with me for a little. I have matters of concern-
ment for you.' She sat at once by his side; he
took her hand and began to talk to her in this
manner.

'It appears, Jehane, that I am something of a
prophet. Your late master, the Melek Richard,
has fallen into the power of his enemies; he
is now a prisoner of the Archduke's on many
charges: first, the killing of your brother Eudo,

Count of Saint-Pol; but that is a very trifling affair, which occurred, moreover, in fair battle. Next, they accuse him — falsely, as you know — of the death of Montferrat. We may have our own opinion about that. But the prime matter, as I guess, is ransom, and whether those who wish him ill (not for what he has done to them, but for what he has not allowed them to do to him) will suffer him to be ransomed. Now, what have you to say, my child? I see that it affects you.'

Jehane was affected, but not as you might expect. With great self-possession she had a very practical mind. There were neither tears nor heart-beatings, neither panic nor flying of colours. Her eyes sought the Old Man's and remained steadily on them; her lips were firm and red.

'What are you willing to do, sire?' she asked him. Sinan stroked his fine beard.

'I can dispose of the business of Montferrat in a few lines,' he said, considering. 'More, I can reach the Melek and assure him of comfort. What I cannot do so easily, though I admit no failure, mind, is to induce his enemies at home to allow of a ransom.'

'I can do that,' said Jehane, 'if you will do the rest.' The Old Man patted her cheek.

'It is not the custom of my nation to allow wives abroad. You, moreover, are not of that nation. How can I trust the Melek, who (I know) loves you? How can I trust you, who (I know) love the Melek?'

'Oh, sire,' says Jehane, looking him full in the face, 'I came here because I loved my lord Richard; and when I have assured his safety I

shall return here.' She looked down, as she
added — 'For the same reason, and for no other.'
'I quite understand you, child,' said the Old
Man, and put his hand under her chin. This
made her blush, and brought up her face again
quickly.

'Dear sire,' she said shyly, 'you are very kind
to me. If I had another reason for returning it
would be that.' Sinan kissed her.

'And so it shall be, my dear,' he assured her.
'There is time enough. You shall certainly go,
due regard being had to my dignity, and your
health, which is delicate just now.'

'Have no fear for me, my lord,' she said. 'I
am very strong.' He kissed her again, saying, 'I
have never known a woman at once so beautiful
and so strong.'

He wrote two letters, sealing them with his
own signet and that of King Solomon. To the
Archduke he said curtly —

'To the Archduke Luitpold, *Vetus de Monte*
sends greeting. If the Melek Richard be any
way let in the matter of his life and renown, I
bid you take heed that as I served the Marquess
of Montferrat, so also I shall serve your Serenity.'

But the Emperor demanded more civil adver-
tisement: he got a remarkably fine letter.

'To the most exalted man, Henry, by the grace
of God Emperor of the Romans, happy, pious,
ever august, the invincible Conqueror, *Vetus de
Monte*, by the same great Chief of the Assassins,
sends greeting with the kiss of peace. Let your
Celsitude make certain acquaintance with error
in regard to the most illustrious person whom

you have in hold. Not that Melek Richard
caused the death of the Marquess Conrad; but
I, the Ancient, the Lord of Assassins, Fulness of
Light, for good cause, namely to save my friend
the same Melek from injurious death at the hands
of the Marquess. And him, the said Melek, I
am resolved at all hazards to defend by means of
the silent smiters who serve me. So farewell;
and may He protect your Celsitude whom we
diversely worship.'

As with every business of the Old Man's, preparations were soon and silently made. In three
or four days' time Jehane strained the young
Fulke to her bosom, took affectionate humble
leave of her master, and left the green valley of
Lebanon on her embassy.

She was sent down to the coast in the manner
becoming the estate of a Sultan's favourite wife.
She never set foot on the ground, never even saw
it. She was in a close-curtained litter, herself
veiled to the eyes. Sitting with her was a vast
old Turkish woman, whom in the harem they
called the Mother of Flowers. Mules bore the
litter, eunuchs on mules surrounded it. On all
sides, a third line of defence, rode the janissaries,
hooded in white, on white Arabian horses. So
they came swiftly to Tortosa, whose lord, in strict
alliance with him of Musse, little knew that in
paying homage to the shrouded cage he was cap-
in-hand to Jehane of Picardy. Long galleys
took up the burden of the mountain roads,
dipped and furrowed across the Ægean, and
touched land at Salonika. Hence by relays of
bearers Jehane was carried darkly to Marburg

in Styria, where at last she saw the face of the
sky.

They took her to the inn and unveiled her.
Then the chief of the eunuchs handed her a paper
which he had written himself, being deprived of a
tongue : — ' Madame, Fragrance of the Harem,
Gulzareen (which is to say, Golden Rose), thus I
am commanded by my dreadful master. From
this hour and place you are free to do what seems
best to your wisdom. The letters of our lord will
be sent forward by the proper bearers of them,
one to Gratz, where the Archduke watches the
Melek, and one to the Emperor of the Romans,
wherever he may be found. In Gratz is he whom
you seek. This day six months I shall be here to
attend your Sufficiency.' He bowed three times,
and went away.

' Now, mother,' said Jehane to the old duenna,
' do for me what I bid you, and quickly. Get me
brown juice for my skin, and a ragged kirtle and
bodice, such as the Egyptians wear. Give me
money to line it, and then let me go.' All this
was done. Jehane put on vile raiment which
barely covered her, stained her fair face, neck,
and arms brown, and let her hair droop all about
her. Then she went barefoot out, hugging herself against the cold, being three months gone
with child, and took the road over barren moor-
land to Gratz.

She had not seen King Richard for nearly two
years, at the thought of which thing and of him
the hot blood leapt up, to thrust and tingle in her
face. She did not mean to see him now if she
could help it, for she knew just how far she could

withstand him; she would save him and then go back. Thus she reasoned with herself as she trudged: ' Jehane, ma mye, thou art wife now to a wise old man, who is good to thee, and has exalted thee above all his women. Thou must have no lovers now. Only save him, save him, save him, Lord Jesus, Lady Mary!' She treated this as a prayer, and kept it very near her lips all the way to Gratz, except when she felt herself flush all over with the thought, 'School of God! Is so great a king to be prayed for, as if he were a sick monk?' Nevertheless, she prayed more than she flushed. Nothing disturbed her; she slept in woods, in byres, in stackyards; bought what she needed for food, attracted no attention, and got no annoyance worthy the name. At the closing in of the fifth day she saw the walls of the city rise above the black moors into the sky, and the towers above them. The dome of a church, gilded, caught the dying sun's eye; its towers were monstrous tall, round, and peaked with caps of green copper. On the walls she counted seven other towers, heavy, squat, flat-roofed fortresses with huge battlements. A great flag hung in folds, motionless about a staff. All was a uniform dun, muffled in stormy sky, lowering, remote from knowledge, and alien.

But Jehane herself was of the North, and not impressionable. Grey skies were familiar tents to her, moorlands roomy places, one heap of stones much like another. But her heart beat high to know Richard half a league away; all her trouble was how she should find him in such a great town. It was dusk when she reached it; they were about to shut the gates. She let them, hav·

ing seen that there were booths and hovels at the
barriers, even a little church. It was there she
spent the night, huddled in a corner by the altar.
  Dawn is a laggard in Styria. She awoke before
it was really light, and crept out, munching a crust.
The suburb was dead asleep, a little breeze ruffled
the poplars, and blew wrinkles on the town ditch.
About and about the walls she went, peering up at
their ragged edge, at the huge crumbling towers,
at the storks on steep roofs. ' Eh, Lord God.
here lies in torment my lovely king!' she cried
to herself. The keen breeze freshened, the cloud-
wrack went racing westward; it left the sky clean
and bare. Out of the east came the red sun, and
struck fire upon the dome of Saint Stanislas. Out
of a high window then came the sound of a man
singing, a sharp strong voice, tremulous in the
open notes. She held her bosom as she heard —

> Al entrada del tems clar, eya !
> Per joja recomençar, eya !
> Vol la regina mostrar
> Qu'el' es si amoroza.

The sun kindled her lifted face, filled her wet eyes
with light, and glistened on her praying lips.
  After that her duty was clear, as she conceived
it. She dared not attempt the tower: that would
reveal her to him. But she could not leave it.
She must wait to learn the effect of her lord's
letter, wait to see the bearer of it: here she would
wait, where she could press the stones which bore
up the stones pressed by Richard. So she did,
crouching on the earth by the wall, sheltered
against the wind or the wet by either side of a

buttress, getting her food sparingly from the booths
at the gate, or of charity.   The townsmen of Gratz,
hoarse-voiced touzleheads mostly, divined her to
be an anchoress, a saint, or an unfortunate.   She
was not of their country, for her hair was burnt
yellow like a Lombard's, and her eyes green; her
face, tanned and searching, was like a Hunga-
rian's; they thought that she wove spells with
her long hands.   On this account at first she was
driven away on to the moors; but she always
returned to her place in the angle, and counted
that a day gained when she knew by Richard's
strong singing that he yet lived.   His songs told
her more than that: they were all of love, and if
her name came not in her image did.   She knew
by the mere pitch of his voice — who so well? —
when he was occupied with her and when not.
Mostly he sang all the morning from the moment
the sun struck his window.   Thus she judged him
a light sleeper.   From noon to four there was no
sound; surely then he slept.   He sang fitfully in
the evening, not so saliently; more at night, if
there was a moon; and generally he closed his
eyes with a stave of *Li dous consire*, that song
which he had made of and for her.

When she had been sitting there for upwards
of a month, and still no sign from the bearer of
the letter, she saw Gilles de Gurdun come halting
up the poplar avenue and pry about the walls,
much as she herself had done.   She knew him
at once for all his tatters, this square-faced, low-
browed Norman.   How he came there, if not as
a slot-hound comes, she could not guess; but she
knew perfectly well what he was about.   The

blood-instinct had led him, inflexible man, from
far Acre across the seas, over the sharp mountains and enormous plains; the blood-instinct
had brought him as truly as ever love led her—
more truly, indeed. Here he was, with murder
still in his heart.

Watching him through the meshes of her hair,
elbowing her arms on her knees, she thought,
What should she do? Plead? Nay, dare she
plead for so royal a head, for so great a heart,
so great a king, for one so nearly god that, for
a sacrifice, she could have yielded up no more to
very God? This strife tore her to pieces, while
Gurdun snuffled round the walls, actually round
the buttress where she crouched, spying out the
entries. On one side she feared Gilles, on the
other scorned what he could do. There was
the leper! He made Gilles terrible; even her
sacrifice on Lebanon might not avail against
such as he. But King Richard! But this strong
singer! But this god of war! Gilles came round
the walls for a second time, nosing here and there,
stopping, shaking his head, limping on. Then
she heard the King's voice singing, high and
sharp and spiring; his glorious voice, keener
than any man's, as pure as any boy's, singing
with astounding gaiety, '*Al entrada del tems
clar, eya!*'

Gilles stopped as one struck, and gaped up
at the tower. To see his stupid mouth open,
Jehane's bosom heaved with pride well-nigh in-
sufferable. Had any woman, since Mary conceived, such a lover as hers! 'Oh, Gilles, Gilles,
go you on with your knife in your vest. What

can you do, little oaf, against King Richard?'
Gilles went in by the gate, and she let him go.
He was away two days, by which time she had
cause to alter her mind.   The prisoner sang
nothing; and presently a man dressed like a
Bohemian came out of the town and spoke to
her.   This was Cogia, the Assassin, bearer of
the letter.

'Well, Cogia?' said Jehane, holding herself.

'Mistress, the letter of our lord has been
delivered.   I think it may go hard with the
Melek.'

'What, Cogia?   Does the Archduke dare?'

'The   Archduke,   mistress,   desires   not   the
Melek's death.   He is a worthy man.   But many
do desire it — kings of the West, kinsmen of the
Marquess, above all the Melek's blood-brother.
One of that prince's men, as I judge him, is with
him now — one of your country, mistress.'

In a vision she saw the leper again, a dull
smear in the sunny waste, scratching himself on
a white stone.   She saw him come hopping from
rock to rock, his wagging finger, shapeless face,
tongueless voice.

'Mistress ——' said Cogia.   She turned blank
eyes upon him.   'I pray,' she said; 'I pray.   Has
God no pity?'

Cogia shrugged.   'What has God to do with
pity?   The end of the world is in His hand
already.   The Melek is a king, and the Norman
dung in his sight.   Who knows the end but God,
and how shall He pity what He hath decreed for
wisdom?   This I say, if the King dies the man
dies.'

Jehane threw up her head. 'The King will not die, Cogia. Yet to-morrow, if the man comes not out, I will go to seek him.'

Early in the morning Gilles did come out, turned the angle of the ditch, and shuffled towards her, his head hung. Jehane moved swiftly out from the shadow of the buttress and confronted him. She folded her arms over her breast; and at that moment the shadow of Richard's tower was capped with the shadow of Richard himself. But she saw nothing of this. 'Halt there, Sir Gilles,' she said. The Norman gave a squeal, like a hog startled at his trough, and went dead-fire colour.

'Ha, Heart of Jesus!' said Gilles de Gurdun.

CHAPTER XII

ONE very great power of King Richard's had never served him better than now, the power of immense quiescence, whereunder he could sit by day or by night as inert as a stone, a block hewn into shape of a man, neither to be moved by outside fret nor by the workings of his own mind. Into this rapt state he fell when the prison doors shut on him, and so remained for three or four weeks, alone while the Fates were spinning. The Archduke came daily to him with speeches, injuries to relate, injuries to impart. King Richard hardly winked an eyelid. The Archduke hinted at ransom, and Richard watched the wall behind his head; he spoke of letters received from this great man or that, which made ransom not to be thought of; and Richard went to sleep. What are you to do with a man who meets your offers and threats with the same vast unconcern? If it is matter for resentment, Richard gave it; if it is a matter which money may leaven, it is to be observed that while Richard offered no money his enemies offered much.

These letters to the Archduke were not of the sort which fill the austere folios of the Codex Diplomaticus as bins with bran, or make Rymer's book as dry as Ezekiel's valley. They were pun-

gent, pertinent, allusive, succinct, supplementing,
as with meat, those others. The Count of Saint-
Pol wrote, for instance, 'Kinsman, kill the killer
of your kin,' and could hardly have expressed
himself better under the circumstances. King
Philip of France sent two letters: one by a herald, very long, and chiefly in the language of the
Epistle of Saint James, designed for the Codex.
The other lay in the vest of a Savigniac monk,
and was to this effect: ' In a ridded acre the hus-
bandman can sow with hopes of good harvesting.
When the corn is garnered he calleth about
him his friends and fellow-labourers, and cheer
abounds. Labour and pray. I pray.' Last came
a limping pilgrim from Aquitaine, whose hat was
covered with metal saints, and in his left shoe a
wad of parchment, which had made him limp.
This proved to be a letter from John Count of
Mortain, which said, ' Now I see in secret. But
when I am come into my kingdom I will reward
openly.' The Archduke was by no means a wise
man ; but it was not easy to know something of
European politics and mistake the meaning of
letters like these. If it was a question of money,
here was money. And imagine now the Archduke, bursting with the urgent secrets of so many
princes, making speeches about them — through
all of which King Richard slumbered ! ' Damn
it, he flouts me, does he ? ' said Austria at last ;
and left him alone. From that moment Richard
began to sing.

Let us do no wrong to Luitpold: it was not
merely a question of money, but money turned the
scale. Not only had Richard mortally affronted

his gaoler; he had innumerably offended him.
The Archduke was punctilious; Richard with his
petulant foot stamped on every little point he
laboured, or else, like a buttress, let him labour
them in vain.   He did not for a moment disguise
his fatigue in Luitpold's presence, his relief at his
absence, or his unconcern with his properties.
This galled the man.   He could not, for the life
of him, affect indifference to Richard's indifference.   When the messenger, therefore, arrived
from the Old Man of Musse, the insolence of the
message was most unfortunate.   The Archduke,
angry as he was, could afford to be cool.   He
played on the Old Man the very part which Richard had played on him — that is, treated him and
his letter as though they were not.

Then he broke with Richard altogether; and
then came Gilles de Gurdun with secret words
and offers.

The Archduke drained his beer-horn, and with
his big hand wrung his beard dry.   He winked
hard at Gilles, whom he thought to be a hired
assassin of deplorable address sent, probably, by
Count John.

'Are you angry enough to do what you propose?' he asked him.   'I am not, let me tell you.'

'I have been trying to kill him for four years,'
said Gilles.

'And are you man enough, my fellow?'   Gilles
cast down his eyes.

'I have not been man enough yet, since he
still lives.   I think I am now.'   Then there was
a pause.

'What is your price?' asked Luitpold after this.

Gilles said, 'I have no price'; and the Archduke, 'You suit my humour exactly.'

Richard, I say, had begun to sing from the day he was sure that the Archduke had given him up. Physical relief may have had something to do with that, but moral certainty had more. What made him fume or freeze was doubt. There was very little room for doubt just now but that his enemies would prove too many for Austria's scruples. His friends? He was not aware that he had any friends. Des Barres, Gaston, Auvergne, Milo? What did they amount to? His sister Joan, his mother, his brothers? Here he shrugged, knowing his own race too well. He had never heard of the Angevin who helped any Angevin but himself. Lastly, Jehane. He had lost her by his own fault and her extreme nobility. Let her go, glorious among women! He was alone. Odd creature, he began to sing.

Singing like a genius to the broad splash of sunlight on brickwork, Gilles de Gurdun found him. Richard was sitting on a bench against the wall, one knee clasped in his hands, his head thrown back, his throat rippling with the tide of his music. He looked as fresh and gallant a figure as ever in his life; his beard trimmed sharply, his strong hair brushed back, his doublet green, his trunks of fine leather, his shoes of yet finer. The song he was upon was *Li Chastel d'Amors*, which runs —

> Las portas son de parlar
> Al eissir e al entrar :
> Qui gen non sab razonar,

2 A

Defors li ven a estar.
E las claus son de prejar:
Ab cel obron li cortes —

and so on through many verses, made continuous
by the fact that the end of each sixth line forms
the rhyme of the next five. Now, Gilles knew
nothing of Southern minstrelsy, and if he had,
the pitch he was screwed to would have shrilled
such knowledge out of him. At ' *Defors li ven a
estar*,' he came in, and sturdily forward. Richard
saw him and put up his hand: on went the ham-
mered rhymes —

E las claus son de prejar:
Ab cel obron li cortes.

Here was a little break. Gilles, very dark, took a
step; up shot Richard's warning hand —

Dedinz la clauson qu'i és
Son las mazos dels borges . . .

On went the exulting voice after the new rhymes,
gayer and yet more gay. *Li Chastel d'Amors* has
twelve linked verses, and King Richard, wound
up in their music, sang them all. When at last
he had stopped, he said, ' Now, Gurdun, what do
you want here?'

Gilles came a step or two of his way, and so
again a step or two, and so again, by jerks.
When he was so near that it was to be seen what
he had in his right hand, the King got up. Gilles
saw that he had light fetters on his ankles which
could not stop his walking. Richard folded his
arms.

' Oh, Gurdun,' he said, ' what a fool you are.'

Gurdun vented a sob of rage, and flung himself
forward at his enemy. He was a shorter man,
but very thickset, with arms like steel. He had
a knife, rage like a thirst, he was free. Richard,
as he came on, hit him full on the chin, and sent
him flying. Gurdun picked himself up again, his
mouth twitching, his eyes so small as to be like
slits. Knife in hand he leaned against the wall
to fetch up his breath.

'Well,' said Richard, 'Have you had enough?'

'Yes, you wolf,' said Gurdun, 'I shall wait till
it is dark.'

'I think it may suit you better,' was the King's
comment as he sat down on the bed. Gurdun
squatted by the wall, watching him. After about
an hour of humming airs to himself Richard lay
full length, and in a short time Gilles ascertained
that he was asleep. This brought tears into the
man's eyes; he began to cry freely. Virgin
Mary! Virgin Mary! why could he not kill this
frozen devil of a king? Was there a race in the
world which bred such men, to sleep with the
knife at the throat? He rose to his feet, went to
look at the sleeper; but he knew he could not do
his work. He ranged the room incessantly, and
at every second or third turn brought up short
by the bed. Sometimes he flashed up his long
knife; it always stayed the length of his arm,
then flapped down to his flank in dejection. 'If
he wakes not I must go away. I cannot do it so,'
he told himself, as finally he sat down by the
wall. It grew dusk. He was tired, sick, giddy;
his head dropped, he slept. When he woke up,
as with a snort he did, it was inky dark. Now

was the time, not even God could see him now.
He turned himself about; inch by inch he crept
forward, edging along by the bed's edge. Pain-
fully he got on his knees, threw up his head.
'Jehane, my robbed lost soul!' he howled, and
stabbed with all his might. King Richard, cat-
like behind him, caught him by the hair, and
cuffed his ears till they sang.

'Ah, dastard cur! Ah, mongrel! Ah, white-
galled Norman eft! God's feet, if I pommel you
for this!' Pommel him he did; and, having
drawn blood at his ears, he turned him over his
knee as if he had been a schoolboy, and lathered
his rump with a chair-leg. This humiliating
punishment had humiliating effects. Gilles believed himself a boy in the cloister-school again,
with his smock up. 'Mea culpa, mea culpa!
Hey, reverend father, have pity!' he began to
roar. Dropping him at last, Richard tumbled
him on to the bed. 'Blubber yourself to sleep,
clown,' he told him. 'Blessed ass, I have heard
you snoring these two hours, snoring and root-
ling over your jack-knife. Sleep, man. But if
you rootle again I flog again: mind you that.'
Gilles slept long, and was awoken in full light by
the sound of King Richard calling for his breakfast.

The gaoler came pale-faced in. 'A thousand
pardons, sire, a thousand pardons ——'

'Bring my food, Dietrich,' says Richard, 'and
send the barber. Also, the next time the Archduke desires murder done let him find a fellow
who knows his trade. This one is a bungler.
Here's the third time to my knowledge he has
missed. Off with you.'

Gilles lay face downwards, abject on the bed. In came the King's breakfast, a jug of wine, some white bread. The King's beard was trimmed, his hair brushed, fresh clothes put on. He dismissed his attendants, crossed over the room like a stalking cat, and gave Gilles a clap behind which made him leap in the air.

'Get up, Gurdun,' said Richard. 'Tell me that you are ashamed of yourself, and then listen to me.'

Gilles went down on one knee. 'God knows, my lord King,' he mumbled, 'that I have done shamefully by you.' He got up, his face clouded, his jaw went square. 'But not more shamefully, by the same God, than you have done by me.'

The King looked at him. 'I have never justified myself to any man,' he said quietly, 'nor shall I now to you. I take the consequences of all my deeds when and as they come. But from the like of you none will ever come. I speak of men. Now I will tell you this very plainly. The next time you cross my path adversely, I shall kill you. You are a nuisance, not because you desire my life, but because you never get it. Try no more, Gurdun.'

'Where is Jehane, my lord?' said Gurdun, very black.

'I cannot tell you where the Countess of Anjou may be,' he was answered. 'She is not here, and is not in France. I believe she is in Palestine.'

'Palestine! Palestine! Lord Christ, have you turned her away?' Gilles cried, beside himself. Again King Richard looked at him, but afterwards shrugged.

'You speak after your kind. Now, Gurdun,
get you home. Go to my friends in Normandy,
to my brother Mortain, to my brother of Rouen;
bid them raise a ransom. I must go back. You
have disturbed me, sickened me of assassination,
reminded me of what I intended to forget. If I
get any more assassins I shall break prison and
the Archduke's head, and I should be sorry to do
that, as I have no grudge against him. Find Des
Barres, Gurdun, raise all Normandy. Find above
all Mercadet, and set him to work in Poictou.
As for England, my brother Geoffrey will see to
it. Aquitaine I leave to the Lord of Béarn. Off
now, Gurdun, do as I bid you. But if you speak
another word to me of Madame d'Anjou, by
God's death I will wring your neck. You are not
fit to speak of me: how should you dare speak of
her? You! A stab-i'-the-dark, a black-entry
cutter of throats, a hedgerow knifer! Foh, you
had better speak nothing, but be off. Stay, I will
call the castellan.' And so he did, roaring through
the key-hole. The gaoler came up flying.

'Conduct this animal into the fresh air, Dietrich,'
said King Richard; 'send him about his business.
Tell your master he will now do better. And
when that is done, let me go on to the leads that
I may walk a little.'

Gurdun followed his guide speechless; but the
Archduke was very vexed, and declined to see
him. 'I decide to be a villain, and he makes me
a vain villain,' said the great man. 'Bid him go
to the devil.' So then Gilles with head hanging
came out of the gate, and Jehane leaped from her
angle to confront him.

To say that he dropped like a shot bird is to say wrong; for a bird drops compact, but Gilles went down disjunct. His jaw dropped, his hands dropped, his knees, last his head. 'Ha, Heart of Jesus!' he said, and covered his eyes. She began to talk like a hissing snake.

'What have you done with the King? What have you done?' King Richard on the roof peered down and saw her. He turned quite grey.

'I could do nothing, Jehane,' Gilles whimpered; 'I went to kill him.'

'You fool, I know it. I saw you go. I could have stayed you as I do now. But I would not.'

'Why not, Jehane?'

She spurned him with a look. 'Because I love King Richard, and know you, Gilles, what you can do and what not. Pshutt! You are a rat.'

'Rat,' says Gilles, 'I may be, but a rat may be offended. This king robbed me of you, and slew my father and brothers. Therefore I hated him. Is it not enough reason?'

Her eyes grew cold with scorn. 'Your father? Your brothers?' she echoed him. 'Pooh, I have given him more than that. I have burned my heart quite dry. I have accepted shame, I have sold my body and counted as nothing my soul. Robbed you? Nay, but I robbed myself, and robbed him also, when I cut him out of my own flesh. From the day when, through my prayers against blood, he was affianced to the Spanish woman, I held him off me, though I drained more blood to do it. Then, that not sufficing to save him, I gave myself to the Old Man of Musse; to be his wife, one of his women, do you understand? His wife, I say. And you talk now of father and brothers and your robbery, to me who am become an old man's toy, one of many? What are they to my soul, and my heart's blood, to my life and light, and the glory that I had from Richard? Oh, you fool, you fool, what do you know of love? You think it is embracing, clipping, playing with a chin: you fool, it is scorching your heart black, it is welling blood by drops, it is fasting in sight of food, death where sweet life offers, shame held more honourable than honour. Oh, Saint Mary, star of women, what do men know of love?' Dry-eyed and pinched, she looked about her as if to find an answer in the sullen moors. If she had looked up to the heavy skies she might have had one; for on the tower's top stood King Richard like a ghost.

'Listen now to me, Jehane,' said Gilles, red as fire. 'I have hated your King for four years, and three times sought his life. But now he has beaten me altogether. Too strong, too much king, for a man to dare anything singly against him. What! he slept, and I could not do it; and then I slept, and he awoke and let me lie. Then once again I woke and thought him still sleeping, and stabbed the bed; and he came behind me, stealthy as a cat, and trounced me over his knee like a child. Oh, oh, Jehane, he is more than man, and I by so much less. And now, and now, he sends me out to win his ransom as if I were an old lover of his, and I am going to do it! Why, God in glory look down upon us, what is the force that he hath?'

Gilles now shivered and looked about him;
but Jehane, having mastered her breath, smiled.
'He is King,' she said. 'Come, Gilles, I will
go with you. You shall find the Abbot Milo,
and I the Queen-Mother. I have the ear of
her.'

'I will do as I am bid, Jehane,' said the cowed
man, 'because I needs must.'

As they went away together, King Richard on
the roof threw up his arms to the sky, howling like
a night wolf. 'Now, God, Thou hast stricken
me enough. Now listen Thou, I shall strike if
I can.'

After a while came Cogia the Assassin ; to
whom Jehane said, 'Cogia, I must take a journey
with this man. You shall put us on the way, and
wait for me until I come again.'

'Mistress,' replied Cogia, 'I am your slave.
Do as you will.'

She put on the dress of a religious, Gilles the
weeds of a pilgrim from Jerusalem. Then Cogia
bought them asses in Gratz and led them down to
Trieste. They found a ship going to Bordeaux,
went on board, had a fair passage, passed the
Pillars of Hercules on their tenth day out, and
were in the Gironde in five more. At Bordeaux
they separated. Gilles went to Poictiers in a
company of pilgrims; Jehane, having learned
that Queen Berengère was at Cahors, turned her
face to the Gascon hills. But she had left behind
her a prisoner to whom death could bring the
only ransom worth a thought.

CHAPTER XIII

OF THE LOVE OF WOMEN

'Ask me no more how I did in those days,' writes Abbot Milo. 'Mercy smile upon me in the article of death, but I worked for the ransom of King Richard as (I hope) I should for that of King Christ. Many an abbey of Touraine goes lean now because of me; many a mass is wrought in a pewter chalice that Richard might come home. Yet I soberly believe that Madame Alois, King Philip's sister, was precious above rubies in the work.'

I think he is right. That stricken lady, in the habit of a grey nun of Fontevrault, came by night to Paris, and found her brother with John of Mortain. They had been upon the very business. Philip, not all knave, had been moved by the news of Richard's immobility. He had had some of De Gurdun's report.

'Christ-dieu,' he said, 'a great king calm in chains! And my brother Richard. Yet God knows I hate him.' So he went muttering on. The Count edged in his words as he could.

'He hates you, indeed, sire. He hates me. He hates all of us.'

'I think we could find him reasons for that, my friend, if he lacked them,' said Philip shrewdly. 'Do you know that De Gurdun is in Poictou, come from Styria?'

Count John said nothing; but he did know
it very well. When they announced Madame
Alois the King started, and the Count went
sick white.

'We will receive her Grace,' said Philip, and
advanced towards the door for the purpose. In
she came in her old eager, stumbling, secret way,
knelt in a hurry to kiss her brother's hand, then
rose and looked intently at John of Mortain.

The King said, 'You visit us late, sister; but
your occasions may drive you.'

'They do drive me, sire. I have seen the
Sieur Gilles de Gurdun. King Richard is in
hold at Gratz, and must be delivered.'

'By you, sister?'

'By me, sire.'

'You grow Christian, Madame.'

'It is my need, sire. I have done King Richard a great wrong. This is not tolerable to me.'

'Eh,' says Philip, 'not so fast. Was no wrong
done to you?'

'Wrong was done me,' said the white girl,
'but not by him.'

'The wrong lies in his blood. What though
the wrong-doer is dead? His blood must answer it.'

Alois shivered, and so, for that matter, did
one other there. She answered, 'I pray for his
death. Dying or dead, his blood shall answer
it.'

'You speak darkly, sister.'

'I live in the dark,' said Alois.

'King Richard has affronted my house in you,
sister.'

But she said, 'I have affronted King Richard through his house.'

'Is this all you have to say, Alois?'

'No, sire,' she told him, with a fierce and biting look at Mortain; 'but it is all I need say now.'

It was. A cry broke strangling from the Count. 'Ha, Jesus! Sire! Save my brother!' The wretch could bear no more. The woman's eyes were like swords.

King Philip marvelled. 'You!' he said, 'you!' John put out his hands. 'Oh, sire, Madame is in the right. I am a wicked man. I must make my brother amends. He must be saved.'

King Philip scratched his head. 'Who is in the dark if not I? I will deal with you presently, Mortain. But you, Madame,' he turned hotly on the lady, 'you must be plainer. What is your zeal for the King of England? He is your cousin, and might have been your husband.' Alois flinched, but Philip went roughly on. 'Do you owe him thanks that he is not? Is this what spurs you?'

She looked doubtfully. 'I owe him honour, Philip,' she said slowly. 'He is a great king.'

'Great king, great king!' Philip broke out; 'pest! and great rascal. There is no truth in him, no bottom, no thanks, no esteem. He counts me as nothing.'

'To him,' said Alois, 'you are nothing.'

'Madame,' said Philip, 'I am King of France, your brother and lord. He is my vassal; owes fealty and breaks it, signs treaties and levies war; hectors me and laughs, kills my servants and laughs. He is my cousin, but I am his suzerain.

I do not choose to be mocked. There will be no rest for this kingdom while he is in it.' He stopped, then turned to the shaking man. 'As for you, Count of Mortain, I must have an explanation. My sister loves her enemies: it is a Christian virtue. I have not found it one of yours. You, perhaps, fear your enemies, even caged. Is this your thought? You have made yourself snug in Aquitaine, Count; you are not unknown in Anjou, I think. Do you begin to wish that you might be? Are you, by chance, a little oversnug? I candidly say that I prefer you for my neighbour in those parts. I can deal with you. Do me the obedience to speak.'

'Sire,' said the Count, spreading out his hands, 'Madame Alois has turned me. I am a sinner, but I can restore. My brother is my lord, a clement prince——'

'Pish!' said King Philip, and gave him his back.

'Madame, go to bed,' he said to his sister. 'I shall pay dear for it, but I will not oppose my cousin's ransom. Be content with that.' Alois slipped out. Then he turned upon John like a flash of flame.

'Now, Mortain,' he said, 'what proof is there of that old business of my sister's?'

John showed him a scared eye — the milky eye of a drowned man. 'Ah, God, sire, there is none at all — none — none!' He had no breath. Philip raised his voice.

'Look to yourself; I shall not help you. Leave my lands, go where you will, hide, bury your head, drown yourself. If I spoke what lies bottomed

in my heart I should kill you with mere words.
But there is worse for you in store. There will
be war in France, if I know Richard; but mark
what I say, after that there shall be war in England.'   The thought of Richard overwhelmed
him: he gave a queer little sigh.   'See, now,
how much love and what lives of women are
spent for one tall man, who gives nothing, and
asks nothing, but waits, looking lordly, while they
give and give and give.   Let Richard come, since
women cry for wounds.   But you!'   He flamed
again.   'Get you to hell: you are all a liar.
Avoid me, lest I learn more of you.'

'Dear sire,' John began.   Philip loathed him.
'Ah, get you gone, snake, or I tread upon you,'
he said; and the prince avoided.   So much was
wrought by Alois of France.

No visitation of a dead woman could have
shocked Queen Berengère more suddenly than
the apparition of a tall nun, when she saw it
was Jehane.   She put her hand upon her heart.
'Ah,' she said, 'you trouble me again, Jehane?
Am I never to rest from you?'

Jehane did not falter.   'Do I have any rest?
The King is chained in Styria; he must be
redeemed.   It is your turn.   I saved his life for
you once by selling my own.   Now I am the
wife of an old man, with nothing more to sell.
Do you sell something.'

'Sell?   Sell?   What can I sell that he will
buy?' whined Berengère.   'He loves me not.'

'Well,' said Jehane, 'what has that to do with
it?   Do you not love him?'

'I am his miserable wife. I have nothing to sell.'
'Sell your pride, Berengère,' says Jehane.
Berengère bit her lip.
'You speak strangely to me, woman.'
Says Jehane, 'I am grown strange. Once I
was a girl dishonoured because I loved. Now I
am a wife greatly honoured because I do not
love.'
'You do not love your husband?'
'How should I,' said Jehane, 'when I love
yours? But I honour my husband, and watch
over his honour: he is good to me.'
'You dare to tell me that you love the King?
Ah, you have been with him again!' Jehane
looked critically at her.
'I have not seen him, nor ever shall till he
is dead. But we must save him, you and I,
Berengère.'
Berengère, the little toy woman, when she saw
how noble the other stood, and how inflexible,
came wheedling to her, with hands to touch her
chin.
'Jehane, sister, let it be my part to save
Richard. Indeed I love him. You have done
so much, to you now he should be nothing. Let
me do it, let me do it, please, Jehane!' So she
stroked and coaxed. The tall nun smiled.
'Must I always be giving, and my well never
be dry? Yes, yes, I will trust you. No; you
shall not kiss me yet; I have not done. Go to
the Queen-Mother, go to the King your brother.
Go not to the French King, nor to Count John.
He is more cruel than hyænas, and more a coward.
Find the Abbot Milo, find the Lord of Béarn,

find the Sieur des Barres, find Mercadet. Raise
England, sell your jewels, your crown; eh, God
of Gods, sell your pretty self. The Queen-
Mother is a fierce woman, but she will help you.
Do these things faithfully, and I leave King
Richard's life in your hands. May I trust you?'
The other girl looked up at her, wistfully, still
touching her chin.

'Kiss me, Jehane!'

'Yes, yes, I will kiss you now, Frozen Heart.
You are thawed.'

Jehane, going back to Bordeaux, found Cogia
with a ship, wherein she sailed for Tortosa. But
Berengère, Queen of England, played a queen's
part.

CHAPTER XIV

The burning thought of Jehane cut off, sixty feet below him, yet far as she could ever be, swept across Richard's mind like a roaring wind, and ridded the room for wilder guests. In came stalking Might-have-been and No-more, holding each by a shrinking shoulder the delicate maid of his first delight, Jehane, lissom in a thin gown; Jehane like a bud, with her long hair alight. Her hair was loose, her face aflame; she was very young, very much to be kissed, fresh and tall — Oh, God, the mere loveliness of her! In came the scent of wet stubbles, the fresh salt air of Normandy, the pale gold of the shaws, the pale sky, the mild October sun. He felt again the stoop, again the lift of her to his horse, again the stern ride together; saw again the Dark Tower, and all the love and sweet pleasure that they made. The bride in the church turning her proud shy head, the bride in his arm, clinging as they flew, the bride in the tower, the crowned Countess, the nestling mate — oh, impossibly lost! Inconceivably put away! Eternally his lover and bride!

Pity, if you can, this lonely heart, this king in chains, this hot Angevin, son of Henry, son of Geoffrey, son of Fulke, this Yea-and-Nay. He who dared not look upon the city, lest, seeing, he should risk all to take it, had now looked upon the bride unaware, and could not touch her. The fragrance of her, the sacred air in which a loved woman moves, had floated up to him: his by all the laws of hell, in spite of heaven; but his no more. Such nearness and such deprivation — to see, to desire, and not to seize — flung his wits abroad; from that hour his was a lost soul. Hungry, empty-eyed, ranging, feverish, he lashed up and down his prison-room, with bare teeth gleaming, and desperate soft strides. No thought he had but mere despair, no hope but the mere ravin of a beast. He was across the room in four; he turned, he lunged back; at the wall he threw up his head, turned and lunged, turned and lunged again. He was always at it, or rocking on his bed. No hope, nor thought, nor reckoning had he, but to say Yea against God, Who said him Nay.

So, many times, had he stood, fatal enemy of himself. His Yea would hold fast while none accepted it, his Nay while no one obeyed. But the supple knees of men sickened him of his own decree. ' These fools accept my bidding: the bidding then is foolishness.' So when Fate, so when God, underwrote his bill, *Le Roy le veult*, he scorned himself and the bill, and risked wide heaven to make either nought.

If Austria had murdered him then, it had perhaps been well; but his enemies being silenced, his friends did enemies' work unknowing, by giving him scope to mar himself. The ransom was raised at the price of blood and prayers, the ransom was paid. The Earl of Leicester and Bishop of Salisbury brought it; so the Leopard was loosed. With a quick shake of the head, as if doing violence to himself, he turned his face westward and pushed through the Low Countries to the sea. There he was met by his English peers, by Longchamp, by his brother of Rouen, by men who loved and men who feared; but he had no word for any. Grim and hungry he stalked through the lane they made him, on to the galley; folded in his cloak there, lonely he paced the bridge. He was rowed to the west with his eyes fixed always on the east, away from his kingdom to where he supposed his longing to be. His mother met him at Dunwich: it seemed he knew her not. ' My son, my son Richard,' she said as she knelt to him. 'Get up, Madame,' he bid her; ' I have work to do.' He rode savagely to London through the grey Essex flats; had himself crowned anew; went north with a force to lay Lincolnshire waste; levelled castles, exacted relentless punishment, exorbitant tribute, the last acquittance. He set a red smudge over the middle of England, being altogether in that country three months, a total to his name and reign of a poor six. Then he left it for good and all, carrying away with him grudging men and grudged money, and leaving behind the memory of a stone face which always looked east, a sword, a heart aloof, the myth of a giant knight who spoke no English and did no charity, but was without fear, cruelly just, and as cold as an outland grave. If you ask an Englishman what he thinks of Richard Yea-and-Nay, he will tell you:— That was a king without pity or fear or love, considering neither God, nor the enemy of God, nor unhappy men. If the fear of God is the beginning of wisdom, the love of Him is the end of it. How could King Richard love God, who did not fear enough; or we, who feared too much?

He crossed into Normandy, and at Honfleur was met by them who loved him well; but he repaid them ill. Here also they seemed remote from his acquaintance. Gaston of Béarn, with eyes alight, came dancing down the quay, to be the first to kiss him. Richard, shaking with fever (or what was like fever), gave him a burning dry hand, but looked away from him, always hungrily to the east. Des Barres, who had thrown off allegiance for his love, got no thanks for it. He may have known Abbot Milo again, or Mercadet, his lean good captain: he said nothing to either of them. His friends were confounded: here was the gallant shell of King Richard with a new insatiable tenant. So indeed they found it. There was great business to be done: war, the holding of Assise, the redressing of wrongs from the sea to the Pyrenees. He did it, but in a terrible, hasty way. It appeared that every formal act required fretted him to waste, that every violent act allowed gave him little solace. It appeared that he was living desperately fast, straining to fill up time, rather than use it, towards some unknown, but (to him) certain end. His first act in Normandy, after new coronation, was to besiege the border castles which the French had filched in his absence. One of these was

Gisors. He would not go near Gisors; but conducted the leaguer from Rouen, as a blindfold
man plays chess; and from Rouen he reduced
the great castle in six weeks. One thing more
he did there, which gave Gaston a clue to his
mood. He sent a present of money, a great sum,
to an old priest, curate of Saint-Sulpice; and
when they told him that the man was dead, and
a great part of the church he had served burnt
out by King Philip, his face grew bleak and
withered, and he said, ' Then I will burn Philip
out.' He had Gisors, castle, churches, burgher-
holds, the whole town, burned level with the
ground. There was not to be a stone on a stone:
and it was so. Gaston of Béarn slapped his thigh
when he heard of this : ' Now,' he said, ' now at
last I know what ails my King. He has seen his
lost mistress.'

He did so ruthlessly in Normandy that he went
far to make his power a standing dread to the fair
duchy. On the rock at Les Andelys he built a
huge castle, to hang there like a thunder-cloud
scowling over the flats of the Seine. He called
it, what his temper gave no hint of (so dry with
fever he was), the galliard hold. ' Let me see
Chastel-Gaillard stand ready in a year,' he said.
' Put on every living man in Normandy if need
be.' He planned it all himself ; rock of the rock
it was to be, making the sheer yet more sheer.
He called it again his daughter, daughter of his
conception of Death. ' Build,' said he, ' my
daughter Gaillarda. As I have conceived her
let the great birth be.' And it was so. For a
bitter christening, when all was done, he had his

French prisoners thrown down into the fosse;
and they say that it rained blood upon him and
his artificers as they stood by that accursed font.
The man was mad. Nothing stayed him: for the
first time since they who still loved him had had
him back, they heard him laugh, when his daughter Gaillarda was brought forth. And, 'Spine of
God,' he cried, 'this is a saucy child of mine, and
saucily shall she do by the French power.' Then
his face was wrenched by pain, as with a sob he
said, 'I had a son Fulke.' Gaillarda did saucily
enough, to tyrannise over ten years of Philip's
life; in the end, as all know, she played the
strumpet, and served the enemies of her father's
house, but not while Richard lived to rule her.

He drove Philip into a truce of years, pushed
down into Touraine, and thence went to Anjou,
but not to sit still. He was never still, never
seemed to sleep, or get any of the solace of a man.
He ate voraciously, but was not nourished, drank
long, but was never drunken, revelled without
mirth, hunted, fought, but got no joy. He utterly
refused to see the Queen, who was at Cahors in the
south. 'She is no wife of mine,' he said; 'let her
go home.' Tentative messages were brought by
very tentative messengers from his brother John.
Good service, such and such, had been done in
Languedoc; so and so had been hanged, or gib-
beted, so and so rewarded: what had our dear
and royal brother to say? To each he said the
same thing: 'Let my good brother come.' But
John never came.

No one knew what to make of him; he spoke
to none of his affairs, none dared speak to him.

Milo writes in his book, ' The King came back
from Styria as one who should arise from the grave
with all the secrets of the chattering ghosts to brood
upon.   Some worm gnawed his vitals, some maggot had drilled a hole in his brain.   I know not
what possessed him or what could possess him
beside a devil.   This I know, he never sent to
me for direction in spiritual affairs, nor (so far as
I could learn) to any other religious man.   He
never took the Sacrament, nor seemed to want it.
But be sure he wanted it most grievously.'   So,
insanely ridden, he lived for three years, one of
which would have worn a common man to the
bones.   But the fire still crackled, freely fed ; his
eyes were burning bright, his mind (when he gave
it) was keen, his head (when he lent it) seemed
cool.   What was he living for ?   Did Death himself look askance at such a man ?   Or find him
a good customer who sent him so many souls ?
Two things only were clear : he sent messenger
after messenger to Rome, and he returned his
wife's dowry.   Those must mean divorce or re-
pudiation of marriage.   Certainly the Queen's
party took it so, though the Queen herself clung
pitifully to her throne ; and the Queen's party
grew the larger for the belief.

Such as it was, the Queen's party nested in
Aquitaine and the Limousin, with all the turbulent
lords of that duchy under its flag.   Prince John
himself was with Berengère at Cahors, biting his
nails as was usual with him, one eye watching for
Richard's vengeance, one eye wide for any peace-
offering from the French King.   He dared not
act overtly against Richard, nor dared to take up

arms for him. So he waited. The end was not very far off.

Count Eustace of Saint-Pol was the moving spirit in these parts, grown to be an astute, un-scrupulous man of near thirty years. His spies kept him well informed of Richard's intolerable state ; he knew of the embassies to Rome, of the fierce murdering moods, of the black moods, of the cheerless revelry and fruitless energy of this great stricken Angevin. ' In some such hag-ridden day my enemy may be led to overtax himself,' he considered. To that end he laid a trap. He seized and fortified two hill-castles in the Limousin, be-tween which lay straggling a village called Chaluz. ' Let us get Richard down here,' was his plan. ' He will think the job a light one, and we shall nip him in the hills.' The Bishop of Beauvais lent a hand, so did Adhémar Viscount of Limoges, and Achard the lord of Chaluz, not because he desired, but because he was forced by Limoges his suzerain. Another forced labourer was Sir Gilles de Gurdun, who had been found by Saint-Pol doing work in Poictou, and won over after a few trials.

Now, when King Richard had been some four, nearly five, years at home, neither nearer to his rest nor fitter for it than he had been when he landed, he got word from the south that a great treasure had been found in the Limousin. A man driving the plough on a hillside by Chaluz had upturned a gold table, at which sat an emperor, Charles or another, with his wife and children and the lords of his council, all wrought in fine gold. ' I will have that golden emperor,' said Richard, ' having just made one out of clay. Let him be sent to me.'

He spoke carelessly, as they all thought, simply to get in his gibe at the new Emperor of the Romans, his nephew, whom he had caused to be chosen; and seeing that that was not the treasure he craved, it is like enough. But somebody took his word into Languedoc, and somebody brought back word (Saint-Pol's word) that the Viscount of Limoges, as suzerain of Chaluz, claimed treasure-trove in it. 'Then I will have the Viscount of Limoges as well,' said Richard. 'Let him be sent to me, and the table with him.'

The Viscount did not go. 'We have him, eh, we have him!' cheered Saint-Pol, rubbing his hands together.

But the Viscount, 'Be not so very sure. He may send Gaston or Mercadet. Or if the fit is on him he may come in force. We cannot support that. I believe that you have played a fool's part, Saint-Pol.'

'I am playing a gentleman's part,' replied the other, 'to entrap a villain.'

'Your villain is six foot two inches, and hath arms to agree,' said the Viscount, a dry man.

'We will lay him by the heels, Viscount; we will lop those long arms, cold-blooded, desperate tyrant. He has brought two lovely ladies to misery. Now let him know misery.' Thus Saint-Pol, feeling very sure of himself.

The Queen was at Cahors all this time, living in a convent of white nuns, probably happier than she had ever been in her life before. Count John kept her informed of all Richard's offences; Saint-Pol, you may take my word for it, was so exuber-

antly on her side that it must be almost an offence
in her to refuse him. But she, in a pure mood
of abnegation, would hear nothing against King
Richard. Even when she was told, with proof
positive, that he was in treaty with Rome, she
said not a word to her friends. Secretly she
hugged herself, beginning (like most women) to
find pleasure in pain. ' Let him deny me, let him
deny me thrice, even as Thou wert denied, sweet
Lord Jesus!' she prayed to Christ on the wall.
' So denied, Thou didst not cease from loving. I
think the woman in Thee outcried the man.' She
got a piercing bliss out of each new knife stuck
in her little jumping heart. Once or twice she
wrote to Alois of France, who was at Fontevrault,
in her King's country. ' Dear lady,' she wrote,
' they seek to enrage my lord against me. If you
see him, tell him that I believe nothing that I
hear until I receive the word from his own
glorious mouth.' Alois, chilly in her cell, took
no steps to get speech with King Richard.
' Let her suffer: I suffer,' she would say. And
then, curiously jealous lest more pain should
be Berengère's than was hers, a daughter's
of France, she made haste to send assuring
messages to Cahors. Still Berengère sweetly
agonised. Saint-Pol sent her letters full of love
and duty, enthusiastic, breathing full arms against
her wrongs. But she always replied, ' Count of
Saint-Pol, you do me injury in seeking to redress
your own. I admit nothing against my lord the
King. Many hate him, but I love him. My will
is to be meek. Meekness would become you
very well also.' Saint-Pol could not think so.

Lastly came the intelligence that King Richard in person was moving south with a great force to win the treasure of Chaluz. The news was true. Not only did he dwell with the nervous persistency of the afflicted upon the wretched gold Cæsar, but with clearer political vision saw a chance of subduing all Aquitaine. 'Any stick will do, even Adhémar of Limoges,' he said, not suspecting Saint-Pol's finger in the dish; and told Mercadet to summon the knights, and the knights their array. Before he set out he sent two messengers more — one to Rome, and one much further east. Then he began his warlike preparations with great heart.

CHAPTER XV

JEHANE, called Gulzareen, the Golden Rose, had
borne three children to the Old Man of Musse.
She was suckling the third, and teaching her
eldest, the young Fulke of Anjou, his Creed, or
as much of it as she could remember, when there
came up a herald from Tortosa who bore upon
his tabard the three leopards of England. He
delivered a sealed letter thus superscribed —

'La très-haulte et ma très chère dame, Madame
Jehane, Comtesse d'Anjou, de la part le Roy
Richard. Hastez tousjours.'

The letter was brought to the Old Man as he
sat in his white hall among his mutes.

'Fulness of Light,' said the Vizier, after pros-
trations, 'here is come a letter from the Melek
Richard, sealed, for her Highness the Golden
Rose.'

'Give it to me, Vizier,' said the Old Man, and
broke the seal, and read —

'Madame, most dear lady, in a very little while
I shall be free from my desperate nets; and then
you shall be freed from yours. Keep a great heart.
After five years of endeavour at last I come
quickly. — Richard of Anjou.'

The Old Man sat stroking his fine beard for

some time after he had dismissed his Vizier. Looking straight before him down the length of his hall, no sound broke the immense quiet under which he accomplished his meditations of life and death. The Assassins dreaming by the walls breathed freely through their noses. As a small voice heard from far off in these dreams of theirs, the voice of one calling from a distant height, came his words, ' Cogia ibn Hassan ibn Alnouk, come and hearken.' A slim young man rose, ran forward and fell upon his face before the throne. Once more the faint far cry came floating, ' Bohadin son of Falmy of Balsora, come and hearken '; and another white-robed youth followed Cogia.

' My sons,' said the Old Man, 'the word is upon you. Go to the West for forty days. In the country of the Franks, in the south parts thereof, but north of the great mountains, you shall find the Melek Richard, admirable man, whom Allah longs for. Strike, my sons, but from afar (for not otherwise shall ye dare him), and gain the gates of Paradise and the soft-bosomed women of your dreams. Go quickly, prepare yourselves.' The two young men crawled to kiss his foot; then they went out, and silence folded the hall of audience once more like a wrapping.

Later in the day a slave-girl told Jehane that her master was waiting for her. The baby was asleep in the cradle under a muslin veil; she kissed Fulke, a fine tall boy, six and a half years old, and followed the messenger.

The Old Man embraced her very affectionately,

kissed her forehead and raised her from her knees. 'Come and sit with me, beautiful and pious wife, mother of my sons,' said he. 'I have many things to say to you.'

When they were close together on the cushions of the window, Sinan put his arm round her waist, and said, 'For a good and happy marriage, my Gulzareen, it is well that the woman should not love her husband too much, but rather be meek, show obedience to his desires, and alacrity, and give courtesy. The man must love her, and honour that in her which makes her worth, her beauty, to wit, the bounty of her fruitfulness, and her discretion. But for her it is enough that she suffer herself to be loved, and give him her duty in return. The love that seeds in her she shall bestow upon her children. That is how peace of mind grows in the world, and happiness, for without the first there can never be the second. You, my child, have a peaceful mind: is it not so?'

'My lord,' Jehane replied, with no sign of the old discontent upon her red mouth, 'I am at peace. For I have your affection; you tell me that I deserve it. And I give my children love.'

'And you are happy, Jehane?'

She sighed, ever so lightly. 'I should be happy, my lord. But sometimes, even now, I think of King Richard, and pray for him.'

'I believe that you do,' said the Old Man. 'And because I desire your happiness in all things, I desire you to see him again.'

A bright blush flooded Jehane, whose breath also became a trouble. By a quick movement she drew her veil about her, lest he should see her unquiet breast. So the mother of Proserpine might have been startled into new maidenhood when, in her wanderings, some herd had claimed her in love. Her husband watched her keenly, not unkindly. Jehane's trouble increased; he left her alone to fight it. So at last she did; then touched his hand, looking deeply into his face. He, loving her greatly, held her close.

'Well, Joy of my Joy?'

'Lord,' she said, speaking hurriedly and low, 'let me not see him, ask it not of me. It is more than I dare. It is more than would be right; I ask it for his sake, not for mine. For he has a great heart, the greatest heart that ever man had in the world; also he is sudden to change, as I know very well; and the sight of me denied him might move him to a desperate act, as once before it did.' She lowered her head lest he should see all she had to show. He smiled gravely, stroking her hand and playing with it, up and down.

'No, child, no,' he said, 'it will do you no harm now. The harm, I take it, has been done: soon it will be ended. You shall hear from his own lips that he will not hurt you.'

Jehane looked at him in wonder, startled out of confusion of face.

'Do you know more of him than I do, sire?' she asked, with a quick heart.

'I believe that I do,' replied the Old Man; 'and take my word for it, dear child, that I wish him no ill. I wish him,' he continued very deliberately, 'less ill than he has sought to do himself. I wish him most heartily well. And you, my girl, whom I have grown wisely and tenderly to love; you, my Golden Rose, Moon of the Caliph, my stem, my vine, my holy vase, my garden of endless delight — for you I wish, above all things, rest after labour, refreshment and peace. Well, I believe that I shall gain them for you. Go, therefore, since I bid you, and take with you your son Fulke, that his father may see and bless him, and (if he think fit) provide for him after the custom of his own country. And when you have learned, as learn you will, from his mouth what I am sure he will tell you, come back to me, my Pleasant Joy, and rest upon my heart.'

Jehane sighed, and wrought with her fingers in her lap. ' If it must be, sire —— '

' Why, of course it must be,' said the Old Man briskly.

He sent her away to the harem with a kiss on her mouth, and had in Cogia, and Bohadin son of Falmy of Balsora. To these two rapt Assassins he gave careful instructions, which there was no mistaking. The Golden Rose, properly attended, would accompany them as far as Marseilles. She would journey on to Pampluna and abide in the court of the King of Navarre (who loved Arabians, as his father before him) until such time as word was brought her by one of them, the survivor, that they had found King Richard, and that he would see her. Then she would set out, attended by the Vizier, the chief of the eunuchs, and the Mother of Flowers, and act as she saw proper.

Very soon after this the galley left the marble quay of Tortosa upon a prosperous voyage through blue water. Jehane, her son Fulke of Anjou, and the other persons named, were in a great green pavilion on the poop. But she saw nothing, and knew nothing, of Cogia ibn Hassan ibn Alnouk or of Bohadin son of Falmy of Balsora.

CHAPTER XVI

THE CHAPTER CALLED CHALUZ

WHEN King Richard said, without any con-
firmatory oath, that he should hang Adhémar of
Limoges and the Count of Saint-Pol, all who heard
him believed it. The Abbot Milo believed it for
one. Figuratively, you can see his hands up as
you read him. ' To hang two knights of such
eminent degree and parts,' he writes, ' were surely
a great scandal in any Christian king. Not that
the punishment were undeserved or the executioner
insufficient, God knoweth ! But very often true
policy points out the wisdom of the mean; and
this is its deliberative, that to hang a bad man
when another vengeance is open — such as burning
in his castle, killing on his walls, or stabbing by
apparent mistake for a common person — to hang
him, I say, suggests to the yet unhanged a way of
treating his betters. There are more ways of killing a dog than choking him with butter; and so
it is with lords and other rebels against kings. In
this particular case King Richard only thought to
follow his great father (whom at this time he much
resembled): what in the end he did was very
different from any act of that monarch's that I
ever heard tell of, to remember which makes
me weep tears of blood. But so he fully pur-
posed at that time, being in his hottest temper of
Yea.'

He said Yea to the hanging of Saint-Pol and
Limoges, and made ready a host which must infallibly crush Chaluz were it twenty times prepared. But he said Nay to the sacrifice of
Jehane on Lebanon, and to that end increased
his arms to overawe all the kingdoms of the South
which had sanctioned it. Vanguard, battle and
rear, he mustered fifteen thousand men. Des
Barres led the van, English bowmen, Norman
knights. Battle was his, all arms from Anjou,
Poictou, and Touraine. Rearguard the Earl of
Leicester took, his viceroy in Aquitaine. When
the garrison of Chaluz saw the forested spears on
the northern heights, the great engines piled
against the sky-line, the train of followers, pennons of the knights, Dragon of England, Leopards
of Anjou, the single Lion of Normandy, the wise
among them were for instant surrender.

'Here is an empery come out against us!'
cried Adhémar. 'If I was not right when I told
you that I knew King Richard.'

'The filched empery of a thief,' said Saint-Pol.
'Honesty is ours. I fight for my lady Berengère,
the glory of two realms, my sovereign mistress
till I die.'

'Vastly well,' returned the other; 'but I do
not fight for this lady, but for a gold table with
gold dolls sitting at it.' Such also was the reflection of Achard, castellan of Chaluz, looking
ruefully at his crazy walls.

Two grassy hills rise, like breasts, out of a
rolling plain of grass. Each is crowned with
a tower; between them are the church and vil-

lage of Chaluz, which form a straggling street.
Wall and ditch pen in these buildings and tie
tower to tower: as Richard saw, it was the
easiest thing in the world to cut the line in
the middle, isolate, then reduce the towers at
leisure. Adhémar saw that too, and got no
comfort from it, until it occurred to him that
if he occupied one tower and left the other to
Saint-Pol, he would be free to act at his own
discretion, that is, not act at all against the
massed power of England and Anjou. Saint-
Pol, you see, fought for the life of Richard,
and Adhémar for a gold table, which makes
a great difference. He effected this separation
of garrisons; however, some show of resistance
was made by manning the walls and daring the
day with banners.

King Richard went softly to work, as he always did when actually hand in hand with war.
Warfare was an art to him, neither a sport nor
a counter-irritant; he was never impetuous over
it. For a week he satisfied himself with a close
investiture of the town on all sides. No sup-
plies could get in nor fugitives out. Then, when
everything was according to his liking, he advanced his engines, brought forward his towers,
set sappers to work, and delivered assault in
due form and at the weakest point. He succeeded exquisitely. There was no real defence.
The two hill-towers were stranded, Chaluz was
his.

He put the garrison to the sword, and set the
village on fire. At once Viscount Adhémar and
his men surrendered. Richard took the treas-

ure — it was found that the golden Cæsar had
no head — and kept his word with the finders,
hanging the Viscount and castellan on one
gibbet within sight of the other tower. 'Oh,
frozen villain,' swore Saint-Pol between his teeth,
'so shalt thou never hang me.' But when he
looked about him at his dozen of thin-faced
men he believed that if Richard was not to
hang him it might be necessary for him to
hang himself. More, it came into his mind that
there was a hand or two under him which might
be anxious to save him the trouble. Being, however, a man of abundant spirit, he laughed at
the summons to surrender so long as there was
a horse to eat, man to shoot, or arrow for the
shooting. As for fire, he believed himself impregnable by that arm; and any day succour
might come from the South. Surely his Queen
would not throw him to the dogs! Where was
Count John if not hastening to win a realm;
where King Philip if not hopeful to chastise a
vassal? Daily King Richard, in no hurry, but
desperately reckless, rode close to the tower and
met the hardy eyes of Saint-Pol watching him
from the top. Richard was a galliard fighter,
as he had always been.

'Come down, Saint-Pol,' he would say, 'and
dance with Limoges.'

'When I come down, sire,' the answer would
be, 'there will be no dancing in your host.'

Richard took his time, and also intolerable
liberties with his life. Milo lost his hair with
anxiety, not daring to speak; Gaston of Béarn
did dare, but was shaken off by his mad master.

Des Barres, who loved him, perhaps, as well as any, never left him for long together, and wore his brain out devising shifts which might keep him away from the walls. But Richard, for this present whim of his, chose out a companion devil as heedless as himself, Mercadet namely, his brown Gascon captain, of like proportions, like mettle, like foolhardiness; and with him made the daily round, never omitting an exchange of grim banter with Saint-Pol. It was terrible to see him, without helm on his head, or reason in it, canter within range of the bow.

'Oh, Saint-Pol,' he said one day, 'if thou wert worth my pains, I would have thee down and serve thee as I did thy brother Eudo. But no; thou must be hanged, it seems.' And Saint-Pol, grinning cheerfully, answered, 'Have no fear, King, thou wilt never hang me.'

'By my soul,' said Richard back again, 'a little more of this bold gut of thine, my man, and I let thee go free.'

'Sire,' said Saint-Pol soberly, 'that were the worst of all.'

'How so, boy?'

'Because, if you forgave me, I should be required by my knighthood to forgive you; and that I will never do if I can help it. So I should live and be damned.'

'Have it then as it must be,' said Richard laughing, and turned his back. Saint-Pol could have shot him dead, but would not. 'Look, De Gurdun,' he says, 'there goes the King unmailed. Wilt thou shoot him in the back, and so end all?'

'By God, Eustace,' says Gilles, 'that I will not.'

'Why not, then?'

Gurdun said, 'Because I dare not. I am more afraid of him when he scorns me thus than when his face is upon me. Let him lead an assault upon the walls, and I will split his headpiece if I may; but I will never again try him unarmed.'

'Pouf!' said Saint-Pol; but he was of the same mind.

Then came a day when Des Barres was out upon the neighbouring hills with a company of knights, scouting. There had been rumours of hostile movement from the South, from Provence and Roussillon; of a juncture of Prince John, known to be in Gascony, with the Queen's brother of Navarre. Nothing was known certainly, but Richard judged that John might be tempted out. It was a bright cold day, cloudless, with a most bitter north-east wind singing in the bents. Des Barres, sitting his horse on the hill, blew upon his ungauntleted hand, then flacked it against his side to drive the blood back. Surveying the field with a hunter's eye, he saw King Richard ride out of the lines on his chestnut horse, Mercadet with him, and (in a green cloak) Gaston of Béarn. Richard had a red surcoat and a blown red plume in his cap. He carried no shield, and by the ease with which he turned his body to look behind him, one hand on the crupper, Des Barres was sure that he was not in mail.

'Folly of a fool!' he snorted to his neighbour, Savaric de Dreux: 'there pricks our lord the King, as if to a party of hawks.'

'Wait,' said Savaric. 'Where away now?'

'To bandy gibes with Saint-Pol, pardieu.
Where else should he go at this hour?'
'Saint-Pol will never do him a villainy,' said
Savaric.
'No, no. But De Gurdun is there.'
'Wait now,' says Savaric again. 'Look, look!
Who comes out of the smoke?'
They could see the beleaguered tower perfectly,
brown and warm-looking in the sun; below it,
still smoking, the village of Chaluz, a heap of
charred brickwork. They saw a man in clean
white come creeping out of the smoke, stooping
at a run. He hid wherever he could behind the
broken wall, but always ran nearer, stooped and
ran with bent body over his bent knees. He
worked his way thus, gradually nearer and nearer
to the tower; and Des Barres watched him
anxiously.
'Some camp-thief making off——'
'Look, look!' cried Savaric. The white man
had come out by the tower, was now kneeling
in the open; at the same moment a man slipped
down a rope from the tower-top. Before he had
touched earth they saw the kneeling man pull a
bowstring to his ear and let fly. Next the fellow
on the rope, touching ground, ran fleetly forward
and, springing on the white-robed man, drove him
to the earth. They saw the flash of a blade.
'That is strange warfare,' said Des Barres,
greatly interested.
'There is warfare in heaven also,' said Savaric.
'See those two eagles.' Two great birds were
battling in the cold blue. Feathers fell idly, like
black snow-flakes; then one of the eagles heeled
over, and down he came.

But when they looked towards the tower again
they saw a great commotion. Men running,
horses huddled together, one in red held up by
one in green. Then a riderless chestnut horse
looked about him and neighed. Des Barres gave
a short cry. 'O God! They have shot King
Richard between them. Come, Savaric, we must
go down.'

'Stop again,' said that other. 'Let us sweep
up those assassins as we go. There I see another
thief in white.' Des Barres saw him too. 'Spur,
spur!' he called to his knights; 'follow me.'
He got his line in motion, they all galloped across
the sunny slopes like a light cloud. But as they
drove forward the play was in progress; they saw
it done, as it were, in a scene. One white figure
lay heaped upon the ground, another was running
by the wall towards him, furtively and bent, as
the first had come. The third actor, he of the
tower, had not heard the runner, but was still
stooped over the man he had evidently killed,
groping probably for marks or papers upon him.

'Spur, spur!' cried Des Barres, and the line
went rattling down. They were not in time.
The white runner was too quick for the killer of
his mate: he did, indeed, look round; but the
other was upon him before he could rise. There
was a short tussle; the two rolled over and over.
Then the white-clad man got up, raised his fallen
comrade, shouldered him, and sped away into the
smoke of Chaluz. When Des Barres and his
friends were within bowshot of the tower one
man only was below it; and he lay where he
had been stabbed. The white-robed murderers,

the living and the dead, were lost in smoke.
The King and his party were gone. Out of the
tower came Saint-Pol with his men, unarmed,
bareheaded, and waited silently in rank for Des
Barres.

This one came up at a gallop. 'My prisoner,
Count of Saint-Pol,' he called out as he came;
then halted his line by throwing up his hand.

'The King has been shot, Sir Guilhem,' Saint-
Pol said gravely; 'not by me. I am the King's
prisoner. Take me to him, lest he die before I
see his eyes.'

'Who is that dead man of yours over there?'
asked Des Barres.

'His name is Sieur Gilles de Gurdun, a knight
of Normandy and enemy of the King's, but dead
(if dead he be) on the King's account. He killed
the assassin.'

'I know that very well,' says Des Barres, 'for
I saw the deed, which was a good one. I must
hunt for those white-gowns. Who might they
be?'

'I know nothing of them. They are no men
of mine. Their robes were all white, their faces
all dark, and they ran like Turks. But what can
Turks do here?'

'They must be found,' said Des Barres, and
sent out Savaric with half of his men.

They picked up Gilles, quite dead of two
wounds, one in the back of the neck, another
below the heart. Des Barres put him over his
saddlebow; then took his prisoners into camp.

King Richard had been carried to his pavilion
and put to bed. His physicians were with him,

and the Abbot Milo, quite unmanned. Gaston of Béarn was crying like a girl at the door. The Earl of Leicester had ridden off for the Queen, Yvo Tibetot for the Count of Mortain. Des Barres learned that they had pulled out the arrow, a common one of Genoese make, but feared poison. King Richard had been shot in the right lung.

CHAPTER XVII

THE KEENING

In the wan hours left to him came three women, one after another, and spoke the truth so far as they knew it each.

The first was Alois of France in the habit of a grey lady of Fontevrault, with a face more dead than her cowl, and hair like wet weed, but in her hollow eyes the fire of her mystery; who said to the watchers by the door: 'Let me in. I am the voice of old sorrow.' So they held back the curtains of the tent, and she came shuffling forward to the long body on the bed. At the sound of her skirts the King turned his altered face her way, then rolled his head back to the dark.

'Take her away,' he said in a whisper; so Des Barres stood up between him and the woman.

But Alois put her hands out, as a blind man does.

'Soul's health, Des Barres; I purge old sins. Avoid, all of you,' she said, 'and leave me with him. Save only his confessor. What I have to say must be said in secret, as it was done secretly.'

Richard sighed. 'Let her stay; and let Milo stay,' he said. The rest went out on tip-toe. Alois came and knelt at the head of the bed.

'Listen now, Richard,' said she; 'for thy last hour is near, and mine also. Twice over I have

396

sought to tell thee, but was denied. Each time
I might have done thee a service; now I will do
thee good service. Thou art not guilty of thy
father's death, nor he of my despair.'

The King did not turn his head, but looked up
sideways, so that she saw his eye shining. His
lips moved, then stuck together; so Milo put a
sponge with wine upon them. Then he whispered, 'Tell me, Alois, who was guilty with
thee?'

She said, 'Thy brother John of Mortain was
that man. A villain is he.'

A moaning sigh escaped the King, long-drawn,
shuddering, very piteous. 'Eh, Alois, Alois!
Which of us four was not a villain?'

Said Alois, 'What is past is past, and I have
told thee. What is to come I cannot tell thee,
for the past swallows me up. Yet I say again,
thy brother John is a sick villain, a secret villain,
and a thief.'

'God help him, God judge him,' said Richard
with another sigh. 'I can do neither, nor will
not.' He moaned again, but so hopelessly, as
being so weary and fordone, that Abbot Milo
began to blubber out loud. Alois lifted up her
drawn face, and struck her breast.

'Ah, would to God, Richard,' she cried, 'would
to God I had come to thee clean! I had saved
thee then from this most bitter death. For if I
love thee now, judge how I had loved thee then.'

He said, with shut eyes, 'None could love me
long, since none could trust me, and not I myself.' Then he said fretfully to the abbot, 'Take
her away, Milo; I am tired.'

Alois, kneeling, kissed his dry forehead.
'Farewell,' she said, 'King Richard, most a king
when most in bonds, and most merciful when
most in need of mercy. My work is done.
Remains to pray and prepare.' She went out
noiselessly, as she had come in, and no man of
them saw her again.

Next came Queen Berengère, about the time
of sunset. She came stiffly, as if holding herself
in a trap, with much formal bowing to Death;
quite white, like ivory, in a black robe; in her
hands a great crucifix. At the door she paused
for a minute, the Earl of Leicester being with
her.

'Grief is quick in me, Leicester,' she said;
then to the ushers of the door, 'Does he live?
Will he know me? Does he wake? Does he
not cry for me now?'

'Madame, the King sleeps,' they told her.

'I go to pray for him,' said the Queen, and
went in.

Stiffly she knelt at his bedhead, and with both
hands held up the crucifix to her face. She began to talk to it in a low worn voice, as though
she were asking the Christ to reckon her misery.

'Thou Christ,' she complained, 'Thou Christ,
look upon me, the daughter of a king, crucified
terribly with Thee. This dying man is the King
my husband, who denied me as Thou, Christ, wert
denied; who sought to put me by, and yet is
loved. Yet I love him, Christ; yet I have
worked for him against my honour, holding it
as cheap as he did. When he was in prison I

humbled myself to set him loose; when he was loosed I held his enemies back, while he, cruelly, held me back. I have prayed for him, and pray now, while he lies there, struck secretly, and dies not knowing me; and leaves me alone, careless whether I live or die. Ah, Saviour of the world, do I suffer or not?'

She awoke the sick man, who opened his eyes and stared about him. He signed to Milo to draw nigh, which the snuffling old man did.

'Who is here?' he whispered. 'Not —— ?'

'No, no, dearest lord,' said Milo quickly. 'But the Queen is here.'

'Ah,' said he, 'poor wretch!' And he sighed. Then he said, 'Turn me over, Milo.' It was done, with a flux of blood to the mouth. They stayed that and brought him round with aqua vitæ.

The Queen was terribly moved to see his ravaged face. No doubt she loved him. But she had nothing to say. For some time their eyes were fixed, each on the other; the Queen's misty, the King's fever-bright, terribly searching, terribly intelligent. He read her soul.

'Madame,' he said, but she could scarcely hear him, 'I have done you great wrong, yet greater wrong elsewhere. I cannot die in comfort without your pardon; but I cannot ask it of you, for if I still had years to live, I should do as I have done.' A sob of injury shook the Queen.

'Richard! Richard! Richard!' she wailed, 'I suffer! You have my heart; you have always had it. And what have I? Nothing, O God! Nothing at all.'

'Madame,' said he, 'the wrong I did you was
that I gave you the right to anything. That was
the first and greatest wrong. To give it you
I thieved, and in taking it again I thieved again.
God knoweth —— ' He shut his eyes, and kept
them shut. She called to him more urgently,
'Richard, Richard!' but he made no answer, and
appeared to sleep. The Queen shivered and
sniffed, turned to her Christ, and so spent the
night.

The last to come was Jehane in a white gown;
and she came with the dawn. Eager and flushed
she was, with dawn-colour in her face; and
stepped lightly over the dewy grass, her lips
parted and hair blown back. She came in exalted
with grief, so that no wardens of the door, nor
queens, nor college of queens, could have stayed
her. She was as tall as any there, and went past
the guard at the door without question or word
said, and so lightly and fiercely to the bed. There
she stood, dilating and glowing, looking not back
on her spent life, but on to the glory of the dying.
The Queen knew that she was there, but went
on with her prayers, or seemed to go on. Jehane
knelt suddenly, put her arms out over Richard,
stooped and kissed his cheek. Then she looked
up, desperately triumphing, for any one to question her right. None did. Berengère prayed
incessantly, and Jehane panted. The words broke
from her at last. 'Dost thou question my right,
Berengère,' she said fiercely, 'to kiss a dead man,
to love the dead and speak greatly of the dead?
Which of us three women, thinkest thou, knoweth

best what report to make concerning this beloved,
thou, or Alois, or I? Alois came, speaking of old
sins; and you are here, plaining of new sins:
what shall I do, now I am here? Am I to speak
of sin to come? Thou dear knight,' and she
touched his head, 'there is no more room for
thy great sins, alas! But I think thou shalt leave
behind thee some spark of a fire.' She looked
again at Berengère, who saw the glint of her
green eyes and the old proud discontent twisting
her lip, but did nothing. 'Look, Berengère,' said
Jehane, ' I speak as mother of his child Fulke of
Anjou. I had rather my son Fulke sinned as his
fathers have sinned, so that he sinned greatly like
them, than that he should grow pale, scheming
safety in a cloister, and make the Man in our
Saviour ashamed of His choice. I had rather the
bad blood stay, so it stay great blood, than that it
should be thin like thine. What is there to fear,
girl? A sword? I have had a sword in my
heart eight years, and made no sound. Let the
son pierce what the father pierced before. I am
a lover, saying not to my beloved, " Stroke my
heart, dearest lord "; but instead, " Stab if thou
wilt, my King, and let me bleed for thee." So I
have bled, sweet Lord Jesus, and so shall bleed
again!' She stooped and kissed his head saying,
'Amen. Let the poor bleed if the King ask.'
The Queen went on praying; but Richard opened
his eyes without start or quiver, looked at Jehane
leaning over him, and smiled.

'Well, my girl, well,' he said, 'thou art in good
time. What of the lad?'

'He is here, Richard.'

2 D

'Bring him to me,' says the King. So Des Barres stole out to the Moslems at the door, and came back leading Fulke by the hand, a slim, tall boy, fair-haired, and frank in the face, with his father's delicate mouth and bold grey eyes. Jehane turned to take him.

'This is thy father, boy.'

'I know it, ma'am,' says young Fulke, and knelt down by the bed. King Richard put his hand on his head.

'What a rough pelt, Fulke,' he says, 'like thy father's. God send thee a better inside to it, my boy. God make a man of thee.'

'He will never make me a great king, sire,' says Fulke.

'He can make thee better than that,' said his father.

'I think not,' answered Fulke. 'You are the greatest king in the whole world, sire. The Old Man of Musse said it.'

'Kiss me, Fulke,' said Richard. The boy put his face up quickly and kissed his father's lips. 'What a lover!' the King laughed; and Jehane said, 'He always kisses on the lips.' Richard sighed, suddenly tired; Fulke looked about, frightened at all the solemnity, and took his mother's hand. She gave him over to Des Barres, who led him away.

The King signed to Jehane to bend down her head. So she did, and even thus could barely hear him.

'I must die in peace if I can, sweet soul,' he muttered. They all saw that the end was not far off. 'Tell me what will become of thee when I am gone.' She stroked his cheek.

'I shall go back to my husband and children, dear one. I have left three behind me, all sons.'
'Are they good to thee? Art thou happy?'
'I am at peace with myself, wife of a wise old man; I love my children, and have the memory of thee, Richard. These will suffice me.'
'There is one more thing for thee to give me, my Jehane.' She smiled pityingly.
'Why, what is left to give, Richard?' He said in her ear, 'Our boy Fulke.'
'Ah,' said Jehane. The Queen was now watching her intently between her hands.
'Jehane, Jehane,' said King Richard, sweating with the effort to be heard, 'all our life together thou hast been giving and I spending, thou miser that I might play the prodigal. For the last time I ask of thee: deny me not. Wilt thou stay here with Fulke our son?'

Jehane could not speak; she shook her head, and showed him her eyes all blind with tears. The tears came freely, from more eyes than hers. Richard's head dropped back, and for a full minute they thought him gone. But no. He opened his eyes again and moved his lips. They strained to hear him. 'The sponge, the sponge,' he said: then, 'Bring me in Saint-Pol.' The cold light began to steal in through the crannies of the tent.

The young man was brought in by Des Barres, in chains. Jehane, now behind Richard's head, lifted him up in her arms.

'Knock off those fetters,' says the King. Saint-Pol was free.

'Eustace,' says Richard, 'you and I have

bandied hard words enough, and blows enough. My chains will be off before sunrise, and yours are off already. Answer me, is Gurdun dead?'

Saint-Pol dropped to his knees. 'Oh, my lord, he died where he fell. But as God knows, he had no hand in this, nor had I.'

'If I know it, I suppose God knows it too,' said Richard, smiling rather thinly. 'Now, Eustace, I have a word to say. I have done much against your name; to your brother because he spoke against a great lady and ill of my house; to your sister here, because I loved her not well enough and myself too well. Eustace, you shall kiss her before I go.'

Saint-Pol got up and went to her. Brother and sister kissed each other above the King's head. Then said Richard, 'Now I will tell you that I had nothing to do with the death of your cousin Montferrat.'

'Oh, sire! oh, sire!' cried Saint-Pol; but Jehane looked at her brother.

'I had to do with that, Eustace,' she said. 'He laid the death of the King, and I laid his death at the price of my marriage. He deserved it.'

'Sister,' said Saint-Pol, 'he did deserve it; and I deserve what he had. Oh, sire,' he urged with tears, 'take my life, as your right is, but forgive me first.'

'What have I to forgive you, brother?' said Richard. 'Come, kiss me. We were good friends in the old days.' Saint-Pol, with tears, kissed him. Richard sat up.

'I require you now, Saint-Pol and Des Barres, that between you you defend my son Fulke.

Milo has the deeds of his lands of Cuigny. Bring
him up a good knight, and let him think gentlier
of his father than that father ever did of his. Will
you do this? Make haste, make haste!'

The Queen broke in with a cry. 'Oh, sire! oh,
sire! Is there nothing for me?' Madame!' she
turned to Jehane and held her fast by the knees,
'have pity, spare me a little, a very little work!
O Christ! O Christ!'—she rocked herself about
—'Can I do nothing in the world for my King?'

Jehane stooped to take her up. 'Madame,
watch over my little Fulke, when his father is
gone, and I am gone.' The Queen was crying
bitterly.

'I will never leave him if you will trust me,'
she began to say. Richard put his hand out.
'Let it be so. My lords, serve the Queen and
me in this matter.' The two lords bowed their
heads, and the Queen tumbled to her sobbed
prayers again.

The King's eyes were almost gone; certainly
he could not see out of them. They understood
his moving lips, 'A sponge, quick.'

Jehane brought it and wiped his mouth; she
could not see either for tears. He gave a strong
movement, wrenched his head up from her arm,
then gave a great gasp, 'Christ! I am done!'
There followed on this a rush of blood which
made all hearts stand still. They wiped it away.
But Jehane saw that with that hot blood had gone
his spirit. She lifted high her head and let them
read the truth from her eyes. Then she put her
lips upon his, and so stayed, and felt him grow
cold below her warmth. The fire was out.

They buried him at Fontevrault as he had directed, at the feet of his father. King John was there with the peers of England, Normandy, and Anjou. The Queen was there; but not Alois (unless behind the grille), and not King Philip, because he hated King John much worse than he ever hated Richard. And Jehane was not there, nor Fulke of Anjou with his governors, because they had another business to perform.

Not all of King Richard was buried there, where the great effigy still marks the place of great dust. Jehane had his heart in a casket, and with Fulke her son, Des Barres, her brother Saint-Pol, Gaston of Béarn, and the Abbot Milo, took it to the church of Rouen and saw it laid among the dead Dukes of Normandy; fitting sepulture for a heart as bold as any of theirs, and capable of more gentle music when the fine hand plucked the chords. After this Jehane kissed Fulke and left him with the Queen, his uncle, and Guilhem des Barres. Then she went back to her ship.

In the white palace in the green valley of Lebanon the Old Man of Musse embraced his wife. 'Moon of my soul, my Garden, my Treasure-house!' he called her, and kissed her all over.

'The King died in peace, my lord,' she said, 'and I have peace because of that.'

'Thy children shall call thee blessed, my beloved, as I call thee.'

'The prophecy of the leper was not fulfilled sir,' says Jehane.

Ah,' replied the Old Man of Musse, 'all these things are in the hands of the Supreme Disposer, Who with His forefinger points us the determined road.'

Then Jehane went in to her children, and other duties which her station required of her.

EPILOGUE OF THE ABBOT MILO

'When I consider,' writes the Abbot Milo on his last page, 'that I have lived to see the deaths of three Kings of England, wearers of the broom-switch, and of the manner of those deaths, I am led to admire the wonderful ordering of Almighty God, Who accorded to each of them an end illustrative of his doings in the world, and so wrote, as it were, in blood for our learning. King Henry produced strife, King Richard induced strife, and King John deduced it. King Henry died cursing and accursed; King Richard forgiving and forgiven; King John blaspheming, and not held worthy of reproof. The first did evil, meaning evilly; the second evil, meaning well; the third was evil. So the first was wretched in death, the second pitiful, the third shameful. The first loved a few, the second loved one, the third none. So the death of the first was gain to a few, that of the second to one, that of the third to none; for he that loves not, neither can he hate: he is negligible in the end. But observe now, the chief woe of these kings of the House of Anjou was that they hurt whom they loved more than whom they hated.

'King Henry was a great prince, who did evil to many both in his life and death. My dear master, lord, and friend might have been a greater, had not his head gone counter to his heart, his

generosity not been tripped up by his pride. So
generous as he was, all the world might have loved
him, as one loved him; and yet so arrogant of
mind that the very largess he bestowed had a sting
beneath it, as though he scorned to give less to
creatures that lacked so much. All his faults and
most of his griefs sprang from this rending apart
of his nature. His heart cried Yea! to a noble
motion. Then came his haughty head to suggest
trickery, and bid him say Nay! to the heart's
urgency.

'He was a religious man, a pious man, the
hottest fighter with the coolest judgment of any I
have ever known; a great lover of one woman.
He might have been a happy man if she had been
let have her way. But he thwarted her, he played
with her whole-heart love, blew hot and cold;
neither let her alone nor clove to her through
all. So she had to pay. And of him, my
friend and king howsoever, I say from the bottom of my soul, if his death did not benefit
poor Jehane, then it is a happy thing for a
woman to go bleeding in the side. But I know
that she was fortunate in his death, and believe
that he was also. For he had space for reparation, died with his lovers about him, having
been saved in time from a great disgrace. And
it is a very wise man who reports: *Illi Mors
gravis incubat, qui notus nimis omnibus, ignotus
moritur sibi.* But King Richard knew himself
in those last keen hours, and (as we believe)
won forgiveness of God.

'God be good to him where he is! They say
that when he died, that same day his soul was

solved from purgatorial fires (by reason, one may suppose, of his glorious captaincy of the armies of the Cross), and he drawn up to heaven in a flamy cloud. I know nothing certainly of this, which was not revealed to me; but my prayer is that he may be now with Hannibal and Judas Maccabæus and Charles the great Emperor; and by this time of writing (if there be no offence in it) with Jehane to sit upon his knee.

'UPON WHOSE TWO SOULS, JESU, HAVE MERCY!'

EXPLICIT